ICE UNDER FIRE

Quietly assessing their feelings about being in one another's arms, Omunique and Ken stood motionless. The atmosphere hissed with tangible tensions: mental tension, physical tension, sexual tension. Their breathing came in uneven spurts, short gasps. As she tried to move away, he held her tighter, then bent his head and consumed her mouth with a fire hotter than Hades had ever been described. Hunger, deprivation, wantonness, all the things they'd experienced over the past weeks, seemed to belong to the past as they devoured, and recklessly gleaned what they so desperately needed from one another. Conversation simply wasn't necessary. Apologies weren't needed. Explanations weren't called for. They could see, feel, and hear what each needed to say to the other. Their eyes saw, their bodies felt, their hearts rejoiced.

BOOK YOUR PLACE ON OUR WEBSITE AND MAKE THE ARABESQUE ROMANCE CONNECTION!

We've created a customized website just for our very special Arabesque readers, where you can get the inside scoop on everything that's going on with Arabesque romance novels.

When you come online, you'll have the exciting opportunity to:

- View covers of upcoming books

- Learn about our future publishing schedule (listed by publication month and author)

- Find out when your favorite authors will be visiting a city near you

- Search for and order backlist books

- Check out author bios and background information

- Send e-mail to your favorite authors

- Join us in weekly chats with authors, readers and other guests

- Get writing guidelines

- AND MUCH MORE!

Visit our website at
http://www.arabesquebooks.com

ICE UNDER FIRE

Linda Hudson-Smith

ARABESQUE

BET BOOKS

BET Publications, LLC
www.msbet.com
www.arabesquebooks.com

ARABESQUE BOOKS are published by

BET Publications, LLC
c/o BET BOOKS
One BET Plaza
1900 W Place NE
Washington, D.C. 20018-1211

First Printing: January, 2000
10 9 8 7 6 5 4 3 2 1

Printed in the United States of America

This book is dedicated to the loving memory of
my beautiful parents,
Jack and Bernice Alice Hudson

Mommy and Daddy,
Although you're not here to rejoice in my triumph,
I know that you share in my joy as you watch over me.
Thank you for teaching me the power of love, humility,
forgiveness, and benevolence.

I love you and miss you.

In memory of my beloved brothers, Maurice, Richard, and
Oscar

In memory of my dear brother-in-law, R.J.

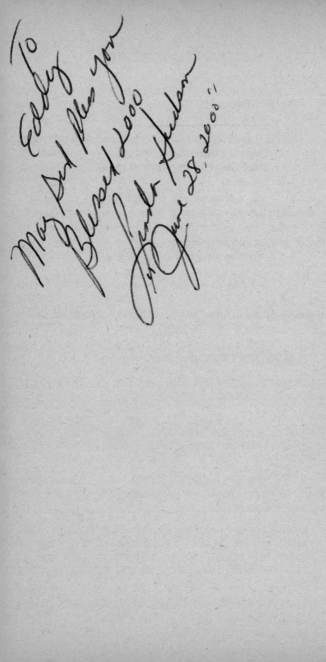

To
Eddy
May God Bless you
Blessed 2000

Sandra Sheldon

June 28, 2000!

ACKNOWLEDGMENTS:

My Father in heaven, who holds me near and dear: Thank you for being everything that I need, for everything that I am.

My husband, lover, best friend, and my hero: Rudy, this book was made possible because of your love, patience, understanding, and altruistic spirit. You are truly the wind beneath my wings, my anchor in the port of storms. I love you always, soulfully.

My sons, Greg and Scott. Children of my extended family, Kristina and Kevin: You each have a unique talent. Dare to use it. I love you individually and collectively.

My grandchildren, Joshua, Kerai-shawn, Gregory III, and Omunique: I love you.

My sisters, Marlene, Donna, Candy, and Sherry: Thanks for the love, encouragement, support, and all the special memories that we hold as sisters. Each of you has played a significant role in my writing accomplishments. I love you all.

My in-laws, Edward and Thomasine, Thank you for my greatest gift ever, your son.

My mother's family, Aunt Ethel, Aunt Josephine, Aunt Renee, Cousin Violet: An honorable mention for your love and supporting counsel. Thank you for the wonderful memories.

My long-term girlfriend-confidantes, Denise, Beverly, Marion, Bonnie, and Brenda: We have a very long history together. When all else fails, I can always turn to you for love and comfort.

My special sister-girl friends, Diane, Judyann, Darlene, Nedra, Sylvia, and Donna: Thanks for being there. I love our "reach out and touch" relationships.

My special brother-friends, Rocky, Antonio, John, Jimmy, Matt, E.L., George, and Ed: Each of you has touched my life in a special way. Thanks to you who read my work before it ever met the public eye. You're all living proof that men and women can be just friends.

Editors, Monica Harris and Karen Thomas: Thanks for all your encouraging comments.

My writer-angel, Angela Benson: Your halo never fails to shine. Thank you for all the time and effort you put into critiquing my project. You're a godsend.

My writer-friend, Alice Lane: Your instant belief in me helped me to keep writing.

My greatest love of all: Thank you for all the wonderful things you taught me to expect from a man . . . and for the types of things that I should never accept from one. I love you, infinitely.

Chapter One

Dressed in a navy blue wool blazer and matching skirt, Omunique Philyaw hoped Mr. Maxwell would think her attire was the epitome of class. As she rushed down the long corridor inside the high-rise building that housed Maxwell's Athletic Corporation—a company that manufactured athletic wearing apparel—she glanced at her gold wristwatch. A few minutes late for her meeting, totally breathless, she swept into the reception area of the suite of offices occupied by Kenneth Maxwell Sr., founder and Chief Executive Officer of Maxwell's.

"It's about time you got here," a sultry, baritone voice boomed in her ear, causing her entire anatomy to tingle.

As she turned around to look at the man behind the voice, she nearly fainted from pure desire. His complexion, the color of melted caramels, looked smooth and creamy. While rating his body a ten plus, she imagined him melting in her mouth as well as in her hands. Though he was much taller than her own five-foot frame, about fifteen inches taller, she felt no discomfort at tilting her head upward at an awkward angle to meet his steady gaze. In sheer bewilderment, she stared boldly into his eyes—mesmerizing eyes of autumn-gold.

He felt his body heat intensify under her bold scrutiny. "I'm glad you're finally here. Maybe we can get some work done now. Why is it all of you temps seem to be late?"

Omunique's pulse raced wildly as this beautiful man with the powerful physique crossed the room and stopped right in front of her. Surprising her, he thrust a manila folder into her hand. "I need these forms typed right away. I'm taking a meeting for my father, but I've only had two hours notice."

Agitation flashed in her smoky-gray eyes now that she realized he was the son of the owner, and that he thought she was the temporary secretary. In an instant she decided to play along. She couldn't wait to see the expression on his face when he learned who she really was.

He waved the endorsement contract he'd been working on in the air. "I think it's ludicrous to pay this type of money for endorsement contracts. Athletes have big enough egos as it is. I guess they need bank accounts to match."

Omunique's eyes signaled storm warnings as she ran agitated fingers through her shiny, shoulder-length almond-brown hair. She'd had about enough of his arrogance. Although she itched to tell him what she thought of his attitude, she refrained, knowing she desperately needed what his company had to offer her. As she patiently waited for his tirade to end, she opened the folder and briefly glanced at its contents.

He pointed at the forms she'd begun to peruse. "Look, I don't mean to be rude, but we've got to get down to work. Although he's already late, my appointment should be here any moment. Lateness has become fashionable these days, but I find it downright irresponsible. If Mr. Philyaw doesn't get here in the next five minutes, he may find himself without a sponsor. In the meantime, these figures need to be typed in the appropriate places."

Omunique laughed inwardly. *So, he thinks I'm a man, as well. This is going to be too good,* she contemplated with glee.

Gee, he's handsome. Too bad he doesn't have a matching disposition.

"Would you like me to make some coffee before I get started on this assignment?" she asked with wide-eyed innocence.

"Coffee would be nice. You'll find a machine in my private office. I take mine black."

She smiled innocently. "I'll take care of the coffee. Then I'll have these figures typed in a jiffy." She cast him a guarded glance. "I sure hope this Mr. Philyaw keeps his appointment. I would hate to see him lose out on something that sounds so important."

Inside his private office, Omunique noticed the unopened file folder on his desk, recognizing it as her personal bio from the name on the color tab. *From all indications,* she thought heatedly, *he hasn't given it so much as a glance.* Otherwise he would've known who she was.

Grumbling to herself, she walked back into the reception area. "I'm really sorry I was late, Mr. Maxwell. Freeway traffic was a bear."

Narrowing his eyes slightly, he looked at her and sighed heavily. How many times had he heard that same lame excuse from other employees? "By the way, I didn't catch your name."

She quickly looked at the name scribbled on a half-sheet of paper that lay atop the desk. A name and the words "temporary secretary" were underlined. "Thomasina Bridges," she replied, hoping the real Thomasina didn't suddenly pop her head in the doorway.

He forced a smile to his generous mouth. "Nice to meet you. I hope you'll be on time for the duration of this assignment." He wagged a finger at her. "You really shouldn't be late again. We handle a large volume of business in this office."

Quelling a sudden urge to bend his finger back as far as it would go without breaking, she took a breath and reminded herself that she needed him, not the other way around. "It won't happen again, sir," she promised. If this was the way he normally treated the hired help, she could understand why he was without a permanent secretary.

Omunique turned, startled, when the front door to the swanky offices suddenly burst open and a young woman walked in. Knowing she was probably busted, Omunique swallowed hard.

Omunique figured the woman, who possessed a clear, tawny brown complexion, to be in her mid-twenties. Her sandy brown hair was cut pixie style, and her neatly trimmed bangs met up with professionally arched eyebrows that hovered above dark brown eyes. Omunique saw Ken's eyes go immediately to the practically non-existent brown leather skirt the young woman wore. A tad more discreet, her white blouse hid the uppermost secrets of her svelte figure.

The woman smiled sweetly. "Hi! I'm Thomasina Bridges, the temp," she announced, her voice annoyingly shrill. "Sorry I'm late, but there was a major accident on the freeway."

He narrowed his eyes, looking from one woman to the other. "If she's the temp, then who in the Sam Hill are you?" he demanded, pointing a manicured finger at Omunique.

Stifling a giggle, Omunique cast him a cool, unassuming look. "I'm one of those athletes with a really big ego, but I'm afraid I only have a small bank account. And I'm also the appointment you've been going on and on about." She turned her palms face up and shrugged her shoulders. "But as you can see, I'm not a male. And since I'm not really sure of who you are, either, I guess that puts us on a level playing field."

Smiling smugly, she extended her hand. "I'm Omunique Philyaw." *It's obvious that you haven't seen my bio, nor do you seem to know much about your assignment,* she accused mentally. Although it would have been very easy to tell him where to go and how to get there, not to mention downright satisfying, she couldn't afford to offend one of the men who might hold her very future in his hands.

His eyes seem to spit fire and brimstone, yet his grip was firm and gentle when he took her hand. "I'm Kenneth Maxwell

Jr., second in command to the CEO, who just happens to be my father," he announced, looking a bit chagrined.

Along with finding himself in an embarrassing situation, Ken felt guilty for not having gone over her profile the second it had been handed to him. Rarely was he caught unprepared. Knowing his father would be outraged at his mistake, he vowed never to let something like this happen again. He was much too good an administrator for this.

His entire expression softened. "I'm truly sorry for this inexcusable mistake. I should've taken the time to look over your bio without hesitation. Please come into my private office."

With a full understanding of what was happening here, Thomasina laughed, but was quickly cut to shreds by an icy glance from her temporary employer. Spotting the computer, she smiled weakly and eased around the fine oak furnishings that filled the reception area's computer work center. Ken quickly filled Thomasina in on her assignments, then returned to Omunique.

Ken held the door for Omunique as she walked through. After directing her to a seat at the conference table, he rushed over to the corner of the room, where a wooden sideboard held a variety of refreshments. He poured two cups of the freshly brewed coffee. When he bent over to retrieve something from one of the lower cabinets, Omunique took this opportunity to take a good look at his firm, perfectly rounded rear end. *Baby's got back,* she thought with amusement, mentally humming the lyrics to the Rap song with that title. Like a naughty child who didn't want to be caught at an errant deed, she glanced away when he straightened up. As he walked back to the table carrying two cups of coffee, his confident stride told her a lot about the man. She definitely liked what it told her. Something about him deeply intrigued her.

A slight frown gave way to a broad smile as he placed one of the cups of hot liquid in front of her. His gorgeous smile caused her heart to dance figure eights. *Those autumn-gold eyes, indescribably breathtaking.*

Omunique grinned impishly "I don't do coffee."

His look was one of exasperation. "You sat here and watched me sweating over that hot coffeepot . . . and don't deny it, you were definitely watching me. I smelled the smoke coming from those devious gray eyes of yours. Now you tell me you don't drink the stuff! What's that all about?" *Why me?* he silently asked. Why did he seem to get stuck with all the pains in the butt? She *was* a stunning pain.

While his eyes sent golden plumes of steam her way, he sat in a chair directly across the table from her. He then took a quick swig of coffee from his cup. "Before we get started, is there anything else I need to know about you, Miss Philyaw? It is *Miss*, isn't it?" he asked, raising an eyebrow.

She simply nodded toward the packet that held her bio. This tall, handsome man gave her the absolute chills. Someone with such good looks had to have a much warmer side.

When her suggestion came in clear, he laughed at the obvious as he picked up the bio and quickly perused all the pertinent information. He tried to ignore the giddy delight that tumbled through him when he saw that she was indeed single.

"Miss Philyaw, we have really gotten off to a bad start, and I hold myself entirely responsible for that. I only learned of this meeting two hours prior to the scheduled time. My father was handling this matter, but he was called out of town unexpectedly."

When she didn't offer a response, he touched a finger to his temple. "I have an idea. Why don't you give me time to look your bio over thoroughly? Then we can discuss things over dinner this evening. I promise to come well-prepared. What do you say?"

Her gray eyes twinkled with mischievous glee. "I'm afraid I don't do dinner, either."

As he shook his head from side to side, hell seemed to spout from his golden eyes. "You don't do coffee, you don't do dinner, so what is it that you can do?"

She momentarily cast her eyes to the floor. "I'm sorry for being a tad bitchy. The morning traffic jam is responsible for my bad temperament. What's your excuse, Mr. Maxwell?"

She immediately regretted her last comment. He'd earned it, all right, but this wasn't the time or the place to voice her displeasure. *You need him,* she reminded herself. *You really need him.* Besides, he made her hot and bothered all over, she admitted with alarm.

Ken sighed. "My rudeness is inexcusable. It seems this has been a crazy morning for both of us." He sighed again, only louder.

She couldn't seem to keep her eyes off him. He made her flesh sizzle with yearning, something she'd never before experienced with anyone. "Are you always this intense, Mr. Maxwell?" She smiled to soften the obvious criticism.

Her question directly affected him, but he ignored it. When he looked straight into her eyes, she saw how dangerously hypnotic his own were, but she somehow managed to remain unflinchingly calm.

"Miss Philyaw, it would really make this all so much easier if you'd just agree to have dinner with me. Business is conducted over dinner all the time."

She folded her dainty hands and rested them on top of the table. "All right," she conceded. She knew she really didn't have much choice in the matter, nor did she need to again remind herself that her career was on the line. The fact that she needed a sponsor was entrenched in her soul.

She pointed at the file folder as she got to her feet. "You have my agent's phone number. Call him with the details." She was out the door before he could respond.

Angry with himself, he shoved several folders off the end of the table, watching as the papers flew across the carpeted floor. He loosened his tie, which suddenly felt too tight, thinking of how miserably he'd screwed things up. "What now?" he said, knowing he had botched things up but good. How was he going to get any work completed after that fiasco?

Ken continued to sit at the table with a brooding expression, wondering what type of hi-tech broom Omunique Philyaw traveled on. Without a doubt she was a witch, a beautiful, bewitching one, to boot. After picking up all the scattered papers, he shoved them back in the proper folders. He then sat back in the chair to peruse her bio in depth.

As he opened the file folder, his breath caught at the soulfully beautiful gray eyes that further cast a bewitching spell over him. Involuntarily, he shuddered. Omunique Philyaw, a champion figure skater, an Ice Princess. *How unequivocally fitting,* he thought, looking totally bewildered.

If Miss Philyaw decided to renege on her word to have dinner with him, he would just have to come up with a new plan of action. It was no longer just a matter of company sponsorship. A matter of the heart seemed to be playing the lead role in his inability to concentrate on his tasks, he admitted reluctantly.

Ken lifted the bio from the folder and read it with an interest that grew more intense with each fascinating line. Before him was the beautiful face and the stunning figure of the woman who had so effortlessly turned his hormones into a raging river of pure physical desire—dressed in a very revealing leotard while striking a pose that could thaw the ice she stood on.

He could see that Omunique was an incredibly built female athlete. He marveled at the lean, shapely legs that supported her curvaceous, petite frame. Sighing wearily, he cursed himself for failing at an assignment that normally would be a piece of cake.

He whistled softly as he read her list of accomplishments. She had won more competitions than he could imagine. He couldn't believe she was only twenty-one years old, five years younger than him. She seemed so mature, and too darn sure of herself. After reading all the competitions she'd won, he could see why she was so cocky. *Cocky, but so sensuously soft,* he reflected, envisioning her silky, fawn-brown complexion.

He laughed when he recalled how he'd thought his appointment was with a man. He'd thought Nique was an unusual
spelling for Nick. In his business he'd run into all sorts of
names with all sorts of spellings. "Omunique," he said aloud.
He'd never heard a more beautiful name. He had no idea of
its origin, but she'd certainly shown herself to be unique.

Omunique Philyaw was a woman he wanted to know everything about, a woman he wanted to become more than just a little
acquainted with. He hated to admit it, but he was bewitched,
enthralled with the woman.

Out in the reception area, Ken found Thomasina typing away.
Not wanting to startle her, he called her name softly.

Thomasina looked up and smiled warily. "Yes, Mr. Maxwell.
Is there something I can do for you?" she asked, turning away
from the computer to await his instructions.

Ken handed her a sheet of paper. "Get Bruce Smith on the
phone. That's his number. He's the agent of the Ice Princess
who's responsible for the freezing temperatures in here." To
Thomasina, the tone of his voice equaled his suggested room
temperature, causing her to grow even more wary of him.

He laughed at the expression on her face. "Don't look so
scared, Thom. I'm not nearly as cold as the winter storm that
just blew out of here. Welcome aboard."

Ken couldn't keep himself from smiling despite his chilly
reference to the young woman who had momentarily stolen
the temp's identity. The rather sassy beauty had somehow managed to enchant him. He had gotten something from her he
hadn't bargained for—nor had he liked it—when she'd told
him to contact her agent regarding dinner. If his suspicions
were correct, he was probably suffering from a severe case of
frostbite. Omunique Philyaw had completely blown him and
his self-assurance to smithereens. Nothing like this had ever
happened to him before. He understood it, but he didn't have
to like it.

In a semi-daze, he stared at the front door, as though she
might reappear if he prayed hard enough. No client had ever

walked out on him, and no woman had ever impacted him the way the gray-eyed stunner had. Eager to get down to work, Ken returned to his office.

Lavish and cozy, the coastal house stood only a few hundred yards from the sandy shores of Hermosa Beach. Enclosed in glass and surrounded by a large sweeping terrace, the white stucco house shone brightly under the Southern California sun. Omunique had become its sole occupant when her father moved to Northern California a short time ago.

Entering the house, Omunique threw her purse on the faux-stone sofa table. While surveying the surroundings she'd come to love so much, she walked into the living room. Painted in Navajo-white, swirling textured walls could be found throughout the house, along with gleaming, hardwood floors. Various paintings and portraits, many featuring Omunique on the ice, covered the walls. Exquisitely plush, the ivory chairs and the lavish, pillow back-style sofa had hand-pleated roll arms and fringed pillows, yet the formal area presented a look addressing comfort and relaxation. Cream-colored faux-stone tables and an entertainment center completed the decor.

Still confused from her brief encounter with the insufferable but definitely sexy Kenneth Maxwell Jr., she rubbed a shaking, fawn-brown hand over the back of her neck, hoping to ease the knots of tension. The fact that he hadn't bothered to prepare himself for the meeting still had her incensed, but her gentle side wrestled with the seemingly sincere excuse he'd given. Two hours wasn't a lot of lead time for something so important, she mused, lowering herself into one of the plush chairs. She tried to relax as she thought about how she was going to handle the problems she was faced with. Lack of money was the most complex.

To continue in her quest to earn a spot on the United States Olympic Figure Skating Team, she definitely needed a sponsor. First and foremost, monies were badly needed for her training sessions. There were other needs that had to be met, but none as important as her training needs. When her longtime agent, Bruce Smith, informed her that Kenneth Maxwell, the CEO of Maxwell's Athletic Wear, just might be interested in backing her quest for Olympic gold, she'd had Bruce immediately call him and set up the appointment.

Too bad he was called out of town. She knew she hadn't made such a great impression on the younger Maxwell. She could only hope the decision to sponsor her didn't lie solely with Junior. Since her father knew both Maxwell men, she picked up the receiver and placed a long-distance call to Wyman Philyaw's San Francisco office, hoping he could give her some insight into the younger Maxwell's psyche.

Omunique could almost see the grin that softened Wyman's cocoa-brown face. He was a very impressive man, she thought, envisioning his large but well-proportioned physique. His walnut-brown eyes, charged with an amazing amber glint, often duplicated the grin he usually wore on his handsome face, she mused with a delicious warmth.

At the sound of his daughter's delicate voice, Wyman dropped down in the chair behind his desk. "Nique, how are you? It's good to hear your voice." He then heard her sigh with discontent. "Is it my imagination, or are you piqued at something?"

She wrapped her fingers tightly around the arm of the chair. "You know me too well, Daddy. I drove all the way to Santa Monica, only to find that Mr. Maxwell hadn't even looked at my bio. How can they think of sponsoring someone they haven't bothered to check out? I may have wasted valuable time. I practically walked out on him, but I did agree to discuss business over dinner."

Wyman raised his bushy eyebrows, perplexed by what he'd just heard. "That doesn't sound like the Kenneth Maxwell I know. He's been in business for over thirty years, and I've never known Max to be unprepared for anything. Are you sure you're not just having an 'I'm too unique' sort of a day?"

Omunique laughed easily at their private joke. "Not hardly. It wasn't Ken Sr. that I met with. It was his non-unique son, Ken Jr. The Senior Maxwell is out of town. Apparently he's gone off and left his ill-prepared son in charge." She chewed on her lower lip. "First off, the guy thinks I'm the temporary secretary, and orders me to get to work. I played along, of course. I just couldn't resist."

Wyman snickered, imagining Omunique playing the dutiful secretary. "Sounds hilarious to me, Nique."

She didn't think it funny as she frowned. "Then I find out he thinks the client is a man, which means he didn't even take a peek at my bio. He did mention that he'd only been given the assignment two hours prior, but I'm afraid I wasn't in the mood to be tolerant. At least I wasn't my usual incorrigible self, though I was tempted."

"He's an intelligent young man, Nique. He comes from a good family, with good values. Max is an honorable man, and I'm sure he's instilled the same honor in his son. Like your dear old dad, Max is a widower. Ken Jr. also grew up without a mother."

Omunique wanted to hear more, but the call-waiting feature had clicked. "I've got to run, Dad. That might be Bruce on the other line. I'll call later and fill you in on the dinner details. Love you!"

Apprehension filled her as she clicked over to the other line. She somehow sensed the call wasn't of the social variety. She was sure the prime candidate for membership in the Black Brat Pack had squealed on her to Bruce—louder than a pig being led to slaughter.

Just as she'd expected, it was her agent. Her eyes brightened at the sound of his voice, but when he spoke she could tell Bruce had his agent's hat on, which meant he'd called to strictly discuss business.

"Bruce, I'm so happy to hear from you. What's up?" she asked, attempting to placate him before he jumped on her with both feet.

Her innocent act amused him. "Dinner, Nique. Seven o'clock at Barnabey's, Manhattan Beach. I'm sure you already know with whom. Don't be late . . . and be on your best behavior."

"Seven, it is. I'll be there, but I don't know if I'll be on my best behavior."

"Just stay focused, Nique. We both know what's at stake here. Call me tomorrow." He rang off before she could comment.

Frowning, she cradled the phone. "How am I going to get through dinner with such an arrogant man? I'd sooner throw myself into the cold Pacific than sit across from his smug, smiling face," she grumbled loudly.

She walked through the house and into the bathroom to run a hot bath. Knowing she'd been lying to herself, she laughed. Having dinner with the arrogant Kenneth Maxwell Jr. more than just appealed to her. She was downright excited about it.

She suspected that he could be just as stubborn as she was, and she expected their interactions to be somewhat fiery. If nothing else, the evening would indeed be very interesting. Omunique knew the explosive fireworks between them would be tantamount to two major planets colliding with one another, but she also knew that if she didn't behave herself Ken just might become her worst nightmare. She'd rather have him in her dreams.

With an enchanting smile glowing on her face, she snuggled her petite body down into the frothy, gardenia-scented water. This was one business meeting she was looking forward to handling. Meekly, she promised herself she'd be on her best behavior. Besides, Bruce would have her hide if she didn't perform like a trained seal.

Minutes later, up to her neck in bubbles and feeling very drowsy, she rested her head on the back of the tub. Fond thoughts of her father immediately came to mind. She really missed him. Wyman had only moved out of the house a little over a month ago, but it felt as if she'd been alone a lot longer. What would she have done without him? she wondered. She owed Wyman Philyaw for everything she'd become thus far, for all that she hoped to become. As she recalled the many sacrifices Wyman had made while getting her started in figure skating, she began to tremble. She would never forget how hard it had been for him financially, nor would she ever forget how they were treated when he'd first inquired about skating lessons for her.

Had Leopold Jarvis, the ice arena manager, known about her medical history and how hard Wyman would have to struggle to come up with tuition fees, he probably would've thought twice about enrolling her in the beginning lessons.

"Your daughter can probably learn the basic techniques of figure skating, but don't get your hopes up for much more than that. If you're hoping for your daughter to make a career out of figure skating, you're setting her up for bitter and major disappointments. The two chances that she'll have at attaining noteworthy achievements are slim, and none," he had told them.

That particular memory caused her to flinch. If she lived to be a hundred she'd never forget the way Leopold Jarvis had looked down his nose at them. Those unpleasant experiences were very much a part of the forces that drove her. Her desire to earn a spot on the U.S. Olympic Team was the most important driving force in her life.

Chapter Two

Barnabey's, a small, exclusive hotel and restaurant, was one of Ken's favorite places to dine. The popular English style eatery was quaint and rustic. Adjacent to the dining room, an English pub style bar could be seen from where Ken sat, along with a small dance floor and bandstand. A five-piece band entertained the dining patrons with a variety of soft hit tunes, past and present. Ken felt sure Omunique would like the place. It was a good place to mull over business matters, he thought as he waited for his dinner companion.

Omunique finally arrived, looking exquisite in a black crepe, backless dress with a halter neckline and a slightly flared bottom. A matching wrap fell elegantly about her slender shoulders. A hostess escorted her to Ken's table.

Lost in his thoughts, Ken sat quietly, sipping on a tall, cool drink. The mere sight of the dazzling Omunique left him breathless. Not only was she an incredibly well-built athlete, her beauty was inescapable. Dazed, he stared at her, feeling as though the world was using his stomach to rotate on. Trying to regain his composure, Ken stood up and politely pulled out a chair for her. He helped to remove her wrap, then carefully folded it and placed in on the back of an empty chair before returning to his own seat.

Omunique gazed at the man who set off every single one of her internal alarms, and she didn't even try to hide her approval of his dashing looks and impeccable attire. He looked fashionably scrumptious in his olive-green, double-breasted suit, and she couldn't help but notice how his deep lavender shirt hugged his rippling chest.

He didn't like the fact that he was so nervous around her. *She's just an ordinary woman,* he lied to himself, swallowing hard. "Miss Philyaw, I'm glad you could join me this evening," he charmed with ease.

As if I had a choice, she sang out inwardly, rolling her eyes up to the ceiling. *You're about to blow it,* said an annoying little voice inside her head. "I'm glad to be here. Thank you." Though she was now being polite, her expressively rude eye gesture hadn't gone unnoticed by him.

Ken began to feel even worse about their earlier meeting. He had to somehow convey his deep regret over their misunderstanding. Reluctantly, he reached across the table and put his hand over hers for a brief moment. "I really do feel awful about the way things went this morning, Miss Philyaw. I should've been better prepared. I'm not here to make excuses for myself—I simply blew it. I do hope you'll accept my deepest apology."

Slightly embarrassed by his humble speech, Omunique lowered her long eyelashes to half-mast. He seemed so sincere. How could she not accept his apology? Her brightest smile shimmied across the table. "All is forgiven, Mr. Maxwell."

He had soon learned much about her, and he was amazed by it all. He still couldn't believe how much this young woman had going for herself. She showed an extreme amount of confidence, not to mention her abilities as an athlete. She was bright and articulate. And he found some of the things she'd told him about the problems she'd had with her feet hard to believe.

Though she seemed to be unaffected by her childhood disability and a few childhood memories that she'd cited as bad, he sensed that it had all once impacted her greatly.

"As a child whose mother died during childbirth and someone born with a disability, you've certainly accomplished marvelous feats. You've overcome many obstacles, and you've done it against all odds."

"Thank you for your gracious remarks," she said, smiling. "I was only four years old when my father took me to the ice rink for the first time. He probably wouldn't have done it then, had it not been for my mother's love of the sport. Had she not been in ill health, she would've been the first black ice princess. Spill after spill occurred back then, but I kept at it. Something about the ice connected with my soul. It soon became an extension of my inner self. An extension that seems to be vital to my very existence."

She had the heart and the courage of a lion. *A lioness,* he reminded himself, a female in every sense of the word.

"And what's your claim to fame, Mr. Maxwell?"

A smile curled at the corners of his mouth as he recalled the first day that he began working at his father's company. "I was ten going on thirty. I started from the bottom and worked my way up. I took great pride in emptying the trash and tidying my father's desk. As each new assignment increased in importance, I began to understand how the rungs of success could be easily climbed—hard work and dedication."

After going away to college, where he majored in business administration, he became fiercely independent of the family corporation. But soon after graduation he was magnetically drawn back to his roots, he told her. In business he was every bit as brilliant as his father. His firsthand knowledge of the company, along with his dedication to it, obviously made him a vital part of Maxwell Athletic Corporation. Wise investments had already earned him a small fortune.

Hardly a word was spoken as they consumed a deliciously prepared meal of prime rib and the traditional compliments.

Once the table was cleared, Ken did his best to turn back to the sparkling conversation they'd enjoyed before dinner had been served, but it appeared as though Omunique had her mind on something else. He couldn't help noticing the disinterested look on her lovely face, which set his teeth on edge. He tried to open things up by reverting to questions about her, but her responses seemed dry and terse.

He eyed her with concern. "Are you feeling okay, Miss Philyaw? You seem somewhat distracted."

Omunique looked crestfallen. "You'll have to forgive me, Mr. Maxwell. I'm afraid I'm a little tired. It's been a long day for me." She excused herself under the guise of needing to use the ladies' room. He quickly got to his feet and pulled out her chair. Wondering what alien forces drove her, he studied her intently as she made her way across the room.

Omunique simply needed to regroup. She was more tired than she'd originally thought. She hadn't meant to be rude to him like that. She had acted horribly, she realized, and she certainly didn't want him to think she didn't like him. She liked everything about him, from his beautiful head of dark-brown, curly hair down to his expensive leather shoes. In her opinion, his lithe body was a gift from heaven. No doubt. Those piercing autumn-gold eyes of his absolutely electrified her. When he trained those eyes on her she knew he could easily have his way with her, despite the fact his earlier reception had left her cold.

"Get over it," she chided herself, repairing her makeup. Satisfied with her appearance, she hastily exited the ladies' room. Though her wild attraction to Ken unsettled her, her euphoria over it couldn't be denied.

He rushed over to pull her chair out when she returned. She liked his attentiveness. He seemed to be the type of man who anticipates a woman's every need. Omunique's chilled thoughts about him had thawed at an alarming rate. She figured if she didn't deep-freeze her own attitude, she'd soon be dripping wet.

Opening up like a dew-kissed rosebud, she allowed her sweet charm to drift toward Ken, who unwittingly hung on her every word. "You and your father won't be sorry should you decide to sponsor me. My love for figure skating makes even my hardest workouts pleasurable. Each time I step onto the ice, it's more thrilling than the last. I get feverish and goose bumps all at the same time. It's simply in my blood. You'll easily recognize the depth of passion in my work when you see me skate."

He found her enthusiasm for her chosen sport exhilarating as she again discussed it with zeal. In an attempt to keep her talking, he constantly fired questions her way. As her softly lilting voice lulled him into a false sense of security, he lost himself to her unending charms.

Out of the blue, though, her rude behavior seemed to surface. When she responded to one of his questions in a sharp tone, he believed that she'd been putting up a front, which crash-landed him with a crushing thud.

He cut his eyes sharply at her. "Not only are you an ice princess, you're a darn good actress, as well. I thought we'd found some common ground," he commented drily.

She was as disappointed in her rude behavior as he was. A look of utter bewilderment swept across her soft features.

His heart turned a double flip. Cocking his head to one side, he eyed her curiously. "Is it possible I've misread you again?"

One could have skated on her eyes as they turned to sparkling sheets of metallic silver. She smiled warmly. "Yep, you certainly have. I've gone from a temp to a man, from an ice princess to an actress, all in less than twelve hours. Wow! I'm more unique than I thought. Maybe I can work it all into my next skating program." Her laughter rang out lustily. He laughed, too, when it appeared she was thoroughly enjoying herself. She suddenly felt reenergized. Fatigue just up and left her.

Their conversation quickly turned back to one of animation. Omunique's laughter excited him, and she looked less tense.

The brilliant smile on her face further elevated his optimism. Dazed, Ken listened as she shared some of her experiences on the ice. He couldn't believe how quickly the tide had turned for them, nor could he believe his good fortune. For the time being, he had this fascinating woman all to himself.

She smiled brilliantly at him. "I'm glad we're taking the time to get to know one another, Ken. I think it would be a good idea for us to try to settle our differences."

He was prepared to give her concerns his undivided attention, and his eyes connected soulfully with hers. "Which of our differences would you like to settle first, Omunique?"

The room suddenly crackled with sexual tension as she practically scrambled her brain trying to come up with a response. How could she speak to differences when he looked at her with such desire in his eyes?

"I'm no longer sure what they are, at least not right now. If we should get the opportunity to work together, I'm sure we'll probably rediscover them. But we can work them out as they come up." She took a deep breath. "You apologized for our earlier mishap—and I accepted. Now it's my turn to apologize. I'm sorry I've been less than charming, Ken."

He grinned. "I accept. Do you think it's possible we can just relax now and enjoy ourselves?"

She looked around the room before looking back at him. "I think so. It's kind of nice here . . . and the music is so relaxing. We owe it to ourselves to at least try to make the last part of the evening truly delightful."

He touched her hand. "I couldn't agree more. It is nice here, isn't it?"

As much as he wanted to know if there were other reasons she'd chosen to remain in his company, he let it go. Their relationship, business or otherwise, was just under construction. While it was in its embryonic stage, he didn't want to do anything to endanger its potential for growth. He felt rather encouraged by the fact she wasn't easily brought into the fold.

Most women were immediately drawn to him. This, unfortunately, had saddled him with the title of notorious playboy.

As the evening moved on Omunique noticed how their comments and gestures toward one another had become slightly flirtatious. Their body language seemed to suggest they were comfortable in each other's presences. They were now on a first name basis, and neither of them seemed aware of when the transformation had occurred. Omunique no longer felt as though she needed to be rescued from herself. Though earlier she'd unwittingly displayed a fair amount of disinterest in her host, she had realized an important career opportunity could be lost to her if she continued in that mode. She needed the Maxwell name and money behind her.

But that wasn't the reason she'd stayed beyond dinner. Her personal interest in him summed it up quite nicely. The fear of being alone with such a charming devil no longer concerned her. He turned her emotions inside out. Kenneth Maxwell Jr. had something else she wanted, but she would now have to identify exactly what that was. He offered her a challenge she felt prepared to take.

Omunique stifled a yawn. "I think it's time for me to get home. Would you like to come to my place for dinner tomorrow evening? We could finish our business and then have the dessert we were too full for."

A trickle of undeniable pleasure coursed through him. "I would be delighted, Omunique. What time?"

"Sevenish?"

He beamed his agreement. Reminding himself that she'd said business, he came down from heaven a little, but not enough to cause his spirits to dampen.

Inwardly, he whistled a happy tune as he guided Omunique out into the chilly night air. After making sure she was safe and sound in her own car, he went off to his, still whistling.

* * *

Stretched out in her large bed but unable to sleep, Omunique looked around the massive bedroom. Done in various shades of pink, adorned with frills and lace, it was the room of her childhood dreams. Blush-pink linens caressed the king-size bed intimately.

In hopes of pushing Ken Maxwell Jr. from her mind, Omunique rolled over and switched the radio on. Failing at her mission, she allowed his autumn-gold eyes to drift along the pathway of her memory. His dark brown curly hair looked soft and crushable. His dangerous sexual aura was deeply compelling, his tall, lean frame powerfully masculine.

Scowling, Omunique thought about the dinner invitation she'd extended to Ken. What had gotten into her? She couldn't even cook.

Getting out of bed, she slipped into a robe and tied the belt loosely about her slender waist. Slipping her feet into a pair of slippers, she left the room and headed toward the front of the house.

Easing open the heavy swinging doors, she turned on the light and peeked inside. Glistening with wheat-gold appliances and shiny, ceramic tile counters, it was a large, homey kitchen. The stained oak cabinets were beautifully carved in an intricate design. A variety of copper-bottomed pots and pans hung on racks high above the center island.

She liked the feel of the room. She propped herself on an oak stool at the breakfast bar, wondering what she could possibly prepare for dinner the next evening that would be relatively easy for someone who had no culinary skills whatsoever. "Well, I can follow directions."

She reached for a copy of the *Ebony* cookbook entitled *Date With a Dish*. Broiled steak and baked potatoes was something she might be able to accomplish with ease, she decided before returning to her bedroom.

Back in bed, she let the melodious sounds of the surf relax her as she happily mulled over the wonderful memories she'd recently made with her intriguing dinner companion. Minutes later she fell asleep, with Ken still on her mind.

In the early morning hours Omunique pulled her late model Jeep Cherokee into a parking space at the Palos Verdes indoor ice rink, where she would train for the next several hours. After retrieving her skating gear from the backseat, she entered the building and headed straight for the womens' locker room.

She slipped off her jeans and wrapped a short skirt around the black leotard she wore beneath her attire. Standing at the mirror, she brushed her long, almond-brown hair into a ponytail and secured it with a heavy metal clasp.

Minutes later, when she took to the ice, she noticed Brent Masters, her skating coach, standing off to the side of the railing, both toast-brown hands firmly posted on his slender hips. Slim, with an athletic build, his body seemed to boast its muscled strength. Glancing down at his wristwatch, he scowled over the rim of his metal-rimmed glasses. Skating to where he stood, she greeted him enthusiastically.

His topaz eyes narrowed as he looked from his watch to her. "Where have you been, Nique? If I tell you seven o'clock, I mean just that," he practically growled.

Granted, a minute late is late, however you look at it, she thought, but she didn't think her being late was what really bothered him. Brent had been on edge a lot lately, which was uncharacteristic of him. Normally he was gentle, soft-spoken.

He snorted and gave her an impatient glance. "Do your stretches, then get started." When she opened her mouth to protest, he yelled, "Move it, Nique. Now!"

Casting him a bold look of defiance, she skated to a secluded corner of the ice, wondering what was really eating at him. It couldn't be the measly minute.

Immediately feeling guilty for having needlessly raked her over the coals, Brent shoved a hand through his wavy, dark brown hair. *Get a grip,* he scolded himself.

Sitting down on a metal bench, he thought of the phone calls he'd been receiving. Before leaving his private office he'd received another, one that made his blood curl. The earlier calls had been very complimentary, but the last few had turned malicious. And they were all directed at his champion skater.

Earlier, when Brent had picked up the phone, the familiar, once friendly voice that had once championed Omunique had come over the line. The voice had turned ugly and cold. The caller's breathing sounded labored, as well. The tone had been very accusatory. "Omunique didn't smile at me today. I didn't like it. Is she smiling at someone else? I certainly hope not. Smiles can often turn to frowns!"

Brent shuddered. The caller had used his office number to communicate his grievances. Of course, whoever was doing this had no way of getting her private number. It was unlisted, thank God. The caller was sadly mistaken if he thought he was going to be his message boy, Brent thought with deep anger. The only people Brent was going to deliver those messages to would be the proper authorities. Something had to be done before this nut could make good on whatever his intentions were.

Joining Omunique on the ice, Brent took her aside and apologized for his outburst. Proving her theory, or so she thought, he explained that something personal was bothering him. He instructed her not to be concerned.

She smiled with relief. "It's okay. I understand." She hugged him before she skated off.

She went through her routine with perfect precision, making him proud. Her jumps and turns were fluidly smooth. A little concerned with the triple axel—regarded as the most difficult jump in skating, the only one where the skater takes off from a forward position—he rushed to her side.

"That was a little rough around the edges, Nique. You came up a little short. Take your time, sweetheart," he encouraged with patience and kindness.

Completely accepting of his well-meaning comments, she listened eagerly.

Brent Masters was an authority on the sport. He'd spent twenty years of his life mastering the art. He never made it to the big show. However, he had won several state and national titles. After many years of being a part of professional skating tours, he had taken up coaching. In her opinion, he was a darn good coach, a devoted one.

The next triple axel was much worse than the previous one, landing her hard on the ice. Smiling sheepishly, she pulled herself up and tried it again and again. *All heart,* he thought quietly. She had a determined heart, and he loved her for it.

He beamed when she landed a near perfect triple axle. "Okay, give that one a rest. Go ahead and work through the rest of your program, Nique."

She did, flawlessly. When she didn't give it her all, she was more aware of it than anyone else, including her coach, but Brent Masters didn't miss much. If she got too lax, he didn't have a problem letting her know about it.

Often, she left practice sessions dissatisfied, but not this time. She had worked her tail off. She was fatigued as she wangled the Jeep into the circular driveway, but the thought of having dinner with Kenneth Maxwell Jr. lent her a fresh burst of energy.

The beach house was dreadfully still when she entered. She had gotten somewhat used to living alone, but she really didn't like it. Her father's move up north when one of his insurance agencies began to fail had come without warning. Pushing the loneliness aside, she entered the bedroom and quickly changed clothing. She then grabbed a wool sweater from the hall closet and headed for the sliding glass doors at the front of the house.

While taking the stone steps that led down to the beach, where she always went to unwind and release the stresses of the day, she marveled at the beauty of the open sea. Pulling the metal clasp from her hair, she welcomed the cool breeze that rushed in and vigorously massaged her scalp.

The coastline was dotted with magnificent houses, small and large. A barking dog could be heard off in the distance before she spotted the small animal as it ran alongside its master. *No place on earth is more restful,* she mused. There was no place she enjoyed more when taking time out. Not in any hurry, she walked along the windswept shore. Sand flew, but she remained undaunted. This was her time of peace, when she could shut out the roar of the busy world she lived in, a time that belonged solely to her. Much of her time was spent chasing her seemingly elusive dreams. She would chase those dreams to the end of the world. She'd come too far to give up now.

Nearly tripping over a jagged rock, she began to watch more closely the path she was on. To twist or sprain a limb was the last thing she needed. During her career a few sprains and aches had sidelined her. Thinking of the U.S. National Championships to be held soon, she knew she needed to be in tip-top shape. A top three win would lay the final brick on the red, white, and blue road that led straight to the Olympics, as a member of the United States Olympic Team—her lifelong dream.

The air had gotten cooler, she noted, slipping the sweater around her shoulders. Glancing at her wristwatch, she saw that it was almost five o'clock, nearly sunset. Positioning herself on a large boulder, she waited breathlessly for the now orange sun to plunge into the depths of the dark, mysterious sea. The silver moon was already in place to relieve the sun of its illumination duties. In awe, she waited.

While the moon lighted her path, she made her way back up the stone steps. The mildly sedating night sounds hummed in her ears as she turned to watch a group of seagulls swoop across the softly moonlit sky. The scene before her was a perfect subject for a dazzling work of art. The purple velvet sky, streaked with flashes of gold and orange, further illuminated the wondrous awe in her smoky-gray eyes.

* . * *

She pulled two steaks from the refrigerator. The phone rang just as Omunique ignited the oven to bake the potatoes. Though she didn't know why, apprehension seeped into her soul. She immediately recognized the sultry voice that wreaked havoc on her composure as it came over the line.

"Hi," she greeted with enthusiasm. "I guess you're calling for directions."

A deep sigh of regret came from his end. "No, Omunique, I'm not. Something terribly important has come up. I won't be able to make it." A long silence ensued, and then he heard her suck in a deep breath.

She felt very disappointed. "Oh I see, Ken. Well, I guess it's your loss. Another time, perhaps."

His father hadn't made it back to town, which forced him into taking another of his appointments—a dinner appointment, no less. He'd momentarily toyed with the idea of taking her along. Knowing he wouldn't be able to accomplish a thing in the company of such a stunning distraction kept him from asking.

"You bet it's my loss. Listen, if I can rush through this appointment can I come for dessert?" He crossed his fingers, hoping against hope she'd agree. Slightly familiar with her arrogance, he rather doubted it.

Not wanting to come off too eager, she forced her tone into a casual mode. "We'll see what time it is when you finish. You can call me back then."

She hadn't said no, and that was more than he'd expected. "Just in case, give me the directions while I have you on the line. I'll call you as soon as I can." He wrote down the instructions and rang off.

Omunique put the steaks away, aware that her appetite was all but gone. Snapping a banana from its stem, she stripped it of its yellow jacket. After breaking a piece off, she discarded the skin in the metal wastebasket. Her next stop was the living room, where she stacked the compact disc player and turned on all the speakers. *Another night alone,* she thought sadly, heading for the pink bathroom, where she turned on the hot water.

Pink wasn't even her favorite color, but it had been her mother's. She really didn't have a favorite color, she realized as she thought about it, but she did love bright and showy ones. This was evident in her stylish wardrobe.

When she stepped into the tub, the water, smelling of sweet jasmine, teemed with steaming heat. Scooting down to one end of the tub, she submerged her body deep into the frothy water. Removing the bath sponge from its holder, she dipped it into the hot water and squeezed it over her neck and shoulders. "Wonderful," she gasped. "Simply wonderful."

Relaxing her back against a pink bath pillow, she listened as Mariah Carey belted out one of her favorite songs, "Hero." Would Kenneth Maxwell Jr. become her hero? she wondered wistfully. *Nique, baby, you're getting way ahead of yourself,* she chided, laughing.

Unsure of the type of clothing she should wear, nightclothes being the heavy favorite, she opted for an electric-blue, loose-fitting caftan. Its simple but elegant style was appropriate for company, or for just relaxing alone. She rather suspected the latter would occur.

Many of her nights were spent alone, especially since her father had moved away. Though he visited often, she was still left to her own devices during most evenings and weekends. He was the only male figure she could relate to. Their relationship could hardly be compared with the type of intimate relationship that existed between a man and a woman, the type every woman should've had some experience with by the age of twenty-one.

There weren't any serious male suitors in her life, past or present. She just hadn't had time for any sort of personal relationship. Her busy schedule had practically made her a social recluse, with the exception of career-related functions. In her heart of hearts, figure skating was her true love, her destiny. It would never intentionally hurt her, nor would it cut her to the quick. Only she could do that by being unprepared, or by lacking a strong commitment. She would never even consider that someone else might be a better skater than she was. Such thoughts were self-defeating.

Dressed in the stunning caftan, her hair loose and free, she took up residence on the sofa. She picked up a pen and some paper from the table and began to write. She loved to write poetry. It gave her the opportunity to free her mind when writing about her life experiences, the bitter and the sweet. Omunique always focused in on everything around her, often tucking it away in her mind for later retrieval. Writing about nature exhilarated her. It relaxed her and allowed her mind to flow in any direction it chose. All of God's creations made her feel alive. Her crystal clear vision of their beauty flowed from the pen like a bubbling brook rushing through a lush, green countryside.

Creativity was called to a screeching halt when the doorbell pealed. Startled, she looked at the clock. Two hours had passed, but she'd been too lost in her wordy creations to notice the time.

Chapter Three

Omunique opened the door to Ken, more handsome than she remembered. His green shirt seemed to cast its deep, dark color into the tranquilizing depths of his eyes. His sexy, dazzling white smile made her weak at the knees.

He took her hands in his. "Couldn't find a telephone," he joked, his sultry voice turning her on in ways that shook her foundation.

Her smile came quick and easy. "Liar." Her laughter danced on the seabreeze as she stepped outside and pointed in the direction of a pay phone nearby. She then stepped back inside and made a sweeping gesture to approve his entry.

Ken allowed his breath to escape. Spreading wildfire warmth to every part of her sexual being, his deep, guttural laughter sluiced right through her. "You had me worried there for a minute. The little I know of you, I had to believe you really would've sent me packing. To be honest, I didn't call because I feared you'd say it was too late." He seemed embarrassed by his confession. She thought it was charming.

"Since we're only talking business, I probably wouldn't

have turned you down.'' Business was the furthest thing from either of their minds. Both were critically aware of it.

Omunique led the way into the living room and told him to have a seat anywhere he would like. Spotting the pen and paper on the sofa, he sat right beside it, hoping she would return to where she'd obviously been sitting.

As he looked around the room, he was impressed with what he could see. *Someone has expensive taste,* he mused. He didn't need to tell her what he thought of her home. She could see it from the expression on his handsome face.

She sat down, closer to him than he'd dared to hope. "Ready to get down to business?" she asked, trying desperately to sound professional.

Ken reached into the inside pocket of his dark brown blazer and pulled out a few neatly folded papers. "The terms in this proposal should be easy enough to understand, but you're welcome to have your attorney look it over. In fact, I advise it."

She couldn't believe her good fortune as she ran a quick eye over the proposal for sponsorship. "Lamar Lyons, my attorney, will read me the riot act if I don't present this to him before agreeing to its terms, verbal or otherwise. Lawyers are that way, you know. I'll make an appointment with him and have it back to you as soon as possible." She silently thanked God for answering her prayers as she placed the typed papers on the coffee table. If Lamar approved, the monies offered would more than cover her training needs and end her immediate problems.

He grinned. "We'd like to schedule a screen test for you. How is your schedule for next week?"

Her sleek brow furrowed. "A screen test?"

He nodded his head. "Along with sponsoring you, I'm going to recommend you for the position of spokeswoman for our line of women's athletic wear—that is, when the time comes. I'd just like to get an idea of what you're going to look like in our gear on film." She could barely contain her enthusiasm as she quietly thanked God for the extra added blessing, should it happen. An endorsement contract was every athlete's dream. "If and when my recommendation is approved by the board, we'll need to do a few commercial spots. It's not something we've done a lot of, but we've never had such a multifaceted subject to work with, nor have we ever had the pleasure of working with a figure skater—an African-American one, at that."

He looked slightly abashed. "I really hate to admit this, but we've never used a woman in any of our campaign ads. That's about to change."

"Why is that?" she asked, curious.

"Until recently, we just couldn't afford names like Flo Jo and Jackie Joyner-Kersee. When the time comes, I hope we'll be able to afford you."

Her laughter was soft and tantalizing. "Is it really all about larger than life egos and matching bank accounts?"

"It can get pretty rough. But I guess if we want our sales to continue to go through the roof, we're just going to have to deal with the egos while shelling out the big bucks."

She laughed again. "I do have an ego, but I can assure you it's not larger than life, at least not yet. I'm sure we can reach an amicable agreement. I'll check my ego out once I win that spot on the U.S. team."

"That sure of yourself, huh?"

"You bet! Your organization must be pretty sure of me, as well. If they weren't, I don't think they'd be willing to put all that money behind me."

"Let's just say my father did his homework. This has been his baby from the outset. Besides your ability to skate well, which of course is the most important factor, I'm sure your being a woman and an African-American was greatly appealing to him. We have yet to sit down and discuss you. That's one of the reasons I didn't know who you were." He draped his arm along the back of the sofa. "Well, that was certainly painless. Now, about that dessert. Or do you have some other business matters you'd like to discuss?"

She touched a glossy fingernail to her temple. "Yes, *serious* business. The dessert I'm about to serve you is indeed very serious business, if you like sweet potato pie."

His eyes danced merrily in his head as he rubbed his stomach. "I love it, Omunique. Did you bake it?"

She started to lie, but thought better of it. "Only the baker knows for sure." *The baker at the local pastry shop,* she quipped cerebrally. "Maybe I'll tell you after I see if you like it or not." His laughter enchanted her, causing her to draw in a shaky breath. "I can serve it in here if you like," she offered with a smile.

He got to his feet. "If it's okay, I'll come into the kitchen. That way, you won't have to make a half dozen trips. As you said, sweet potato pie is serious business. Lead the way, Ice Princess." A smile lighting up his face, he followed her into the kitchen.

As she groped for the light switch, he had the urge to wrap his strong arms around her tiny waist and gently bring her to him. He couldn't see her eyes clearly, but he could feel them. The aura around her seemed to be free of hostility. Still, he thought better of making such a bold move on her. It was much too soon. "Why don't we light a candle?" he whispered near her ear.

As far as she was concerned, the brilliance of his autumn-gold eyes was more than enough. With a flick of her wrist, light flooded the kitchen. "I don't do candlelight." They both burst into gales of laughter. Ken now considered the "don't do" statements their very own private joke.

Glad his offhand remark hadn't offended her, he sat on a stool at the breakfast nook, where he watched her every graceful movement. Driving him to distraction was the sensuous scent of her perfume gliding on the air.

After spooning out a whipped concoction, she plopped it on top of the huge wedge of pie. Carrying it over to the breakfast

Linda Hudson-Smith
BET/Arabesque Author
Poetess, Screenwriter
2026C N. Riverside Ave, Box 109
Rialto, Ca 92377
(909) 716-6572

E-mail: lhs4romance@yahoo.com

http://romantictales.com/linda/index.html

Soulful Serenade   ISBN 1-58314-140-5

IN BOOKSTORES AUGUST 2000

Soulful Serenade

Linda Hudson-Smith

bar, she placed the dish in front of him, handed him a shiny fork, then hopped onto the stool beside his.

He looked at her questioningly. "Where's yours? Or are we going to share mine?" She raised an eyebrow, wistfully eyeing the delicious looking dessert. "Oh, let me guess. You don't do dessert, either," he mocked, his eyes traveling heatedly over her curvaceous body. "It does show on your lovely figure."

She smiled at the meaningful reference. "In my profession, I can ill afford to indulge myself in such sweet obscenities. I do cheat now and then, but never with anything I know I can't be satisfied with just a dab of. If I touch that pie, I won't be able to stop myself from overindulging."

Fully understanding her dilemma, he nodded. "Disciplined, huh? I like that." Though it appeared he had understood, it didn't stop him from raising his fork to her lips in an attempt to test her resolve. "How disciplined?" he challenged, mischief twinkling in his eyes.

Omunique threw him an uneasy glance as she picked up the offered bite of pie from his fork and directed it toward her mouth. Instead of eating it, she smeared it in one quick motion all over his succulent lips with her fingers. "How's that for discipline?" she asked smugly, barely able to harness the laughter in her throat.

His eyes registered shock and disbelief. Then, in a movement much quicker than her own, he retaliated. Imagining him using his provocative mouth to spread the pie over her lips, she closed her eyes, gasping inwardly. She wondered how much of a fight she would put up if he tried to kiss her. She already knew she'd hardly be a match for his strength. Her eyes were still closed when she felt his moist tongue push through the slight opening of her mouth. There, in his passionate embrace, her questions were answered. She had no desire to put up a fight, nor did she want to escape his kiss.

Greedily, they sucked at the sweetness of each other's mouths. She molded her upper body against his muscular chest. As he was tender in his explorations of her, she eagerly conducted eye-opening explorations of her own. Eons seemed to have passed before they gained enough control to separate.

Expecting her to be upset with him, however willing it seemed she'd been, he looked deeply into her eyes. "Maybe I shouldn't have done that, but I couldn't seem to help myself."

Sensing his uncertainty, she touched his cheek. "It's okay. Until now, I didn't do kisses, either." *But I'm afraid yours are the kind I can't be satisfied with just a dab of,* she confessed mentally.

Relief washed over him as he expelled a gush of breath. "Until now, I've never been so deeply satisfied by a kiss. And I hope my kisses won't be classified as 'sweet obscenities.' Care to indulge in another?" he inquired breathlessly.

Without the slightest hesitation, she stretched her limber body across the barstool and went into his arms. As she plied his mouth with warm, sensuous kisses, his hands torridly roved over her body, defrosting the ice princess. Abandoning all fears, she permitted him to familiarize himself with her softness. Trusting that he wouldn't go any further than she would allow, she relaxed under his gentle probing. While neither of them dared to analyze what was happening between them, they lost themselves to the moment.

They found their way into the living room, where he dropped down on the sofa first and then pulled her down beside him. With her sense of propriety returning, Omunique put a little safe distance between her and Ken's alluring physique.

Besides, he was a playboy, she reminded herself. The previous night, when she'd remembered reading something about him in an issue of *Ebony Man,* she'd dug the issue out of a pile of old magazines kept in one of the spacious bedrooms that had been transformed into an office. Indeed, he'd been described as single and one of the most eligible bachelors in Southern California. According to the magazine story, though, he simply wasn't interested in marrying—ever.

He nudged her gently. "What are you thinking about?"

Her smile came slow but sure "Nothing important," she lied. *Just that you're not interested in marriage.*

While marriage had no place in her immediate future, she did hope to marry someday. There were times when just the thought of it scared her to death, especially when she thought about what the loss of her mother had done to her father. Twenty-one years had passed, but Wyman still grieved for his precious Patrice. He'd lost his beloved wife only moments after she'd given birth to their only child.

While conversing well into the night, they discovered they had more than just a little in common. Both having grown up with only one parent, they talked about the difficulties they'd experienced by not having a mother around to nurture them. Julia Maxwell, Ken's mother, had died of breast cancer, but he talked very little about the too painful subject. His was still a private hurt. Although both had received quite adequate nurturing from their fathers, they expressed their cravings for the tenderness only a mother could provide.

Two-thirty in the morning, Ken noted as he checked his watch. Sliding his hand under the hair at her nape, he kissed her. Much to her dismay, he kissed her as though he was kissing a friend, but he'd sensed her need for reserve.

"Can I call you later in the day?" he asked, knowing he'd call no matter how she responded.

"Make it later in the evening. I train until four or four-thirty, then I have a few personal errands to run. After seven would be an excellent time. I'm usually wound down by then."

Ken smiled and nodded. "After seven, Miss Philyaw. Thank you for the wonderful company and the delicious pie, especially the part I tasted from your sweet mouth."

He hesitated, mentally preserving the precious memories of the last few hours.

It appeared he didn't want to leave. Omunique didn't want him to go, either. She wanted to undress him and feel his nakedness. She wanted to discover what it would feel like to have a man nestled deeply inside of her.

Just any man would never do. Handsome, intelligent, witty, and sensitive, Kenneth Maxwell Jr. was the man she passionately desired, the only man she'd ever desired in the physical sense, the only man to ever awaken her dormant sexuality. . . .

Ken reluctantly moved out of the door, then sharply turned on his heels and drew her in close. His lips crashed down over hers, taking what he couldn't get enough of, giving her what she no longer wanted to do without. Knowing he wanted to possess her completely, he rushed away without risking another glance at her beautiful face.

Shock waves reverberated through her entire body as she closed the door and leaned against it, trying to steady her wildly pulsating heart rate. She finally dragged herself into the living room. Curling up in the spot he'd just vacated, she felt the warmth he'd left behind. It was delicious warmth, warmth the cold ice would never be able to offer her. While drifting off to sleep, she hoped her dreams would be filled with wondrous, erotic fantasies, starring Kenneth Maxwell Jr.

Without turning on the lights in his posh Venice Beach condo, Ken entered the master bedroom and dropped down on the bed. "What the hell happened out there tonight?" he asked aloud. That little witch had stunned him with a potion deadlier than voodoo. "That's what happened," he concluded incredulously.

Hell, hadn't he hoped for what had occurred between them? Hadn't he gone there with the intention of seducing her? The answers came easily. After sliding his shoes off, he lay back on the dark burgundy coverlet. Thinking of dry ice, he remembered how easily it could burn the skin while sticking to it. She'd stuck it to him, all right, leaving him with third-degree burns. But there wasn't a dry thing about her, he recalled, remembering her moist kisses and the liquid smoke that seemed to rise from those bewitching silver eyes.

Ken looked over at the softly illuminated phone dial. No,

he reasoned. She needed her rest. He needed his, too, but he knew all too well there'd be no rest for him until he held her in his arms again.

While waiting for the screen test to get under way, Omunique tried to calm her nerves by leafing through a magazine, but she couldn't seem to concentrate. She'd been in front of the camera on numerous occasions, but Ken Maxwell's distracting presence hadn't been there to unnerve her. When she'd first arrived at the studio, they'd only had a chance to wave to one another, not enough time for them to break the ice.

Although she'd tried, she just couldn't forget all the intimacy that had passed between them. Ken had phoned a time or two, but they hadn't been able to talk for any length of time. She'd been getting to the ice arena early in the mornings, and his schedule had been quite hectic. She'd learned of the screen test date through her agent.

As Ken eyed her intently from across the room, he realized this wasn't the time or the place for them to discuss personal matters, but he couldn't help wondering if the wonderful kisses they'd shared meant anything at all to her, especially when they meant so much to him. It bothered him that she hardly looked his way, but he was sure she wasn't reading since the magazine was upside down. He nearly laughed, hoping he had everything to do with her seemingly confused state of mind.

Bill Faison, the video cameraman, entered the room. "We're ready for you, Miss Philyaw," he said, smiling as she came toward him. "We're just going to do a few head shots."

Omunique smiled back at him. "Okay. Lead the way."

The camera seemed to love Omunique, Ken observed as she complied with Bill's instructions. Ken watched as she easily turned her head to accommodate the direction of the lens. The wide lens appeared eager to zoom in on her natural beauty. He loved the way she responded to the camera. As Bill happily clicked the shutter over and over again, her natural beauty and elegant grace excited Ken beyond reason.

When Ken later reviewed the video proofs, he found that he could hardly breathe. From the photos he'd already seen of her, he'd expected her to be photogenic, but what he now saw was too incredible for words. Her smoky-silver eyes captivated him, her full luscious mouth teased him relentlessly, and her soft, elegant neck appealed to him sensuously. Omunique was a total athletic package, and her looks alone were worth every penny the corporation would eventually pay her to endorse their products. If her skating was as beautiful as she looked, they had a hands-down winner, Ken marveled happily.

Approaching her with a caution he didn't particularly understand, he handed her the photo proofs. "These pictures are sensational! What do you think?" he asked, closely studying her reaction to the stunning photos.

Though she only made brief eye contact with him, she smiled brightly at the photos. "They are good," she announced, holding them up to the light. "Are you satisfied with the outcome?"

More than you'll ever know. "I am. Are you ready to move on?"

"Yes. What is it you have in mind for me to wear?" she inquired, glancing up at him.

Nothing at all would do just fine, he thought with mischief, conjuring up a nude image of her. "I brought along a few pieces of our workout attire. They're in the dressing room." He pointed her in the right direction. "Everything will be set up by the time you change."

Omunique was nearly breathless as she disappeared into the tiny dressing room. Ken looked better every time she saw him. How she had managed to act so cool and calm was a mystery. She might have looked as though she wasn't hotly bothered by his virile presence, but her quaking insides told an altogether different story.

She could barely move around inside the miniscule dressing room, but limited space was something she'd gotten used to.

While touring on the road, she often found herself in such quarters. Some of the places she performed in didn't have the fancy gym facilities she was accustomed to. Omunique had learned long ago to make the best of every situation, and she could easily adapt to most. In her profession, adaptability was necessary. The unexpected always had a way of rearing its head. Thus far, she'd been able to rise to each and every occasion.

Ken wasn't the only male who stifled a wolf whistle when she returned to the outer studio. The basic black one-piece, knee-length leotard would've been just another piece of spandex without Omunique's magnificent physique poured into it. If she didn't know how darn good she looked, Ken thought someone other than himself should shout it out loud.

A look of pure innocence gleamed in her eyes. "How does it look?" she asked no one in particular. All of the men quickly exchanged wide-eyed, haven't-you-looked-in-the-mirror glances.

The photographer had a hard time finding his voice as he trained the video camera on her upper body. "It looks just great, honey. Can you flex a few muscles for me?"

Laughing, Omunique flexed the small but firm muscles in her arms, then the larger ones in her calves. Taking her cues from Bill, she flitted around the studio, posing as well as any professional model.

The lens of the camera was not the only thing eating her alive, Ken noted. The men's tongues were practically hanging out. Their eyes seemed to devour her.

"That's great, honey. Now show me those beautiful pearly whites," Bill encouraged. "Okay! Now give me a look that says come and get it while it's hot." Her cheeks colored, and the rosy nuance of her blushing innocence gave Bill exactly what he'd been hoping for. "Keep that look, baby. We'll be through in just a few minutes."

Though Ken didn't like all the endearing names Bill showered on Omunique, he made a gallant attempt to hide it. She, on the other hand, seemed to be eating up the endearments.

That annoyed him. At Bill's prompting, her last pose was so seductive it made Ken want to rush over and shield her body from all the lustful eyes, including his own.

There weren't any words to describe the outcome of the project. In fact, Ken didn't think it even needed any editing. He was extremely excited about the video. It was better than good, even without her uttering a single word. What was it going to be like when she actually spoke into the camera's recording device? He could only imagine the favorable response she'd receive. There was little doubt in his mind that she'd be an excellent spokesperson for the company when the time came. Clad in Maxwell's beautifully designed athletic wear, Omunique's body would be a walking advertisement.

Frowning, Ken caught up to Omunique in the underground parking garage and slid his hand under her elbow with ease, turning her around to face him. "Am I missing something here? Why did you take off like that? What's up with the freeze out?"

Breaking eye contact, she lowered her lids. "We were working, Ken. I wasn't sure what to do, given the circumstances."

"If that's all it was, then why don't I believe you?"

Her body tensed as she made direct eye contact with him. "Are you calling me a liar, Mr. Maxwell?"

"I don't recall that particular word coming out of my mouth. If that's all it was, I'm glad, but I somehow get the impression there's more to your quiet disappearance. If there's something on your mind, lady, I think we should at least discuss it, don't you?"

Disliking the sharp edge to his voice, Omunique turned to walk away, but he stilled her with a stiff hand on the back of her shoulder. "Are you feeling guilty about what happened between us last week?"

She turned around to face him. "Guilty? I don't think so. But I am concerned about us mixing business with pleasure.

We hardly know each other, yet we acted like two teenagers in heat. Can you explain our unprofessional behavior? I sure can't?''

He laughed. ''It's called undeniable attraction . . . it's what happens between a man and a woman when they are extremely attracted to one another.'' He took her hand. ''Look, Omunique, I don't normally mix business with pleasure either, but it's not as if we're going to be working together on a day-to-day basis. What's wrong with us becoming friends?''

It was her turn to laugh as she remembered the more than friendly ways he'd rained on her. ''Oh, is that what you want us to become? You certainly weren't acting like you wanted us to be just friends.''

Looking a bit embarrassed, he grinned, giving her face and physical attributions more than a cursory glance. ''Well, I guess you could say that I wasn't just acting friendly that night. But how's a man supposed to act when he's so fiercely attracted to someone? You are one beautiful woman, you know. Just look at you!''

She found it impossible not to smile. ''I'm also a potential business associate, Mr. Maxwell. Do you always pay such special attention to your female associates?''

Perplexed, he scratched his head. ''I don't get it,'' he stated calmly. ''I know you're attracted to me, you know you're attracted to me, yet you seem to want to pretend otherwise. What's the real story, Omunique?''

Smiling, she moved toward the Jeep and leaned against the door. ''You are quite the confident one, aren't you, Mr. Maxwell? I guess you're used to having your way with women. But let me say this—I have more than looks going for me.'' She jabbed lightly at her skull with her forefinger. ''There's a magnificent mind inside this head, and it's signaling me to watch my step around you. Can you give me one good reason why I shouldn't pay attention to the warning signals I'm receiving?''

His smile was disarmingly sexy. ''I can give you dozens of

reasons, but they can best be explained over a drink and something to eat. Will you indulge me with a few minutes of your time? Please.'' His golden eyes seemed to further plead his case.

She frowned. "Right now?"

"This very minute! There's a coffee shop right across the street. We can leave our cars parked here and walk over. What do you say?"

Having a hard time resisting his desirable offer, she looked up at him. Rather than tell him he'd won her over, she turned away from the Jeep and started for the exit that would take them out to the street.

He caught up to her and slipped his hand under her elbow again. "I guess this is your way of saying yes," he commented, smiling broadly.

Turning to face him, she narrowed her eyes until they became shiny slits of silver. "Don't push your luck, Mr. Maxwell. The only reason I'm doing this is because I'm dying to hear your dozens of reasons why I shouldn't listen to my very sound mind."

Seated at a window table in the cheerfully decorated coffee shop, waiting for drinks to be served, Ken wasted no time in telling Omunique, in a very charming way, the dozens of reasons why they should be able to see one another socially. Enchanted with him, Omunique couldn't deny that she enjoyed all the attention he so eagerly lavished upon her. She thought his wit was as sharp as a tack, as refreshing as a cool drink of spring water.

She gave him her brightest smile. "I hate to admit it, but I've somehow forgotten all the reasons why I shouldn't let myself become involved with you. You're quite the charmer."

"There's more to me than charm, Omunique. I pride myself on keeping it real. Like you, I have a darn good head on my shoulders."

During the course of their conversation, the warning signals in her brain were soon drowned out by their effervescent laughter as they enjoyed his ecstatically funny jokes. Once Ken got through telling her all the jokes he could think of, he smoothly launched into some of the future plans he and his father had for their company.

As he talked about the bright future of Maxwell Athletic Corporation, Omunique got a full dose of his fathomless intelligence. His marketing and public relations strategies were nothing less than brilliant. The more he talked, the more interested she became. She found herself wanting to know more about the man behind the brilliant mind, more about who he was as a person. Although she had many questions she was dying to ask him, she decided to leave them for another time.

Looking at her with a serious expression on his face, he gently covered her hand with his. "Have I satisfied your curiosity, Miss Philyaw? Do my many reasons for wanting to see you again meet with your approval?"

Not knowing how she should respond, she glanced away for a fleeting moment. "You've done well for yourself, Mr. Maxwell. While some of your reasons reeked of plain bull, I found the others endearing. I liked it when you said we could take things at the pace I wanted to set. So, yes, most of your reasons meet my approval." Though his playboy label was still in the forefront of her mind, she still decided to keep it wide open. Forming premature opinions about someone without really getting to know them, especially from something she'd only read in a magazine, just wasn't something she normally practiced.

Had it not been for her wild attraction to him, his alleged personal indiscretions wouldn't have even mattered to her. Because she was very interested in him on a personal level, every little and not so little detail about him was important, especially when it could come down to her getting romantically involved with him. Playboy or not, he was intelligent and charming. He made her laugh, which helped her to relax around him even more

Glancing at her watch, she took a sip of her drink. "One

thing is for sure, time for executing the short program has expired, which can only mean that I enjoyed the routine. You have quite a sense of humor, Ken. I can't tell you the last time I laughed so hard, really.'' Her eyelashes fluttered involuntarily. "Notwithstanding your arrogance, I think you're an okay guy.''

He pretended to be disappointed by her mediocre assessment of his character. "Just okay? I've always been told I'm all that and a bag of pork rinds," he joked.

She laughed heartily. 'You see what I mean. I was trying to cut you some slack here, but you're just too arrogant for words. What am I going to do with you?''

A devilish look popped into his eyes. "Are you sure you want the answer to that question? I can think of hundreds of things you can do with me. Shall I run that list down for you, as well?''

She batted her eyelashes playfully. "That won't be necessary, my dear. But at the mention of the word run, I have to do just that. Are you going my way?'' she flirted.

He gave her a candy-coated smile. "Just let me pay the check, then I'll walk you back to your vehicle.''

Smiling broadly, Omunique stayed a short distance behind Ken, watching his sexy swagger as he walked toward the cashier booth. When the female cashier smiled at something Ken had said to her, jealousy burned deep in Omunique. Whatever he'd said to the rather attractive young woman, it was quite obvious she had enjoyed his comment. As the young woman pressed something into Ken's right hand, Omunique thought it might be her phone number, but how could she be sure without coming right out and asking him? She wasn't about to do that. How would she feel it if turned out to be his change, or just the receipt? *Like a darn fool.*

Besides, he wasn't her lover. She didn't have exclusive rights to him. And she wasn't sure it could ever be like that, anyway. So far they'd only shared a few passionate kisses, even if she had felt them right through to the core of her heart.

The walk to the car was made in absolute silence, yet his

arm wrapped loosely around her waist sent intimate messages that came in loud and clear. At the Jeep, Ken took the keys from her hand and opened the car door. As she was about to step inside her vehicle, he moved in front of her, blocking her entry.

"I know what I said about allowing you to set the pace . . . but my desire to kiss you is stronger than I'm capable of handling right now. Is it okay if I give you a more than friendly kiss good-bye?"

In response to his question. she moved closer to him. Instead of allowing him to capture her mouth, she placed a light kiss on both of his cheeks and one on the slight dimple in his chin. Once again, she tried to get into her vehicle, but he pulled her back to him, kissing her full on the lips. Slowly, her mouth opened to receive him. When the kiss grew deeper and more sensuous, she flattened her palms against his chest and backed slightly away from him.

"Whoa, pal," she remarked, laughing. "Looks like you're in danger of executing all the wrong moves before the long program can even begin. You don't want to do that, especially not right in front of the judge. You could be penalized for such a thing."

Looking at her intently, he ached to kiss her until she was breathless. "Are you going to penalize me?"

She took a moment to think about his question before she shook her head. "Not this time. But I'd be careful about the rules if I were you," she warned, wagging her forefinger at him in a playful manner.

He brought her finger to his mouth and pressed it against his lips. "I'll try to remember the rules, but you'll have to keep warning me. Since I don't know what all the rules are, it might be a good idea for you to lay them down as we go."

She climbed into the Jeep. "Great idea. And thanks for the ice tea."

He tossed her an appreciative smile. "Thank you for the company."

As Omunique pulled out of the parking space, Ken stayed rooted to the concrete, happy the prospects for a long program with her just might exist. As he normally did when in a cheerful mood, he whistled the tune of "My Way" while making his way to his own car.

"Yes," he said, "things are finally starting to go my way."

Chapter Four

Flying across the ice like a woman possessed, Omunique tried to concentrate solely on her training session. Ken Maxwell had invaded her dreams the entire night, and she desperately needed to be free. She'd awakened with cramped limbs and a void in her soul, an intimate void that she'd never known to exist—the type of void that could only be filled by the love of a man.

During the drive to the arena she'd wondered if she had been sane to deny herself, for so many years, the opportunity to become intimately involved with someone. The truth was she'd never met anyone she wanted to become intimate with. The ice had been the only intimacy she'd thought she needed.

While executing a double axel, she fell and went sliding across the ice. More distracted than she would've liked, she let out a low, rumbling expletive, blaming Kenneth Maxwell Jr. for the unnerving distraction.

Once she'd finally completed a near flawless run through of her entire program, she skated over to the metal bench, where she sat down and covered the ice blades. As she watched the other skaters perform Brent joined her on the bench, and they began to talk about all the important things she needed to concentrate on.

A frown creased his brow. "I saw something in your performance that I've never seen before. You appeared somewhat distracted. That concerns me."

Uncertainty flashed across her delicate features. "You noticed, huh? I'm sorry. I won't let it happen again. Were you pleased with my final run-through, Brent?"

"Your final executions were done extremely well. I'm just not used to seeing you so distracted. I realize that with the Olympic trials so near there's more pressure on you now. Just hang in there, Nique. You can do it."

As they ventured into other areas of conversation, Omunique told Brent bits and pieces about her blossoming relationship, but she purposely failed to reveal Ken's identity. She knew Brent would probably disapprove, since Maxwell Corporation was involved in her career.

Brent's smile was strained despite his attempt to hide his dismay. He didn't think athletes should have social lives while in training. "Sounds like you're really excited about this guy, Nique. Just keep your career goals in mind. You can't let anything or anyone interfere with your training or your bid for the Olympic team."

She smiled affectionately at the man who had been hired to train her for the upper echelon of competition, but she could feel the tension she'd unwittingly created. "Don't worry, Coach. My barely there social calendar is hardly a problem, and I have no intention of letting it conflict with my career goals." The genuine affection between them was obvious as they embraced warmly. With sore limbs and an exhausted body, she entered the women's locker room, immediately stripped away her practice attire and took a brief, relaxing shower.

* * *

Dressed in denim jeans and a turquoise, handsewn sweater, fully relaxed from her jog on the beach, Omunique ascended the stone steps and sprinted to the entrance of the beach house. Along with the stinging wetness falling from her eyes, the salty ocean spray stung her cheeks. Though she'd just left her special peaceful place, she felt anything but peace. Scared silly of all the new feelings she'd begun to experience, she reflected on the unexpected upheaval that had abruptly turned her otherwise sedate existence topsy-turvy.

The phone rang just as she fell across the bed. Nervousness suddenly befell her, and her hands shook when she reached for the receiver. Instead of picking it up, she only stared at it. Anxiously, Omunique listened.

When Ken's voice came over the recorder, she practically swooned. His sexy, sultry voice seemed to command her to respond. She snatched up the receiver before the message was completed, swallowing the lump in her throat. "I'm here, Ken," she announced breathlessly.

Ken sighed deeply, a huge smile spreading across his smooth, caramel-colored face. "Hello, there. You can't possibly know how disappointed I would've been without a chance to speak directly to you. How are you doing this evening?"

She gasped for air, trying to catch her speeding breath. "I'm good, Ken. Tired, but good."

He wondered if she'd said that to put him off. "Too tired for a friendly walk on the beach?" he inquired despite his thoughts. He dreaded using the word "friendly." Omunique as a friend just wasn't cutting it.

"Never too tired for a walk on the beach, Ken, but you might have to carry me back to the house," she flirted.

The thought of her cradled in his arms made his body burn with desire. "I'm up to the challenge, girl. I'm right around the corner from the phone booth you told me about. Do you need a little extra time?"

Nervously wrapping the phone cord around her left wrist,

she grinned. "No more time than it will take for you to get from there to here," she encouraged eagerly.

His balmy laughter drifted through the phone line. "Close your eyes and count to a hundred." The phone line went dead, and she squealed with delight. Knowing she would see Ken in just a few minutes filled her heart with joy.

Rushing over to the mirrored dresser, she brushed her hair, sprayed on a light fragrance, and dabbed a small amount of blush on her already flushed cheeks. She then removed a navy blue quilted jacket from the spacious walk-in closet. Having forgotten to count to a hundred, she giggled when the doorbell rang.

Counting out loud, after the fact, she hurried to the door and promptly flung it open. He smiled, and it got trapped in her heart. Laughter crinkled her eyes. Unsure of how she should greet him, almost timid, she stuck her hand out for him to shake, much to his dismay.

Not disappointing her, he pulled her to him by her extended hand. "We've passed the handshake stage, Omunique," he whispered close to her ear. "In fact, I'm having that uncontrollable urge again." Tenderly clamping his mouth down over hers, he drew from her the response he'd been dreaming about all day. She knew she was responding to him like the earth to rain after many years of drought, and she didn't feel a single twinge of shame or regret.

He tilted her chin with a closed fist. "The beach awaits us, Princess." Taking the jacket from her trembling hand, he held it while she slipped into it. With the sweltering warmth that flowed from his body, she seriously doubted that she'd need the jacket. Their hands tightly clenched together, they walked out the door.

When they reached the stone steps, he stepped in front of her and carefully guided her down the stony path. It was much colder than she'd anticipated, and her body shuddered in protest of the sudden blast of cold air that assailed her, causing him to wrap his arms snugly around her slender shoulders and pull her in closer to him.

"Tell me about your day," Ken prompted.

She tilted her head and leaned it against his arm. "Training went fairly well. I was too tired to run a few personal errands, so I came straight home. How was yours?"

He bent his head down and rubbed the tip of her nose with his. "Inundated with sweet thoughts of you."

Ecstatic at his response, she couldn't keep her eyes from reflecting the joy she felt. With deep affection ablaze in his golden eyes, he watched as she inhaled a gusty breath of sea air. The sensuous way in which she closed her eyes as she exhaled caused his lower anatomy to throb with aching desire. As the rolling waves crashed and thundered against the rocks, they were compelled into one another's arms. Sure that she wanted them to be more than friends, she made a bold move on him. Her lips, moist and sweet, met hungrily with his, making his body tremble all over.

This is serious, she ruminated with incredulity. *What has happened to me?*

Kenneth Maxwell Jr. happened came her heart's reply. *He had you, heart and soul, from the very first moment you two breathed the same air. This is what it feels like to be in love,* her heart whispered.

Ken laughed at the bewildered expression on her face. "You look as if you've been struck by a bolt of lightning. What's going on in that pretty head of yours, Princess?"

I have, she thought, looking up at him. *A golden bolt of lightning.* "Can we really do this without serious consequences to our careers?" *And will I ever recover from this blow to my heart?* she added in her thoughts.

She felt as though she'd drifted into the wind and somehow landed gently on a cloud. She likened the feeling to what a bee might feel when it lights on a nectar-filled flower—sensationally sweet. *Yes,* she mused, *my passionate encounters with Ken have been sensationally sweet. But what about my career? Can I really have both of my heart's passions?*

Ken studied her intently as he searched his heart for the right words that would reassure, words that mirrored his heart's response. "We most definitely can."

She gave a nervous laugh. "I hope you're right."

Lifting her head so that her eyes met with his, he traced moist kisses from her forehead to the skin exposed at her throat. Like a jungle of wildflowers, she smelled exotic. "I am right."

As the cold wind sliced through their jackets, they huddled close together and retraced their footprints in the sand, which led them back to the house. Their faces were fused with color, but they didn't seem to mind the cold wind striking their skin. It could've been snowing on the beach, Omunique surmised, and in all probability neither of them would've even noticed.

They hung their jackets in the closet before running through the other rooms and into the kitchen, where Omunique immediately put water on to boil for hot chocolate. Seated on one of the bar stools, Ken watched her as she moved about the kitchen. Her smile spoke to him from across the room, and he read it to say that she cared for him in a special way. He cared for her, too, deeply.

Raising himself from the bar stool to help her, he took the lacquer tray from her hands and carried the hot, liquid filled cups over to the table. They sat, facing one another. As steam curled from the cups, they adoringly watched each other through the rising steam.

Ken raised his cup in a silent toast. Deciding it was still too hot to drink from, he returned it to the table. "Omunique, I'd like to take you out tomorrow night to one of the finest Spanish restaurants I know. We can make it our first official date. Will you honor me with your delightful presence?"

Her face crumbled, feeling a tad miserable about the conflict in scheduling. "Oh, Ken, I can't, not tomorrow. I have a meeting with my agent and my attorney. I have to be there. Those two never let me out of any of my commitments, as you very well know," she said, refreshing his memory in regard to his calling Bruce to make sure she'd attend their first dinner meeting. "I'm sorry."

He smiled, but disappointment showed in his eyes. "I'm sorry, too. What are you doing the rest of your life?" She landed an intolerant glance right between his eyes. That line was still as sorry as it was when she'd first heard it, umpteen years ago.

He chuckled. "Sorry I couldn't come up with something more original. You leave my brain numb, girl."

Her smoky eyes softened to a misty gray. "I don't know about the rest of my life, but Friday and Saturday of this week are still open." Every night of her dull social life was open, but she didn't want to enlighten him to that shameful fact.

He finally took a sip of his hot chocolate. "What about seven on Friday evening, and eight on Saturday morning?"

She wrinkled her nose. "Eight on Saturday morning? Why so early?" she asked, not seeming to have a problem with Friday evening.

His smile carried a truckload of charm. "I thought we could have breakfast before taking a long drive up the coast. Coastal drives are pretty romantic, you know."

No, she didn't. The only coastal drives she'd ever taken were with her father, or all alone. In a knowing way, she smiled. Getting up from the chair, she walked over to him and placed a kiss on his smooth brow. "How long a drive?"

While pulling her down on his lap, Ken slid his arms around her waist and boldly ran his tongue across her lower lip. They both shuddered as he drew her tongue into the warm recesses of his mouth. The kiss was deep and passionate, and she wanted it to go on forever. Ken's kisses drove her crazy, and she knew hers had the same effect on him from the way his body twitched when her lips melted on his. He couldn't disguise the way she made him feel anymore than she could disguise her feelings for him.

Later, a blazing sunset found them innocently curled up in

front of the fireplace, where the flames roared and waved their dazzling array of yellow, orange, and bluish hues. With his knees drawn up, Ken was on his back, and his head rested in Omunique's lap. "It's getting kind of late, Princess. Are you tired?"

Lost somewhere between here and there, she didn't hear a word he said. Smiling, he laced his fingers up through her hair, causing her to look down into his eyes. "I hope you're thinking of me. Otherwise I'm going to feel as though I'm being ignored."

She gently ran her thumb across his lower lip. "I could never ignore you, though you have a tendency to think like that. I was just enjoying the fire show. The colors are beautiful, aren't they?"

He raised his head and briefly captured her lips. "Not as beautiful as you. You're even lovelier in the firelight. I like the way it makes your face glow. You look like a golden angel."

She blushed and smiled at the same time. Looking deeply into his eyes, she lowered her head and rested her nose against his. "You really know how to make me feel good, don't you? That was so sweet. I could get used to all these mushy compliments."

He lovingly nipped at her lower lip with his teeth. "They're not just compliments, Omunique. They're facts." He kissed her again. He then got to his feet and pulled her up to stand before him, drawing her into his arms. "As much as I hate to go, it's time. Call me when you return from your meeting with the powers that be?"

She nodded. "As soon as I get home." Just like before, he had a hard time leaving her warmth. It left him feeling cold and empty.

Resting on the sofa, she looked at the business card he'd given her. She already had one from their first meeting, but his home and voice-mail numbers were written on the back of this one. He'd provided her with the private line to his office and his mobile number, something he rarely did. Tingles of ridiculous fear and excitement raced up and down her spine as she placed the card in the pocket of her jeans. Determined not to fall asleep on the couch again tonight, Omunique leaped from the sofa and began the short journey down the hallway to her bedroom.

After a quick shower, she draped her body in a mint-green silk gown, then slipped into a robe to keep the chill away. Walking across the room to the window, she opened the draperies and looked out over the blackened sea. As she thought of Ken and the way he made her feel, she felt an overwhelming peace wash right through to her spirit. If this was what love felt like, it was fuzzy, warm, and sensuously exhilarating—and it scared her senseless.

Though confused by the entire concept of love between a woman and a man, she wanted to experience this crazy notion called love. Ken wanted to see her again. Just the thought made her feel euphoric as her eyes softened and glistened with the moisture of unshed tears.

The phone rang, disturbing her sweet reverie. When she picked up the receiver, she heard only heavy breathing. "Hello . . . hello," she responded, anxiety lacing her tone.

A low, menacing laugh came across the line. "You didn't smile at me today. I was offended by it. Don't let it happen again," the threatening voice rasped. A loud click sounded in her ear, then the line went dead.

She froze, fear gripping her insides. Still holding the receiver, she looked at it as though she expected the cord to wrap itself around her neck and strangle her. Feeling as if she might be overreacting to the anonymous phone call, she attempted to laugh, but it came out terribly strained. Trying to put the call from her mind, she settled herself in bed.

Immediately, the phone rang again. She stiffened as she drew her knees up to her chest and reached over to pick up the receiver. Without offering a greeting, she waited and listened with bated breath, expecting to hear another terrifying message.

"Omunique? Omunique, hello. Are you there?" Ken summoned urgently.

She expelled her tightly held breath. "Oh, it's you," she said, sounding nervous and unsure of herself.

He sounded puzzled, wondering what had happened to her cheerful spirit. "You sound disappointed. Are you? Am I disturbing you"

"No, on both counts. I'm rather pleased to hear your voice. You made it home awfully fast. How much over the speed limit were you flying?" she queried worriedly. It suddenly dawned on her that she didn't even know where he lived. For all she knew, he could live just a few blocks away.

"Sweetheart, Venice Beach is really not all that far from your place."

Venice Beach, she thought. She loved all the craziness that went on there. "I guess it isn't. Twenty to thirty minutes close. I just realized you never told me where you lived . . . and I never asked. I guess we have a lot more to learn about one another."

"And we'll have loads of fun while we do." He paused for a moment, not sure he should pose the question that had just popped into his head. Wanting to make sure everything was okay out there, he decided to ask her, anyway. "Why didn't you say anything when you first picked up the phone?"

She wanted to tell him the truth, but how could she tell him about the terrifying phone call when she didn't know what to make of it? Besides, she reasoned, she barely knew him. "No one calls here this late. Besides that, I was in that state of drowsiness—almost asleep, yet half awake." She found it difficult to lie to him, but she didn't want to put any unnecessary burdens on their budding relationship. The mystery call was probably just a silly prank, anyway. Some teenager might have thought this was a good way to have some fun. But instilling fear had nothing to do with fun.

"I see." For a reason unbeknownst to him, he didn't quite believe her. She sounded much too nervous for someone who claimed to be half asleep. But he would let it alone for now. "I kept you up late last night, and I have no intentions of doing so tonight. Goodnight, Ice Princess."

She was often referred to as the "Ice Princess," but not one single person she knew of effected it quite like Ken. The sultry baritone in his voice melted her insides like heated candle wax. "Goodnight, Kenneth Maxwell Jr.," she cooed softly.

Nestling under the blush-pink comforter, Omunique yawned and tossed her head against the plump pillows. Before she had a chance to close her eyes, the phone rang. She left it for the answering machine to pick up. The same breathing she'd heard earlier came hard and rapid, lasting until the machine clicked the caller off. The message response time was up—and in response to the disturbing call her blood gushed like a rushing waterfall through her veins.

With lightning speed she got out of bed, ran out of her room, and burst into the darkened bedroom Wyman had recently vacated. Though her father wasn't there, just being in his space was enough to soothe her rattled nerves. Scooting into her favorite corner of the bed, she silently prayed her fears away. Knowing God would send a protective angel to watch over her simply because she'd asked that of Him, she relaxed. He'd already answered too many of her prayers for her to start doubting Him now.

Ken's handsome face loomed before her when she finally closed her eyes. Suddenly afraid of her own emotions and how Ken made her body yearn for his touch, she thought it best that she attempt to sort out what was really happening to her. She began to wonder what all these new, wonderful, scary feelings really meant. Could she be in love with him so soon after meeting him, or was she just terribly infatuated? How would these alien feelings impact her career goals? She'd never had to deal with any of these questions before, and she found them distracting, if not downright disturbing.

Was she just fooling herself into believing she could have both a career and a serious love affair? She didn't know how serious it was on Ken's part, but it definitely was on hers. There were no reasonable explanations for her fears about him, she thought with frustration, but the one thing she was sure of was that she wanted to find out just how far her relationship with Kenneth Maxwell Jr. could go.

As for the disturbing phone calls, the mystery caller had no idea who he was toying with, she thought, angry now. She wasn't easily intimidated by cowards.

Returning to her own bedroom at the first sign of dawn, she clicked on the answering machine and played back the message tape. It was jammed with calls just like the one she'd received the previous evening. There wasn't any speech whatsoever, only the same hard, heavy breathing. Different from the time before, she noticed that the strange breathing was fraught with desperation, almost asthmatic. It was an eerie breathing, a chilling breathing that nearly froze her blood solid.

All during practice Omunique was jittery. She'd already made more mistakes in one morning than she'd made in a long while. Simple skating techniques had suddenly become difficult. Spins and turns that were a part of her everyday routine frustrated her, and she couldn't execute them with ease. Though she held Ken in part responsible for her disastrous morning, the unnerving phone calls were the real culprit. In no uncertain terms, Ken had her going in circles, but the strange caller had her in a tailspin. Ken was in her blood, and it appeared he was there to stay, while the anonymous caller's voice turned her blood to ice.

Was she in Ken's blood? Did he feel the same way she did? She didn't know the answer to that question, either, but she knew it was a lot less cocky than her previous answer. When she'd returned to her bedroom at the crack of dawn, she'd come no closer to finding the answers to all the questions she'd entertained the night before.

Ian Swanson—another champion skater, someone Omunique considered a dear friend—swept across the arena. They often practiced together. As he skated toward her, his ash-blond hair fluttered wildly from the whirlwind his speed created. When he flashed in front of her, she took another hard spill, startled by his sudden appearance.

Ian firmly dug the picks of his blades into the ice and came to a smooth halt. He then bent over to help her up. "Girl, you look a little shaky today. I've been watching your performance."

Smiling weakly at him, she tightly gripped his arm. "Tell me about it, Ian. I think I'd better call it a day before I break my tailbone," she said, sounding slightly irritated and nearly out of breath.

Once he steadied her, his olive-green eyes studied her with curiosity and a bit of concern. He could see that she was awfully tense, and he'd felt the tension in her hands when she'd gripped his arm. "I think you'd be wise to call it a day, Nique. Another hard spill like the one you just took, you could find yourself down for the count. I had hoped we'd get a chance to go around a few times, but we can practice together on Monday. By the way, have you given any more thought to skating with me in the charity exhibition?"

His question surprised her. "Are you sure you still want me as your partner after the disastrous performance you just witnessed? Not being an experienced pair skater, I could end up embarrassing you, a lot."

"Nah, that won't happen, Nique. Besides, we've been prac- ticing the none too difficult program for weeks, now, and you've been just great. We all have a bad day or two. I'd still like you to skate with me."

Flattered, she smiled. "Sure, Ian. I'd be delighted. I talked it over with Brent, and he doesn't see any problem with it. However, he is worried about the lifts.''

Ian's gaze became thoughtful. "There's nothing extremely difficult about those particular lifts, but we can eliminate them if it'll make him feel better.''

Animatedly, she bobbed her head up and down. "Eliminating the lifts would definitely make him feel better, Ian. But what about you?''

"Ah, Nique, it's not that big of a deal. Besides, it's only a charity exhibition. We don't have to get too technical with our program.''

She nodded her head. "Okay. I'm in, and the lifts are out. But I don't think the program will work without the first lift. I can manage that one with ease. Let's do a quick run-through. Then I'm off the ice for the weekend,'' she suggested, eager to work with one of the best figure skaters she knew.

The concerned look returned to his face. "Are you sure, Nique? You've already been in one fierce battle with the ice this morning.''

"I need to do this, Ian. I know I'm better than what I've shown here today. If I do well skating with you, it'll help boost my confidence.''

"Whatever I can do to help, my good friend. Let's get it on.''

As though the two skaters were joined together at the hip, they melded together, skating in perfect harmony. The delicate Ice Princess and the good-looking, sinewy Ice Prince began their program with great zeal. Other skaters stopped to watch them as they slashed across the ice with grace and style. Together, they were fantastic.

Just as she'd earlier hoped, she handled the first lift with ease. When Ian lifted her high into the air, she spun two full revolutions and then her body slithered down his as they attempted to effect a perfect landing. Neither of them could have asked for a more precise touchdown. Sliding his long arm around her tiny waist, Ian pulled her back into formation, a smooth transition, neither of them missing a beat while falling back into step with one another.

From a short but discreet distance, a pair of eyes watched their every exciting twist and turn, a pair of autumn-gold eyes that held a spark of envious green.

Unaware that Ken was an observer, Omunique executed the program with all the heated passion of a late night lovemaking session. Ken looked on in awe. The male skater held her as intimately close as he himself had held her the previous evening. Despite the great disparity in height, Ken thought she and Ian positively flowed together, in the same way he hoped she'd soon flow with him. Having come there without any intention of her seeing him, Ken slipped out of the arena with a content smile on his face. He hadn't made physical contact with her, yet he somehow felt as though he had.

Although his visit was more of a professional call than a personal one, he would've liked to have at least said hello to her. Her agent had been instrumental in his gaining access to the practice session. Had his company not been involved in her career, Ken knew he wouldn't have been able to get inside the arena, where security was tight.

Soon, Ken slid under the wheel of his sleek, black sports car and leaned his head against the steering wheel. After a few seconds of silent meditation, he drove out of the parking lot, smiling broadly. Yes, he thought with enthusiasm, Omunique was as good as she'd boasted. In fact, she was much better than good—she was magnificent. . . .

Omunique and Ian sat down on the long metal bench and pulled off their skates, happy with their performance.

Ian flashed her a boyish grin. "You've recovered nicely, Nique," Ian praised. "We'll do well at the exhibition. What are your plans for the evening?"

Frowning, she tilted her head to the side. "I'm having dinner with Bruce and my attorney, but there's someone else I'd much rather be dining with,'' she said with a faraway look in her eyes.

He raised an eyebrow. "Oh? Who might that be?"

"A man who's all that, and a bag of pork rinds, a hunk. I only met him a short time ago," she uttered dreamily. "He's a real suave character. He has loads of finesse and charm, and I hope he's as sincere as I think he is. You know that men have been darn near non-existent in my life, so when I say a guy has got it going on, you know he must be something else."

Ian laughed at the way she playfully swooned. "Does this hunk have a name?" he asked, his tone a bit strained.

"Yeah. Mr. Right. And I'm going to do my best to keep him from turning left." Her laughter drifted into the air, sending soft ripples of pleasure through Ian's hard body.

She would've loved to shout Ken's name from high above the arena's rafters, but it didn't seem right. Having a pleasurable tryst with one of the top executives of a sponsoring company wasn't exactly the in thing to do. In fact, she wasn't sure that it wasn't against the rules. She made a mental note to check out the personal boundaries that might exist, if any, between skater and sponsor. Maxwell Athletic Corporation was well-known throughout the sports world, and she didn't think they needed any negative publicity.

She could see the tabloid headline now: *Ice Princess Philyaw Lands Olympic Sponsor by Sleeping With Maxwell Heir Apparent. No, that would never do,* she thought fearfully.

Sensing that she wanted to keep the anonymity of the man in her life, Ian aborted the probe. He already knew who that someone was, the someone who had somehow managed to turn her lovely head—something he wished he'd had the nerve to try.

Looking slightly disturbed, Ian dropped a kiss into her disheveled hair. "I can only imagine the fit Brent threw when he found out you'd gone social. The guy is way too rigid."

Ian got up from the bench. "Have a great weekend, Nique. See you on Monday."

She knew Ian was right about her coach, but Brent was such a sweetheart. Sweetheart or not, she wasn't so sure he'd come around regarding her having a personal relationship, especially after he found out who with. It would probably be the same no matter who she dated. Brent just couldn't seem to separate a social life from a professional one, not even his own.

Chapter Five

By the time Omunique dragged herself from the arena the sun had set, and its fading rays had already launched ribbons of deep lavender and pale pinks across the now dark blue sky. *This is a perfect evening for lovers,* she thought. A nice moonlit walk on the beach with Ken would do wonders for her fatigue. But no, she had to have a stuffy dinner with a bunch of egotistical males. Her smile was impish. Well, the guys surrounding her career weren't all that bad, she conceded with ease.

Feelings of paranoia were with her as she warily checked over her shoulder on the way to the parking lot. Safely inside the Jeep, she quickly locked the doors. The mysterious phone calls had spooked her more than she would like to admit.

Just as she was about to enter the freeway on ramp, she saw flashing red and blue lights through her rearview mirror. She immediately pulled over to the right shoulder of the road. After shoving the automatic gearshift into park, she jumped out of her vehicle.

"Get back in your vehicle," a heavy voice growled.

Omunique did as she was ordered, but she didn't like the

rough tone of voice the C.H.P. Officer had used in making his demands known. As she sat in the Jeep, she intently watched the gorgeous officer from the sideview mirror, wondering what she could've possibly done wrong. The color of his skin and hair, both a sandy brown, along with his cool blue eyes, made her wonder if he might be of mixed heritage. Then again, blacks came in an array of beautiful shades. She had gray eyes, and she was definitely black, she thought with swelling pride.

Before he advanced toward the car, she saw the officer disengage the baton from his belt. The reason for such a drastic sign of authority completely eluded and unnerved her. She'd never been in a situation like this before, and it made her tremble.

When he reached the car, she rolled down the window and looked up at him, expelling a nervous laugh. "Officer, what did I do?"

"Give me your driver's license and then I'll tell you exactly what you did," he instructed forcefully.

She fumbled in her wallet, pulled out the license, and handed it to him. "I've never received a ticket in all the time I've been driving. Why did you tell me to get back into my vehicle?"

Once he explained the proper procedures, she understood, but she thought it was ludicrous that anyone would perceive her as dangerous.

"Ma'am, you failed to come to a complete stop at a posted stop sign. After I write you the citation, I'll come back and explain everything to you."

"What about just a warning this time?" she yelled out the window as he went back to his patrol car. Although she didn't believe the charges being leveled against her, she knew that once he started writing the ticket he'd have to follow through. She had asked the question in hopes of further dialogue between them, but when he shook his head curtly she accepted defeat.

When he returned with the written citation she tried to tell her side, but he wasn't in the mood for listening. She couldn't imagine what stop sign he was referring to. She certainly hadn't seen one on this route before.

He turned the citation over. "Tell it to the judge! You can appear in court if you don't agree with my observations. You need to sign this right there. Your signature is not an admission of guilt. It just means I've explained the procedures to you, and that you understand them."

This was her first brush with the law, and she broke down and cried. Tearfully, she explained to him how his disengaging his baton had frightened and upset her, and his having mentioned a warrant for her arrest if she failed to appear in court or to pay the ticket had upset her even more. She felt like a criminal. Now she understood all the stories she'd heard from people who felt officers of the law had harassed them without just cause.

Surprising her, Officer Marcus Taylor knelt down beside her open car door. He stared right into her crying eyes, smiling a smile she wouldn't soon forget. He then showed an incredible amount of compassion, something that she'd thought him incapable of. He even gave her his business number, in case she had any more questions.

Inside the Sports Connection, Omunique scanned the tables for her associates. It was difficult to see past the tall heads and wide bodies that blocked her view, but she could see that the place was packed.

The Sports Connection was a favorite hangout for those involved in the world of athletics. Its decor was definitely sports-oriented. Omunique thought it had the same atmosphere as the *Cheers* bar, friendly, warm and cozy. Several posters and pictures of popular sports figures were plastered all over the oak-paneled walls. There was also a gigantic billiards room on the premises.

Bruce saw her first. As she spotted him coming toward her, she smiled brightly. Bruce's muddy brown eyes were slightly red, yet they still carried their familiar joyful glint. What little gray hair he had left stood on end. His tan slacks were baggy, due to recent weight loss, but his rust-colored shirt was a perfect fit.

Bruce's medium-brown complexion glowed as he welcomed her with an enthusiastic bear hug. She hugged him back with the same degree of ebullience. He then steered her toward the table where Lamar Lyons, her attorney, awaited their arrival.

Lamar was a longtime friend of the Philyaw family. His skin was a smooth, lucid, chestnut-brown. Clear as his complexion, his dark amber eyes twinkled in appreciation of Omunique's denim wheat jeans and the formfitting yellow cashmere sweater he thought she wore so well.

Lamar kissed the back of Omunique's hand. "Instead of you wearing that sweater, Om, it's wearing you. You're looking really good. How's it going?"

Although she disliked him calling her "Om," his voice was deep and soothing to her senses. She thought the middle-aged attorney also had excellent taste in clothes, which was evident in the finely tailored, gray pinstriped suit and powder blue silk shirt. His salt-and-pepper hair was cut short and crisply edged on the sides and at the nape.

She sat down in the chair Bruce had pulled out for her. "It's going well, Lamar."

Reaching into her brown leather shoulder bag, she pulled out the proposal she'd received from the Maxwell Corporation. Before handing it to Lamar, she took it out of the envelope and gave it a quick once-over. Then Omunique and Bruce struck up a conversation while Lamar looked over the proposal with well-trained eyes.

Minutes later Lamar looked up from the papers. "Om," he called out, "this is an excellent proposal. I don't see a thing that arouses my suspicious nature. Actually, it's pretty cut and dried. You get adequate monies for training and such, and they get the world's best figure skater to show off their athletic wear. It looks like you might get even more than you were after. You must have lit some fire under the Maxwell men for them to want to do more than sponsor you."

Basking in the delightful memory of at least one of the Maxwell men, the sexy one, she smiled sheepishly.

"Congratulations on the extra added benefit. You're going to make one hell of a spokeswoman. But we need to concentrate on that gold medal for now," he told her, grinning from ear to ear. "Another thing, you should have discussed this new angle with us when it first became known to you. I know it's a future deal, but that's what we get paid for," Lamar chided.

Lamar handed Bruce the proposal. "Give it the eagle eye, my man. Four eyes are always better than two. Tell me what you think when you've finished looking it over."

Bruce grunted as he nodded his head. "Will do."

It was almost as if Omunique hadn't heard Lamar, but she'd heard every word. She just hadn't responded to his chiding way of putting her in her place. Omunique Philyaw knew her place—and it was wherever she decided it to be. She knew he was right in what he'd said, just as she knew he'd never stop calling her "Om."

Once Bruce voiced his thoughts about the proposal, Lamar discussed its most important terms. They also talked about how well the photo shoot went. It shouldn't have happened before they'd agreed to accept the proposal, Lamar was quick to point out. With much humility, Bruce shouldered all the responsibility for that error.

Despite all the delicious smells in the air, Omunique had only ordered a small chef's salad, less the ham. It appeared that Bruce and Lamar had ordered half of a cow. Omunique tackled her salad with much enthusiasm. Between bites she talked about the traffic ticket, and the charity event she was to do with Ian.

Finished with her meal, Omunique pushed back from the table. "Don't order any dessert for me. I'm going to go and wash my hands and freshen my face."

As she walked through the bar area to get to the ladies' room, she heard familiar laughter. Looking in the direction from where it came, her heart skidded to a breaking halt. Leaning against the bar, his head bent low, Kenneth Maxwell Jr. was talking to a fabulous looking woman with short, raven-black hair. He appeared to be enjoying himself. Omunique struggled to choke back a strangling sob.

When the woman with the sienna complexion reached up and stroked Ken's cheek with long fingers, Omunique wanted to torture those same slender digits. Spotting the rock-size diamond on the woman's hand, Omunique became paralyzed by jealousy and fear. The woman was engaged. *To Ken?* As Ken threw his head back in another gale of laughter, Omunique shuddered.

What a ghastly day, she thought, stomping into the ladies' room, where she sat down at the mirrored dressing table and put her face in her hands. Tears fell unchecked. There hadn't been a spoken commitment between them, she realized painfully, but deep inside she'd hoped . . . *Hoped for what? Perhaps an everlasting relationship?* her heart responded.

That particular revelation didn't ease the gut-wrenching pain of the dark shadow that passed over her heart, a shadow that threatened to cast her into its blackness. Maybe she'd trusted too soon, given too much of herself too soon. Whatever the case, she had made a bad error in judgement. At least she wasn't so into him that she couldn't recover, she lied to herself.

On her way back to the table, she looked over at the bar, but her dreamy hunk and his companion were gone. Sickness churned her stomach, and the tears resurfaced. She felt as though the bottom of her world had suddenly dropped right out from under her. Consternation chewed at her insides.

As she neared the table, Bruce noticed how sick she looked. He immediately got to his feet. "What's wrong, Nique? You look like death warmed over," he muttered, worried. "Are you okay?"

She sat down and Bruce returned to his chair. "I'm just in a white mood." Omunique had gotten so sick of everything negative being referred to as "black this or black that" she'd long ago turned the rotten platitude around. "Don't worry yourself. If it's okay with you guys, I'm going to haul my butt home.''

Concerned for her, Lamar got to his feet. ''I'm out of here, too, Om. I'll walk you to the car. Bruce, my man, I'll call you tomorrow.''

Bruce raised his hand in a farewell gesture. ''Okay, you two. Take it slow. I'm going to hang around here and down a few more beers. With Nique's future secure, I at least know where my next meal's going to come from,'' he teased.

Bruce got out of his chair and walked as far as the bar with Omunique and Lamar. He bid them a cheerful evening as they exited.

Lamar slid his hand under Omunique's elbow. He escorted her to the Jeep, then strolled the few steps to his own white Lincoln Town Car.

It seemed to take forever for her to get home, but it really hadn't taken any longer than usual. The freeway traffic had run smoothly, but Omunique's mind hadn't, and she felt very tired and extremely disillusioned.

Cupid had misfired his arrow, and it had come at time when she'd been willing to give this ridiculous notion called love a try, regardless of how much it scared her. The possibility of love might have thawed, she mused, but the ice would still be frozen solid under her feet. Though it might grow thin at times, it would always be there for her, she reflected with sadness.

When Omunique entered the driveway, she saw Ken's car parked off to the side of the circular driveway. Her unbearable disappointment swiftly turned to unmitigated anguish. What was he doing here? How could he just up and leave one woman and go straight to another? As she stepped out of her vehicle, he got out of his.

Omunique nearly dropped dead from the panic that struck a note of disharmony in her heart. Seeing Ken only a couple of yards away from her drove her senses into overkill. Dazed and unable to speak, she looked right past him. Without uttering a word, she sped from his presence and made a mad dash for the stone steps.

Ken looked puzzled and anxious at the same time. "What in the Sam Hill was that all about?" His expression turned to one of grave concern. "I don't know what's going on here, but I'm damn sure going to find out." With his heart beating erratically, he ran down the stone steps.

Be careful with her, he advised himself. *She's probably as fragile as a china doll despite her athletic strengths. Something emotional is going on here.* From the look he'd seen in her eyes he sensed that there were times, like now, when she could possibly turn into a china shop's worst nightmare, a raging bull.

A heavy blanket of fog had rolled in, making it difficult for him to see for any distance. Then he saw her ballerina figure, standing quietly, facing the ocean. He ran to where she stood, but when she turned around to face him, the glacier-cold look in her eyes told him to keep his distance. He looked at her in bewilderment.

"Why did you run away from me like that, Omunique?" His voice was so tender she almost began to cry. But when he moved closer to her, he could easily guess at the outside temperature from the chill in her now icy silver eyes.

She turned slightly away from him. "Why are you really here, Ken? I don't know what you're playing at, but I won't be played like a bad game of checkers," she hissed. Pushing past him, she ran back toward the steps.

"Omunique," Ken shouted, stopping her cold. Moving quickly, he moved to her back and stopped right behind her. "I deserve to know what the hell you're talking about, don't you think?"

Omunique turned sharply on her heel. "You don't deserve the time of day, Kenneth Maxwell Jr. Go back to the Sports Connection and find someone else to play your silly games with. I'm not a child, Ken, but I'm not so sure *you're* not still stuck in puberty," she challenged, standing her ground and glaring at him with barely controlled anger.

Ken roared with laughter, amused by her outburst now that he understood her rage. "The Sports Connection, huh? Is that what this is all about?"

Finding nothing amusing, she continued to glare at him, her eyes turning to silver razors. "You tell me, Ken. You seem to be very amused with yourself, not to mention too darn smug."

Shaking his head from side to side, he laughed again, fully understanding what had happened. "Sweetheart, I can only assume you saw me with Marion Washington. I can assure you that you've jumped to all the wrong conclusions."

Her hands latched onto her hips. "Is that so? Then why were her fingers all over your face?"

Normally he couldn't stand jealous women, but he found Omunique's jealousy so charming he was outright flattered by her obvious display. Her smoky-gray eyes were even more mesmerizing when she was angry, he noted, trying to control his laughter. "For your information, my sweet girl, the woman you saw me with is the fiancée of my best friend, Frank Green. Frank was there with us, but I guess you couldn't have known. What did you do, storm off in a jealous rage?"

Omunique felt like a passenger on the sinking *Titanic* as she stood stock-still, drowning in her own stupidity. Then a hand flew up to her mouth. "Oh, boy, it seems we keep misreading one another. I'm terribly sorry, Kenneth. I'm normally not a jealous person, but jealousy can't begin to describe what I felt when I saw you two. If I'd had a hammer I would've broken her fingers, slowly, one by one."

Gathering her in his arms, he pressed his face against hers. "I'm genuinely flattered, Omunique," he said before closing his mouth over hers. Twisting his fingers in her hair, he gently pulled her head back and looked into her eyes. "I'm not seeing anyone else, Omunique Philyaw. As long as I'm seeing you, I won't be."

Sunshine rapidly peeked through the dark clouds that hung

over her heart as she fervently returned his tender kisses. Molding herself close to his body, she sighed against his lips. "That makes two of us." Omunique felt her tilting world righting itself.

On the way to the house Ken began to tell Omunique about his closest friends. He and Frank had been college roommates, he told her, and they were close as brothers. Frank was a stockbroker; Marion owned her own interior design business. The two were going to be married next spring, and Ken would stand as best man.

He ran his fingers through his hair. "I love Marion like a sister. The three of us are a very close-knit trio. You'll fit into our little group quite nicely," he assured her. "I believe you and Marion will find a lot in common. But let me warn you, she's the mother hen type. She has a tendency to hover over Frank and me like we're small children. It's not such a bad thing. We actually get a kick out of her constant cackling."

Omunique removed her hand from his and placed it around his waist. "They sound like two very nice people, Ken. I look forward to meeting them. I'm really sorry I got the wrong impression. Maybe it was because she was so darn gorgeous. Is Frank as handsome as you are?"

Ken grinned as he opened the front door and stepped aside for her to enter. "To hear him tell it, he's the best looking man on the planet. He's a couple of inches shorter than I am, and his eye color is unusual, almost a burgundy. He smiles all the time, always talks stocks and bonds, and never knows when to shut up."

Omunique looked at him from over her shoulder. "Well, that's one thing for sure you two have in common," she insulted playfully as they walked into the living room and lowered themselves onto the sofa.

Looking at her with feigned injury, Ken cuddled up next to her. "I might talk too much, but I never say anything I don't mean . . . and I always keep my word. In time, you'll learn that about me."

"In time," she said on a sigh. "Time is at the core of everything we do. So often there's barely enough time to get everything done. On the other hand, one can have too much time, like the times when I'm away from you." Silently, she wished that he missed her, too, when they were apart.

"Oh, Omunique, how well I know. Now that you're in my life, time seems to stand still, especially when I'm waiting to see you. But when I'm with you it flies right on by. I came out here tonight because I couldn't wait until the time we'd set for tomorrow. I called first, but you weren't here yet. I didn't think you'd be out too late, so I decided to come here and wait for you."

Comfortable with his reasons, she smiled broadly. "I'm happy you came. After I saw you with Marion and got the wrong idea, my sleep would have been chaotic."

"At least you would've slept," he countered.

Ken looked at her with a cat-that-ate-the-bird grin. "I have to get something I left in the car. Will you be here when I get back?" He laughed at his foolish question. Quite naturally she'd be there. After all, they were at her home, he mused.

"Of course. Just don't take too long. I miss you already." As he disappeared from her sight, she relaxed her head against the sofa back.

He couldn't have been gone for more than a few minutes, but a contented Omunique was already half-asleep when Ken returned. When she felt his presence in the room she looked up, her eyelids drooping heavily. After handing her a small, foil-wrapped package, he snuggled up next to her. Her eyes sparkled as she unwrapped the box.

Tears welled in her gray eyes when she saw the lovely crystal music box. On a tree of pink crystal glass, two gold lovebirds faced each other, their beaks touching. When she wound the box up, the crystal base turned as it sweetly played the tune of "Hero."

Delighted with the gift, she squealed with joy and then planted a juicy kiss on his lips. "It's lovely, thank you, Ken.

I don't remember telling you that 'Hero' is one of my favorite songs.''

Kissing her deeply, he lifted her from the sofa cushion and positioned her on his lap. Omunique purred gently under his expert manipulation of her mouth. "You didn't," he finally responded, his voice husky with passion. "It just happens to be one of my favorites, as well. I hope that someday you'll come to think of me as your hero."

Interesting statement, she mused, recalling wondering the very same thing. *Great minds think alike.* As she was about to tell him what she'd been thinking, the phone rang. Jumping up from the sofa, she dashed across the room and picked up the receiver. Instinctively, she knew it was the mystery caller. Harsh and brittle against her ears, this time the heavy breathing sounded like an angry tirade. Frightened and shaken, she dropped the phone as if it were a ticking time bomb and backed away from where the receiver lay on the floor.

Noticing her reaction, Ken rapidly moved toward her and picked the phone up from the floor. When he put it to his ear and spoke, the line went dead. He reached for her, but she flinched and moved out of his reach. She hadn't gotten very far when he pulled her into the safety of his arms.

Ken looked into her silver-plated eyes, now glazed with fear. "What's wrong, Princess? You look so frightened."

She didn't want to tell him a thing, but somehow her reaction to the call had to be explained. Besides, she couldn't come up with a good enough reason not to tell him. She shrugged her shoulders, a shadow blanketing her eyes that failed to hide the fear. "I think that was a . . . threatening phone call. Then again, it could have been a wrong number." But she knew better, not daring to tell him that this hadn't been the only call of this nature, that they were of malicious intent, aimed directly at her.

She hadn't convinced Ken in the least that it might be a wrong number, yet he sensed her reluctance to go further. It was quite obvious that she was very shaken. He didn't want to force the issue, at least not while she was so upset. Letting the subject drop for the time being, he lifted her up, carried her back to the sofa and positioned her on his lap.

They sat in stone silence, her head cradled against his chest, gently rocking back and forth. It wasn't long before the hypnotic rhythm of his movements lulled her to sleep. When he realized she was asleep, he shifted himself into a more comfortable position, closed his eyes, and fell asleep with his head nestled on her shoulder.

An attractive man was now in her life, but an unwanted swarm of butterflies had arrived with him, and a heavy breather, a maniac of some sort. Was it just a coincidence they all happened along at the same time? She'd often heard that butterflies accompanied love. For her, they were a normal occurrence before and sometimes during skating performances. But the phone messages had nothing whatsoever to do with love, she knew, wondering how they'd impact her career goals.

Surely the presence of these three entities had brought some pressure to bear. In fact, she was already reeling from their roiling effects. Ken's presence was one she most assuredly desired. The butterflies she could deal with. The other, frightening presence was one she wished she'd never made the acquaintance of. Many thoughts and questions traipsed through her mind as she looked up at the sleeping face on her shoulder, the handsome face bathed in the early morning sunlight streaming through the open drapery.

Tilting her head slightly, she brushed her mouth across Ken's full lips. He stirred as he opened his eyes. His smile was so sweet it made her want to consume him with the flame blazing in her femininity and leave no part of him untouched by her innermost secrets.

He jumped, noticing the light of dawn. "What time is it, beautiful? Oh, my God! I've been here all night. It feels as if I just got here." To calm himself, he lowered his head back onto her shoulder. His sigh was audible. "Omunique, you're having a profound affect on me. I'm going to be late for work, yet for the first time in my life I really don't care. What about your training session?''

She wrapped her forefinger around one of his dark brown curls. ''Don't train on Friday, Kenneth. The weekends, either,'' she added. ''Don't worry, though, I put seven days of hard labor into the four days I do train. If you weren't here, I might have been tempted to train, anyway. One can never train too much or too hard, especially when seeking the Olympic gold.''

He smiled up at her, far more than just a bit curious. ''Is Olympic gold the only thing you're seeking in life, Omunique?''

''Until I met you it was the only thing that mattered. Don't misunderstand me ... it still matters, but I'm beginning to realize there are other things that can matter just as much.''

''Such as?''

She laughed softly. ''Such as you. That's what you wanted to hear, isn't it?''

''Is that the only reason you responded the way you did?''

''No, Ken, it was the truth.''

''Ah, truth. How sweet it is. How sweet it is.'' Looking worried, he sat up again. ''Jeez! What are your neighbors going to think about my having been here all night? I hope I haven't posed a problem for you.''

Omunique massaged his cheek with the back of her hand. ''I don't really know what they're going to think. I'm not sure I care, either. I'm fully grown. What I do in my home is my own business.''

With scorching intensity, his eyes slowly scanned her body. ''Yes, you are fully grown, desirably so.''

She felt the color rise in her cheeks, noting it was time to change the subject. ''Would you like some breakfast, Ken?''

He took her hand in his. ''As much as I would like to stay here and eat breakfast with you, I can't. I have several meetings scheduled for later this morning, all of which are very important.''

She was rather glad he'd declined her offer. All she could've offered him was cold cereal and toast. She would have to stop inviting him for meals until she could do a little more than boil water for tea and oatmeal.

He got to his feet and pulled her up from the sofa. "I'm sorry I have to run, but we'll have tonight. I hope you haven't forgotten our first official date. We're going to celebrate this wild attraction between us. We're going to make this relationship work," he announced with certainty.

Marriage didn't suit his lifestyle or his free spirit. He'd had his share of beautiful women, but he'd managed to emotionally keep them at a safe distance. He wasn't one to allow himself to fall prey to feminine contrivances, nor had he ever made a commitment beyond a casual relationship. A few women had tried hard to change his confirmed status, but those who had tried were undoubtedly disappointed. But he was now getting the strangest feeling, a totally unfamiliar one.

He wanted Omunique urgently, and he could only hope that she wanted him half as much, and in the same compelling way. He had to admit that she was at the center of the argument that he was now having with himself on the subject of marriage.

Ken exchanged bewildered glances with Omunique. "We do want this to work, don't we? We seem to be so good together."

As though trying to calm her heart, she placed a hand over its nesting place. "Kenneth ... we're ... the only ones ... who can make it work."

Ken took a deep breath. Her statement had touched him where it mattered the most—his heart. "You've said something neither one of us should ever forget. You're absolutely right ... it's all up to us," he remarked, taking her in his arms for one last kiss.

The kiss was long and deep. It had to be to get him through the rest of day and hold his need for her in check—at least until their early evening date.

Chapter Six

Clean-shaven, wearing a fresh change of clothing and fully revitalized, Ken walked into the reception area of the Maxwell Corporation. He wore a bright smile as he thought about the woman who'd recently brought the sunshine to his days. "Good morning, Thomasina," he boomed in his bass voice with uncontainable joy.

Thomasina picked up a few messages from her desk and handed them to him. "Good morning, Mr. Maxwell. Sir, the nine o'clock appointment cancelled. Mr. Stone said he would call you later to reschedule. His wife is in the hospital."

Ken's eyes grew sympathetic, yet he smiled at her as he picked up a manila file folder from her desk. "Oh, I'm sorry to hear that. I hope it's nothing serious." He looked toward his father's closed office door. "Has my father come in yet? By the way, it's nice to have you here."

She smiled back. "He's in his office, sir. There's also a message from Sandy Wilson. She wants you to call her, but she didn't reveal the nature of her business."

He acknowledged her comment with a nod as he shuffled

through the rest of his messages. He finished reading, then looked down at her. "Sandy's our permanent secretary, as you already know, out on maternity leave. Thanks, Thom, I'll call her soon as I get settled in. Got to have that coffee first."

He stepped away from the reception desk and went into his private office, where he unloaded his briefcase and transferred his private line to his father's office, just in case Omunique gave him a call. He then stepped out into the hallway and closed the door behind him. Without knocking, he entered his father's private office.

With a slight frown creasing his forehead, Kenneth Maxwell Sr., fondly known as Max, looked up from the morning paper spread out on his antique, cherrywood desk. "Morning, Kenneth," he cheerfully greeted his only offspring. "A little late, aren't you, son?"

Max had the same autumn-gold eyes, though much keener than those of his son. His complexion was a slight shade darker than his son's caramel-brown skin, and his hair was a shocking mass of snowy white curls. His closely trimmed beard was the same color as his hair and eyebrows. Kenneth Maxwell Sr. had a well-groomed, distinguished look that spoke to clean living and a peaceful spirit.

Ken looked slightly embarrassed. "Good reason for it, Dad. I would've been a lot later had I known Ray Stone cancelled our meeting." Ken poured himself a cup of coffee, pulled a chair out from the conference table, and propped his feet up on another chair.

Max folded the newspaper and set it aside. "You said you had a good reason for being late. I'd like to hear it." A wry smile curled Max's lips.

Ken laid out on Max's desk the file folder he'd held in his hand. "She's my tardy excuse. Quite a beautiful one, isn't she, Dad?"

"Ah, yes. This is the young lady I was supposed to meet with. Not only was I taken with her beauty, I was impressed with her entire bio. I know her father, Wyman Philyaw, very well. Do you remember Mr. Philyaw, son?''

With his eyes fixated on the stunning picture, Ken nodded. Omunique in the flesh as well as in a photo had a way of simply taking his breath away.

''But how is she responsible for your tardiness?''

Knowing Max wasn't keen on mixing business with pleasure, Ken decided to approach the subject with caution. Until Omunique happened along, neither was he. ''I've been seeing her, Dad—socially.''

Max cast Ken a reproachful glance. ''That could get a little sticky, son, yet I understand why you would want to become acquainted with such a lovely young woman. Kenneth, she's a popular sports figure, and the tabloids could have a field day with this. I know you've just met her, but you sound like you're serious about this girl. Are you? If so, are you prepared to take the heat? In view of the playboy status the press has unfairly labeled you with, there could be plenty.''

''Dead serious! I've thought about the media, too, but I'd be more concerned about her than myself if she wasn't such a feisty little number.'' Ken laughed. ''Dad, believe me, Omunique Philyaw can handle herself pretty darn well. She gave me ulcers the first day I met her. I wasn't as prepared for our meeting as I should've been, and she practically walked out on me. I was stunned. To be honest, I wasn't prepared at all. I hadn't even glanced at her bio. To top it off, I'd mistaken her for the temp. I also thought the client was a man.'' Ken grimaced at the memories of all his major blunders.

Max roared. ''I guess you have me to thank for all your troubles. Sorry. I should've given you more details about her. But I'm sure you were relentless in making your apologies known.''

''Yeah, but she wasn't too thrilled with my tactics. She had agreed to have dinner with me that evening, but to ensure that she'd keep her word I had a chat with her agent. I think she'd already had her fill of me, so you can imagine how perturbed she was. It was rather tense in the beginning, but it turned out to be a great evening.''

Max stroked his chin. ''Hmm. Intriguing story. Just take it easy, and watch out for the media. They're capable of turning this relationship into a three-ring circus. Being a seasoned veteran, I'm sure you'll handle them delicately. I look forward to meeting the young lady. Omunique Philyaw is a fantastic figure skater, and I think she has an excellent chance of making the Olympic team. Maybe you two can take your dear old dads out to dinner one evening.''

Ken grinned. ''We're going out tonight, but I want her all to myself. It'll be our first official date. I'll hook the four of us up at a later date. It should be fun, since you're already well acquainted with Mr. Philyaw. Omunique says he visits quite often.''

Ken was halfway out the door when he turned. ''Dad, I have to discuss some important matters with you. When the time comes, I want to use Omunique as a spokesperson for our female line of athletic wear. I'm already in the process of writing a recommendation to the board.'' He glanced at his watch. ''I'm meeting with Fenton West at eleven, so I'll see you at the board meeting. Afterward, I'll fill you in on the great photo shoot Omunique has already completed.''

Max cast his son an admiring glance, unable to believe how much the two of them were alike. He'd had the very same plans in mind for Omunique Philyaw. ''I scheduled a luncheon meeting for us at one o'clock. We'll get together after that.''

In her bedroom, Omunique pulled out a drawer and carefully placed her freshly laundered lingerie on the sachet-scented liners. She deposited herself in a lounge chair in front of the picture window, facing the coastline, where she began to sort out the mail. An envelope without a return address on it immediately caught her eye. Ripping the envelope open in one quick motion, she began to peruse it. Seconds into the reading, terror filled her expression and twisted her delicate features into a grotesque mask of pain and fear.

Large, gold block print, self-adhesive letters had been haphazardly arranged on a sheet of plain white bond paper. The letters read:

I WARNED YOU, BUT YOU DIDN'T TAKE HEED. THIS IS YOUR LAST WARNING. SMILE AT ME, ONLY ME, OR CRY FORVER.

Muffling a scream, her knees shaking from fear, she dropped the undesirable letter to the floor as though it burned her fingers. Although truly upset, she couldn't help noticing that forever was spelled wrong—it was missing an e. However it was spelled, it meant danger. Looking closely at the envelope, she checked the postmark. It had been mailed from Los Angeles, which didn't necessarily mean that the sender lived there. The lunatic could live right there in her own neighborhood.

She had a very serious problem on her hands. Aware that she needed to tell her father about the situation, she decided to wait until he came down for the benefit. The weekend was the only time Wyman got to relax and enjoy life. Besides, she would feel foolish if it just turned out to be a prank by some teenagers having fun at her expense.

During the course of the day Omunique was as jittery as an expectant father awaiting the arrival of his first child. A glass of orange juice had slipped from her shaking hands, and the pulpy liquid and flying glass had splashed all over the kitchen floor. While readying herself for her dinner date, she'd knocked over a bottle of nail polish remover and ruined two pair of brand new pantyhose. Every time the phone rang, she nearly jumped out of her skin, and her heart pounded steadily like a jackhammer.

She blamed this unidentifiable, unwanted presence in her life for all the mishaps. Her life had always been so settled, she ruminated, pulling on yet another new pair of pantyhose. Besides worrying about an arthritic attack in her feet, breaking or spraining an ankle were the only other fears that had ever really plagued her—until now. She had earned the respect of almost everyone she'd come into contact with, and there wasn't a single person that she could think of who'd want to harm her. Yet this mystery person must know her, or know of her.

How could someone demand that she smile only at them? She smiled at practically everyone she saw. How could she do that, especially when she didn't know the person she was supposed to be smiling at? To suggest that she smile at no one else was absurd. Her smile was as much a part of her as breathing. This person had to be a fool, an idiot. *Or mentally ill, which could be even worse,* she thought, growing more fearful.

Who did this person think she was smiling for? Kenneth Maxwell Jr. came to mind, and she shuddered. She definitely had a special smile for him. A distracting presence, but one that certainly wasn't unwanted. She'd been in the company of many striking males, but never had anyone had the effect on her that Ken had. She couldn't think of a single person, male or female, that she'd ever reacted to in such an uncharacteristic manner.

The calls hadn't begun to occur until she started seeing him. Was it possible that her dating Ken disturbed someone? To think that someone might be actually watching her every move made her skin crawl. There certainly were no jilted lovers in her past. Could there be one in Ken's? *But the caller sounded like a man.* Was this a fatal attraction of some sort? One thing she was sure of—it was a very sick thing.

Despite all the mishaps and her rattled nerves Omunique managed to make herself look spectacular. Wearing a stunning, midnight-blue silk sheath, she looked gorgeous. Deep blue sapphire earrings, inherited from her mother, dangled from her dainty ears. The matching necklace delicately possessed her graceful neck. Her hair, twisted in an elegant style, swirled neatly atop her head. Decorative combs kept it in place.

By the time Ken arrived, Omunique was in such a fragile mental state she had to fight doubly hard to remain in control of her sanity. She'd racked her brain so much over the mystery phone calls it felt as if her brain had slowly seeped from her skull.

Though Ken couldn't have guessed what color Omunique would wear for their date, it looked as though he had. His dark blue suit was an exciting compliment to her attire. The rich nuances in his hand-painted silk tie brought his crisp white shirt to life.

Omunique had been cold and unresponsive to his passionate kiss, Ken recalled as he sat directly across from her. Noticing her zombie-like state, Ken closely observed her seemingly detatched behavior. She'd been practically silent during the drive to the Gates of Seville, yet her brief enthusiasm over the beautiful Spanish restaurant seemed to suggest he'd simply misread her again. But once they'd been seated her detached mood had resurfaced almost immediately.

Ken watched with concern as she poked at her food, taking very small bites of the cheese enchiladas and barely touching her Spanish rice. When she laid down her fork and broodingly stared out over the Santa Monica coastline, he placed his hand over hers.

"There's something terribly wrong here, Omunique. Would you mind telling me what's bothering you? Is the food okay?" His tone was strained, yet his hand gently massaged the back of hers.

Managing to pull off a halfway convincing smile, she placed her other hand on top of the gentle hand covering hers. "Everything was divine, Ken, and I don't have room for another single calorie," she told him before returning her attention to the outside view.

He knew that something was bothering her, though. The look in her eyes was only one of several things that confirmed his suspicions. "You didn't answer my first question, Omunique, so I'll repeat it. Would you mind telling me what's bothering you? I'd like to know what it is." He now massaged the back of her other hand.

She looked up at him briefly, and turned her gaze back to the coastline. "It's nothing for you to worry about, Ken."

He moved closer to her. "Is it something to do with us?" He lifted her hair and kissed the side of her neck. "You can discuss anything with me, you know. I'm a good listener," he whispered against her ear.

It took every ounce of her strength not to fall apart in his arms, but she couldn't let that happen. Their relationship was much too new to burden it with such a heavy weight. "It has nothing to do with us, Ken, but it's very personal." *It just might have everything to do with us.*

Though unsatisfied with her response, he kissed her cheek. "I don't like seeing you like this. Does it have something to do with your profession? If so, maybe I can help."

At this point, she knew she needed to say something to calm his suspicions. She also knew she should come clean with him about her concerns, but she couldn't bring herself to unload her burdens on him. "There are a couple of things that I'm concerned about, Ken. I've been brooding about an exhibition I'm going to do with my friend, Ian Swanson. I've never skated with anyone in an exhibition, or when on tour. I'm worried about screwing things up for Ian. I'm also a little worried about how people are going to perceive our relationship, especially the media. Have you given the issue any thought?"

He grinned. "Much thought, Omunique. I know there could be a lot of gossip and unfounded rumors about our professional and personal relationship, but I think we're both mature enough to handle it. We're both pretty strong. I'm sure you've already faced some adverse publicity, and I'm hardly a stranger to it. I hope you're up to the challenge, young lady." Stroking her hair, he guided her head onto his shoulder. "I have a confession to make."

Misinterpreting his comment, she looked up, startled, and gazed into his eyes. She didn't want to hear his confession, especially if it was somehow going to hurt. She couldn't bear another ounce of disconsolation. Her sanity was already hanging by a single thread.

She cleared her throat. "Where there's been no commitment, there's no need for confessions."

Her last comment made him nervous. He thought they'd made a commitment when they'd talked about not seeing anyone else as long as they were involved. To busy himself, he pushed a loose strand of her hair behind her ear. "Trust me, it's nothing like that, Omunique," he said, unsure of what she'd really meant. "I came to watch you practice yesterday." She truly looked surprised. "You were wonderful, Princess! You and the guy you skated with are perfect together—as skaters, mind you. I felt a little envious of him. He's sharing something with you that I never can. I can learn to appreciate or even love your sport, but I'll never have it my blood the way you both obviously do."

Tears sprang to her eyes. "I'm touched, Ken. That you would take time out of your busy schedule to watch me skate astounds me. You must not have seen my earlier performance. I was absolutely disastrous." She released a sparkling stream of laughter. "My rear end still stings from all its ice-kissing mishaps."

Her laughter was infectious, making him laugh, too. "I guess I didn't. All I saw were two beautiful skaters who have a rare and magnificent talent. You shouldn't let an exhibition upset you. If it were the Olympic trials, then I could understand. But Princess, it's only an exhibition. You'll be just great. So will our relationship."

Tossing him a dazzling smile, she nodded. She then bit down on her lower lip. "Maybe I am worrying about nothing. I should just relax and enjoy being here with you." She kissed his cheek. "You've calmed the storm, Ken." *For now,* she added in her thoughts, *but what am I going to do when I'm alone, and the phone calls start up?* "Thanks for the pep talk."

As piped-in music drifted through the lovely, Mediterranean-style restaurant, he found himself wanting to feel her body next to his. "How about us taking advantage of all this good music? Would you like to dance with me, Omunique?" he asked, eagerly anticipating an intimate interlude with the woman who took his breath away.

Her smile was brilliant. "I would love to, Ken, but I think it's only fair that I warn you about my two left feet."

"If you're feeling what I'm feeling, your feet won't even touch the floor. For someone who was so defiantly bold the first day we met, you suddenly seem so shy and delicate." Ken stood up and reached for her hand, which she placed in his without hesitation. A few admiring heads turned their way as they strolled the few yards to the dance floor.

The moment his body made contact with hers, he knew there was no other place on earth he'd rather be. When her arms closed tenderly around his neck, he knew he wanted to hold onto her forever. . . .

Later, she pushed her chair back from the table, smiling adoringly at him. "If you'll excuse me, I have to use the little girls' room. I won't be gone too long."

Ken slid out of the booth and remained standing until she walked away. The gentle sway of her hips excited him. He smiled when nearly every head in the restaurant turned and followed her graceful retreat.

Though she'd said he'd convinced her that everything would be okay, he sensed that there was more to her strange behavior than any exhibition. From what he'd seen of her and Ian's performance, he couldn't understand why she would have any doubts about her abilities. He'd never seen a finer skating program. Something else was at work here. *Something complex,* he mused, vowing to find out what that something was.

Sitting in one of the stalls, Omunique tried to convince herself that Ken had accepted her reasoning. *Has he really?* she wondered. She didn't think he was gullible in any way, but she'd been desperate to lead him afield. If he didn't believe her, he'd certainly convinced her that they could have both a professional and personal liaison. She wasn't going to let her silly worries ruin their first official date.

She was going to go back out there and relax and enjoy the company of the man she could so easily fall in love with—if she hadn't already. Maybe he wouldn't return her feelings, but she wasn't going to worry about that, either. At this stage of the game, worrying about what could or couldn't happen between them was ludicrous. *Just let whatever happens happen naturally,* she concluded, promising herself to bask in his attentiveness the rest of the evening.

A sudden noise outside the stall frightened her. The hairs on the back of her neck bristled, and her heart began to pound in her chest like that of a wild, captive bird. For a few seconds she sat motionless, listening for any signs of someone lurking about.

A few more minutes had passed before she finally got the nerve to leave the confines of the stall. The size of saucers, her eyes looked all around the room for evidence of someone having been there. She saw none. If someone *had* been there, they'd already left. *After all, this is a public restroom,* she thought, laughing at her own silliness.

When she turned toward the lounge area of the restroom, she noticed a piece of white bond paper attached to the dressing table mirror. Her laughter died in mid-air. Undoubtedly, the paper hadn't been there before. Timidly, she removed the note from the mirror, opening it slowly and then dropping it rapidly.

YOU'VE SMILED YOUR LAST SMILE leaped at her from the sheet of plain white paper.

Nausea launched a jab right into her midsection. Fear engulfed her in an apocalyptic funnel cloud. A blood-chilling scream wrenched free from her throat as the floor appeared to rise up to meet her.

*   *   *

Omunique didn't know where she was when she came to, but she smelled a familiar scent, a man's aftershave or cologne. She saw that she was in a strange bed, in an unfamiliar room. As she tried to sit up, she gasped. A sharp pain had torn through her right temple, casting her into total darkness. Then she heard the shuffling of feet, which seemed to stop right in front of where she lay. Someone was standing over her. Just the sound of their breathing frightened her, causing her to truckle into a fetal position.

As gentle hands lifted her head. she slowly opened her eyes. Recognizing Ken, she threw her arms around his neck. The sudden movement caused a wave of nausea to surf on her stomach's contents. The distressing look on her face told Ken that he needed to lay her head back against the pillow, slowly and gently.

"Oh, Ken!" she cried, "Where . . . am I? What has happened to me? I feel so . . ."

When her voice trailed off, he stretched out beside her on the bed and carefully drew her head onto his chest "You're safe, Omunique. You're in my bedroom." She gave him a questioning look. "At the restaurant, do you remember leaving the table to go to the restroom?"

Her head throbbed like an abscessed tooth as she struggled to remember. Gingerly, she nodded her head, wincing in pain. Soothingly, he rubbed the lump on her right temple.

"You were in the ladies' room when screams echoed throughout the restaurant. Several people ran in the direction of the screams. Knowing you were in the same vicinity, I followed the others. We found you unconscious, on the floor. You have a pretty nasty bump on your right temple." He kissed the large lump. "Princess, do you remember whether your screams came before you hit your head, or afterward? Do you recall what happened in there? Did something or someone frighten you?"

As she tried to recall the events that led up to her being flat on her back and in acute pain, a patch of dense fog appeared before her eyes. Her entire body shook as she recalled the threatening note. "Oh. God, somebody is trying to hurt me," she moaned, the pain in her head nearly causing her to black out again.

Shocked by her outburst and gravely concerned for her health, Ken tightened his arms around her to bring comfort. He sensed that she didn't remember anything. "Shh, shh, you're safe, Princess. No one is going to harm you. You have a slight concussion. When I took you to the hospital, you still hadn't completely come around. Dr. Greer said you were going to be just fine, but you need plenty of rest."

"No," she shouted in frustration, "you don't . . . understand. Someone wants to hurt me. Didn't you see the threatening note?" she inquired tearfully. "Didn't anybody see it?"

Realizing that whatever she had experienced was very real to her—rather than imagined or a direct result of the concussion—he grew even more concerned. He had to control his own panic. Otherwise, she might sense the strong current of fear he himself now felt.

He raised up on one elbow and looked down at her. "I didn't see a note, Omunique. What did it say, and how did you get it? Was someone else in the bathroom at the same time you were in there?" His voice quaked as he questioned her.

Starting at the very beginning, with the first terrifying phone call she'd received, she explained everything to the best of her recollection. Bits and pieces of the bathroom tale were shady, but she told him, with clarity, those things that had occurred prior to the latest incident.

He listened in stunned silence, feeling a tight fist knot up in the pit of his stomach. "You should've told someone about this sooner, Nique," he gently scolded, calling her by her nickname for the first time. Coming from him, it sounded like a term of endearment. "Something terrible could've happened to you. No one would have been the wiser. We've got to contact the police, and we should probably call your father.''

She gripped his hand tightly. ''Ken, please, I don't want to involve my father. He has enough to worry about. I didn't tell you because I didn't think I should involve you in something this deep. Our relationship is just beginning,'' she moaned.

To think that she wanted to protect him from involvement only made him care for her all the more. He kissed the top of her head. ''Oh, Omunique, it sounds as if you didn't think I cared enough about you to help you through this. My beautiful Ice Princess, you were so wrong. I couldn't walk away from you if I wanted to. I care deeply for you. Don't ever doubt my feelings.''

Exhausted and traumatized, she looked drained of all color. Using a wet towel, he wiped the sweat from her brow and the tears from her eyes. ''Rest, Princess,'' Ken soothed. ''I'm going to make all the appropriate calls from the other room. Your situation has to be dealt with, swiftly . . . by any means necessary,'' he stated firmly.

She clutched at his arm as he raised up from the bed. ''No, please don't leave me all alone. I couldn't bear it.''

The terror in her voice made him shudder. When he lay back down on the bed, she immediately curled up against him. ''I'm here, Omunique. I won't leave you.''

Chapter Seven

Under the natural warmth of Ken's lustrous smile Omunique seemed to blossom, despite what she'd been through. "I owe you an apology, Ken. I realize I've been very moody. I've been a nervous wreck all day. I'm sorry if I shut you out. It really wasn't my intention. While I was getting ready for our date, everything that could go wrong did. But the truth of the matter is, besides all these horrifying occurrences, I'm not used to much dating. I just don't know how I'm supposed to act." She laughed at her own naivete. "I hate to admit it, but my social calendar is completely blank."

There, she thought with satisfaction. A good dose of honesty just might cure what ailed her with regard to their romantic involvement.

He ran his index finger up and down her bare arm, causing her to shiver with delight. Her remarks titillated him. "Though I find it hard to believe that men aren't knocking down your door, I'm relieved to know that I'm not responsible for your earlier mood."

More responsible than you could possibly know, she mused.

As much as the phone calls instilled fear in her, her feelings for him caused a different type of fear, the fear of loving someone who might not be able to return those feelings.

"Well, it's not so much that men haven't been knocking down my door. I think it has more to do with my unwillingness to answer the bell," she said, her confidence restored.

He threw his head back in laughter. "I like that, Nique. That was real honesty mingled with your great sense of humor. Until you enlightened me about what's been happening, I was beginning to think you weren't all that interested in me."

Wondering how he'd reached such a totally inaccurate conclusion, she stared at him, her eyes bright with surprise.

"And that would be such a shame," he continued, "since you have exclusive rights to all my personal interests. As far as how you're supposed to act goes, Omunique, just be yourself—it's a large part of your attraction. I think I've gotten more than a glimpse of the real Omunique Philyaw, especially the one who knocked me off my high horse. You were treacherous on our first meeting."

Her eyes widened. "I hope I wasn't that bad, Ken. At any rate, I have to warn you—you might have to exercise overabundant patience with me. I have so many things going on career wise, and I'm going to have to do some fancy finagling to keep abreast of everything."

Her voice was now more confident. He was elated to learn that her earlier moods hadn't meant she wasn't interested in him, but he detested the real reasons for her distractions. He realized she was going to have to adjust to having a man in her life, as well as this threat to her safety. He had no intention of removing himself from the scheme of things, but the threat to her safety would be foremost, he vowed.

"I can understand that. I just want you to know that I'm an easy person to get along with. Especially when things are going my way," he added on a chuckle. "I have a lot of career things going on, as well, so we'll both have to learn how to finagle things." Even without the candles that lit up the room she would've glowed. Leaning over her, he aligned his mouth with hers and gently probed her sweetness.

Savoring his last kiss, Omunique touched two fingers to her moist lips. "Now that we've come to an understanding, I'm afraid you have me at a disadvantage here. My bio has provided you with a lot of information about me, personal and professional, but I'd like to know more about Kenneth Maxwell Jr., the man."

He grinned widely, though he felt this conversation was a way for her to take her mind off the previous unsettling events. He also suspected she was trying to keep him from making certain phone calls.

"Oh, so you want to talk about my favorite subject," he joked easily. "There's not a lot more to reveal. I'm open, honest, and sensitive. I love to laugh and I'm not ashamed to cry. And I know what I want out of a relationship before getting involved. Nique, I know exactly what I want out of this one."

Omunique arched her eyebrows sharply. "Oh? And what might that be, Ken?"

Ken loosely entwined her fingers with his. "I want something from this relationship I've never desired from any other. Permanence."

Astonished, she gasped.

He grinned. "Hold on now, don't let that comment scare you away. I may want permanence, but I know that that's something that has to be built from the ground up. It's kind of like setting a goal knowing you have to work hard at achieving it, for however long it takes. I'm sure you're quite familiar with that concept."

She nodded. "I'm very familiar with being goal-oriented, but I guess I've never thought about it in terms of building a personal relationship." So he did feel the same things she felt, she thought, feeling giddy inside. First, she'd feared that he wouldn't return her feelings. Now that he'd exposed his hand, why was she quaking in her silk stockings?

He placed his hand on the side of her face. "Omunique,

you're the type of woman that makes a man want to discard all the rules he's played by. I never thought I'd see the day when I'd feel the need to revise my old rulebook, but it's here. In other words, I want to see if we have what it takes to build a solid future together. Have I made my intentions clear?''

''Abundantly,'' she breathed shakily.

Appearing anxious, Ken took her hand and raised her fingertips to his lips. ''Is that all you're going to say on the subject, Princess?''

She covered his hand with her own. ''For now. You've given me a lot to think about. And I do appreciate your candor.'' She felt it best to hide her elation. They sat in silence for several minutes, which gave Omunique the opportunity to ponder his voiced intentions. She liked how straighforward he was. He certainly hadn't beat around the bush regarding his feelings. A sudden need to use the bathroom came over her. It made her uncomfortable when she thought of how to tell him. ''I need to go to the bathroom, Ken.'' Feeling embarrassed, she paused for a moment. ''I . . . need help . . . getting there.''

Seeing that her request embarrassed her, he pushed back the deep burgundy coverlet. Lifting her from the bed, he carried her into the adjoining bathroom and set her down on the covered toilet seat. ''I'll be right outside if you need me. If you get dizzy, yell out. Sweetheart, take it easy and be careful.''

If he didn't hurry up and leave there'd be no reason for her to be careful. Her bladder would overflow. Noticing her discomfort, he hurried from the room and strode over to the bed and sat down on the side of it. He then picked up the phone and called his father, hoping he had Wyman Philyaw's San Francisco phone number.

With trembling hands, she fumbled with her pantyhose. Using the wall for support, she stood up and lifted the toilet seat. Although dark spots appeared before her eyes, she managed to sit down before the dizziness could overcome her.

The doorbell rang just as Ken finished writing down the

phone number his father had given him for Wyman Philyaw. Not knowing what to do, he looked anxiously at the bathroom door. She hadn't called out to him thus far. If he left the room he wouldn't hear her if she did need him, yet he had to answer the door.

Walking over to the bedroom door, he knocked. "Are you okay in there?"

"I'm fine, Ken."

"Good. I need to answer the doorbell. I'll be right back. You stay put until I return. Don't try to go it alone."

Dr. Columbus Greer, a medium-build black man with a mahogany complexion indented with small patches of grayish cracked skin, extended his hand to his old friend, his widely spaced dark brown eyes revealing fatigue.

"Ken, sorry I'm so late getting here, but I wasn't able to get away from the hospital before now. How is your girlfriend? You were really stressed over the lump on her head when I saw you two in the emergency room earlier. Is she feeling any better than she did?"

His girlfriend. Ken mulled that over in his mind. How nice that sounded. It did seem a little adolescent, but he did feel like an adolescent when he was with her—an adolescent who was discovering all the intriguing qualities of his first serious relationship with a girl.

"Come on in the living room, Columbus. We can talk in there, but first I need to check on Omunique. She's in the bathroom. Let me get her settled back in bed."

Columbus meandered across the room and sat down on the forest green and burgundy awning-stripe sofa. He placed his medical bag on the smoked-glass coffee table. Though he'd been in Ken's place on many occasions, his dark brown eyes carefully studied the character of the spacious, exquisitely decorated condo.

In the bedroom, Ken busied himself making Omunique comfortable. "Dr. Greer has arrived, and he'll be right in to see you." He kissed the tip of her nose. "I'll be right back, Princess."

Ken returned to the living room and sat down on the opposite end of the sofa from the doctor. He then turned at an angle to face his friend. "She's feeling a little better, Columbus. She's been communicating easily enough, but I'm still concerned with the lump on her temple." Ken told Columbus how he thought her head injury occurred, but he didn't give the nasty circumstance regarding why she had fallen.

Ken escorted Columbus into the bedroom and sat in a chair while Columbus reexamined Omunique. Columbus had recognized her at the hospital, which surprised Ken, since his friend wasn't into any type of sports. He'd often expressed his dislike for what he thought to be "dangerous living." But who could ever forget the inescapable beauty of Princess Philyaw? All someone needed to do was see her just once, Ken thought, and her lovely features would remain forever engraved in their mind.

Columbus sat on the side of the bed. "It's nice to see you, Omunique, though I wish it were under different circumstances. You were in no shape for me to tell you this earlier, but I've read a lot about you. All of it was quite spectacular." Omunique smiled a quiet thanks before thanking him aloud.

"I'm going to do another routine exam, nothing too painful. I'm going to further assess your condition to see if you might need any other medical tests. Ken, could you blow out the candles and turn out the overhead light? I want to examine Omunique's eyes."

Using a small penlight instrument, he shone light in her eyes. "Your eyes are just fine, Omunique, but I need to check a few more things before I decide whether to send you back to the emergency room for admission."

His long fingers probed her head tenderly as he checked the lump on her temple. He then did a partial neurological exam.

"Let me help you get back in bed, Omunique. I don't want to tax you any further. I don't see any real cause for alarm.

Your skull X rays and brain scan didn't show anything out of the ordinary, but I'll have the official radiology report sometime tomorrow. If you'll give me the name of your sports physician, I'll be glad to discuss your case with him or her.'' He smiled and patted her hand. "However, I think you're going to be just fine. After a few days rest, you'll be good as new."

His tone and methods had been so gentle and soothing that Omunique had to wonder if he'd ever hypnotized anyone. He truly had a wonderful bedside manner. She smiled back, sighing with relief. "Thank you, Dr. Greer."

"I prefer Columbus, especially coming from those I consider friends."

"I take that as a compliment. Thank you. You've been very kind and gentle with me. I appreciate it."

"You're very welcome." Columbus turned to face Ken. "We're all done here. I'm sure you're anxious to get back to your evening, but I have a suggestion to make before I leave." He encompassed both Ken and Omunique in his concentrated gaze. "Because I don't want you moving about, Omunique, I think you should remain here for the night. Riding around in a car is only going to make you feel worse than you already do. You can go home tomorrow, but should you have any major discomfort Ken needs to bring you back to the hospital. Do either of you have any questions?" Ken and Omunique shook their heads.

"In that case, I'm on my way. You have my home phone number, Ken. If I'm not in, just tell my exchange it's an emergency. They'll contact me right away."

Wyman was distraught. "How could she keep something so serious from me, of all people? I don't understand it, Ken. She normally tells me everything—or at least I thought so."

"Sir, in the beginning I don't think she thought it was all that serious, but when it continued I think she finally realized the imminent danger she might be in. If the incident at the restaurant hadn't occurred, I strongly believe she would've continued to keep it to herself. She hadn't told me because she didn't want to burden our relationship, and she thinks you have enough to worry about with the problems in your San Francisco insurance agency.''

"That's so ridiculous," Wyman charged impatiently. "There's nothing in my life that's more important than my daughter . . . and she knows it. I'd go insane if something were to happen to that girl.'' Wyman took a moment to collect himself. "I'd like to know what the doctor said about her condition.''

Ken filled Wyman in on all the details. When Wyman asked to speak with his daughter, Ken seemed reluctant. He hadn't promised Omunique he wouldn't call her father, but she didn't yet know that he'd gotten the number, let alone that he'd actually placed the call.

"Sir, if you could give me time to tell her I've phoned you, it would make things easier. As it is, she's going to feel betrayed by me. But I promise you this, your daughter is in good hands. I'm going to stick to her like glue, and that's something she's just going to have to deal with. Either she's staying here at my place, or I'm staying with her—that is, until we can come up with some other viable solution.''

Wyman felt instant relief. "Though I would be more comfortable looking after her myself, I'll trust you'll take good care of her. I'm going to get there as soon as I can, but having you to look after her will allow me a little more time to get this agency through this critical stage. You do have to work, you know. I'm not worried about her when she's at the arena. There's plenty of security around that place. We might want to consider hiring private security to protect her.''

"That's a good thought, but for now I'm going to take her to the arena before I go to work and pick her up afterward. Besides, with that lump on her head she's going to be off for a few days, anyway. That will give me time to put a few plans into action. I'll keep you posted. I know it will be hard, but don't worry about your daughter. I will protect Omunique with my very life. She has become very important to me, in a way that has nothing to do with company sponsorship.''

Wyman heard more than just admiration for his daughter in Ken's voice. He remembered feeling the same way about the woman he'd married, the same girl who'd been his high school sweetheart, the same woman he'd lost to death only moments after she'd given life to Omunique. Patrice had won his love the instant they'd met. He couldn't be sure, but it sounded as though his daughter had already stolen this young man's heart.

''Young man, if you're anything at all like your father, you're a man I can trust. Have Omunique call me when she's up to it. You must tell her you've told me. She doesn't like to have things kept from her. I'm sure you'll do what's right by her.''

''I'll take everything you've said under advisement. Have a good evening, sir,'' Ken said before cradling the receiver.

Ken stepped quietly into the room, surprised to find Omunique wide-awake, lying on her side and staring into space without expression. He hoped she hadn't heard any of his phone call.

His presence seemed to fill the room as she turned over on her back, smiling in his direction. ''Can you believe I'm here in your bed, without any coaxing on your part?''

She is feeling better, he thought happily. ''I can see that no damage has been done to your sense of humor. As for you being in my bed, you're too easy, Miss Philyaw. I thought it would take much longer than this to have you spend the night with me. However, you're a bit overdressed.''

Opening a dresser drawer, he pulled out a large, silk T-shirt and a pair of gray silk boxer shorts, holding them up for her to see. ''Now, this is my idea of comfort. I'll fix you a hot cup of tea while you slip into these. Of course, I can stay and help you undress if you'd like,'' he teased, arching his eyebrows in a suggestive manner.

She laughed. ''I'm a big girl. I can get dressed and undressed all by myself,'' she responded haughtily.

He tossed the clothing her way. "Can I interest you in a small sip of brandy?"

"Sounds nice, but put it in the tea. Disguising the taste will help me get it down."

"As you wish. I'll be back in a jiffy. Make yourself comfortable. I won't be long."

As she surveyed the magnificent surroundings, she pulled back the burgundy coverlet and stretched her cramping limbs. *He favors burgundy and green,* she mused, recalling the colors in the bathroom. She had to wonder if the front of the house carried the same color scheme. The room was so well maintained that if it weren't for the masculine decor she would've thought a woman resided on the premises. Omunique figured that there were very few males who kept their residences so orderly and sparkling clean, but there were very few men like Kenneth Maxwell Jr.

Sitting on the side of the bed, she stripped out of her clothes, slipped into the boxer shorts, and pulled the T-shirt over her head. As she climbed back into bed, Ken came through the door carrying two cups of steaming liquid. Placing one on the nightstand nearest to where she lay, he slid it within easy reach.

Here's a couple of Tylenol, should you need them." He laid the white pills on the nightstand. "Before I go to bed I'll bring you a glass of water."

"Where are you going to sleep?" she asked timidly.

"Where do you want me to sleep?" he countered softly.

Without thinking of the consequences of such a bold move, she patted the far side of the bed. "Only if you can control yourself," she asserted, smiling innocently.

The autumn-gold eyes smiled mischievously. "It will be very, very hard, but for you I can do just about anything," he assured, blowing a kiss in her direction. "Be right back," he flung over his shoulder in parting.

Picking up the cup of tea, she sipped on it methodically, happy that she wasn't going to have to be alone. It wasn't long before she felt the effects of the small amount of brandy. Her eyelids became heavy, but she fought the idea of sleep, fearful that she'd be troubled with nightmares. Fear was the real reason she'd wanted Ken in the same room with her, and if she hadn't been so frightened she would've insisted on going home—home, where she'd find comfort in familiar surroundings, comfort in her own bed.

Ken slipped into the far side of the bed. When she scooted over and nestled her head onto his chest, nothing could've prepared him for the earth-shattering sensations that rushed through him. Able to feel her softness through the silk T-shirt, he closed his eyes, trying his best to will his manhood into an unresponsive state.

Unaware of how she affected him, Omunique shifted her body around, trying to make herself more comfortable. Each of her movements caused shock waves to rumble through his irrepressible maleness. Obtaining her desired position, she lifted her head and glanced down at him. His eyes were closed shut. She thought he was asleep, and she placed an airy kiss on his mouth.

Ken was busy exercising all the control he could muster. He tried desperately not to respond to her kiss. It worked—that is, until she turned her back and her bare legs and firm, silk-clad rounded bottom brushed against the throbbing in his loins. Exhaling a deep breath, he turned over on his side and snuggled up behind her. Encircling her tiny waist with his arm, he pulled her in close to him and wrapped one leg over her hip.

Tilting her head back, she sought out his mouth, kissing him deeply. When reality set in, she pulled away quickly. "This isn't working, is it?" she whispered softly.

He laughed huskily. "No, it isn't. Do you . . . want me to . . . go into one of the other bedrooms?"

"No," she responded in haste. "I'd be terrified if you left me all alone. Besides, I'm not used to your house. It's a lot different from staying in hotels."

"In that case, we have to make it work. Go to sleep, Princess," he gently commanded.

Though their eyes were closed, both were very much awake. They could sense their passionate need for one another, yet neither of them was willing to be the first to act on it. Their breathing was even, because they struggled to keep it that way. Thoughts of making love were close at hand, so close they could envision themselves intimately entwined.

Restless and aroused to the point where he no longer thought he could control himself, Ken rolled over on his side and clicked on the light. Pretending to be asleep, Omunique fervently prayed that he wasn't going to leave her all alone. Her eyelids were so tightly squeezed together he easily recognized their unnatural fluttering.

He laid a tender hand on her arm. "I know you're not asleep, Omunique. Maybe we should discuss what we're both feeling."

Holding her breath, she didn't move a muscle. Then her eyelids slowly fluttered open, exposing bewilderment. "We should." She paused briefly. "It's very hard sleeping next to someone you're so physically attracted to. My body craves your intimate touch, but my sense of morality won't allow me to satisfy those cravings. Yet I'm afraid if you leave me, I'll be terrified. Do you have any suggestions?" she asked, her voice shy.

He propped himself up in bed. "Well, we could shut out the morality issues and satiate our bodies. We could rid ourselves briefly of any hang-ups that could hamper us. But I know our relationship is too damn important to just throw caution to the wind. If it physically happens for us, I want there to be no regrets. So, with that in mind, I'm going to get a sleeping bag and make a pallet right here by the bed. That way you won't be alone, and we won t be tempted to do something we might later regret. Will just having me in the same room with you calm your fears?"

"Tremendously," she responded, a mixture of relief and regret in her voice. "Since this is your bed, I think I should be the one to sleep on the pallet."

His smile was tender. "I won't hear of it. Your physical

condition demands that your body be pampered and well-rested. Sleeping on the floor is hardly my idea of pampering. I'll get the sleeping bag and come right back.'' He kissed her eyelids. "We're going to make it through this night, after all—together. Physically apart, but soulfully connected. May your dreams be filled with my presence. I know mine will be filled with yours.''

Chapter Eight

Awakened by an acrid smell emanating through the room and burning his nostrils, Ken jumped up from the floor. Noticing that Omunique wasn't in the bed, he became worried. For fear that the house was burning down, he began to check.

As he neared the kitchen, the acrid smell of sulfur became unbearable. He rushed into the smoke-filled kitchen, where he found Omunique sitting at the table with unchecked tears streaming down her lovely face.

He rushed to her side. "Hey," he said softly, "why all the tears?"

She began to sob loudly. "I've ruined one of your pans, not to mention . . . the entire kitchen."

Surveying where her finger pointed, he saw that the pan was severely burnt. He laughed lightly. "What happened?"

Her cheeks fused with color "I intended to surprise you with breakfast, but I forgot one important detail." He looked at her questioningly. "I don't know . . . how to cook." Picking up a paper napkin, she wiped her tears, but more fell to replace the ones she'd wiped away.

Ken couldn't contain his laughter despite feeling he shouldn't take her anguish lightly. "Really now," he commented, laughing. "You mean there's something the Ice Princess hasn't mastered? But why would you attempt to make breakfast if you know you can't cook?" he grilled in a teasing manner, stifling another outburst of laughter.

She rolled her eyes. "I thought boiling a couple of eggs would be a piece of cake. If I hadn't decided to shower while they boiled, it might have been okay. I don't think I put enough water in the pan. When I returned from the bathroom the pan had burned, and the kitchen had filled with smoke." She moaned painfully. "I feel like an idiot. Who burns water?"

He couldn't let that question go unanswered no matter how hard he tried. He smoothed her hair back with his palm. "Someone who can't cook," came his joking response.

She didn't find any humor in his statement. The narrowing of her eyes drove her point directly home.

He kissed her forehead. "Don't be offended, sweetheart. I'm only trying to lighten your mood. Not knowing how to cook is nothing to be ashamed of. Don't let this insignificant mishap ruin your day. I'm flattered that you even wanted to cook me breakfast. I'm an excellent cook, and I'd be happy to teach you. Besides, you shouldn't be doing anything but resting. Columbus did instruct you to rest a few more days."

Wiping her tears away, she smiled brightly. "I am making too much of this, aren't I?"

Sympathetically, he agreed.

"Well, you've learned something else about me. I'd rather you hadn't learned it in this way, but what the heck. It's done now. We need to get out of this smoky room. My head is already splitting."

Grasping her hand, he gently pulled her up from the chair and guided her into the living room. After opening all the windows, he drew her down onto the carpet.

"I'll get dressed, then I'll take you out to breakfast. Afterward, we'll take our postponed coastal drive." He touched the shrinking injury to her head. "Your lump has practically disappeared. Are you up to going out for breakfast and the drive, though? Maybe we should postpone it a while longer."

She ruffled his hair. "I'm hungry, Ken, and I do have to eat somewhere. As far as the drive goes, it'll be therapeutic. Except for the one day we went to the house to retrieve clothes for me, I haven't been outside for over a week. It's time for me to rejoin the living, don't you think?"

'You've got a point. With you back on the ice come Monday, we might not get this opportunity for a long while. If I know you, you're going to try to make up for all the training time you've lost. So we'll go ahead and do it," he conceded.

"You're so right. I'm not going to push myself too, too hard, but I do need to get back to where I was. I imagine it's going to be rough going for a few days. Brent will see to that. He's been anxious for my return."

Putting a fluffy pillow under her head, he kissed her, and went off to shower and dress. Once he was out of earshot, she had a good laugh over the kitchen incident. Ken had been a good sport about it, but she still felt a little embarrassed. Though the fresh sea air blew in through the open windows, it would take a windstorm to clear all the rooms of the pungent odor.

Omunique got up from the floor and pulled a chair in front of the living room window. The sea breeze rushed in, filling her nostrils with the scent of salty sea air. Ken had a spectacular view of the ocean and the Venice boardwalk. The boardwalk was a big tourist attraction, which made it a lot noisier than her quiet beach community. Still slightly embarrassed over the burning eggs, Omuniqué turned her mind back to the incident.

Ken had said she shouldn't be ashamed of not knowing how to cook, but she was. Everyone should know how. While there were a lot of things she could prepare to keep from starving, they were mainly salads, sandwiches, canned soups, and things that could be popped into the microwave or the deep fryer. Though Omunique had watched Wyman and her grandmother, Ava Philyaw, who had helped raise her, prepare meals, she'd always been too busy studying or too tired from training to get involved with the preparations.

Now it was costing her. Now that she'd found a man she'd love to prepare breakfast, lunch, and dinner for, and especially a romantic candlelight dinner, she would have to learn to cook. She thought of the many things she'd missed out on in life while working to achieve her educational and athletic goals. They'd never really concerned her until now. Being around Ken made her realize just how much she'd truly missed out on.

Dating was what a lot of teenagers lived for, but she hadn't had much experience there, either. She'd always seen boys, then young men, as unnecessary distractions. As far as she'd been concerned, needing a man in one's life was akin to needing an emotional crutch. But now that she was learning what it really meant to have a man to lean on, she found herself in an unfamiliar position, one that excited and frightened her at the same time.

Then she thought about the things she had experienced. She'd traveled around the world to exotic places, something a lot of youths and many adults would never get to experience, had made many international friends through her travels and athletic ventures. Nothing seemed to compare to what she'd been feeling since Ken came into her life, though.

Ken was altogether a new, exciting adventure, and she sensed that he was a very special kind of man. What she felt with him was good and wonderful. Every time he smiled at her, she felt as though she'd been placed on top of the world. And when he kissed her, the incredible rush of joy and passion that spread all the way through to her soul was unrivaled.

Walking up behind her chair, Ken rested his chin on her shoulder and nuzzled her ear, gently lavishing each lobe with moist kisses. "Are you still hungry, Princess?"

Omunique rubbed her cheek against his. "More than you could possibly know." She was hungry all right, but her hunger had nothing to do with food.

"Well, let's get out of here. I'm in the mood for pancakes and lots of syrup," he told her, helping her up from the chair. "What about you?"

"Sounds divine, Ken, but I need to stick to my diet. I can't be overweight when it's time for my next competition. But I'm sure you can manage to eat enough for both of us. And please don't try to tempt me. I'm not that strong. When it comes to sweets, my willpower has a hard time kicking in."

"I won't, but I can't promise you that I won't try to tempt you in other ways." His eyes seem to devour her, as though she were his desired meal.

"I'm going to hold you to that promise."

Over breakfast at the International House of Pancakes, Ken closely watched Omunique as she ate her grapefruit and cold cereal with gusto. Each time she stuck her spoon into her mouth he wished that it were his tongue slipping past the sweetness of her ripe lips. His manhood involuntarily responded to every single movement she made. Omunique had no idea of how her ever-blooming sensuality affected him. If just watching her eat from a spoon made him respond in such an ardent way, then what would it be like to have a complete physical connection with her?

Having had her in his bed that first night had given him some indication of what it would be like, which was one of the reasons he'd opted to sleep on the floor. Had he stayed in bed with her he would've gone totally insane. Being next to her in bed was like being cooked alive on the broiling pan of an oven—too hot to survive.

Of all his experiences with women, he'd never had one come this close to blowing his mind the way Omunique did. The girl simply had "whip appeal." If she had any idea of what she did to him, the way she made him think and feel, she'd probably run for cover. No matter how long, or even how far, she'd try to run from him, though, he'd find her. Destiny was incapable of failure.

Maybe they'd been right to be afraid of what they might

have gotten themselves into over the past days of wonder and surprise, not to mention the galvanizing nights they'd spent together under the same roof. At this very moment his thoughts made him afraid of himself.

More than his fear of himself was the fear that had been placed in her heart by this heavy breathing maniac. When they'd gone to the beach house to retrieve clothing for her, without her knowledge he'd checked the answering machine. The only sound on it was the ragged breath of a deranged stranger. Because there were no messages, he'd erased the calls and withheld the destructive information from her. When she finally got around to checking the machine, the once blinking message indicator had been stilled.

Keeping her safe was first and foremost. All else would have to remain secondary until whoever was responsible for this reign of terror was behind bars.

It was a beautiful day despite the fog that shrouded the coastline. Darting in and out of the pink-tinged clouds, the sun appeared to be playing a game of peekaboo. Large grayish rocks looked as though they grew right out of the sea. The coastal waters were dotted with windsurfers, their neon-colored sails fluttering in the heavy sea breeze as they mastered their windsailing equipment. The colorful scenery was picturesque all along the magnificent Southern California coast.

With one hand resting on Omunique's left knee, Ken revved up the sleek, black sports car, racing it at high speeds. The engine purred as the powerful car raced down the open road. Ken had total control, much like the tight control he normally kept on himself.

The sun caressed Omunique's skin, bathing her in its serenity. Under its warmth, she blossomed like a newly budding spring flower. Her gray eyes sparkled like diamonds, Ken observed with an awestruck smile on his handsome face. He moaned inwardly at her wholesome beauty, stealing minute glances at her whenever he could. He'd never seen anyone as beautiful as the woman who sat next to him. As well as her outer beauty, her inner beauty reached out to him, making him feel blessed to be alive.

Contented at just being with him and feeling at one with the universe, she smiled over at him, completely awed by him and their surroundings as they sailed along the highway in peaceful harmony.

Several miles later Ken pulled the car off the road and into the parking area of a fantastic lookout point, where he parked and exited the car. He then walked around to the passenger side and opened Omunique's door. With his arm slung around her shoulders, they walked to the guardrail where they stood in silence, looking out over the sea. The fog had lifted considerably. They were now able to see for quite a distance. Unlike the city air that was normally lost to the smog, the air here was fresh, crystal clear, and briskly clean.

Ken kissed her left temple. "I love it out here in the open. What about you?"

Adoration shining in her eyes, she smiled up at him. "Oh, Ken, it's perfect. It's seems so natural to spend a day discovering the beauty of nature. I love it when I get a chance to skate at an outdoor ice rink. The ice rink in Central Park is my idea of a skating paradise. When not too severe, the New York winter winds feel so good on my face."

Ken bent his head and nibbled playfully at her ear. Then he kissed her deeply. When the cold wind rustled through his hair, he drew her even closer. Splaying his strong fingers across the muscles in her back, he massaged them gently. His mouth was so tender against hers that she tightened her grip on his slender waist, drowning herself in the sensuality of his passionate kisses—kisses that could make her hair curl.

He loosened his hold on her. "We need to keep going. We have a lot of road to cover before we stop for lunch."

She allowed him to guide her to the car. "I'm not ready to go, but I know that we should. I could stay in a serene place

like this forever.'' Before getting into the passenger seat she
pulled his head down, kissing him with something akin to
desperation, needing to feel the peace that being one with him
brought to her soul.

Bright yellow and blue splashes of paint lent a cheerful
ambience to the small coffee shop where they'd dropped in for
lunch. To Omunique it looked as though the splashes of bright
colors had been carelessly slung against the glossy walls,
reminding her of the fingerpainting she'd once created as a
child. The entire place was lively, much like the waitress who'd
taken their order.

When salads and cold drinks were placed before them, they
relaxed and engaged in amicable conversation between bites.
Ken even found himself comfortable enough with Omunique
to talk about his mother, Julia Maxwell, and how she'd died.
She could see that he was still deeply affected by the loss of
the woman he and his father adored; yet his somber mood
passed rather quickly. Ken had openly revealed another compelling side of himself, a very compassionate side, Omunique
reflected quietly.

It appeared as though nothing could shatter their peace—
that is, until Ken leaped out of his seat and ran across the room
like a charging bull who'd been taunted by the waving red cape
of a matador.

Omunique watched in horror as Ken nearly knocked someone
over in his flight toward a man who held a very expensive
camera. Before the man could snap a picture of Omunique,
Ken covered the lens with his hand. In that instant Omunique's
fears rushed her calm. She was sure the cameraman was from
the press, or worse, from one of those sleazy tabloid papers.
She wondered if he had followed them there.

No one knew who was who these days, she thought, especially in a place where masquerading was the norm rather than
the exception. Everyday living in Southern California was often

like one gigantic masquerade ball, though one could rarely tell the difference between those in costume from those who were au naturel. "Land of fruits and nuts" was a very fair assessment of California and some of its eccentric citizens.

As if there hadn't been enough drama for one day, the waitress suddenly appeared out of the blue and handed Omunique a folded piece of paper. White bond paper. Before Omunique could open the note, Ken was there beside her, removing it from her trembling hand.

"Who gave this to you?" he demanded of the waitress.

The waitress, looking mystified, turned around and pointed at what was now an empty seat. "The person who gave me this note was sitting right there. I don't know where he disappeared. He told me she was an old friend of his, and that he wanted to surprise her."

Omunique's entire body began to shake like a leaf.

With rage burning in his eyes, Ken looked around the restaurant. Then, without warning, he raced out the front door. As he reached the outdoors, a blue van peeled out of the parking lot, churning up dust and gravel in its hasty departure. The black sports car could've easily caught up to the speeding van, but he wasn't about to leave Omunique unprotected. The van could've been just a decoy to draw him away. Had the cameraman been a part of this weird scenario? Had he drawn his attention for the sole purpose of distracting him, for this occurrence to take place?

Before Ken returned to the table where Omunique waited for him, he and the man with the camera seemed to have come to an amicable understanding. When the man opened the camera and took out the film, which he handed to Ken, Omunique sighed with relief. Ken had also apologized to the man, whom he'd nearly flattened. Wearing a concerned look, she watched the men shake hands.

Omunique looked scared to death by the time Ken finally returned to the table, though he'd kept a constant eye on her while he'd been across the room, wanting to murder the person who'd placed the painfully haunted look in her eyes.

He looked at the waitress, who appeared to be frozen in time. "Can you describe the person who gave you this note?"

Unblinking, she looked back at him "No, I'm afraid I can't, but I do remember how strange his eyes looked. They didn't seem real. Perhaps colored contacts." Ken looked puzzled. "Maybe it was the blue eye shadow," the waitress explained. "I thought it was unusual, but a lot of men are wearing makeup these days."

The waitress, now known to them as Sable, looked around the restaurant for a moment. She turned back to face the distraught couple. "That's it," she said, snapping her fingers. "The lips. The lips appeared very feminine."

Her comments made Ken wonder if the culprit had been a woman dressed up like a man. Fear gnawed at his stomach. Anyone could disguise his or her voice.

Ken handed the waitress his business card. "Thank you, Sable. If you see that person in here again would you please call this number, but not before you alert the authorities. Whoever it is, they're responsible for terrorizing my companion."

Sable touched Omunique's shoulder. "I'm sorry for you. I hope they catch the person. I'll do all I can to help. I've been a victim of a stalking, and I know exactly how it feels. I didn't really know the jerk, yet it turned out to be a customer that I served daily. I didn't have a clue that he was dangerous. He's behind bars now. Thank God!"

Omunique shivered. Though Sable had tried to calm her, it had had the opposite effect. "Thank you. I'm glad they apprehended the person who disrupted your life. I feel confident that this person will be caught, too." Confident, she wasn't, but she knew she had to try to be brave.

Omunique's false bravado had not been lost on the man at her side, the man who was rapidly falling in love with her.

Ken got to his feet and held his hand out for Omunique. "Come on, sweetheart, we need to get back. I can see how frightened you are, but I won't let anything happen to you. I swear it on my mother's grave! This son of a b—'' he charged—biting off the expletive to show respect—''has no idea what he's gotten himself into. I'm taking this very personally.''

So I should be, he thought.

Seated inside the car, Omunique felt numb from trying to figure out who was behind the malicious acts. It was no longer just a control or power issue. It was sheer trepidation, shattering her in ways she couldn't begin to explain. Looking over at Ken, she felt protected, felt safe in the knowledge that he was there for her, that he didn't seem to want to be anywhere else. He wasn't put off by the danger that had invaded her life, and she felt guilty for having thought he might run from it.

She didn't know exactly what her true feelings for him were, but she had a serious inkling that she was falling in love with him. She knew she could fall hard, if she wasn't already in love with him. She had to wonder how damaging the fall might be, and if it would leave her broken.

They drove the long miles toward home in complete silence, each lost in his own thoughts. Omunique's head rested on Ken's shoulder, but she couldn't have purchased a nap. Her thoughts were way too tumultuous for her to even consider falling asleep, though sleep was what she needed most.

When she suddenly looked up at him in bewilderment, he misinterpreted the mystifying look in her eyes for fear. He had no idea she might be in love with him, though it was what he would've hoped for, which might have explained why he thought he'd seen fear there. He had also spent time assessing the enormity of his feelings for her, and had come to the conclusion that he had already fallen hard.

He caressed the back of her hand. ''Would you like to go out for dinner this evening, Omunique? Somewhere quiet.''

She considered his offer. No, she wouldn't. She might not ever want to go out in public again. ''I don't think I want to go out, Ken, but I would love to spend another quiet evening with you. I hate to admit it, but I'm starting to get a little gun-shy about going out in public."

"It's nice to know you want to be with me. I hope you realize you're going to be spending every evening with me. I'm not letting you stay alone, not until this nut case is caught. Your place or mine?"

"I'll leave the decision up to you. But at some point I'd like to listen to your extensive collection of oldies, especially those recorded by Gladys Knight and the Pips."

"There's no better time than this evening. We'll stop by your place for a few minutes. You may want to pick up a few more of your things. Don't you think it's time you talked to your father about all this? He needs to hear from you."

She rolled her eyes back. "Not if I have a choice. Dad will go nuts over this. I know it's wishful thinking on my part, but I'm hoping all this bad stuff will simply go away, and that the perpetrator will tire of this cruel game. I'm a public figure, and I can't hide out in fear of my life. I just can't imagine myself doing that."

"This is not a game, Nique. This is for real. We're going to have to take every necessary precaution to help ensure your safety."

"I understand that, but if this person thinks he's been success-ful in his form of intimidation he'll only continue. But if he thinks he's failed, he might just give up. It's all about power and control—though I'm frightened, I won't allow him to have either over me."

Ken didn't agree at all with her assessments. "I don't want to frighten you any further, but this person obviously believes the phone calls have fallen short of his intentions. It's getting much nastier, Omunique. This person is not rowing with both oars in the water. I know you want to be free to come and go about your activities, but Princess, this thing has really gotten dangerous."

She had grown impatient, and it showed in the way that she shifted her body. "I intend to be very cautious, but I don't intend to be intimidated by anyone!'' she shouted with indignation. ''Enough of this, already. Can we just drop the subject?''

Looking defeated, Ken shrugged his shoulders, though he wasn't giving up. Just having her phone lines tapped wasn't enough to give her a sense of security, he decided. The numbers should be changed altogether, before a tracer was put in place. If the lunatic somehow managed to get the new numbers, the tracer would already be in working order. Through modern technology it would be an easy enough task to achieve. His godfather, Ralph Steele, a retired police captain, came to mind. Uncle Ralph would provide him with some good, sound advice.

When Ken spotted the rental car in Omunique's driveway, he suspected that Wyman had come home. Now he'd have to tell her that he'd informed him of the situation. D day had come, much sooner than he'd anticipated. He had to be up front with her, and he had to do it before they entered the house.

He parked the car and turned to face her. ''Sweetheart,'' he began, ''I know you're not going to like what I'm about to say, but I hope you'll try to understand it. I called your father and told him about the horrendous things that have occurred. I'm aware that I've gone against your wishes, but if you were my daughter I'd want someone to tell me about the danger you'd been placed in.''

With an odd expression etched on her face, she stared openly at Ken. ''I'm *not* your daughter, Ken, and I resent the fact that you decided to take matters into your own hands.'' She paused, her anger subsiding. ''I do understand why you did it. I just hope it doesn't make things worse for me. Knowing my father as I do, I'm sure he's had a lot of anxious hours over this.'' Frowning, she looked over at the parked car. ''Did you only tell me this now because you saw the rental car?''

He looked abashed. ''If you recall, I've been trying to get you to call your father from the moment I learned of this unfortunate situation. But, yes, I saw the car, and I wanted you to hear the truth from me before you saw him. He might not give me away, but I think he will give himself away. No loving parent would be able to hide their anxieties from their child, not in a situation like this one. His concern for you will be written all over his face, and you'll know something is up."

Everything he'd said rang with truth. "It's done now, so I'd better go in and face the music. My father is not going to be too happy about my decision to keep this away from him."

"Would you like me to leave so that you can talk with him in private?" Ken asked, stroking her face with the gentleness of a butterfly.

She smirked. "Are you kidding? I'm not letting you off that easy."

Inside, Wyman protectively wrapped Omunique in the safety of his arms, anxiously searching her face for any signs of distress. When he saw that she looked fine despite the emotional trauma she'd gone through, he released her and turned to Ken. Prepared to keep Ken's secret, he greeted him as if hadn't spoken to him recently. He'd met the young man a long time ago, through Max. "It s nice to see you, son. It's been a long time. Do you recall meeting me at your father's office?"

Ken extended your hand. "Yes, sir, I do. It's nice to see you again, as well."

The trio passed through the foyer and entered the living room, where each took a seat. Wyman sat in a chair directly across from Ken and Omunique, who'd seated themselves on the sofa.

Omunique stifled a wry smile. "What brought you down so soon, Dad? I wasn't expecting you to come down until the weekend of the charity skating event."

At a loss for words, Wyman telegraphed Ken a questioning glance, hoping for a sign that said he'd already told Omunique of their conversation. The look in Ken's eyes, along with a slight nod of his head, provided him with that answer. "I think you already know why I'm here, young lady. Don't be coy with me," he scolded.

Moving out of his seat, Wyman lovingly folded his daughter into his arms, kissing her satiny cheek. "You've been a bad girl, Nique, but we'll discuss that later. However, don't you ever attempt to keep something so seriously important from me. You know that I'd give my very life for you. How *are* you feeling, Nique?''

"Much better, Daddy. Ken has taken very good care of me. I know I should've told you about the phone calls, and all. I'm really very sorry that you had to hear it from Ken.''

"I'm glad to hear that, Nique,'' he said, returning to the chair. "Ken's a good man. He only did what he did because he's worried about you, my dear. I'm just sorry I wasn't here when you needed me most.''

Omunique shook her head. "You've always been there for me. Don't go putting yourself on a guilt trip. It appears this would've happened no matter where you were. We can't control the thoughts and actions of others. You taught me that a long time ago.''

"You're right, I did. Though we can't control others, we can do our best to make damn sure they don't get our power. I'm prepared to stay here as long as you need me. That is, if that's the way you want it.''

Omunique shook her head. "No, Dad, you need to take care of your business. It's not that I don't want you here—I always want you around. But I'm going to be okay. Ken has agreed to stay with me until this matter is solved. You just said we have to make sure we don't give others our power. If we rearrange our lives, we've already conceded defeat and they've won. As much as I don't want to have someone watching over me, I know it's necessary right now. Ken has agreed to be my bodyguard, if you will, so you can rest assured that no harm will come to me.''

Ken scooted to the very edge of the sofa. "She's right on target, Mr. Philyaw. I give you my word. Omunique will be protected.''

Wyman looked straight at Omunique. "I'd like to hire an around-the-clock security team, Nique. As much as he'd probably like to be, Ken can't be with you every second of the day, honey.''

"No," she objected loudly. "No security, period. I have enough of that at the arena. I couldn't stand the thought of someone constantly tailing me."

"Okay, Nique. For now, we'll do it your way, but I hope we don't come to regret this decision."

As they got into lighter topics of conversation, Ken brought up the breakfast mishap.

Wyman arched a surprised eyebrow. "Nique fixed you breakfast? And you're alive to tell about it?"

Picking up the daily newspaper from the coffee table, Omunique hurled it at Wyman. "There was an insult in that comment! He's alive because he didn't get to eat it. I burned it beyond recognition. Now go ahead and have a good laugh at my expense. I certainly won't mind," she remarked with sarcasm. "I'm going to pack a few things." She strolled off in a feigned huff. No sooner had she left the room than Wyman and Ken practically laughed their heads off.

Chapter Nine

It didn't take long before they'd gotten themselves settled in at the Venice Beach condo. Omunique had changed clothing, and Ken had told her she looked gorgeous in forest green slacks and a soft, wool sweater of the same color. Her skin glowed with a healthy freshness. Spilling out over her shoulders like a glossy curtain, her long hair bounced with luscious body.

Ken had already taken a shower and was now in the kitchen preparing a stir-fry combination of fresh shrimp and vegetables. Omunique sat on the living room floor playing her favorite oldie tunes.

When Ken called her into dinner, she was ravenous. Over a quiet dinner, they once again laughed about the earlier breakfast mishap, but there wasn't a trace of the offensive smoke that had smothered the condo rooms.

Once the kitchen was restored to its normal condition, they retired to the living room. Omunique looked on as Ken built a cozy fire. He then poured two glasses of chardonnay and handed one to her, hoping to further relax her. It had been a harrowing day for her, he knew.

She smiled at him. 'I'd love to accept that, but I can't. I rarely touch alcohol. The brandy I drank the first night was under rare circumstances. I really don't like the taste of alcohol.''

Ken stroked her hair with a gentle hand. "I fully understand. As a minority athlete in a sport dominated by whites, how are you received?'' he asked, curious.

She picked up one of the burgundy-and-green-striped sofa pillows and placed it in her lap. "I've had my share of scoffers, and those who have done their best to discourage me. There's been plenty of racist propaganda left on my assigned gym lockers, and some of my peers keep me locked out of their close-knit circles. But I've always been determined to overcome racial slurs and the devious pranks. While ignoring the ignorance and narrow minds of those involved in such pettiness, I keep my mind on the sport.

"I've never even considered giving up figure skating, and I won't allow others to decide my destiny. I'm the master of my destiny. I relentlessly pursue my goal of becoming one of the best figure skaters to hail from my native America.''

Ken was impressed by her determination. "I'm glad that you don't allow others to control you. Your strength is one of your greatest assets.''

"Over the course of the years I've surrounded myself with the best coaches, trainers, choreographers, and others important to my success. I'm confident of my abilities, and I believe I can achieve the ultimate—a spot on the United States Olympic Team.''

He looked at her with admiration. "You are indeed unique, Princess. I wish you all success, and I hope the rest of your career will be rewarding.''

She kissed his chin. "Thank you. Although it seems that some unknown assailant has put the *ice under fire,* I'm determined to stay clearly focused on my mission. It seems there's a hidden agenda, for someone other than a possible obsessed fan. My competing in Denver, to make the team, may be threatening to someone. It's a very big competition. I've been known to be wrong, so I won't omit any possible reason that someone might have for doing this."

She's being very brave, he thought, *maybe too brave for her own good.* It worried him that her will and determination could put her directly in the path of danger.

Thoughts of the 1994 Winter Olympic Games held in Lillehammer, Norway, came to Ken's mind. A media circus, just one of many that the media had created with sensationalized journalism. The crimes of the media seemed almost as bad as the ones committed against a single figure skater by a group of brain-dead perpetrators.

Steering his mind clear of all negative thoughts, Ken lifted Omunique's head and guided it higher onto his chest. He then cradled her in his arms. Closing his eyes, he took possession of her inviting mouth, making fiery love to her lips with his own.

She gasped as his tongue hungrily sought out hers. Throwing her arms around his neck, she moaned, pressing her lips urgently against his fire-breathing mouth.

Sliding his hand under her sweater, he touched all the nakedness that wasn't caressed by her wispy, intimate apparel. A shudder of ecstasy passed through her as his fingers ignited a fire beneath her rose petal-soft flesh. Slightly bold in their explorations of each other, they cautiously tugged at one another's clothing. After loosening a couple of buttons on Ken's shirt, Omunique poked her delicate hand in the small gap, teasing his thick mass of curly chest hair, which caused his kiss to grow intense.

When panic flared inside her, she pushed her fears away. Reaching an impassioned point, at which neither knew how much further the other wanted to go, they stopped and stared questioningly into one another's eyes. Her body was in no mood to be denied, yet her eyes gleamed with fearful uncertainty. No longer the self-assured, confident young woman he'd first met, she was now rendered vulnerable by lust, fiery passion, and the man she most assuredly desired.

Ken smothered the inside of her palm with sensuous kisses. "Are you afraid of what's happening between us?" he asked, his tone husky.

Briefly, she looked away from him. "Only afraid that . . . it may be happening too soon," came her shy response. *Afraid that you'll go away. Thus, a broken heart,* she added silently.

He whispered kisses onto her lips. "We'll wait, then. I don't want you to be afraid of anything. The only thing I know is that I'm falling in love with you." *And that you may not be able to return those feelings,* he continued in his thoughts.

He's falling, and I've fallen, she thought in wondrous astonishment.

"Perhaps, for the rest of the evening we should just share our hopes, our dreams, maybe dance to some soft music, and laugh at each other's jokes. How does that sound to you, Miss Philyaw?"

"Like a brilliant idea," she said, capturing his face between her hands.

The hours rushed by, yet the time between them stood still as they lost themselves to the things each of them wanted to share about themselves.

Though Ken had admitted that he might be falling in love with Omunique, he hadn't admitted to himself or to her that he feared what was happening to him. Fear wasn't something he normally allowed himself to feel. For the most part, he'd been able to keep his emotions out of personal relationships. In the past there'd been only a couple of times when he'd come close to letting his defenses down, but when he was with Omunique he couldn't even rouse his defense mechanisms. In fact, there wasn't any defense strong enough to ward off the powerful effect she had on him.

While Omunique talked about the death of her mother, and the guilt that sometimes plagued her—especially those times when she blamed her birth on her mother's death—Ken grew very quiet. By listening to the things Omunique had felt over the years he was able to sort out some of his own feelings, feelings he'd suppressed.

It was only now that he understood why he hadn't let anyone get inside his soul. It all had to do with the loss of his mother. Unlike Omunique, he'd had his mother for the first fifteen years of his life. He had very vivid memories of their time together. His mother had been the apple of his eye. For sure, he'd been the apple of hers. Julia Maxwell had doted on her husband and their only child. When Julia died, a part of Ken Sr. had died with her.

"During the first few months after her death, all my father could do was sit and cry," he told Omunique. "There was a time when he spent more time at the cemetery than he did at home. He was only able to pull himself together after I dared tell him how neglected I felt. Not only had I lost my mother, it seemed as though I'd lost my father, too."

It was during that awful time that Ken had vowed to never love someone so deeply, so completely, lest they should go away, in the same way his mother had.

Feeling his pain, Omunique rested her head on his shoulder. "I can imagine how you must have felt. My father still mourns my mother. To my knowledge he's never gotten involved in any type of relationship with another woman. I can't ever remember him bringing another woman home, other than my godmother, Mamie Gordon. She was my mother's best friend. I'd really like to see my father and Aunt Mamie get together, but I'm afraid the love they have for me is their only common bond."

He looked at her as though he'd just stepped into the Garden of Eden. The discovery of something that held such magnificent beauty nearly leveled him. Omunique could give him what he now knew he'd been afraid of. She could give him what Max had told him to hold out for when looking for his soulmate— someone he could love unconditionally, someone who would only want the same unconditional love in return. The same kind of love his parents had had.

It was that kind of love he hoped to find with Omunique, that same kind of love he was more than willing to share with his fascinating Ice Princess. Although the thought of her going away forever shook him right down to the core of his heart and soul, the thought of not having her in his life at all was even more frightening. . . .

"I think it's time for us to retire for the night," Ken suggested. "We both have busy schedules for tomorrow."

Omunique cast him a thoughtful glance. "I'm extremely tired, but I'm going to call Dad before I go to bed. He's leaving first thing in the morning, and I want to have a last minute chat with him. He's been such a good sport about my staying here tonight instead of being there at the house with him. I feel guilty for leaving him all alone."

"You have a very understanding father. He told me he thought it best that you come back here with me. He trusts me to take good care of you. He said he'd return for the charity benefit. It'll all work out just fine. I'm going to leave you alone so that you can have a private conversation with your Dad. I'll be in the bedroom until you finish talking on the phone."

Brent Masters and Omunique sat on a metal bench discussing his concerns over the numerous mistakes she'd made during the grueling training techniques he'd just put her through.

"I know I've been hard on you today, Nique, but it was necessary. You seemed lackadaisical and unfocused while executing your routine," he said, worried about what was interfering with her ability to skate well.

"It's okay, Brent. I have some things going on that I haven't yet come to terms with," she explained.

"Is it the guy you're seeing? How deep have you gotten yourself involved in this new relationship?"

She looked him square in the eye. "I have something to tell you that you might not like, Brent. I seem to be falling in love with the person I've been seeing, but I don't think I'm distracted because of him. He understands what I have to do as an athlete. I don't know why I didn't tell you this long before now. I guess I didn't know how to."

Fury glared in Brent's hazel eyes. "You know exactly why you didn't tell me, Nique. You knew I would disapprove of you becoming romantically involved with someone at this critical point in your career. It's not a smart move on your part—or his, for that matter."

Trying to decide if she should tell him the real problem, she lowered her lashes to half-mast. Her real problems were so far removed from any romantic involvement.

"You're dead wrong, Brent. My romantic involvement has nothing to do with my distractions. Brent, someone has been threatening me with nasty phone calls, and a few other distasteful forms of intimidation."

Brent looked up, startled. So, he thought, her home phone number had somehow fallen into the hands of the maniac who'd been calling his office. He wrestled with the idea of telling her he'd been receiving the same sort of calls. Seeing how fragile she looked, he decided not to mention the calls he'd received. It would only cause her to become more distracted. Her plate was full enough for the moment.

He draped his arm around her shoulder, fearing she'd lose herself to her newly acquired phobias. "I'm sorry about this, honey. I know you're suffering. It shows in your performance. But I can't allow you to lose sight of your goals. We've worked too hard, too long, and we've come too far as a team to give it all up now."

After taking a few minutes to think about the danger that faced his star athlete, he knew that something had to be done, but he just couldn't bring himself to discuss it with her. It was something he just wasn't prepared to deal with at the moment. Instead, he decided that he wasn't going to stand by and watch his champion skater go up in flames . . . and he had to find a way to distance her from the man she'd fallen victim to. Getting her out of this destructive relationship was going to be his top priority.

"Brent, the things you've mentioned are not going to happen. Winning a spot on the Olympic team is the most important thing in my life. Trust me on that account."

With her legs so weak that she could hardly stand, Omunique sat on the floor in the locker room, pulling on her jeans. Every muscle ached as she lifted her buttocks to pull the jeans over her slightly curvaceous hips. She was too tired to shower, but a long, hot soak in the tub was imminent.

Minutes later, as though in a trance, she climbed into the Jeep. Ken had wanted her to leave her vehicle at home, but she had effectively stated her case about wanting her car at the arena should something unexpectedly come up. He had followed her there in his car, and she had promised to wait until he came back to escort her home, but now she had the desire to get home as quickly as possible. He wasn't expected at the arena for another couple of hours, which would give her time to call him and inform him of the change in plans.

Tightly gripping the steering wheel with both hands, exhausted, she lowered her head onto the steering mechanism. Hearing a light tapping on the window, she looked up, gasping when she saw a face meshed against the window. It felt as though she'd stopped breathing. She then blew out a ragged breath of relief as she recognized the face of her longtime friend, Sara Davies. Breathless, she rolled down the window. When she'd first seen the face she was sure she'd smiled her last smile.

"Sara, you scared me to death! What are you doing out here all alone?"

Sara Davies was a twenty-one-year-old woman who was always watching and waiting for a chance to talk with the other skaters. Severely torn ligaments had sabotaged her dreams of becoming a champion skater. The accident had occurred over a year ago, but she still showed up at the arena every single day.

Of all the many skaters who frequented the arena Omunique and Ian Swanson were Sara's idols.

Sara blinked her cornflower-blue eyes. "Lately, I haven't been able to talk to you, Nique. You always leave before I can catch up to you. You don't seem to be smiling very much these days, and I miss talking with you," Sara said, running her hand through her heavy, spun-gold hair.

Her comments seemed to smack Omunique right in the face, causing her skin to pale. "What did you say about my not smiling anymore?" Omunique asked, hating herself for what she was thinking. Sara was harmless, wasn't she?

"It's just that you seem so intense nowadays. Have I done something to offend you?"

Omunique felt terrible. She'd always made it a point to interact with Sara, but with so much turmoil going on in her life she'd simply forgotten how important she'd become to her. "I'm so sorry, Sara. I've just been so preoccupied with other things. It was never my intention to ignore you." Sara looked so dejected Omunique felt a sharp pain strike a soft spot in her heart. "Want to get together after my next training session?"

Sara's blue eyes brightened, and her milky white skin took on a hint of color. "Oh, yes, Omunique. I'll wait for you by the refreshment stand. I have to go now. My parents are waiting supper for me." Sara waved as she limped toward her parked car.

"Be careful, Sara," Omunique yelled from the Jeep's open window. "I'll be looking forward to us getting together tomorrow."

Omunique watched as the crippled woman reached the safety of her late model sedan. Though Sara was an adult by age, she was still very much a childlike innocent. Her emotional maturity was that of a teenager. Even though she no longer suspected Sara of being behind the malicious phone calls, something about Sara still bothered her. Sara had a strange way about her, and this wasn't the first time she'd thought about it.

Sara had a strong crush on Ian, but he didn't seem to be

aware of it. Could Sara be jealous over the fact that she practiced with Ian? Omunique wondered. Realizing she was probably overanalyzing Sara, and that she hadn't completely exonerated her as a suspect, Omunique attempted to put the young woman from her mind.

Traffic was horrendous, as it was most of the time in Southern California, but at least she didn't have to crawl through traffic to get home, which she considered a miracle. It normally took her a lot longer to reach the beach house. Too afraid to walk alone on the beach, she hurried into the house she'd come to miss like crazy. Staying at Ken's had been nice, but this was what she knew as home. First she'd call Ken. Then she'd take that long, hot bath she'd dreamed about.

Ken sat at his desk, his head lowered over a legal document Max had given him to look over. Unable to fully concentrate on his reading, he set the document aside, reflecting on the conversation he'd had with his godfather, Ralph Steele.

The retired police captain had told him there really wasn't anything that could be done about the malicious acts against Omunique at this point, which had stunned and outraged him. Until the person responsible attempted to harm Omunique, he couldn't be arrested. Ridiculous, Ken thought, yet he knew before they could arrest anyone that they did first have to learn the identity of the perpetrator.

However, Ralph advised him that he would see to it that a tracer was placed on the two lines in the Philyaw home. Although he was retired, he had many connections as an active-duty reserve officer. Even with all his contacts, he told Ken that an official police report needed to be filed by Omunique. Until that was done, his hands were tied.

Still, Ken was dissatisfied. Was Omunique going to have to be attacked, or worse, before anyone did anything about it? He just didn't understand the laws. They seemed to be designed to protect the criminal and not the victim. How could the laws in this country have gotten so out of control? These were downright malicious acts against an innocent person. *Inexcusable acts,* Ken thought with disgust.

Picking up the phone, Ken used the intercom line to summon Thomasina. Before he could hang up the phone, she appeared in the doorway, her yellow blouse revealing more of her than he cared to see of his newly acquired, permanent secretary. When Sandy had resigned her position to stay home and take care of her new baby, he'd offered the job to Thomasina.

"Have you been able to reach anyone at the ice arena?" he asked, scowling. He had tried calling several times, but the phone had gone unanswered.

Thomasina nodded her head. "Her coach told me that she'd already left. He said she should be at home by now."

Ken caught his lower lip between his teeth, wincing when he bit down too hard. "That can't be. She was supposed to wait until I got there."

"I've tried both of the numbers you gave me for her home, but no one answered. The recorder didn't even come on."

Ken was so upset that he threw a rather large dictionary across the room, just missing an antique vase that had once belonged to his maternal grandmother. When he cursed and stomped his feet on the plastic runner under his desk, Thomasina backed out of the office.

Squinting his eyes, he put a finger to his lip, wondering how Thomasina knew the Philyaws had more than one line in their home. He could only remember giving her Omunique's personal line, regardless of what she'd just said. Thomasina had shown a definite interest in him, but thus far he'd refused to address it.

He gathered that her short, sexy clothes were worn for his benefit, but he detested some of the things she wore in the office. How to tell her without hurting her feelings was a major concern for him, yet he knew he'd have to discuss it with her. He hoped his father would get around to it first, since Max had also expressed his concern about her wearing apparel. The type of clothes she wore had no place in the offices of Maxwell Athletic Corporation. Just as his thoughts turned back to Omunique, the intercom line buzzed.

"It's Miss Philyaw," Thomasina informed him.

"I miss you," she stated simply.

Though thoroughly irritated with her, he couldn't keep a smile from lighting up his face. He'd been standing, but when he'd heard her voice he dropped down into the chair behind his desk. "I miss you, too, but where the hell are you? I've been trying to reach you for the past couple of hours. Why haven't you called?"

"I'm calling you now," she countered. "I'm at home, but I can better explain myself in person."

"I'll be right there, but you'll have to count to a thousand this time." He wanted to tell her to make sure all the doors and windows were locked, but he didn't want to put any more fear in her heart. Since she'd been foolish enough to go to the beach house alone, perhaps she wasn't as afraid for her safety as he was, which brought him no comfort whatsoever.

"I'm counting," she whispered.

Feeling as though she could fall asleep standing up, Omunique slipped into a pair of loose, comfortable lounging pajamas. The plump bed pillows looked fluffy. Extending their inviting warmth and pleasantly summoning her was the clean smell of the fresh bed linens. The thought of a cup of hot chocolate roused her palate but she was too tired to take another step. Falling across the bed, she loosened her hair and laid her head on the floral scented pillow slip.

Sara had been right about her being intense lately, she thought. An unexplainable sadness and explainable fear had ruled her entire day. Being home alone wasn't helping matters. She should've waited for Ken. Leaving the arena without an escort hadn't been a very smart thing to do, she now realized. She didn't know that Wyman had ordered a twenty-four hour surveillance team to patrol the beach house and discreetly watch over her despite her objections. He knew his daughter better than anyone, and he knew she'd quickly tire of having someone underfoot at every turn—even the man she seemed to be falling in love with.

Her arms ached to be filled with the man who ruled her heart. She felt as if she were on a fluffy cloud, and she gave herself up to the downy softness. Her arms felt numb and the rest of her body felt weightless. Ken's calming eyes caressed her face as she got caught up in a delicious fantasy.

Ken had a way of making her come alive. She ached to be in his arms, craved the sultry voice that made her shiver with delight, yearned for the touch that set her soul on fire. The night would go on forever if she couldn't feel him next to her.

The ringing doorbell created a tingling sensation in her dulled senses. Half asleep, she turned the bedside lamp on. *He's here,* she thought, arriving in the place she'd longed to be, in his world, a world that was a masterpiece of his own creation.

Just about the time his anxiety had begun to take him for a serious ride, she opened the door. Moving with the swiftness of a thoroughbred, his heart pounding heavily in his chest, he moved inside the house. The essence of innocence stood before him, looking beautiful as ever. His thundering heart did a swan dive into the swirling, liquid smoke of her gray eyes. Everything about her looked soft and warm, and he ached to hold her. The sky-blue lounging pajamas caressed her softness, and the moonlight coming in from the skylight appeared to dance a waltz in her almond-brown hair.

Kicking the door shut, Ken reached out and pulled her into his arms. The sweetness of his breath engulfed her, submerging her in a wave of ecstasy. In a fiery burst of passion, his lips slowly undulated over hers, bringing her into the reality of his world. Though she could barely breathe, she didn't care. Knowing she could draw her next breath from his own, she allowed the sweet massacre of her lips to continue on and on, on into oblivion.

Holding her away from him, he looked deeply into her wondrous eyes. "I reached a thousand ages ago, but I kept on counting. I would've gone crazy had I stopped. I've been so worried about you, Om.''

Although she detested it when Lamar chopped up her name, coming from Ken it sounded heavenly, but she wasn't going to let him get away with it, either. "Omunique or Nique, but never Om," she scolded gently. "Om sounds like part of a chant. Listen. Om, Om, Om," she chanted, pressing her lips together in rapid succession.

His laughter rang out. "I see what you mean, Princess. I'll try to remember that.'' From the dark, curling smoke in her eyes, he knew he'd better not forget it.

Omunique curled up beside him on the sofa. "I'm really sorry I didn't wait for you to come to the arena. I'm so used to being independent, it's hard for me to act otherwise.''

"Independence is one thing, safety is another matter altogether. I hate to ask this, but are you taking these threats seriously? If not, you should be.''

She looked injured. "Of course I do. But what am I supposed to do about it?''

He smoothed her hair back from her face. "File a police report. I talked with my godfather, a retired police officer. He told me that a police report had to be filed before any kind of investigation could begin. He's looking into tapping your phone lines, but the police report has to be filed first. Only you can do that.'' He saw the hackles of her indignation give rise right before his eyes.

"Did you know there's really nothing they can do in cases like this, at least not until an attack on your person has been committed? It's ludicrous,'' he practically spat out, sighing heavily. "When you're not in the security patrolled confines of the arena someone should be with you at all times,'' he said, unaware that Wyman had already hired around-the-clock security.

"So I'm to become a prisoner, even though I haven't done one thing to deserve such a punishment?'' The thought of someone being with her all the time made her realize how much she'd taken freedom for granted. Freedom was important to her. "No such thing is going to happen. I don't want someone underfoot at my every turn. If this looney tunes character has any intention of harming me physically, he's had plenty of opportunity. As I said before, this is about intimidation, power, and control. These are the acts of a coward!"

Dropping the subject was starting to become all too familiar for him, but that's what needed to be done at the moment. All this talk about security had practically made her hostile toward him. He might drop the subject, but his plans to see that she was fully protected wouldn't be dropped until this nightmare was over, he vowed.

He threw up his hands. "Let's talk about something else, Nique. You and I are never going to see eye to eye on this issue. We can agree to disagree. I remember reading in your bio something about a community service you're involved in. Why don't you tell me about it?" he coerced patiently, hoping to calm her down.

Being in a stubborn mood, she wanted to continue with the subject they'd gotten into, but she also saw the necessity to move on to lighter topics. Bickering over this matter wasn't going to solve anything. Amicably, she agreed.

"Several of us skaters work with physically and mentally challenged youth. We donate several hours each month to the center that sponsors them. Our group goes to a special ice arena where we teach simple skating techniques to those interested in figure skating. We hope that one day they can compete in the Special Olympics program. On the days we offer the training I get home very late. I try hard not to neglect this special group of kids. Can you forgive me for being negligent today?"

He propped a pillow behind her back. "Forgiven, Nique. It seems that you're involved in a wonderful community service. You should be proud of yourself. How long have you been involved with this particular group of kids?"

"For about nine months. The center is called Magnolia

House. A group called M.A.D., which stands for making a difference, heavily backs the center. It's very worthwhile.''

"Sounds like it. Perhaps Max and I can donate some equipment . . . or money—whatever you feel is needed the most.''

"That would be terrific, Ken. We can discuss what's needed later. I just want to be in your arms right now. Will you hold me?'' she practically pleaded, rubbing her palms up and down the length of his arm. "I need to feel the comfort your arms bring to my soul.''

Vulnerability shone in her eyes, and there was no way he could've denied her request. At the moment he knew she could get him to agree to almost anything. Ken kissed her lightly on the mouth, but she wanted more of his commanding power. Overcoming her shyness, Omunique showed him exactly the type of kisses she needed from him. Passion was ignited within seconds of her falling into his arms. Their loudly beating hearts mingled together created a thunderous melody that sounded like the hoofbeats of steeds racing across the desert plains.

He stretched himself out on the sofa and pulled her on top of him. As his hands stoked the fires of her desire, his need for her became greater than his need for air. Their desire blocked out all reason, casting them into an unconscious state of mind that wouldn't allow for any boundaries.

Kissing her throat, he unbuttoned her pajama top, lowering it onto her shoulders. As he sprinkled her bare shoulders with weightless kisses, her body involuntarily gyrated across the lower half of his. The feel of his maleness against her thigh made her feel as though her blood had exploded into millions of tiny bubbles. When he reached down to remove her slippers, she instantly recoiled.

"No, leave them on,'' she said anxiously, sounding panic-stricken.

He looked at her incredulously. "Whatever for, Nique?''

She turned away just before tears fell from her eyes. Composing herself, she willed herself to look down at him. "I'm ashamed of my feet, Ken. They're not a pretty sight, in fact, they're ugly.''

"So what if they are? Mine aren't anything to crow about. I want to make love to every part of you, Nique," he assured her with calm.

Keeping his eyes focused on her face, he gently drew one of her feet into his hands and removed the slipper from her right foot. Though he didn't look down at her feet, he could feel the thin, hardened ridges of scar tissue. Lowering his head level with her foot, he tenderly outlined the thin scars with his lips. "Do you want to talk about it, Nique?"

She heaved a deep sigh. "Those are surgical scars, Ken. I've had several operations on my feet, due to birth defects in the bone structure. I've already told you about that. When I was a child my father and I were told I'd never be able to participate in any strenuous activities, especially athletics, at least none that would put stress on my already fragile bone structure. Running and jumping could be done only in light moderation. I guess I've proved them wrong on all accounts. However, I do suffer with serious bouts of arthritis from time to time. The condition causes severe swelling, and has wreaked havoc on my training schedule more than a few times. So far it hasn't kept me out of an important event."

His eyes glistened with moisture. "You're one incredible human being, Princess. I remember some of the things you said you'd gone through, but I had no idea it was so much. I kind of thought you'd been pampered and spoiled rotten—that is, when we first met. Getting to know you has been one marvelous revelation after another. I have a much better understanding of why you're so intensely driven. And, Princess, your feet are not ugly. There's nothing ugly about you, period.''

She rested her cheek against his. "That's kind of you to say. But for me, those scars represent years of pain and suffering. The scars may appear thin, but I see them in an entirely different light. But in a way, I'm glad they're there, as a constant reminder of the things I should never forget. When you're forced to wear corrective shoes to elementary school, you don't exactly get votes of confidence." When she lifted her head, her smoky-gray eyes merged with his autumn-gold ones. "Kids can be cruel. I was the butt of every kind of joke you can imagine. The jokes and the name-calling seemed endless. Now, some of those same people claim to have been best friends with me back then. I wonder why?"

"I think we both know the answer to that one." He kissed the bottoms of her feet. "I want us to get back to where we were, back to the passion we had ignited between us."

Pushing aside the emotional scars and no longer feeling awkward about the physical ones, she relaxed and allowed Ken to satisfy her deepest emotional needs. Ken made her feel beautiful all over. The depth of his compassion simply blew her mind. Wanting desperately to return them to the idyllic place they'd been, his lips branded her skin with an intense heat that crept into her very soul. Once the fire had been rekindled, she saw no way of escaping the burning flames of passion, nor did she desire escape. She was right where she longed to be.

Reaching the point of no return, they recklessly tore each other out of the restraints of their clothing. Twenty nervous fingers traveled over the white-hot flesh of their intimate zones. No longer of this world, they floated into a seemingly unrealistic one, yet the avid responses of their steamy bodies felt realistic, indeed. While his breathing quickened at her ardent responses to his heated touch, Ken lifted her from the sofa and carried her into her bedroom. She felt still as death, yet so positively alive.

With no distance between them, they landed atop the firm mattress. The final hurdle was yet to come, the hurdle that would bridge any minute gap that may have been left unclosed. Once the gap was bridged, they both knew they could never turn back.

Dizzying questions regarding her innocence suddenly swirled in his mind. Though he desired her like crazy, he knew he had to regain his control. Looking for the answers in her bewitching gray eyes, he traced her hairline with his index finger.

"It's okay if we don't go through with this, Nique. You already make me feel complete. I want you more than I can adequately express, but I don't want to risk losing you in the process, nor do I want to lose you to a delayed bout of regretful hysteria. You mean far too much to me for that. You are afraid of this, aren't you, Nique?"

Omunique momentarily buried her face in his neck before looking up into his eyes. "Yes, I am afraid, but I'm more afraid of the way you make me feel." *More afraid that I might not be able to satisfy you.*

He frowned. "What do you mean by that?"

"Don't get me wrong. You make me feel wonderful despite the fact I get nervous and confused when I'm near you like this. I'm inexperienced in this area. I fear that I may not be able to satisfy you," she confessed from the heart.

He was deeply touched by her heartfelt confession. "Oh, sweetheart, you have no clue. I don't need to make love to you in order to be satisfied with you. You satisfy so much more inside of me than any physical contact could ever come close to. You satisfy my very soul, Omunique Philyaw."

Several minutes of roaring silence passed between them before she slowly threaded her trembling fingers through his hair. "I want you every bit as much as you want me, Kenneth Maxwell Jr." An erotic moan trilled from her throat. "In the midst of finding one another, let's not talk about losing. I, for one, don't want to lose the magic of this moment. I want to know what a woman feels like on the morning after. Make love to me, Ken," she whispered breathlessly, drawing his lower lip between her teeth. This was just another request from her that he couldn't possibly refuse.

A wide-eyed Omunique watched as he sheathed himself, his golden eyes engulfing her in the undeniable power they held over her. As he began the journey that would fulfill her whispered request, his fingers tenderly glided into her moistness.

Aching painfully for all that she imagined he was capable of giving her, she slowly closed her eyes, savoring the touch that brought the sort of peace she'd never known before.

Fine tuning the keys of her erotica, Ken strummed the taut strings of her sweet femininity with a tantalizing gentleness. Sensations, alien in nature, coursed through her trembling body as he deflowered the firstborn blossom of spring. The sudden piercing pain caused her to muffle a gasp, then it was gone as quickly as it had come.

The music of his tender thrusts created a harmony so powerful that she melodiously screamed out his name to the tune which his rapturous body expertly scored. Rising up to meet each mind-blowing thrust, she wrapped herself around his manhood like ribbons of steel. Gripping him tightly as his fullness swept through her, she joined in the timed rhythms flowing majestically from him. When she screamed out his name again, he slowed the rhythms until she began to score her own sweet, shy rhythms, which soon became wild and daring. Schooled only by the natural responses of her body and the gentle teachings of his, she freed her mind and soul to receive and give untold pleasures.

Engulfing her in exquisite tenderness, Ken tenderly drove in the final strokes that bounded homeward. There, inside her pool of sweltering heat, he found unadulterated ecstasy. Manipulating her inner sanctum with long, slow, frenzied strokes, he exacted his own pleasures from the depths of her moisture filled canal.

At the same time that her explosion spread through him, he released a long, intense shudder. With breathtaking explosions careening recklessly through her body, she trembled all over. She was now a woman, his woman, a woman satiated, satiated by the only man she'd ever loved.

Chapter Ten

They lay quietly, yet their burning emotions loudly communicated their euphoria. With her head tucked into the well of his arm, his hands tenderly stroked her back.

Turning onto his side, he gazed into her silver, moonstruck eyes. "You felt so good ... Hell, what am I talking about? You *feel* good! Remember when I said I thought I was falling in love with you?" Blinking, she nodded. "I'm *in* love with you, Omunique Philyaw. I've known it long before tonight. In fact, I've known it almost from the start of our relationship. I do love you," he confessed, tears brimming in his eyes.

She loved him, too, yet she was afraid to tell him—afraid that he might disappear, like in some of the stories she'd heard from other young women. "Once they know you love them and know that they got your heart, they leave you," she'd heard one skater say. Lifting her head from the well of his arm, she kissed his mouth deeply. Though he would've preferred to hear her say that she loved him, too, he kissed her back with the same intensity.

Omunique had never felt this good, this alive, in her entire

life. She didn't have to wait until the morning after to know
what it felt like to become a real woman. Tears born of mixed
emotions ebbed in her eyes. Releasing them felt good, but not
nearly as good as the riotous release Ken had effected from deep
down inside of her, a release that made her body exclusively his.

Ken brushed her tears away. "Regrets already?"

Blushing like a schoolgirl, she felt a silly smile caress her
lips. "If this is regret I feel, then I'm in big trouble. Whatever
you've drugged me with is highly addictive, and I can't wait
to get my next fix." Omunique didn't doubt there might be
later regrets, but now was not the time to allow them in. She
felt way too good.

Relieved to know she had no regrets, Ken tenderly worried
her bottom lip with his thumb. The passion burning in her eyes
stroked his ego. "Junkie, huh? I've never thought of myself
as a drug dealer, but as your exclusive supplier I promise
to keep you from ever going through the wicked pains of
withdrawal."

Omunique shaped her lips into an oval. "Ooh, I like the way
you negotiate a deal, Mr. Maxwell. I can see why your father
has such confidence in your negotiating abilities, even though
you were no match for me at our first meeting." Noticing the
time on the Sony clock radio, she gasped. "Oh God, Ken, I
have to get some sleep. I had no idea it was this late."

"Calm down," he chided. "Would I be pushing the envelope
if I asked to sleep here in the bed with you for the remainder
of the night?"

The thought of sleeping next to her all night titillated him.
Now there wasn't a reason for him to sleep on the floor in his
bedroom or in one of her guest rooms. All night in the same bed
with Omunique would be like a night in heaven, he pondered
excitedly.

Omunique smiled up at him, but her face was a mask of
perplexity. "Do . . . you think . . . that's such a good idea?
Neither of us will get any sleep, and I have to be up super
early."

Ken trailed kisses up and down her spine, causing her to shiver with longing. "I promise to let you get plenty of sleep, but right now I just want to be inside of you."

Rolling on top of her, he smothered her body with luscious warmth. Omunique moaned and cooed her answer as he claimed her once again, wanting her to feel how much love he was capable of giving her, assiduously, consummately.

As the breaking of dawn peeked through the windows, Ken propped himself up on one elbow, marveling at the sleeping portrait of beauty beside him. Neatly curled up in a ball, she had her delicate hands folded between her knees, which were drawn up to her chest.

She's so beautiful, he thought, *so very beautiful.* He couldn't stand the thought of someone hurting her, and he was grateful she'd agreed to file the police report before they'd fallen off to sleep. It had lifted a heavy weight off his shoulders.

"I know an angel resides inside her soul," he whispered into the silence.

Moisture suddenly gathered in his eyes. Women like Omunique were the kind men married, not the type to just have a frivolous affair with. There was nothing frivolous about the love he felt for her. It was as pure as the innocence she'd so lovingly bestowed upon him. His love for her was like the rainbow that sometimes appeared after the rains, so alive and colorful. Unlike the rainbow, it would never disappear even if dark skies returned to the heavens above.

Knowing he didn't want to go on without her, couldn't go on without her, he pushed his sobering thoughts aside. Promising himself to always be there for her, no matter what the circumstances, he snuggled up close to her. Laying his head next to hers, he shared her pillow.

Awakening moments later, Omunique didn't appear to have any visible signs of regret about the previous evening of exquisite lovemaking. Her skin glowed with a blush of passion as the tip of her nose touched the nose of the man she'd dreamed of. Parting her mouth, she brushed his full lips with a moist, feathery kiss. Inflamed by her gentleness, he nestled her into his arms, ready to arouse a passion to greet the dawn of a new day, a new era, a new life.

Feeling more exhilarated than ever before, Omunique spun around on the ice, skating to "Hero" as it drifted softly from the overhead speakers. Before losing herself in the touching music, she bowed gracefully.

She first went through an array of technical moves. Then she put the *ice under fire,* whirling and spinning as she skated a fantastic artistic program. If her performance were being judged, she would've received extremely high marks, she knew, hoping she would skate as well in the exhibition.

In the middle of the song, Ian skated onto the ice. Catching up to Omunique, he slid his arm around her waist and fell into perfect rhythm with her movements. Expressionless, she tilted her head against his broad chest and immediately felt the steady thumping of his heart. As though no one else existed, they glided across the ice, allowing the music and the rhythms of their bodies to take them to heights unknown. Hypnotized by their own gracefully seductive movements, the Ice Princess and her charming Prince created a fairy tale of mystery and magic atop the ice. The arena was their castle, the ice castle of their childhood dreams.

In the grand finale, Ian lifted her effortlessly and held her slightly above his head as he spun around. Her delicate hands swayed with beautiful, ballerina-like gestures. When he brought her down slowly, they huddled closely together and ended the program with a breathtaking pirouette. Ian was so mesmerized by their superb performance that he raised her head and planted a sweet, lingering kiss on her lips.

Nearly out of breath, Omunique gulped in some air and blew it out in a gush that swept across his parted mouth. Stunned and embarrassed, she looked at Ian through startled eyes. "Where did that . . . come . . . from, Ian?"

Ian's cheeks flushed a deep rose as he tried to hide his own embarrassment. "My lips, Nique. Where else?" He gently touched her cheek. "Just a friendly kiss," he assured her. "I guess I can blame it on the music and the moment."

Feeling a little more composed, she laughed. "Do you kiss all your friends that way, Ian?"

"Only special friends, Nique. You're a very special friend." Out of the corner of his eye he could see someone waving at them. He focused in on the subject. "There's Sara, Nique. I think she's trying to get your attention," he said, glad for the timely interruption. Things had become awkward for them. *It was only an innocent kiss,* he told himself, knowing he was so good at lying to himself.

Omunique joined Sara at the exit railing, where Sara had been watching her favorite figure skaters. Sara giggled loudly when Omunique approached her.

"My, my, Sara, you're in a good mood," Omunique exclaimed. "What did you think of our performance? We only went through part of the routine we're going to use when we perform at the benefit."

Sara kissed Omunique's cheek. "You and Ian are the best, Nique," she gushed. "I'm always in a good mood after I watch you skate. I'd kill to have the opportunity to skate with Ian," Sara commented, her eyes glazed over with something akin to passion.

Maybe it was just a poor choice of words on Sara's part, thought Omunique. *Stop being so paranoid,* Omunique scolded herself. "Let's get our hot chocolate and grab a table. I want to hear about everything you've been up to, Sara."

While Omunique and Sara chatted and sipped their hot drinks, they watched Ian work an extraordinary artistic program as he skated to Quincy Jones's "Everything Must Change."

Omunique listened to the words of the song, aware that something had changed for Ian. She didn't know what had changed, she just knew that something had. Was it possible that Ian had more than a friendly interest in her? If Ken hadn't come into her life, could something have happened between them? Ian was a very charming man, and he loved the world of ice as much as she did. The fact that they weren't of the same race had no bearing whatsoever on their close friendship.

Ian's fluid movements were always exciting to watch. His body was strong and lithe. Omunique admired the way he put himself through strenuous workouts every day. His dedication to the sport equaled her own. But, like her, Ian didn't have much of a social life. She couldn't remember him ever having a girlfriend. Maybe that's the reason he'd kissed her that way.

Kenneth Maxwell Jr. knew he had changed, too. Deep in thought, trying to get a grip on his emotions, Ken paced his office floor. All through his early morning meetings his mind had stayed on Omunique and the evening they'd spent together. He had relived every touch, every kiss, and the feel of every inch of her soft flesh. He'd told her he loved her, which was true enough, yet he somehow felt as though he hadn't thoroughly convinced her of how much. Was he ready to pay the ultimate price for unwittingly leaving his heart exposed?

When Thomasina sashayed into the room in yet another skimpy outfit, he put his thoughts on hold.

"Ken, I'm leaving for the day," she announced. "Is there anything I can do for you before I take off?"

Pressing his hands against the desk, he stood up. "Yes, Thomasina, there is something. Have a seat, if you will."

A bit puzzled, Thomasina took a seat at the conference table.

Moving from behind his desk, Ken propped himself on the end of the table, hoping to handle this matter tactfully. "I'm very pleased with your work, Thom, and so is Max. You're very efficient. However, we're not pleased with the way you dress. We have a reputation to uphold here at Maxwell. Your style of dress is inappropriate for the image we've worked so hard to achieve."

Embarrassed to no end, Thomasina looked dumbfounded.

She had no idea the Maxwell men felt this way. "I don't . . . know what . . . to say," she stammered. "I always thought men enjoyed this sort of dress. Don't you like the way I look, Ken?"

Her very direct question stunned him. "We're not discussing my personal preference here. We're discussing the image of this company. It doesn't matter what I like or dislike in this instance."

"In that case, I'll dress to fit the company image. Off the record, what do you like to see your women wearing?"

This conversation has gotten very sticky, Ken thought impatiently. "No disrespect intended, but that's kind of personal. Since you've agreed to dress appropriately, we can call this meeting to an end. Thank you very much, Thom."

His quick dismissal grated on her nerves, he saw, but she vacated his office without further comment. He had firmly put her in her place, but he knew she'd deserved it. She'd had a crush on him from the moment she first walked in. Up until now, he'd refused to deal with the issue at all.

Now that she knew he wasn't the least bit interested in her, maybe she could concentrate on her job, instead of trying to get the attention of the man who only had eyes for one very beautiful Ice Princess. He hoped Thomasina found no fault in his candor, and he hoped she wasn't a sore loser. A sudden look of panic crossed his face as he thought of how the waitress had described Omunique's stalker, the feminine lips.

Ken wiped the sweat from his brow. Could Thomasina be behind all this? *No chance,* he told himself, but she'd certainly been more direct than he'd expected. He was glad he'd straightened things out with her, apparently in more ways than one. He was sure he hadn't given her any reason to think he'd be interested in her on a personal level. If she *had* imagined it, the record was straight on that account as well, he hoped.

As for her question about what he liked to see his women in, he thought about Omunique. He loved the colorful, fashionable style of dress she chose. Now that he'd seen the bare facts of her hidden beauty, he knew he preferred her in absolutely nothing at all. She had the most beautiful, silky skin he'd ever touched—he couldn't wait to touch her again and again.

Sitting down at his desk, Ken picked up the phone to call Ralph Steele. The issues regarding Omunique's safety still hadn't been completely worked out. Wyman Philyaw had called him that morning, informing him of the security he'd hired to protect his daughter at home and away from home. For that bit of information, Ken was glad. It was what he himself had planned to do. He thought it might make it easier for Omunique to take if it had come from her father, and not him, when she did find out.

After another disastrous practice session, Omunique sat in the bleachers inside the ice arena, feeling miserable. She had performed wonderfully with Ian, but since then everything had gone downhill. *This has to stop,* she told herself. *If I perform like this at the trials, I can bid the Olympic team a sad farewell.* The passion seemed to be absent from her performances. It was the passion that made it all come together. Without it, she was just another run-of-the-mill figure skater.

After all the passion she'd shared with Ken, she'd thought for sure she would come and set the arena on fire, but the flame hadn't been strong enough to light even a simple candle.

Plopping down in a seat next to Omunique, Brent looked as miserable as she felt.

Omunique could see the displeasure in his eyes, which made it hard to make eye contact with him. "I didn't do so well, huh? I don't know what's wrong with me, Brent. I know I'm a much, much better skater than this," she practically wailed.

Looking straight at her, Brent cleared his throat "Why didn't you tell me you were dating Maxwell? Was it because you knew what I'd say about it?"

Trying to digest what she'd just heard, Omunique briefly

closed her eyes. "Maybe we shouldn't have this conversation. I don't want an explosion, Brent," she stated dispassionately.

Brent rolled his gold watchband around his wrist. "His company sponsors you, Nique. That alone should tell you this relationship is taboo. Your emotional attachment to him already shows in your performance. You're totally distracted, Nique. Maybe you're no longer interested in fulfilling your dreams. I don't know. You tell me. You're the only one who knows."

Omunique sucked in a ragged breath. "Let's not blow this all out of proportion, Brent. You know about what else is going on in my life. If I had to blame my distraction on anything, it would be on the maniac who seems bent on putting me through hell." She looked at him thoughtfully. "By the way, how did you find out I'm dating Maxwell?"

He rolled his eyes at her. "I have my sources. And it won't be long before the whole world knows about it. The press would love to get their hands on this story. When they do, don't expect it to be pretty. Think about it, Nique."

The call from Ken's secretary had revealed more than just a working relationship between Omunique and her sponsor. His secretary had mentioned how upset her boss was that he hadn't been able to get hold of Omunique, and that he was beside himself with worry, Brent reflected. If Maxwell knew about the threatening distraction in her life, that would explain his concern, but Brent had gotten the impression from the secretary that there was something more going on between her boss and his star, something intimate.

Feeling he'd said enough on the subject to make her think seriously about what she'd gotten herself into, Brent got up from his seat and walked away. He could only hope she wouldn't make the same mistakes he'd made. A person could have one or the other, but never both. He knew, firsthand. He hoped Omunique would figure it out before it was too late for her to do anything but fail.

* * *

Brent had gotten her attention, all right. Through her shower and during the drive home, all she could think about was what he'd said. Though she didn't agree with all his remarks, she knew he'd been right about her emotional attachment to Ken. Since they'd made love, her emotional attachment to Ken was that much stronger. She was in love with Kenneth Maxwell Jr. and she was in love with competing. Was it necessary for her to choose?

There were a lot of sports figures who had both love affairs and careers, she considered, thinking about all the pair-skaters who'd fallen in love and had even gotten married. Why should it be any different for her? There were a lot of skaters who married partners who weren't even in the same field of work. At least Ken was a part of the sports world, she reasoned. If two people were in love, why should it matter? Anything was possible. Then again, Brent could be right.

Although it was late in the evening, Ken still worked in his office. Knowing Omunique had twenty-four hour protection at home and in the arena helped him keep his sanity. He knew he had no choice but to give her the private space she required.

After a few more minutes of mulling over her situation, he picked up the phone to call her. The last time they talked she was still in agreement about them spending their nights together, but she'd made it perfectly clear that she didn't want anyone underfoot twenty-four-seven—including him.

"How about going out for a late dinner?" he asked when she answered.

She battled with her response, believing that she might have gotten in too deep with him. Unable to fully concentrate on her Olympic goals, she had regrettably accepted that her love affair with Ken was in part responsible.

"I don't think I can make dinner, Ken. I'm really tired.

Maybe it's not a good idea for us to stay together tonight. I know I agreed to this arrangement earlier, but I've had second thoughts. I need to get plenty of rest before the charity benefit tomorrow. Besides that, Ken, I think we're making a big mistake as far as us being involved with one another this way.''

"Mistake? What are you trying to tell me, Omunique?''

"That we may have gone too far, too soon. Our affair is interfering with my professional goals. I thought I could have you and my career, but I'm starting to think that I can't,'' she announced sadly, blowing him away in the process.

Brent had been so adamant about her getting her mind back on her skating, despite the intrusive phone calls and her affair with Ken, that she now doubted that she could be in any sort of personal relationship at all. Both the dangerous intruder and her love affair with Ken were the main reasons she stayed so preoccupied. She heard Ken's sharp intake of breath.

"I don't believe what I m hearing,'' he responded flatly. "I thought we were on the same wavelength. When did you decide all of this, Omunique? You certainly haven't had a lot of time to think this through. It's only been a few hours since we last talked.''

"I thought we were too, Ken. I've never been involved this way with anyone, and to tell you the truth it has me scared to death. I think we need to cool off first, then assess what we're really doing. I can't give up my dreams.''

He was stunned at the unfair assessment it seemed she'd already made. "I don't know what to say now. Are you saying that we shouldn't see each other again?'' he asked, hoping against hope that he'd simply misread her again for the hundredth time.

The issues were now confusing to her, and she felt confused. "Honestly, I don't know what I'm saying. I just think we should take a time-out. Ken, I put in very long hours on the ice, and I'm just not able to be there for you at a moment's notice. My training schedule would be just plain unfair to you.

Do you understand what I'm trying to say?'' *How could he?* she thought. She didn't even understand it herself.

Frantic at the thought of losing her, he slipped out of the chair and began pacing back and forth in front of his desk. ''This is all so crazy, Nique. I'm not asking you to give up your dreams. I understand all that you're up against here, but I don't understand why we can't work this out. Why don't we go ahead and have dinner so we can discuss this face-to-face?''

''Okay,'' she conceded without any difficulty. She wanted to be with Ken as much as he seemed to want to be with her. ''I can't be out late, and I hope our discussion won't turn into an ugly confrontation if we aren't able to agree on everything. I couldn't deal with that.'' Assuring her that he had no intention of allowing any argument to ensue between them, no matter what their differences might be, he hung up, and quickly grabbed his suitcoat from the back of the chair.

In less than ten minutes Ken escaped the huge office building and rushed to the parking garage, where he jumped into his black sports car and sped out into the darkened streets. During the drive out of the city, all he could think about was Omunique. Their affair had only begun, he thought moodily, wondering how she could even entertain the idea that it should be over. Sure, he'd had several dates that hadn't progressed past the first couple of dates, even if sex had been involved, but from the very beginning he'd never thought of Omunique as someone to just have sex with. He wasn't going to allow her to think that way, either, if that was what she was thinking.

Had he done something to make her think that their relationship was nothing more than a casual affair? Hadn't he gone to great lengths to show her how he truly felt about her? Did she really feel this way, or were those damned phone calls responsible for this new turn of events?

Noticing the vehicle parked on the opposite side of the street, Ken pulled into the circular driveway of the beach house. Though the body of the dark vehicle was unmarked, he recognized the kind of special license tags issued to security vehicles.

Satisfied that it was a security team, he parked the car and rushed up to the front door.

When she opened the door, he pulled her into his arms without the slightest hesitation. ''I don't know what's going on in that lovely head of yours, but I certainly intend to find out. We're too good together to have things end like this.'' Taking her coat from her hand, he helped her put it on.

While guiding her to the car, he kept her close at his side. Before opening the passenger door, he kissed her. When she responded the way she normally did, he found a reason to be optimistic.

Although she hadn't yet uttered a word, he wondered if she might be regretting their earlier conversation. ''You're so quiet, Nique. Want to tell me what you're thinking?''

''I'm just thinking about tomorrow. Ian is counting on me. I don't want to let him down. Whether it's a charity benefit or an important competition, I take my job very seriously. So does he.''

He smiled at her ''I know that you both do. I don't ever want to be the cause of your not performing well. Do I distract you that much, Miss Philyaw? If so, is that why you're having doubts about our relationship?'' he asked, pulling into the parking lot of the Golden Whale restaurant.

Placing her hand on his, she looked over at him, wanting to kiss all his fears away. Afraid that her feelings for him could get in the way of her recent decision, she wouldn't allow herself to do that. ''Why don't we go inside and get a table? Then we can talk.''

Inside the intimately lit restaurant, the hostess led them to a table that overlooked the ocean, but it was much too dark outside to see anything but the rolling whitecaps. After ordering their meals, the couple sat in stone silence, both fearing the things that needed to be said. Omunique's mind was in absolute turmoil. Ken's wasn't in any better shape.

A short time later the hot seafood dishes were placed in front of them. Omunique had ordered grilled salmon and Ken had asked for fried red snapper, both of which looked to be cooked to perfection. The silence remained as they ate, yet their eyes appeared to carry on an emotional conversation of their own accord.

Less than an hour later, when the waiter finally removed the empty plates and all they had left to finish was their hot tea, Ken pulled his chair closer to Omunique's.

He kissed the tip of her nose. "Now, about the questions I asked you in the car. I think our feelings for one another can get us through any crisis. So why are we going through all this, Princess?"

"I don't know," she said timidly. "It all seems so silly now." Quizzically, he raised an eyebrow, prompting her to continue. "I'm here with you, and I can't think of any place I'd rather be. However, Brent has raised some questions about my performance, which made me think I might be allowing our relationship to interfere with my training. Brent won't put up with anything less than my full concentration and dedication. He's a perfectionist."

"Listen," Ken began, "I know exactly what an athlete has to concentrate on. I played high school and college basketball. I wasn't looking to make a career of it, but I dedicate myself to everything I take on. For that reason, among others, I won't stand for you being anything but dedicated, either. After all, Maxwell sponsors you. We're in this business to make money; not lose it. Trust me not to screw up your goals. I want you to realize your dream. I want to see you on the next winter Olympic team."

Her heart thumped like crazy inside her chest. "Oh, Ken, that's what I live for. I've put so much energy into my sport. I'd want to die if I came up on the short end of the stick just because I was unprepared. Do you know what it means to me as a black woman to be able to represent my country and my people in such a prestigious way? I can tell you. It means *everything*!"

Lifting her hand, he pressed his lips into the center of her palm. "I can see the passion in your eyes, Nique. It's going to happen for you, just the way you've dreamed about it. Speaking of our people, why do you think so few blacks are involved in the sport?" He had his own ideas, but he wanted to hear her take on it.

"That's an easy enough question. Like ice hockey, whites dominate figure skating. I don't think anyone has ever encouraged our people to become involved in the sport. If my mother hadn't been involved in it, I'm not sure my father would've ever taken me to an ice rink. It always surprised him that my mother loved it so much. In the past, blacks just haven't taken to the ice. But if I have my way, all that's going to change. Are you aware of the young black woman, Surya Bonaly, of France? She's an athletic wonder, very gymnastically inclined."

"To be honest, I've not paid a lot of attention to the sport, yet I know about Debi Thomas, the bronze medal winner of the nineteen eighty-eight Olympics held in Calgary. As I mentioned before, we've never sponsored a figure skater until now. Track and Field has always been our main interest. You mentioned something about things changing if you got your way. What did you mean by that?"

Omunique looked embarrassed. "I have another dream, Ken, one that I've failed to mention. Sometimes I feel it's far-fetched, but it's one of the things that keeps me going. It keeps me focused. One day I want to operate my own ice arena. I'd like it to be located in the inner city. I want to be a role model in the black communities."

Ken's eyes lit up "Wow, that is an awesome dream," he said, finding it hard to contain his excitement over how much they had in common. Her dreams simply mirrored his.

She laughed lightly. "I know I'm shooting for the moon here, Ken, but I can't help it. I want minority boys and girls to have the same opportunities I had, only with a lot less hassle. I don't want them to have to live their dreams vicariously," she uttered passionately.

Ken hugged her fiercely. "I don't think wanting your own

ice arena is at all far-fetched. In fact, it's a marvelous idea. There's nothing wrong with shooting for the moon, especially when you're talented enough to land among the stars. Max used to say to me, 'Shoot for the moon, son, you might get lucky enough to land among the stars.' '' He smiled. "You seem more relaxed now. Can it mean that we don't have to put the skids on our budding romance?"

She lowered her lashes. "This relationship stuff is complicated, and I just can't allow anything to interfere with my goals. Ken, if I don't rise to the occasion, I don't stand a chance in hell of being financially able to help anyone. Winning lands endorsement contracts. Endorsement contracts put money in the bank, money I can invest in the future of our children and in our communities."

Ken blew out a ragged breath. "Look at me, Nique. Look into my eyes and tell me you don't want me as much as I want you. Tell me you really believe I can't be a part of your dreams. They're really not that different from my own. Nique, we're good together. Together, we can make more of a difference than we could separately."

Omunique pulled her eyes away from his intense gaze. "I won't lie to you, Ken. I do want you, and I want you to share in all my dreams," she said, close to tears.

"But?"

"There are no buts, Ken."

"Are you saying you want things to remain the way they are between us, which is damn good in my opinion?"

A single tear cascaded down her face. "I think it's safe to say that. But I do have to stay at the top of my game. If you'll just be patient with me, I'm willing to give our relationship every chance to thrive. I do love being with you, Ken. That was never the issue."

He swiped at the beads of perspiration on his forehead. "You don't know how good that makes me feel. Just tell Brent Masters that I'm not out to take you away from your chosen field. I'm here to encourage you every step of the way." He glanced at his watch, noting how late it had gotten. "Are you ready for me to take you home? It's close to ten o'clock."

Sliding her arms around his neck, she kissed him. "I think that would be wise. I have an early training session, and then I have to rehearse with Ian before the benefit. Are you planning to come to the event?"

"Are you inviting me?" he countered.

"Most definitely. My sponsors should see what they've gotten themselves into. Your tickets will be at will call, but I'm surprised you don't already have them."

Sliding his hand into the breast pocket of his suit jacket, he pulled out two tickets, holding them up for her to see. "I hope you didn't think I'd miss your performance. The other ticket is for Max, of course, but I'm not sure he'll make it. I know he's going to try." He stood up and held his arm out to her. "Max can't wait to meet you, though he feels as if he already knows you. I talk him to death about you."

Before leading her to the entrance, Ken kissed her passionately. Inside the car, the silence returned, but their fears about their personal relationship had been put to rest. They both were simply tired.

Omunique fell asleep on the drive home, but Ken felt alert and exhilarated, happy that things had turned out favorably. He was aware that he'd have to be careful not to demand too much of her time, though he hoped they'd find adequate time to be together. As for the problem with the stalker, he was totally stumped by the whole thing.

When they reached the beach house, he awakened her with a soft kiss. "Are we—"

Smiling, she silenced him by putting one of her fingers to his lips. She then took his hand and put it in hers. "Yes, we're spending the night here together."

"How did you know what I was going to ask you?"

"Let's just say I've already learned to read your expressions."

Softly whistling the tune to "Hero," Ken helped her out of

the car. Arm in arm, they walked the short distance to the house.

As Omunique readied for bed, she wondered how she was going to keep everything in proper prospective. It wouldn't be easy, but she had to try—for everyone's sake. As Ken had stated, they were good together. She wanted Kenneth Maxwell Jr. in her life.

For now . . .

For always . . .

Chapter Eleven

The amber spotlight had the appearance of a golden moon slipping into the blackened sky. While the audience waited in eager anticipation for the final figure skating performance to begin, in awe of what they'd already seen, not a single whisper could be heard. The music, dramatic in quality, echoed throughout the ice arena.

In a rolling motion, the spotlight crashed into the center of the ice, where it caressed and illuminated the two intimately entwined figures, causing their black and silver costumes to launch silvery rays of dazzling light.

With his hands placed snugly on Omunique's hips, Ian gently lifted her. While spinning around on the blades of his skates, he held her high above his head. When he released her, she spun two revolutions and executed a perfect landing. Omunique sighed. The hardest part of the routine was over, which really hadn't been hard at all. She simply wasn't used to being lifted. *The audience didn't seem to notice,* she thought, encouraged by their loud cheers.

In a soft flurry of spins and turns, the two skaters mesmerized their audience with enough zest to whet their appetites, which only left them craving for more. When the music turned slow and dreamy, Omunique and Ian engaged in a seductive waltz. As they danced in perfect harmony to the music, their synchronization was nothing short of excellent. Her ballerina-like gestures exhibited grace, and his sensual moves aroused the passions of the audience.

Skating backward, their energy levels overflowing with promptitude, Omunique and Ian skirted along the outer perimeters in a flirtatious style of ice dancing.

Lowering his head level with Omunique's, Ian brought his mouth close to her ear. "Shall we give Brent a heart attack?" he whispered, smiling devilishly. At that exciting moment she would've agreed to fly to the moon, which was exactly what Ian had in mind. Having received her nod of approval, Ian carefully lifted Omunique over his head. On a quick release, he tossed her high into the air.

With his face twisted into a stunned mask of horror, Brent Masters held his breath as he jumped to his feet. When she landed safely back in Ian's arms, he blew out a gust of audible relief. Brent saw that he hadn't been the only person compelled from his seat. The entire crowd had stood up. Wyman appeared ecstatic over their flawless effort, Ken observed, when he finally calmed down enough to look in his direction.

Back on solid ice, Omunique and Ian whirled into a fantastic finish. The camel spin was one of their favorite endings, only this time they followed it with a sit spin. Continuing to flow across the ice, waving and blowing kisses to their deeply moved fans, Omunique curtsied repeatedly as Ian bowed from the waist. The arena rained colorful showers of roses and other resplendent blooms, thrown by fans in the bleachers who were caught up in a frenzy. Carefully watching each step they took, Omunique and Ian bent over to gather up several of the flowers. Waving them in the air, they showed joy in their triumph.

Patiently, Ken waited at the exit railing for Omunique to make her way from the center of the ice, cognizant of the danger that could exist in a large crowd. His eyes darted everywhere, watching for any unusual activity from those around her. Smiling, she rushed into his outstretched arms and basked in the loving kisses he showered all over her face.

Holding her face between his palms, he held her at arm's length. "You were fantastic, Princess. Absolutely wonderful!" Noticing Ian standing by quietly, with an odd expression on his face, Ken reached over Omunique's shoulder and extended his caramel-brown hand to her partner. "Brilliant, Ian," Ken praised with sincerity. "You two should consider taking your show on the road. You make an excellent ice dancing team."

"Thanks, but her coach would never allow it. As far as Brent's concerned, Omunique is a 'one star' attraction," Ian stated, taking inventory of the man that held Omunique so possessively close.

Omunique thought she could read the expression on Ian's face as well as his thoughts. He now knew who her secret lover was, but she didn't assign it a care as she formally introduced them. Surprised to see that Wyman wasn't close by, she looked around for him. He was always there after one of her performances.

"Where's Daddy?" she asked Ken.

Ken took a cursory look around the arena. "I know he's here—we sat together. I saw him just a minute ago," he told her, continuing his search for the man who couldn't easily lose himself in a crowd. *His size alone would make it impossible,* Ken thought.

Fearful of leaving Omunique's side, Ken had reluctantly offered to go in search of Wyman when he suddenly appeared, his expression full of fatherly pride.

"Starlight, star bright, Omunique Philyaw has shone her brightest light," Wyman sang out sweetly, handing her a dozen of yellow baby rosebuds. His smiling, walnut-brown eyes embraced his daughter and Ian. "You both expressed yourselves so beautifully. If I didn't know better, I would think you two were madly in love. It was a well-executed performance, kids. Congratulations!''

Severely jealous of the statement Wyman had made, Ken's neck snapped back in a jerking motion as he bit back the retort that would tell exactly how he felt about it.

Several others expressed their sincere congratulations to the two figure skaters, but Brent Masters wasn't one of them. To Omunique he looked more than upset. It looked as though he was too upset to speak. Noting the tight set of Brent's jaw, she knew she was in for a major scolding.

Walking up to Brent, she slid her hand into his. ''I know we upset you, coach, but we felt confident that everything would turn out just fine. Ian and I practiced that last lift so many times we could've done it with our eyes closed,'' she explained, hoping to appease him. They hadn't practiced that particular lift, at all. When Ian put her to the test out there, she'd quickly decided she could do it.

Brent tossed her an impatient glance. ''You're not a pair skater, Nique. What you two did out there was dangerous, practice or not. You can't afford to take such risks for an exhibition.'' In spite of the disdain he felt for the lack of maturity they'd displayed, he smiled, squeezing her fingers tightly. ''Though I hate to admit it, you two skated an excellent program. But don't scare me like that ever again,'' he berated, unable to keep a smile at bay. Her eyes seemed to make him a solemn promise to do as he'd requested.

When Omunique attempted to introduce Ken to Brent, his reluctance to shake Ken's hand outraged her. Then her outrage turned to embarrassment. Brent's face had hardened once again, making his adverse feelings for Ken plain. This wasn't the same Brent Masters she'd come to know. His direct snub of Ken wasn't something she would've ever expected from the man she'd come to love and revere. His demeanor reeked of downright antagonism.

Brent's rudeness made Ken wonder if his feelings for Omunique extended beyond the realm of their professional relationship. Brent was thirteen years Omunique's senior, but age had little to do with anything when the heart became involved. Ken explored the possibility of Masters having a romantic interest in his star athlete. Stranger things than a coach falling for his star had certainly happened.

Discreetly, Omunique and Ken slipped away from the crowd as soon as she'd accepted all the congratulations and other well-meaning comments. They had plans to meet with Ken's best friends, Frank and Marion, who awaited them at Frank's place.

Out in the parking lot a tall, dark figure suddenly rushed Omunique. In a split second, Ken wrestled the man down to the ground, twisting his arm behind his back. Scared stiff, Omunique pressed her back against a parked automobile. When she got a good look at the man's face, her hand flew up to her mouth to muffle a scream.

"Ken," she shouted, "let him go! I know him. He's a friend."

Ken looked back and forth between her and the young man, who appeared to be in severe pain, not to mention a state of shock. "Who the hell are you?" Ken asked, his tone rough and gravelly. "Why did you come at her like that?"

To no avail, the young man tried to loosen the tight grip Ken still had on his arm. "My name's Brian. I've known Nique for a long time. I work part-time at the arena." Biting back an expletive, Ken freed the young man's arm.

Weak in the knees. Omunique approached the two men. Kneeling down, she made eye contact with sixteen year old, blond and blue-eyed Brian Terry. "I'm sorry about this, Brian, but you came at me so fast. Out of nowhere. I didn't recognize you. Your unpredictable behavior caused my friend to react the way he did. Why didn't you come up to me while I was still inside?"

Brian rubbed the arm Ken had released. "It was impossible to get near you. It looked as though you had an army surrounding you, Nique. I'm sorry if I frightened you. I just wanted to say hello, and to congratulate you on another great performance.''

''Thanks for the compliment. And I'm sorry, too. It's been one big misunderstanding.'' Still trembling from the experience, she reached for Ken's hand. ''Brian, this is my friend, Kenneth Maxwell Jr. I know he's sorry he hurt you. We both are.''

Ken wasn't the least bit sorry. The kid had gotten what he deserved. He shouldn't have come at Omunique the way he had, way too aggressively. Whether he knew her or not, his approach had been all wrong. ''You need to be careful, young man, how you approach someone, especially women. Your behavior displayed aggression. You could've gotten hurt worse than you did. I saw you as a major threat.''

Ken offered Brian his hand, helping him to his feet. ''If you're smart, you won't ever approach anyone the same way you just approached Miss Philyaw. Is your arm okay? I twisted it pretty good.''

''You practically broke it off, mister. If you weren't Nique's friend, I'd sue you for causing me bodily injury.''

Omunique stepped between the two men when it looked as though Ken might give Brian a busted lip to go along with his twisted arm. ''That's enough now,'' she scolded. ''Brian, you run along. I can assure you my friend didn't intend to cause you any real harm, but you should heed his advice. I'll see you at the arena next week.''

''Keep smiling, Nique,'' Brian shouted in parting. He gave Ken the finger and ran away as fast his long legs would carry him.

''That kid's a real menace,'' Ken told Omunique, as he steered the car out of the parking lot gates. ''How well do you know him?''

''He's pretty harmless, despite the fact he normally hangs out with a bunch of hoodlums. I see him as a wannabe. He also lives in an extremely tough neighborhood.''

Scowling, Ken glanced over at Omunique. ''Just because he

lives in a tough neighborhood doesn't mean he has to be involved with a group of roughnecks. He could do a lot of other things. It's all about choices. What else do you know about him?''

"He has a rather troubled home life. His father is an absentee parent who rarely visits his five children. His mother works all the time to try to make ends meet. The father provides no monetary support—or any other support, for that matter. When Brian's not working, he's home taking care of his four siblings, all of whom are much younger,'' she said, her voice cracking with compassion.

Ken reached across the seat and touched her cheek. When a single, unexpected tear fell from her eye, Ken wiped it away. "I'll see what I can do to help the family, Nique. Because of Maxwell Corp's heavy involvement with inner city families, we have all sorts of resources at our disposal. Can you find out his address for me?''

"I don't know the exact address, but I know where he lives. I can take you there. Dad and I have taken food and money over there. That's kind of you to want to help out.''

Ken shook his head. "I'll be more comfortable if you just provide me with the address. Some neighborhoods aren't safe for brawny men, even those who consider themselves street-smart, let alone a petite woman like you. I'll take care of it.'' She would've argued the point had he not pulled into Frank Green's driveway.

Frank didn't live that far from Ken's Venice Beach condo. From the arena it had taken them less than thirty minutes to make it to Frank's house.

Just as they mounted the steps of a marvelous tri-level home, the front door flew open. Frank and Marion stepped out onto the porch to greet their guests.

"Hey, pal," Frank called out, "we thought you guys would never get here.''

Ken turned to Omunique. "What did I tell you about these

two? Go ahead and tell them what I told you,'' he prompted, nudging her shoulder.

Omunique smiled brightly at Ken's friends. ''Ken said you two would be looking out the window for us. I see he's right. I hope you weren't worried about him. He's a pretty safe driver, most of the time,'' Omunique teased, breaking the ice with ease.

Ken put his arm around Omunique's waist. ''Guys, this is the girl of my dreams,'' Ken said. He then formally introduced them.

Marion stepped forward and offered her hand. ''Hello, Omunique. We've heard a lot about you. It's so nice we're finally getting a chance to meet you.''

''Yes, it is,'' Frank chimed in. ''We had started to think you were a figment of our boy's imagination, though Marion and I definitely knew of you. We follow your career. Come on into the house,'' Frank offered kindly.

The tri-level house was warmly decorated in tones of earth and wood. Some of its contents were similar to those found in a greenhouse. A variety of lush plants and beautiful orchids, in an array of colors, created an atmosphere that spoke to nature. The walls, painted a glossy beige, boasted a collection of antique stocks and bonds. Worth a small fortune, the magnificent collectibles, showcased in heavy wooden frames, hung on the walls throughout the house. The plush carpet was a mixture of dark and light earth tones.

Frank sat his guests down, in the contemporary style living room, for an evening of chitchat and fun. Excusing herself, Marion went off to the kitchen to bring out the snacks she'd prepared. Aware that Omunique had special dietary needs, Marion had opted to serve lightly grilled chicken breasts and a variety of seasonal fresh fruits and raw vegetables, along with two homemade vegetable dips, creamy cucumber and dill.

When Marion returned to the living room, laden with pastel-tinted glass trays, Frank rushed over to help her place them on an antique mahogany dining table—an heirloom that once belonged to his deceased grandparents, he told their guests.

Marion summoned her guests into the dining area. She sat down, facing Frank, after their guests had been comfortably seated. While munching away on the healthy finger foods, Frank and Marion delighted in their opportunity to get acquainted with Omunique. The two women seemed to take an instant liking to one another, Ken observed.

A quarter of an hour later, full and happy, Ken and Frank disappeared into Frank's computer room, much to Marion's dismay. Frank wanted to show off to Ken his new computer program. Omunique and Marion moved back into the comfortable living room, where they sat on opposite ends of the winter white sectional sofa.

"So," Marion began, "you've certainly bowled over our dear friend. He's very taken with you, Omunique. Frankly, I've never seen him this happy. Ken's a good man."

"I think so, too," Omunique shared happily. "Did he tell you that I was jealous of you, Marion?"

Marion looked surprised. "Of me? Whatever for?"

Omunique laughed. "Late one evening, I saw you with him at the Sports Connection. Of course, I jumped to all the wrong conclusions. I thought you two were an item," she revealed with refreshing honesty. "When I spotted the huge engagement ring on your finger, I burned with jealousy."

Marion took her turn to laugh. "Oh, yes, he did mention something about that, but he didn't go into that much detail. I'd actually forgotten about it until you mentioned it. I don't think he's going to give you any cause to be jealous. He tells us he's in love with you," Marion tossed out purposely. Sitting back in her chair, Marion closely observed Omunique's nervous reaction to her statement.

Thinking the conversation had turned a little too personal, Omunique looked uncomfortable. "I don't know about all that, but I certainly would be flattered if it were true. Even though he's said as much to me, we've only known each other a short time. I'm not sure about this concept called love, but I know my feelings for him run very deep. Actually, I'm terrified of all these new emotions.''

Her emotions weren't the only thing that terrified her, Omunique quietly reflected, remembering that Brian had mentioned something to do with her smiling. Her fears had made her unfairly suspicious of everyone she came into contact with, and she hated that.

Marion noticed the expression of fearful uncertainty on Omunique's face. Deciding it had to do with the new emotions she'd spoken about, Marion thought it best not to probe any deeper into her emotional fears.

''Well, just give it time,'' Marion advised her. ''Time always tells the story. Tell me, that's if you don't mind, how did you become involved in figure skating? It's not the kind of sport African-Americans normally choose.''

Marion listened intently to Omunique, who responded with an in-depth story about her love for the sport and how it had all begun. Enchanted with the magical stories of Omunique's experiences on the ice, truly interested in what she had to say on the subject, Marion encouraged her to reveal a lot more about her experiences than she had intended. Marion had tears in her eyes by the time Omunique finished.

While Marion talked excitedly about her interior design business, her upcoming marriage to Frank, and their plans to move in together before the wedding, the two men returned. Their loud chatter disrupted the two women's conversation, but Marion didn't seem to mind, Omunique observed.

''You're back,'' Marion remarked. ''I left the dishes for you to tackle, Frank.''

Smiling, Frank dropped down on the sofa beside Marion. ''What else is new?'' he joked, jostling Marion playfully.

Ken made himself comfortable next to Omunique. Tossing his arm around her shoulder, he pulled her closer to him. ''Marion, I know I've asked you this a thousand times, but how do you deal with this computer nut? If it had been up to him, we'd still be in the computer room. Now me, I prefer something soft and beautiful,'' Ken said, nudging Omunique flirtatiously. ''I admit they're a valuable asset, especially for business purposes, but computers just don't turn me on.'' *Nothing turns me on the way Omunique does,* he thought.

Smiling, Marion looked at Frank in adoration, her ebony eyes flashing signals that only he could interpret. ''It's hard at times, Ken, but he knows when I need him to be attentive to me. The computer is just his hobby. I'm his full-time job.''

''You can say that again,'' Frank interjected, smiling back at the woman he seemed to adore. ''When Marion gives me that sister girl head action, I immediately turn that bad boy off. She's made it perfectly clear that she has no intention of competing with any electronic device. She only had to tell me once that it can't hardly satisfy a man's most fundamental needs, the kind of needs only a woman can fulfill.'' Everyone laughed, Frank the loudest.

Although Omunique felt completely relaxed with Ken's friends and enjoyed their discussions on a wide range of interesting topics, intermittent panic attacks seemed to come at her from every direction. Simply because of the remarks they'd made regarding her smiles, both Sara and Brian had given her cause for grave concern. Paranoia wasn't normally a part of her psyche, but she thought she had good reason.

''How about a game of Spades?'' Frank asked his guests.

Ken got to his feet. ''Sorry, but we have to beg off, pal. I made some promises to this young lady, and I've got to keep them.'' He pulled Omunique up from the sofa. ''This here beautiful girl is a star athlete, and I promised to let her get plenty of rest so that she can be on top of her game. Isn't that right, Princess?'' he asked, kissing her forehead.

Blushing, Omunique smiled at Ken's open affection for her in front of his closest friends. ''That's what we agreed on,'' she said, reaching her hand out to Marion. ''But I really hate our little get-together to end. I've had such a wonderful time.

I want to thank both of you for opening up your home and yourselves to me in such a warm way. It's been wonderful.''

Marion grasped Omunique's fingers with her own. ''You're more than welcome. We'll have to do it again. As soon as possible.''

At the front door, the two couples promised to see each other in the near future. Marion hugged Omunique, while Frank and Ken exchanged a few more humorous comments.

''Good night, you two,'' Frank shouted from the porch as he and Marion watched Ken maneuver the car out of the driveway.

Ken and Omunique waved before the car had completely backed out.

Before Ken could walk Omunique to the front door of her house, she grabbed his hand and directed him toward the stone steps. Not wanting her to miss out on proper rest, he started to object, but thought better of it. She wanted to take a walk, and he didn't think it was wise to try to become a dictator. If he refused, she'd probably go alone, he figured—not a safe thing for her to do. At any rate, it was a perfect night for a stroll in the moonlight.

''Are you warm enough, Princess?''

Her smile rivaled the brightness of the stars. ''I am.'' *I'm always warmer than warm around you,* she added in her thoughts.

Eyes bright with unshed tears, Omunique walked alongside Ken, feeling wonderfully alive. Ken made her happy, filled the void of bitter loneliness, made her see all the things she'd missed out on by not taking time out for fun. Ken could make her laugh, even at herself. He had a way of bringing sunshine to her heart. He was her solace when troubled waters ran deep. And he kept her from constantly dwelling on the dangerous negativity that she'd suddenly found herself surrounded by. Above all, he made her feel like a real woman.

Stopping dead in her tracks, she wrapped her arms around

his waist. Silently, she offered him her mouth. Reading her like an open book, he bent his head and took fervent custody of her mouth, to which her entire anatomy responded wildly.

As the moon shone down on the two intimately entwined figures, the shadows of their love for one another surrounded them. While they exchanged kisses, their pulses began to race. Had they been in private, Omunique sensed, they undoubtedly would've given in to the desires that their bodies had longed for the entire evening.

Looking into her glistening eyes, he took her hands and placed them against his chest. "So," he began, "this is what serenity is all about. I feel so at peace when I'm with you. I'm glad you're here with me. I see many nights like this one in our future. I love you," he whispered, drugging her senses with an onslaught of impassioned kisses. *Yes,* he decided, *peace and Omunique are what I need most in my life. They seem to be one and the same.*

Twisting his fingers in her hair, he slowly undid the tightly fashioned braid, immersing his fingers in its thickness as the loosened hair cascaded into his trembling hands.

Staring into the eyes that captured her soul, Omunique stroked his jaw. His skin felt baby soft, and she never could get enough of touching him like that. "I don't know what the future holds for us, but I know that I want to share many more nights just like this one with you. You bring me joy and laughter. As much as I've enjoyed this entire evening, we must bring it to a close," she uttered with remorse. She then drew his head down, urging his lips to attend yet another meeting with hers—a meeting he was more than willing to attend.

Feeling no need for conversation, they walked back toward the house. At the door, where they found it difficult to separate from one another, they kissed goodnight. As long as Wyman was staying at the house with his daughter, Ken knew she'd be safe.

Wyman was still up, sitting in the living room, when he

heard Omunique enter the house. "Hello, Nique," he called out. "How was the rest of your evening?"

"Hey, Dad," she responded, hanging her jacket in the hall closet.

She walked into the living room, dropped tiredly into a reclining chair, and adjusted the chair back to a more comfortable position. "I had a nice time with Ken and his friends. Marion and I hit it off pretty well. They're a nice looking couple. She's a raven-haired beauty. He's quite handsome, and has odd colored eyes—burgundy."

Wyman smiled. "She may be a beauty, Nique, but no one is as beautiful as my girl. You shone perfectly tonight. I still can't get over your performance with Ian. You and he are great together. Maybe you should consider teaming up with him. Pair skating is so fascinating."

Omunique momentarily pondered his comments. "I don't know. I do like skating with Ian, and pair skating is so romantic. I get so emotional when I watch them do their thing. They have great synchronization. While Ian and I skate well together, I'm not sure I could do it full-time. Some of the lifts are very difficult, and I'd be in constant fear of our ice blades getting tangled together, which could possibly cause injury to one of us, or both. I think I'll stick with the singles. I might consider it later on in my career. But it'll be like starting all over again."

Wyman nodded. "I understand all of what you've said. Anyway, I love seeing you perform solo. When you become one with the ice it's so exciting to watch. It appears that the ice is just another of your extremities. It seems to move right along with you. You and the ice are as one. Keep doing what you do so beautifully, daughter."

Omunique got to her feet. "Thanks, Dad, for all your encouragement."

"Are you ready to go to bed?"

She ran her fingers through her hair. "Yes. I'm bushed. But

first I'm going to take a long, hot bath. My calf muscles are a little tight.'' Bending over, she dropped a kiss on Wyman's lips. ''See you in the morning, big guy. I wish you didn't have to leave tomorrow, but I know you're needed up north. I really appreciate you coming down for the benefit, Daddy.''

He hugged her to him ''I wouldn't have had it any other way, Nique. I'm sorry I have to leave, too, but I'll be back. The holidays are just around the corner. I'd like you to invite the Maxwells for Thanksgiving dinner. Mamie and I will act as host and hostess. You know how your Aunt Mamie loves to cook.''

Omunique grinned. ''That would be super nice. Ken has mentioned the four of us getting together for dinner. Your suggestion will make him happy.'' She kissed him again. ''Good night, Mr. Philyaw. Pleasant dreams,'' she cooed.

Ken felt good when he reached home. A quick steamy shower made him feel even better. In bed, he reflected on the evening and how well it had gone. Marion had been an absolute angel, the perfect hostess. Although Marion was like a mother hen where he and Frank were concerned, she meant well. She always worried that some unappreciative female might hurt him. She could never get it through her lovely head that he wasn't an easy man to take advantage of. Taking everything into account, it had been one fabulous evening.

Omunique was also recalling the wonderful evening. With her head resting against the rim of the tub, she closed her eyes. It felt so good to have someone who cared deeply for her. She had enjoyed Ken's friends. She thought Marion and Frank were very friendly, but she could see that Marion was very protective of both men, just as Ken had told her. She then thought about how attentive Frank had been to Marion. It had been easy for her to see why Ken and Frank were such good friends. For sure, they had each other's back.

Because of her career, she'd missed out on having a truly close friend. But now that Ken was in her life, she hoped they'd become so much more than lovers. Maybe they had put the cart before the horse, but she felt that they were rapidly becoming best friends. For sure, he had her back. Just as he had Frank's. And he utterly fulfilled her in every way.

Chapter Twelve

A chill raced up and down Omunique's spine as she dragged herself out of bed and wrapped herself in a warm robe. *Where has September gone?* she wondered, shivering from the unusual chilling temperatures that October had brought. Contrary to popular belief, California could get very cold during the late fall and winter.

Plopping down on the side of the bed, she looked over at the answering machine and smiled. No phone calls, no letters, no nothing, from the menace-to-sanity, she thought with much joy. Her life was practically back to normal, with the exception of Brent staying on her case over her love affair with Ken. That, too, shall pass, she mused, sighing with content.

Ken had warned her not to become too complacent about things. Just as quickly as the threatening situations had started and then stopped, they could start all over again, he kept reminding her. But she was sure it was over, and that it had all been just a bad hoax.

Getting up from the bed. she trudged through to the front of the house and turned the heat on, glad that the central heating unit had already been checked and serviced, in preparation for the coming winter months. Due to the sea air, it was much colder in the beach cities than in the inland ones.

In the kitchen she lit the fire under the teapot. Just as she removed the wheat bread from the refrigerator the kitchen clock chirped, announcing the five o'clock hour. At seven o'clock she was due on the ice. Not on her way to the arena, not coming out of the locker room, but *on the ice*, per Brent, who was such a stickler for time. So was she.

Omunique popped a slice of bread into the toaster. She then opened the refrigerator and pulled out the plastic butter tray and a glass pitcher of grapefruit juice. With the skim milk being the last item to be retrieved, she closed the door. When the teapot whistled its readiness, Omunique poured the hot water into a colorful mug and dropped in a cinnamon-apple teabag.

Carrying her scant but nourishing breakfast over to the table, she sat down to polish it off. While eating, she thought about Ken, and her eyes twinkled with merriment. She then thought about the upcoming holidays. Thanksgiving would be the first official holiday they'd spend together, and she couldn't wait for it.

At five-thirty Omunique placed the dirty dishes in the sink. She then dashed to the bathroom for her morning shower. As she passed through the hallway, she lowered her head and smelled the fresh red roses that sat atop the credenza. She smiled when she remembered how Ken had presented them to her the previous evening. Down on bended knee, he'd told her how much he loved her, then given her the roses.

After towel drying the last drops of water from her body, she pulled on a navy blue leotard, covered it with a gray wool wraparound skirt and buttoned the side closure. Taking a gray sweater from the dresser drawer, she slipped it over her head and folded it under at the hemline. She then stepped into a pair of flat-heeled shoes. Before tackling her hair and makeup, she smoothed the sheets and tucked them in. Lastly, she straightened out the comforter and tossed the pillows back in place.

Once she'd selected a change of clothing to wear after her workout, she packed them in her gym bag, along with powder and deodorant. After a quick brush through her hair, a touch of moisturizer to her skin, and a dab of lip color, she was off and running for the door.

The cold wind slashed into Omunique's face as she stepped out of doors. After throwing her gear in the backseat, she situated herself behind the Jeep's steering wheel, started the engine, and pulled out of the driveway.

Happy thoughts of the holidays were still with her as she turned onto Pacific Coast Highway. This time of year she participated in numerous skating events. When she thought of all the holiday gala affairs that would take place, she made a mental note to check out the holiday skating schedule kept on the arena bulletin board.

The arena was a lot more crowded than usual, she noted, skating onto the ice. Several skaters that she didn't recognize whirled around the ice. Giving it no more thought, she skated to her favorite spot and began her normal workout paces.

Brent was late, she realized when he appeared on the ice at seven forty-five. Skating to where Omunique practiced, he greeted her in a voice like the growl of a bear with a sore tail. *Another PMS day,* she thought wickedly, laughing at Brent's newly acquired moody attitude, which she mischievously referred to as Preposterous Mood Swings.

"What's so funny?" he mumbled under his breath.

"Oh, nothing," she replied cheerfully. "I'm just in a good mood. She glanced at the large clock that hung on the back wall. She then looked back and forth between Brent and the clock, in the same way he did her. "Get stuck in traffic?" she nagged.

"No, Nique, I was not stuck in traffic," he countered impatiently. "Young lady, it will serve you well to remember who's in charge here. You know I'm rarely ever late."

Determined not to let Brent's funk get under her skin, she let a bright smile quickly soften the scowl on her face. "Don't get your ice blades all in a tangle, Brent. I was just joking. I thought I might be able to get you to laugh.'' *Something you've been doing very little of lately,* came her churlish thought. Her glance swept the arena. "Do you know why this place is so crowded?''

"They're part of the ice show that's taking place in the Sports Arena tonight. I thought you kept up with all the happenings. I remember a time when you attended every ice show around town that you could find.'' *That is, before you became so enthralled with your sponsor,* she finished for him in her thoughts.

Brent didn't have to voice his boorish thoughts. The implication was made clear by his tone. He didn't have to tell her what she already knew—that she shouldn't have gotten herself so hung up on Kenneth Maxwell Jr. With her future destined for brightness, she shouldn't be emotionally hung up on any man, Brent had told her. It was too late for that bit of advice. And she wasn't going to beat herself up about it. She wouldn't change her circumstances if she could, nor did she want to. Omunique completely ignored her thoughts and Brent's adolescent behavior.

"Speaking of ice shows, I see I'm on the schedule for *Expressions on Ice.* I can't imagine how I forgot that one, since I've participated in it for the last two years.''

"I can,'' came his dry response. Omunique ignored that sarcasm-laced comment, too. "Since you're already working on the program, I don't suppose you'll forget the Christmas show. By the way, Jake should be here in a few minutes. He has choreographed a new routine for you, hoping you might use it in your *Expressions on Ice* performance. In fact, there's Jake now,'' he said, spotting the powerfully built man skating toward them.

"Good morning, you two,'' Jake Neilson greeted, coming to a halt in front of Omunique. "How's our star performer?''

"Hi, Jake. I'm fine, but I'm not so sure about my coach.

He's been giving me the blues,'' she joked, rolling her eyes around.

"Don't listen to her, Jake,'' Brent muttered. "Lately, Nique's been having a hard time staying focused. She's all yours. Maybe you can whip her back into shape before she's too far gone.'' Denying Omunique the chance to respond, Brent skated off.

"What's eating him?'' a curious Jake queried.

Omunique shook her head, chuckling out loud. "It's a long story. A very complicated one.'' She touched Jake's shoulder. "Are you sure men don't have monthly cycles?''

When Jake smiled, the rugged olive skin at the corner of his eyes crinkled. "I'm sure we have some kind of biological screw up, but I think it occurs more than once a month. I'm in a snit at least three to four times a week.'' They laughed hysterically at each other's attempts at racy humor.

"There isn't anything that should prove too difficult for you in the new routine,'' Jake told her when they got their laughter under control. "I choreographed it based on those techniques you're most effective at, and most comfortable executing.''

Jake then took Omunique through the new ice dance program. Over and over again, he coached her on the new routine. Two of the three songs he'd chosen were moderately slow and seductively tantalizing. While Whitney Houston's "I Have Nothing'' enchanted her, she was beside herself with excitement over being able to skate to Toni Braxton's "Breathe Again'' and her more upbeat tune, "Just Another Sad Love Song.''

Omunique loved to show off her modern ice dancing skills. Skating to the Top Forty was the new rage among the latest generation of skaters. The words to "Breathe Again'' mirrored her feelings about Ken. If their love ended, she was sure she'd never breathe again.

"Although you're going to have to practice more diligently on the upbeat tune, I have no doubt that you'll drive the audience wild with your flash dance style.''

"Thanks for the vote of confidence. You know I'll do my best, Jake.''

"Brent knows it, too. Whatever's going on with you two, try not to sweat it. He knows you're one of the world's best figure skaters, Nique."

Brent came over to where she practiced and relieved her earlier than usual, much to her surprise. "You've done enough for today. Don't want you to overtax yourself."

"Thanks, Brent. I could use an early breather. Jake worked these skates today."

"It's my way of rewarding you for a job well done. There are still several kinks in the program that need to be worked out, but I know your tenacity and relentless pursuit of perfection will see you through the most difficult program."

If she puts her full attention on the tasks that lay ahead, she could easily secure a spot on the Olympic team, he thought, looking after her as she skated off the ice. He could see that getting her to stay steadfast to her goals was going to be a major problem as long as Maxwell was entrenched in her life.

It looked to Brent as though Maxwell had dug a permanent haven for himself. Right inside Omunique's heart.

When Omunique came upon the freeway entrance, her desire to see Ken overwhelmed her. Deciding to pay him a surprise visit at his office, she headed the Jeep in the direction of Santa Monica. She could've stayed on Pacific Highway most of the way to her destination, but she didn't want to be bothered with the tedium of traffic lights.

The lively music coming from the radio kept her energy flowing at a high level. She was somewhat tired, but she was too keyed up to rest. The new skating routine was in part responsible for her effervescent mood. Ken was responsible for the laughter that flowed within. He made her realize the truly wonderful benefits that were reaped from laughter. Yes, laughter was definitely an upper. Grateful to find the freeway traffic moving at a steady pace, she relaxed and concentrated on the road.

While looking in the rearview mirror before making a lane change, she noticed a white car tailing her much too closely. She detested tailgaters.

As she moved into the next lane, the white car moved in right behind her. Panic struck a powerful blow to her stomach. Thinking of the safety of others, she decided not to put the pedal to the metal. Besides, she didn't want the driver of the white car to think he or she intimidated her in any way. The windows of the white car were so heavily tinted—a violation of the law—that she couldn't see if the driver was male or female.

When she exited the freeway, the white car followed her down the exit ramp.

As she turned right at the light, the car turned right, too, falling in behind her. *It's just two short blocks to Ken's office,* she thought. *Keep going and see what happens,* she told herself. Without flashing her turn signal, she quickly swerved the Jeep into the parking garage, causing the white car to sail right past her.

Although she knew the parking garage was security patrolled with physical manpower as well as security cameras, the knowledge offered her little comfort. Getting to Ken's office in one piece was uppermost in her mind. Whoever was following her—if in fact she was being followed—was probably annoyed by her quick maneuver. When she saw three women walking toward the elevators, she quickly dashed from the Jeep, sliding into the elevator just as the door started to close. *Safety in numbers,* she thought with relief, glad the three women had happened along.

As her mind shifted gears, she wondered if it was fair to drop in on Ken without prior notice. When the elevator came to a halt on the floor where his offices were located, she dismissed the troubling question from her mind. She was here now, and she desperately wanted to see the smiling face of the man she adored. And she was anxious to see the look on his face when he saw her, hoping it would be a pleasant one.

Taking a deep breath, she exited the elevator and walked the few steps to the office entry. Paranoia had set in again, she noticed. Trying to calm herself, she sucked in a ragged breath and blew it out in a shaky stream.

Thomasina was busy at the computer when Omunique tapped on her desk.

Thomasina turned around. "Hello, Miss Philyaw," she greeted, smiling politely at Omunique. "Are you here to see Ken?"

"Yes, I am. But it's nice to see you again, too. Ken told me he hired you full-time. How do you like working for the Maxwell men?"

Thomasina thought it was kind of funny that Omunique referred to them as the Maxwell men, the same as she did. "They're great to work for. I like my job very much." In spite of the crush she had on Ken, Thomasina couldn't help responding warmly to her rival. "Would you like me to let Ken know you're here? He didn't mention that he was expecting you, Miss Philyaw."

"He isn't. And please call me Nique. I wanted to surprise him. Is it okay if I just pop my head in his office door?"

Thomasina smiled warmly, shrugging her shoulders. "It's okay by me, Nique. He's not with a client." Omunique gave Thomasina the thumbs-up sign as she moved rapidly toward Ken's office and knocked on the door.

She entered on his command. "Hi," she greeted enthusiastically. Surprised but definitely pleased, Ken hurried around the desk and planted a staggering kiss on her mouth.

"Am I dreaming, or what? You *are* a living portrait of God's love. You look wonderful, Princess." He fully appreciated the way her outfit hugged her ballerina figure. How he'd love to be as close to her as the clothing she wore. "Come over here and sit down." Taking her hand, he led her over to the sofa that sat a few yards from his desk.

She sat down beside him and wrapped her fingers around his. "I hope you don't mind my dropping in on you like this.

Brent let me go early, so I thought I'd use the time to pay you a surprise visit.''

He kissed the side of her neck. ''A wise thought, Miss Philyaw. I was beginning to think I had kinetic powers. I've been thinking about you all day, wishing we were off somewhere together.'' He raised an eyebrow. ''Brent must be going soft. What's up with the early out?''

She laughed. ''You make it sound as if I'm in prison. Brent was pleased with the progress I made with a new routine, so he gave me the rest of the day off. Brent's a taskmaster, but he's also fair. What are you working on?''

Grinning, Ken raked his hand through his hair. ''An endorsement contract. One of those athletes with a really big ego! A track star.''

Her smile was smug. ''That comment is going to get you into trouble, yet. All athletes don't have big egos. I know many that are very humble. I'm one of them.''

''You certainly are. That's one of the things I find so refreshing about you. Believe me, I've run into some real egomaniacs in this business. We try to stay clear of those types.''

He stood up. ''I think it's high time you met Max. He's sorry his schedule has kept him so busy. He's been dying to meet you. It's unusual for Max not to meet with the people we sponsor, but it's really been hectic for him.''

Before she could respond, he bent over and stole a quick kiss, which turned into a few lingering ones. When he pulled her to her feet, she clung to him. His potent kisses made her feel feverish all over. As usual, they swept her breath away.

She had to take a moment to catch her breath. ''I'd love to meet your father. Dad holds him in high esteem . . . as he does you. Are you sure we won't disturb him?''

''He'll be disturbed if we don't. But I'll buzz him first to make sure he's free. Can I have another kiss to savor until I make it back over here to you?''

Omunique threw her arms around his neck and offered him her mouth. ''Kiss me, babe,'' she whispered onto his lips.

When he finally did make it back to his desk, he picked up the phone and dialed a two-digit code. "Dad, do you have a few minutes? I'd like to see you."

"Sure, son. I'm never too busy for you. I'll be waiting for you."

"Come on, Princess. He's free."

Ken held the door as she passed through, closing it behind them. They walked a few yards and turned left at the end of the hallway. Without knocking, Ken opened Max's door, allowing Omunique to enter first.

Smiling broadly, Max got to his feet. "No introductions are necessary. I know exactly who this stunning young woman is," Max charmed. "I would know who she was even if we hadn't pursued her for sponsorship. I've seen many pictures of you, sweetheart. Hello, Omunique, it's so nice to see you at last." Max moved swiftly from behind his desk. Face-to-face with Omunique, he embraced her affectionately. "You're even more stunning in person. How's that father of yours?"

"He's doing just fine, Mr. Maxwell. Thanks for asking. I'm happy we're finally meeting, too, although I feel as if I already know you. Dad and Ken often sing your praises."

Max pointed at the lavish reception area located on the far side of the office. "Let's sit right over there and get better acquainted. Please call me Max. Mr. Maxwell makes me feel much older than I am."

While Omunique and Max delved into conversation, Ken filled two ceramic cups with steaming coffee. Remembering that Omunique didn't do coffee, as she'd so smugly put it, he made her a cup of orange-spice tea. Placing the cups on a lacquered tray, he carried it across the room and set it down on an oval shaped coffee table.

In a matter of minutes Omunique felt as though Max had known her all her life. He knew quite a bit about the Philyaw family. She was flattered by his knowledge of her and her numerous skating triumphs. She was sure Wyman had told him a lot of the things he knew. The rest had probably come from research, she guessed, but she was still impressed that he'd retained the knowledge. He certainly knew more about her than his son did on their first meeting. She found Max to be as charming as his son. His genuine warmth and loving smile further endeared him to her.

An important phone call drew Max away from the company he was enjoying so much.

Ken noticed how anxious Max looked when he returned to the reception area. "What is it, Dad? You look worried."

Max sat down and placed his hands on his knees. "Son, I'm afraid you're going to have to represent Maxwell in Seattle. I have to go to Detroit. It's very important to our business that we try to get the Seattle account. That Michigan ball club is ready to sign on the dotted line. We've finally landed the contract."

Ken jumped up as Max's announcement hit home. "That's great! We worked hard for that contract. I can't believe they've finally accepted our bid to design and manufacture their new uniforms. We've been working on this for close to a year now. Congratulations to us!"

Max cleared his throat. "About Seattle, son, you'll have to be there for several days. And you'll have to leave tomorrow." Aware of the danger Omunique had been plagued with, he looked over at her. His eyes seemed to apologize for sending Ken out of town, also knowing what it was like to be young and under the magical spell of love.

When Ken finally caught Max's drift, his excitement died on his lips. How could he go to Seattle and leave her unprotected? He had enough trouble keeping up with her as it was. From what Wyman had told him, the security team struggled with the same problem. Since Max was going to be in Detroit, he was the only man for the Seattle trip. Therefore, security would have to be heightened. It was the only workable solution.

"I'm sorry about this, Princess. I know we had plans for the new gospel play, but we may have to cancel. I promise to make it up to you."

Omunique clicked her tongue. "Don't give it another thought. There will be other gospel plays. I know what it means to have to go on the road. I'm used to this sort of thing. Besides, your business is more important than any play. I'll allow you to make it up to me," she said, flirting with her eyelashes. Ken's eyes told her that he would've leaped to the challenge if Max hadn't been in the room.

"Sorry, kids, this is a tough business we're in. When the eagle flies, we have to be packed and ready for takeoff. Now if you two will excuse me, I have to attend an outside meeting."

Max took Omunique's hands into his, kissing the back of each. "We'll be getting together again, young lady. That's a promise. I just hope we can do it before our Thanksgiving engagement. If not, we'll certainly see one another over the holidays."

"I'm looking forward to it, Max. It was a pleasure meeting you," Omunique cooed, accepting Max's warm hug with open arms.

Max straightened his tie as he left the office. When he winked at his son on his way out the door, Ken knew it was his way of showing his approval of Omunique.

Omunique turned to Ken. "Look, I'd better be going, as well. I'm sure you have a lot of things to take care of before your flight to Seattle. Will you call me tonight?"

Ken frowned. "If you'll let me, maybe I can do one better than that. Why don't I try to get tickets to see the play this evening? We can have dinner at my place afterward."

Omunique smiled, thrilled by his offer. "I don't want you to go to all that trouble, knowing you have to leave town tomorrow. We can do it when you get back."

"Who said it would be any trouble? You just be ready at six. I'll take care of the rest," he commanded, pulling her into his arms for another lingering kiss.

On the way home Omunique wondered why Ken had to come into her life now, of all times. Their schedules would always get in the way of their romance. He'd be here, she'd be somewhere else, so on and so forth. They needed time to nurture their relationship, time to discover hidden secrets, time to lose themselves to the madness of love. He'd come into her life at a time when she needed to concentrate on her goals, at a time when the slightest distraction could be her undoing.

Her thoughts wrapped around the white car. Once the Seattle trip had been announced, she didn't have the heart to tell Ken she thought she'd been followed to his office. He already seemed torn about leaving her alone, and she just couldn't add any more drama to his life—especially when she wasn't sure if she'd truly been followed.

She muttered an oath. "How could something so right be timed so wrong?"

Was it possible she was taking things much too seriously? After all, neither had promised forever. But one thing was for sure—they'd made a promise for tonight, a promise she wasn't about to renege on.

Forgetting about the danger she might be in, when she got out of the Jeep she headed straight for the beach. Several children played along the shoreline, which made her wonder what it would be like to have her own kids—with Ken, of course.

Children would have to come much later in life, she knew. There was no time to raise a family now. When she did become a mother, she wanted to be there for them. She wanted to give them all the things she'd missed out on by not having her mother. A husband, a home, and motherhood were such appealing prospects.

Retracing her steps to the house, she thought about the promised evening that lay ahead. Not wanting to miss out on a second of the time she was about to share with Ken, she rapidly picked up speed.

Chapter Thirteen

Earning rave reviews, *Whose God Shall We Serve?* was the latest black gospel play to burst onto the live stage. Omunique had read the reviews, all favorable, which was one reason she was eager to see it.

Seeing it with Ken was the main reason.

According to the synopsis in the entertainment section of the local Sunday newspaper, the play was about a husband and wife of different religious backgrounds. Before marriage, they'd discussed the possibility of their different beliefs becoming a problem in their marriage, but both felt that their love could overcome all obstacles.

The husband had attended the wife's church for fifteen years, but when he decided to return to the roots of his own faith, a breakdown occurred within the marriage, causing them to become at odds with one another. The wife had never dreamed religious preferences would become a core problem in their marriage. When the controversy continued for months, the wife began to ask herself, Whose God shall we serve? Believing there was only one God, and that man designed denominations, she set out on a mission to find the answer to her burning questions.

The play was scheduled for seven o'clock at the Wilshire Ebell Theater, in Los Angeles. They'd see the play, then have an intimate candlelight dinner at his place. Smiling, she settled down for a much-needed nap.

The alarm, as annoying as it was, was a vital piece of equipment in the Philyaw home. Without it, Omunique would have been late for her own funeral. She slept so soundly that she would've often been late had the clock not been equipped with a dead-waking buzzer. Stretching her hand over to the nightstand, Omunique shut the alarm clock off, leaving on the radio but turning the volume down. Her first coherent thought was of Ken, then of what she'd wear to the play.

After climbing out of bed, she straightened the pink comforter and matching sheets, placing all the sham pillows at the head of the bed. Walking over to the mirrored wardrobe, she slid the door back and took a quick inventory. A teal, washed-silk dress caught her fancy. She pulled it from the rack and removed the clear plastic covering. Fashioned with a shawl collar, the double-breasted dress fell above the knee, and its rich teal color was what she liked most. After hanging the dress on a wall hook, she looked it over closely, making sure there weren't any hard to detect spots on it. Silk was so hard to keep clean, but she loved its feminine softness. Ken loved silk, too. Most of his shirts were made of it.

Although she'd showered before her nap, she went into the bathroom and freshened up, powdering and perfuming her body with a delightful gardenia scent. Before slipping into the silk dress, she searched the shoe store in her closet, smiling when she found her teal suede pumps. Once she'd loosened her French braid, she brushed her hair out vigorously, left it to fall softly below her shoulders, then sprayed on a light oil sheen that left it with a high gloss.

A sudden loud noise caused her to jump. Her heart beating rapidly, a baseball bat in one hand, she cautiously crept out of the bedroom. In the hallway, she stood quietly, listening for any sounds. Hearing nothing unusual, she slowly made her way to the front of the house.

When she saw that the wind had knocked over a lamp, she scolded herself for being careless enough to leave the patio door open. It would take an extremely long ladder to reach the balcony, but when somebody wanted something enough they'd go to any lengths to get it. The balcony did face the beach, so that should pose a problem for someone trying to make an unlawful entry.

Hating herself for being so jittery, she sat down on the sofa and cried, feeling ridiculous. *There haven't been any phone calls for weeks, now, and you can't be sure that the white car was following you. Drivers in California tailgate all the time. You've got to get a grip here, or you're going to have a nervous breakdown.*

At five forty-five the doorbell rang, startling her. She looked at the clock and saw that it was a bit early for Ken. Using caution, she made her way to the front door. Instead of opening the viewing window, she looked out the picture window. The black sports car was there. She sighed, relieved that it was him, and that she was ready to go.

When she opened the door, he immediately took her in his arms. His warm hugs and kisses captivated her and helped to calm her down. Moving slightly away from him, she critiqued his attire. You're looking good in that gray pinstripe suit, Mr. Maxwell.'' She fingered the pink silk shirt he wore. ''Nice threads, my brother,'' she complimented, drinking in the magnificence of his extraordinary physique. He wasted no time voicing his praises for how stunning she looked.

The traffic was good, allowing him to reach the theater in plenty of time to find a great parking space. On the drive into the city, the two of them chatted away like two lovebirds, as if they needed to cram in all the things they wanted to say before Ken left for Seattle.

Ken felt lucky when he found a good parking spot right on

the front row, nearest to the main entrance. He cut the engine, got out of the car, and walked around to open Omunique's door. He couldn't resist kissing her, and she didn't mind. Since food and drink weren't allowed in the theater, Ken ordered a tea and coffee from the catering trucked parked in front of the theater.

While they were sipping the hot drinks, Ken gave Omunique a tentative rundown of his Seattle itinerary. "I'm going to be very busy. The time will pass rather quickly. Then I can get back here to you."

She beamed at his last remark. "I'm going to be busy, too. I'm working hard to perfect a new program. It's all I've been able to think about."

Frowning, Ken raised an eyebrow. "That's *all*?"

Omunique fussed with a loose tendril of her hair. "Well, no." A rivulet of laughter followed her teasing smile. "As the song goes, I only think of you on two occasions—day and night."

He tickled her under the chin and brought her to him for a passionate kiss. "Now that's what I wanted to hear. The sentiment is mutual. You *own* my thoughts, woman. If you want my dreams, you can possess them, too. You know you make me happy, don't you?"

She blushed. "I try to. It works both ways, you know. I always thought I was the happiest person on this planet. Then came you," she said, her voice low and seductive.

He smiled all over. "It's time to go in, but I want to talk more about this subject later. I want to know exactly what happened when I came along."

As the crowd began to move toward the entrance, Ken threw their empty cups into a nearby trashcan. Holding Omunique's hand, he guided her inside to the lobby of the theater, where he purchased programs for souvenirs. He handed one to Omunique, then handed the flashlight-bearing attendant their tickets. While shining her light in the aisle, she led them to their seats, located in the orchestra section.

Omunique shrewdly opted for the aisle seat, knowing she wouldn't be able to see the stage if a tall person sat in front of her. On the aisle, she'd be able to see by looking straight down at the stage. However, she didn't want Ken to know she was a little self-conscious about her height. When he winked at her and laughed, color arose in her cheeks. It appeared that he knew exactly why she'd chosen the aisle seat. She was thoroughly embarrassed, but all she could do was laugh along with him.

As the lights dimmed and the orchestra ceased to play, Omunique shifted to a more comfortable position, keeping her eyes trained on the cast of characters entering from the left side of the stage. Quickly becoming absorbed in the on stage activity, Omunique blocked out all distractions except the handsome one seated next to her. Although she'd gotten pretty comfortable, she leaned over and nestled her head on Ken's broad shoulder. In response, he innocently rested his hand on her right thigh. Smiling, she laid her hand on top of his.

The religious dilemma of the once very happy couple was deeply moving. As the gospel singers belted out a very old tune—''Swing Low, Sweet Chariot,'' classified as an old Negro spiritual—tears formed in Omunique's eyes, along with the flood of sweet memories she had of her grandmother. Ava's angelic voice had been powerful. Though she'd been very young, she could still remember her grandmother singing gospel music while she tended to the chores. Ava, as a member of the church choir, never missed a single rehearsal. The church choir always performed on the first and third Sunday of each month.

Omunique recalled how she could be found fidgeting in her seat as Wyman's tender hands had tried to calm her hyperactivity. But when the choir performed, she'd become pindrop-still. Gospel music had struck a chord deep within her soul. When the choir at First Baptist Church sang, that old building rocked and rolled, she recalled with fondness.

As the curtain fell on the last act, tears streamed from Omunique's eyes. Now she understood why the church members hadn't been able to stay in their seats. During this performance, she hadn't been able to stay in hers, either. In fact, throughout the play, very few people remained seated. The music had been that compelling. Anyone who'd stayed seated, Omunique believed to be half-dead, or just plain lazy.

Everyone was in an excited buzz, as she stood to join the much deserved standing ovation, drying her eyes with the back of her hand, noticing others who did the same, including a number of males. As the theater emptied, Ken and Omunique remained seated.

The story had ended happily. The couple resolved their religious differences by deciding there was only one God. As long as they believed in a power greater than themselves it didn't matter whose church they worshipped in, as long as they kept their eyes focused on God.

Whose God Shall We Serve was a smashing success!

Deeply moved by her tears. Ken put a gentle hand under Omunique's elbow and guided her out to the parking lot. "Now that's what I call a Sunday-go-to-meeting, good old-fashioned time," Ken enthused. "It sure reminded me of many special times we had in our home. I think I'm going to have to see this play again." He already knew Omunique was overcome with joy by her tears.

She became extremely excited. "It was the most compelling play I've ever seen. I'd like to see it again, too. Thanks for working it all out. The play might not have been the same for me had you not been here with me. I'm glad we saw it together."

He took the liberty of kissing her passionately. "You're more than welcome, Princess. I don't think it would've been the same for me, either."

As much as she was going to miss Ken, his going out of town wouldn't be such a bad thing. She needed to refocus, to reclaim her seemingly dwindling drive and determination, to put everything back into proper perspective. Love was grand, but it wouldn't win her a gold medal. Without a medal-winning performance, she could all but forget her own ice arena.

Dead tired, Omunique fell asleep in the car only minutes after Ken pulled out of the parking lot. She'd trained harder and longer than she should have, she'd told Ken before nodding off. She was determined to master the new program by the set deadline, and she'd be right back at it in the early morning hours.

By the time Omunique and Ken arrived at his place he was overly anxious to be alone with her. They'd had such an incredible time that he'd just about forgotten his untimely departure schedule. Although he'd arranged for heightened security, it didn't bring him much solace.

Sudden thoughts of her all alone had scared him colorless. His face looked pale and drawn when he opened the front door to the condo and switched on the lights.

Worry touched her eyes when she noticed the grayish tone of his skin. "Are you okay?" she asked, feeling his forehead for sign of a fever. "I always thought we'd die the same color we were born, but you look positively gray, Ken. However, you don't feel hot."

Masking his fear, he grabbed her around the waist, hugging her so hard she thought he'd break her in half. "I'm hot, all right—hot for you."

She wriggled from the grip of steel. "You don't know your own strength, do you?"

Tenderly, he hugged her again. "Sorry, beautiful."

Ken directed her into the living room, sat down on the sofa, then pulled her down beside him. "I hate to admit this, but thinking about you being all alone has me a little panic-stricken. In fact, I can't even stand to think about it. Are you going to be okay?"

She lazed her finger down the side of his face. "I'll be just fine. All the bad stuff is over," she tried to assure, though she wasn't sure herself. There was no use upsetting him by telling him someone might be following her, not when he had important business to tend to. She wasn't going to be the cause of him losing a deal worth millions. "I've also gotten used to being alone again. You know we have an alarm system. I just have to keep reminding myself to turn it on when I'm inside the house. I remember being scared all the time when Dad first moved out, especially at night. Now I just pray and go to sleep. Everything is going to be fine. You'll see.''

"I'm sorry, Princess. I don't know what I'm thinking about here.''

"I do. You were thinking about getting me into bed,'' she charged sweetly, trying to lighten his mood. That was all she could think of herself. Though she would love to, she just couldn't bring herself to tell him that all day she'd hoped they'd end the evening by making love. They'd only made love twice, and she wanted to feel those magnificent feelings over and over again. Since that early morning he hadn't attempted to make love to her again, which made her wonder if she'd really satisfied him. *Chill,* she scolded. *He's still here, isn't he?*

Laughing at her very much on target observation, Ken buried his lips in the soft crease of her neck. "Hungry?''

"Famished.''

He got to his feet. "Good. Go to the table while I get the food warmed up. I have to be careful about dining with you. I'm starting to lose weight. All this low-cal food is taking its toll on me.'' He pulled his shirt out of his dress slacks. "Look, you can see my ribs.'' Omunique laughed as he disappeared into the kitchen.

Moisture sprang to her eyes when she looked at the dining room table. It was so beautiful. He'd pulled out all the finery. How had he managed to work all day, cook, and set a lovely table, all before he'd picked her up? *And on time,* she marveled.

A tiny, foil-wrapped package sat in the center of one of the expensive looking china plates. Should she open it, or wait for him to present it to her? she wondered, feeling breathless. The accompanying card did have her name on it. For several seconds she looked back and forth between the package and the kitchen entry, wishing he'd hurry up and return. Unable to wait another second, she picked up the package and unwrapped it, only to put it back down. She would read the card first.

To My One and Only Ice Princess; the kind of ice that never melts. Love, Ken.

"Oh my God, he didn't go there, did he?" she whispered, thinking it might be an engagement ring. It was much too soon for that. Wasn't it?

Before she could open the box, Ken came back into the room carrying a white china bowl, which he placed on the table. "Go ahead and open it, Omunique. I thought I'd given you enough time to do so. It's just a small token of my love for you."

Smiling, she opened the tiny box. Gasping with delight, she picked up the gold ice skate charm by the delicate link at the top. Set in the blade, four rows of crusted diamonds sparkled like midnight stars. Tears swam in her eyes, and a lump arose in her throat as she kissed him softly on the mouth.

She swallowed hard. "It's so delicate. I love it. I have two empty spaces on my charm bracelet. One is for the replica of the gold medal . . . now I have something to fill the other space. Standing on tiptoe, she kissed him tenderly. "Thank you so much."

She had mixed emotions over the absence of an engagement ring. Nonetheless, the symbolic gift touched her deeply. Even Wyman hadn't ever thought of giving her an ice skate charm; win or lose, he did present her with a small token after each and every one of her performances. She kissed Ken again, wondering how much the charm had cost. The diamonds alone had to be worth a small fortune. Taking the charm from her hand, he placed it back in the box, then set it aside.

Gathering her against his chest, he drank deeply from the sweet nectar of her inviting mouth. He didn't know what to do now—set out to seduce her, or set the rest of the food out. The feel of her firm flesh beneath his hands sent electric tremors through him, and the sweetness of her lips enraptured him.

Somehow she found the strength to push him away, giving

him a bewitching smile. "I don't know about you, but I'm still famished. I just might have to devour you if you don't hurry up and feed me, boy," she menaced, using a Caribbean accent.

"That isn't such a bad idea, girl." Laughing, he wiped his brow. "Sit down, little girl. Papa has just what you need." He pulled out her chair and waited for her to be seated before retreating to the kitchen.

When he returned he placed a huge lobster tail on her plate, along with a small vessel of drawn butter. She watched him in adoration as he darted in and out of the kitchen, making several trips before he sat down to join her. They both bowed their heads as he passed a blessing on the food.

Omunique didn't waste any time digging into the well-prepared feast. The vegetables, tender but crunchy, were cooked just the way she liked them. As she buttered a half a slice of sourdough bread, the melted butter trickled down her fingers. Sensuously, he licked them clean. While he gently nipped at her fingertips, she felt a moist heat on her inner thighs, making it difficult for her to concentrate on eating. As hard as it was to get through the rest of the meal, she finally polished it off. When would he stop testing her resolve? *Hopefully never,* came the whispered response of her heart.

Ken began clearing the table. When he carried the dishes into the kitchen, she followed along behind him and sat on a nearby stool. Refusing to allow her to help, he busied himself, stacking the dishwasher.

While watching him work, the obviously expensive gift weighed heavily on her mind. It had cost way too much, she guessed. "Ken," she began, "I really love the gold charm, but I'm having second thoughts about keeping it," she uttered, hoping he didn't think her ungrateful. He turned around and looked at her, a dubious expression crossing his handsome face.

"Why?'

"It's so expensive! I'm afraid I'm very frugal when it comes to spending. Dad had to scrape for every single dime, and he taught me to respect the value of a penny before moving on to the nickel. There are so many people who don't have anything . . . sometimes I feel guilty for having so much, though it hasn't always been that way. Do you understand what I'm trying to say? Please don't think I'm ungrateful.''

He sat down on one of the other stools and swiveled it around to face her. ''I understand, Princess, but I gave you the gift, and I can afford it. Max worked hard, too. As a black man he had so many obstacles shoved in his way, but, like Wyman, he was able to tough it out. He accepted jobs that a lot of black men wouldn't even consider today. But for Max, feeding his family came before pride.

''In fact, in those days a man had to set his pride aside entirely, but that didn't mean he wasn't proud. Max is one of the proudest black men I know. And he's taught me to be proud. I'm not a poor man, Princess,'' he said with much humility. ''I earned it the hard way. I've never been scared of a hard day's work.''

Omunique rocked back on the stool. ''I know about being proud. If Wyman hadn't taught me to stand up for myself, my rights, to be the best at whatever I set my sights on, I might have allowed those who thought a black girl had no place on the ice chase me away. I decided a long time ago that my place is wherever I choose, as long as I'm not infringing on the rights of others.''

He grinned, kissing her cheek. ''As it should be, Nique.''

''Getting back to the gift, Ken. Do you understand why I'm anxious over it?''

''I do, but if I were you I wouldn't worry about what I paid for it. This conversation has proved to me how much you'll truly appreciate it. Will you keep it?''

She smiled brightly. ''There's no way I can turn it down now. Knowing we have many of the same values is comforting. I'll wear it with pride.'' Once she rewarded his extravagant generosity with a sweet kiss, she told him she was going to go into the living room so he could finish up his tasks. She was in a hurry to have his undivided attention.

Lazily, she stretched, looking around for somewhere comfortable to lay her head. The rug in front of the fireplace was plush enough. Fondly, she thought of the times she and Ken had curled up in front of a toe-warming fire. Grabbing a loose pillow from the sofa, she dropped down to the floor and pulled the pillow under her head.

Finished with his chores, Ken walked into the living room. Finding her curled up in front of the unlit fireplace, he quietly studied her ballerina figure, his eyes dancing with sheer delight.

Dropping to the floor, he curled up behind her and pulled her hips back against his throbbing sexuality. While brushing her hair with his fingers, he trailed kisses along her jawbone, and upward to her temple. The throbbing intensified as he gyrated against her firm buttocks while rubbing his hands up and down her hips. Pushing her hair aside, he teased the column of her neck with moist, tissue-soft kisses.

Turning over on her side, she pressed herself against him. Drawing his lower lip between her teeth, she nipped gently, her flattened palm journeying across his muscled thigh. Reaching around to his buttocks, she pulled him in closer to the core of her growing need.

His hands spiraled up under her sweater and undid the front clasp of her bra. Cupping a satiny mound of firm flesh in his palm, his thumb and forefinger tweaking a pebble-hard nipple, he drew a strangled gasp from deep within her throat. The crisp jeans he'd changed into were much too tight for her to maneuver over his hips on her own. Releasing her for a moment, he wriggled out of them, then removed most of her attire.

As the growing friction torched the heat of their passion, white cotton briefs connected torridly with foam-green silk bikinis. Boldly, Omunique enclosed her hand around his need, stroking and squeezing him with a tenderness that sweetly tortured his loins. Drowning in intoxicating sensations, yet unafraid of them, she allowed Ken to cover her like a second skin.

Their breathing quickened with every fiery caress. When his

lips claimed her inner thigh, she didn't think she could take any more, but he proved her wrong—she could take all night if he offered it. When she guided him inside of her, something he would've never expected from the morally correct Ice Princess, it thrilled him senseless. Omunique kept him intrigued with delicious surprises, and he loved every one of them. He loved her more than he'd ever thought he could ever love anyone.

As he slowly moved over her, her fingers splayed across the taut muscles of his flat abdomen, then moved down to tangle in the soft, curly hair that surrounded his maleness. His slow pullback movements afforded her the opportunity to explore his tender spots more thoroughly. Uneducated in all the ways to please a man, she relied on the urgent callings of her love-starved body to guide her path.

Before he could launch the next arresting thrust, she raised her hips up to meet his breadth with a few power thrusts of her own. They were soon unable to keep from responding to their body's demand for utter fulfillment. Their movements grew intense, causing their needs to rival. As their explosive eruption arrived simultaneously, spreading through them like wildfire on a parched hillside, frantically, they screamed out each other's names.

Rolling over on his back, he pulled her into his arms and drizzled lazy kisses on her swollen lips. "Stay with me tonight," he requested, his voice low and husky.

Her smile dazzled him. "I was hoping you'd ask," she cooed, her eyes sparkling with unbridled passion. An urgent need to possess her again tugged at his insides. The thought of not seeing her for several days caused him to respond wantonly to the pressing demands of his uncontrollable longing.

The alarm clock sounded much too soon for Ken. He slammed his hand down over it, disarming it before Omunique could be disturbed. He looked at the almond-brown hair tumbled in disarray, marveling at the nakedness scorching his composure. Amazed that Omunique had chosen him to be her first lover ever, he laughed inwardly, feeling he was the luckiest man on the planet. Of all the men in the world she had chosen him.

He tried to imagine life without her, something he never wanted to contend with. He grew somber when he thought of Wyman's security team sitting outside all night. He tried to imagine what their thoughts had been when she failed to come out of the building. Of course, they knew she was safe with him. According to Wyman, he'd put Ken's name and address on the security list.

It was so unjust that she would be tailed like a common criminal, but it was necessary. As far as he was concerned, Omunique wasn't taking this as seriously as she should. Maybe it was all over, as she'd expressed earlier. But why had it begun in the first place? No one seemed to have the answers.

He was well aware of the many popular sports figures and other celebrities who were plagued with the same injustice. Celebrities paid a high price for the spotlight. What would happen when Omunique won the gold? Chilling visions made him flinch. After seeing her performances it was no longer an "if" question. She'd probably become an unwilling target for every unscrupulous journalist in the country, along with every misguided idiot who owned a camera of some sort. Would their relationship crack under the pressure? he wondered, unprepared to entertain any kind of response to that question.

When had the world become so violent, so uncaring, and impersonal? Tabloids were another form of injustice, often printing bitter lies, not caring who got hurt. Didn't they realize celebrities had families and friends who got hurt along with their loved ones? Sure, there were those who sought that type of sick attention, for one reason or another, but Omunique Philyaw wasn't one of them, and would never become one.

Quietly, he slipped out of bed and disappeared into the bathroom.

Expecting to cuddle up to the warmth of his lithe body, Omunique turned over on her back, disappointed to find his space empty. Opening one smoky-gray eye, she looked over at the spot he'd occupied all night long. Stretching her arm out, she touched the still warm spot, wondering how she was going to get through the next several days. He'd be in Seattle, and she'd be home alone with three days off. Of course, she would work on the skating program, but at the moment the idea wasn't very appealing.

"Princess," he called out as he rapidly closed the distance between them and slid in next to her. "Did you miss me?"

She drew his head into the well of her arm, and he snuggled against her breast. "Take a wild guess," she responded drowsily, kissing him to show just how much.

Both fearful of touching on the subject of his leaving town, they lay in silence. Unable to draw any closer, without exercising the ultimate in closeness, they held one another, wishing the clock could come to a complete standstill for the next seven or eight years.

Omunique remembered something an old friend, Elester Latham, had told her: Time was the world's largest bank, only a fool would ask it for a loan. Time sailed on, something neither of them could control. Had control been possible, they would seal time in a bottle and launch it into the mysterious depths of the sea in hopes of later retrieval—much, much later.

Ken shifted his position and laid her head on his chest, stroking the length of her glossy hair. "I have to pack," he uttered regrettably, shuddering at what those words really meant. *I have to leave you. We have to be apart for a while.* Then it came to him. If they couldn't borrow time, why couldn't they just steal it? "Come to Seattle with me?"

She looked up at him, her eyes bright with a meaning he couldn't interpret. "I can't." A broken sob wrenched free of her lips.

As her body twitched against him, he felt her struggling to control her emotions. "Can't, or won't?"

"Both," she countered firmly, without an explanation. There simply wasn't one. Sensing that the subject of her going to Seattle was a dead issue, he turned on his side, drawing her full against him. Slipping his tongue past her even white teeth, he tried to find comfort in what little time they did have left. Whether it was freely given, taken, or stolen, time marched on.

Ken climbed out of bed. Feeling miserable, he just stood there, looking down on her. Her eyes were closed, but he knew she wasn't asleep. He saw the tears that rolled downward across her cheek. Bending over, he kissed the salty liquid away. He then made a hasty retreat toward the bathroom.

She heard the shower teeming full blast, wanting so much to join him under the steamy water, but he hadn't asked.

As though he'd somehow read her mind, he appeared before her, stretching his hand out for her to take. In slow motion, she slid across the bed and reached for his extended hand. Lifting her in his strong arms, he carried her into the bathroom and into the downpour of steamy rain. Before bathing one another, they made love, completely oblivious to the stinging torrent pounding against their naked flesh. . . .

Chapter Fourteen

With the exception of one very lonely figure skater, the ice was deserted. Filling the mammoth arena with its gentle seduction, ''Breathe Again'' floated out from the sound system. Ken had been away less than twenty-four hours, but to Omunique it seemed as if a decade had passed. Losing herself to the only other lover she'd ever known, Omunique engaged the ice in a tantalizing slow dance, moving over its polished smoothness with quiet deliberation. In perfect harmony with the tempo of the music, the sweet rhythms of her body guided her through the inspiring routine. Imagining a full house, she performed for the silent audience like the brilliant champion she aspired to be.

When ''I Have Nothing'' impressively serenaded her ears, a haze appeared in her eyes as she transcended time and space and moved into the exosphere of her own creative mind. She simply wouldn't have heard the cheers and applause had there been a live audience. Omunique had been transported to a world of musical magic. She could hear only the sounds of her skates, the rhythms of her body, and the words of the song that somehow seemed to be sympathetically tuned into her being out of touch with the world. While she was turning, spinning, jumping, her delicate hands and emoting eyes spun the saga of a woman in love, a woman who had nothing if the man she loved was lost to her forever. . . .

As she hearkened to the words of the song, she interpreted its meaning in her own way, translating it to the silent audience through the extraordinary language of her seductively swaying body and hands. Her body appeared weightless as she spiraled through the arena like a gusty, wintry wind.

Yes, he could share her life. No, she wouldn't change her colors for him. Yes, he could take her love, nor would she ask for too much in return—just all that he was, and everything that he did. No, she didn't want to have to look much further, or go where he wouldn't follow, came her inward response to the song's soulful lyrics.

The funky sort of cha-cha beat of the tune "Another Sad Love Song" transformed her into a sultry seductress, in by far the most challenging number she'd have to master. The ice show was only a few short weeks away, but Brent had assured her that if she wasn't comfortable with the new routine by then she could use an old standby.

By the time a group of kids showed up for a late afternoon skating lesson, Omunique could barely move another muscle, which made her think of what she could've been doing instead of burning herself out on the ice, physically and emotionally. She could be in Seattle with the extremely handsome and very sexy man she couldn't get out of her head. Although he would've been busy during the day, they could've shared the cool Seattle evenings. When totally alone, they could've further explored their dreams and each other's fascinating minds and warm bodies. She somehow got the feeling they'd never stop discovering all the magical things that existed between them.

"Hey, little girl," Andy Tarpley, the head maintenance technician, called out to her from the exit railing. "You sure know how to tell an awesome story on those skates of yours, a very romantic one at that," he complimented, his sable-brown eyes soft with tenderness.

In charge of arena maintenance, Andy kept the ice in perfect condition. At sixty, he still had a head full of smoked-silver curls. Wrinkle-free, his skin was the color of finely aged cognac. His medium frame, physically fit, boasted a healthy diet and plenty of exercise.

A shadow of a smile teased the corners of her mouth as she skated toward Andy. Omunique leaned over the railing and placed her delicate hand in his large, rough one. "Thanks, Mr. Tarpley. I always appreciate your comments. When I've evoked this type of response from you, I know I'm on the right track. How Mrs. Tarpley?"

He snorted. "Well enough to spend my hard-earned money," he drawled in a heavy Southern accent. "Tell me, what do you womenfolk do in them shopping malls for hours on end? Claretha has a new career. Shopping. I cancelled all that plastic money, but do you think that stopped her? Nooo. 'I'll just put it on layaway,' she said in that haughty, sistertude way."

Omunique laughed until tears rolled down her cheeks. Andy had moved his head in what Frank referred to as sister-girl-head-action, putting her in stitches. Trying to contain her laughter, she stretched across the railing and gave Andy a tender hug. "It's going to be all right. You two have been married for thirty-seven years. If you've put up with it all this time, there's a good chance you'll put up with it another thirty-seven."

"If we live that long," he countered, smiling. "But you're right, I wouldn't give up that woman for all the peanuts in Georgia, and you know how I love my peanuts. I'm going to mosey on, now . . . I got work to do. You keep going the way you're going, girl, you're not just going to find yourself on that Olympic team, you're going to be the smack dab center of it. Stay grounded, honey."

* * *

Feeling like something the cat dragged in, Omunique tiredly carried herself into the bedroom and fell across the bed. The second her head hit the pillow the phone rang. Although she hadn't received any threatening phone calls of late, she was hesitant. When she heard the sultry voice of the man whose handsome face loomed in front of her at every turn, her fears quickly dwindled, her energy miraculously restored. "Ken, I'm so excited to hear your voice. How's Seattle?"

"Hectic," came his weary reply as he stood at a payphone in a restaurant. "I miss you, Princess. I thought I was the one who was dead tired, but you sound extremely fatigued. What have you been doing with yourself?"

"What I do best, sweetie, but I'm afraid I may have overdone it. I've been working on my new routine since early this morning. I shouldn't work out on my days off, but then again, I'm so much further ahead than I would've been. I love this new program. Jake is wonderful!"

Jealousy stabbed him right in the center of his heart. "Jake? Who's Jake?"

Though flattered by the jealousy she heard in his tone, she never wanted to do anything to make him feel that particular emotion. It wasn't a good feeling. She propped her head on a pillow. "I thought I had mentioned him to you before. He's my choreographer."

Ken smiled. "In that case, I guess he needs to be wonderful. Otherwise he shouldn't be working with you. You're wonderful, too, you know."

"I am, aren't I? But you wouldn't think that if you could see me. I look and feel like yesterday's garbage."

"Girl, if I could see you, I doubt that I'd be thinking at all. You *do* have that type of power over me, Miss Philyaw. Listen, I talked to Frank this morning and he suggested that you have dinner with him and Marion this evening. They even offered to pick you up. What do you think?"

She moaned. "That I'm very tired. However, I don't want your friends to think I'm snobbish. After a short nap, I should be just fine."

"No, no. I don't want you to do anything you're not up to. They'll understand if you're too tired to go out this evening. Maybe you can go another night, Princess."

"That might be best. Tell them I'll make it up to them. Do you have any idea how much I miss you, Mr. Maxwell?"

He grinned. "I'm starting to, but I miss you more. Have you heard from your Dad?"

"He called last night. He really became anxious about me when he learned you were out of town. Aunt Mamie invited me to come and stay with her. I didn't go last night, but I'm seriously considering going tonight." *Why flirt with danger? And why stay alone, when there are places I'd feel safe?*

Ken was puzzled by what she'd said about Wyman. Before leaving town, he'd talked to him. He had called Wyman to inform him that he'd arranged for the security around Omunique to be tightened. Maybe it was Wyman's way of protecting his involvement in deceiving her.

"That sounds like a good idea, Nique. I'm sure she would love the company."

"What are you going to do this evening. Ken?"

He groaned loudly. "I have a business dinner at seven-thirty. Old Mr. Warner is a trip. If Max is correct, he'll try to take me to one of those topless bars he loves to frequent. At seventy-three years old, he's still hanging out in bars. Must be a lonely man."

"And if he does?" Omunique queried, her tone suspicious. "If he does what?"

"Try to take you to a topless bar," she responded with indignation. When Ken laughed, the delicious sound of it made her tingle all over, making her miss him all the more.

"Well, I'll have to go. Then I'll have to suffer through the night watching a bunch of size fifty-two DS dirty dance with a pole."

"Oh, how horrible that will be for you," she quipped. "You have my deepest sympathy. While you're there just remember what you have waiting at home for you. A fool and his woman will eventually part company."

He laughed. "I love it when you act like a jealous she cat. All joking aside, I won't be going to any sleazy bar."

"I haven't the faintest idea why, but I feel a smile coming on."

"Good. You get some rest now. And don't worry about me playing host at some freaky breast convention. I know exactly what's waiting for me at home . . . and I can't wait to get back to her. I'll talk with you later tonight. "I love you," he breathed with longing.

"I . . . I'll be waiting for your call." She'd almost told him she loved him, too, she realized. She did, but just didn't know why she couldn't bring herself to tell him.

"Omunique," he shouted before she disconnected, "before I go out, I'll call Frank and tell him you can't make it."

"Why don't you just give me Frank's office number and I'll make the call. That way, you can spend your long distance phone money talking to me."

"Aren't you the thoughtful one? Keep me on your mind, Princess." Before hanging up, he gave her Frank's home and office numbers. She had barely drawn her next breath when the phone rang again.

"It's me again, Princess. I forgot to give you the phone number at my hotel. Call if you need anything, or nothing at all." She wrote down the phone number and his room number. After a brief exchange of words, he rang off, promising to call again later.

Once she'd called Frank, Omunique made herself comfortable in bed. A few minutes later, feeling restless, she picked up the latest issue of *Ebony*. She thumbed through it for a while, then got up and went into the kitchen.

After removing a can of low-salt chicken noodle soup from the pantry, she opened it and poured it into a saucepan, then set it on the burner and turned the gas flame on. While waiting for the soup to heat, she grabbed a box of Ritz crackers and carried it over to the table. Before she could sit down, the phone bell jingled.

"Are you free this evening, Nique?" Brent asked. "We need to talk."

Omunique sighed wearily. "Is it something, that can wait until morning? I'm eating now, then I'm going to Aunt Mamie's for the night. I want to get there before dark."

Brent heard the impatience in her voice. "I see. Nique, there are some matters we need to discuss. I see things in your performance that concern me. I've talked to you about this on several occasions, but I don't see much improvement. I'll let you off the hook this evening, but first thing in the morning we're having this conference."

Omunique snorted. "Okay, Brent. I'll stop by your office before I go to the locker room. See you." Not bothering to wait for his response, she cradled the receiver. "Great! Just what I need—another long, boring lecture on the pitfalls of dating while in training. Enough is enough, is enough," she lamented. *Isn't Brent ever going to stop this?* she wondered, feeling a bad mood coming on. She just couldn't believe his antiquated way of thinking.

Was it possible Brent just plain didn't like Ken? She knew there wasn't any valid reason for him to dislike Ken, especially since Ken had gone to great lengths to deal with the issue of her dating her sponsor. He had completely pulled himself out of the business end of their relationship, turning it back over to Max. She'd never been seriously involved with anyone before now, so she had no way of knowing if Brent would've reacted to someone else in the same manner. He'd been downright rude to Ken when he'd officially met him after the charity benefit. It was so unlike Brent.

It seemed as if Brent had turned into an ogre overnight. She didn't like his new personality at all, but she couldn't afford to lose him as her coach, nor did she want to. Therefore, she'd have to find a way to make everyone happy. *Good luck,* she told herself.

Omunique walked down the hall to the bedroom that served as an office, where she pulled from the filing cabinet a green file folder and carried it back to her bedroom. After situating herself in the middle of the bed, she opened the folder and perused its contents. The folder contained handwritten notes regarding the ice arena she hoped for. Hope wasn't enough to make the arena a reality, she knew. She had to work hard, and come up with a good marketing plan. She also needed financial backing, which meant writing a darn good proposal.

Endorsement contracts and television commercials, among other marketing endeavors, would help her accumulate the funds she'd need to build an arena, or buy an existing one. Purchasing such a real estate holding would take tons of money, but she wasn't averse to leasing an existing site, the right one, in the right community. Easy access to the arena was a must, due to the existing transportation problems in the inner cities. Another problem was finding figure skaters to work in the arena. There were very few figure skaters from the Southern California area, which meant advertising in major newspapers all across the country.

Omunique rocked herself back and forth as she envisioned realizing her dream. She could see it all so clearly, but she didn't have any illusions about it being an easy feat. It would be awfully difficult, but she felt confident her goals could be attained with a workable plan if she worked hard and stayed focused. Before any of her dreams could be realized she had to give that medal-winning performance, she reminded herself.

As impatience and irritation flashed in his autumn-gold eyes, Ken lightly drummed his fingers on the hardwood table, located in the hotel dining room. Bored beyond comprehension, he listened to Nelson Warner drone on and on about his flashy cars, tight-dressed women, and his I-can-get-it-anytime-I-want-it sex life. Hoping he'd get back to his room before it would be too late to even think of phoning Omunique, Ken furtively glanced at his watch.

At seventy-three, Nelson Warner was an amazing fireball who possessed an incredible amount of energy, which had nothing to do with Geritol. His once gray hair was now dyed a dark brown, and it looked pretty good on him. Nelson owned a huge portion of a major league baseball team.

Nelson picked up his full glass of Chablis, raised it up, and took a long swallow. "This is my fountain of youth." Watching him closely, Ken saw that his pale blue eyes had turned brick red. "Now ... let's ... get back ... to business." Nelson slurred. "Son, I like you," he patronized. "I liked you the first time we met. I think we can do a lot of business together. That sly fox you call Dad is one hell of a businessman. I'm sorry he couldn't make it to Seattle this time around."

"Max sends his sincere regrets, Mr. Warner. He was looking forward to this meeting. But I can assure you that your business will be handled properly."

"I have no doubts about you, young man," Nelson flattered knowingly. "However, do you think you can rework those figures we've been discussing?"

Ken thoughtfully pondered the question though he'd already made up his mind, then looked the older gentleman straight in the eye. "Sir, those figures are bottom line dollars. You're not going to find anyone willing to go any lower. If you can find a company able to offer the same quality of service, I suggest you award them the contract. If we went any lower we'd be working for free. Maxwell is in business for profits, not losses."

Ken smiled wryly. "Let me ask you something, Mr. Warner." Nelson nodded. "If Max were here, would you have asked him the same question you just asked me?"

Nelson's complexion turned a brighter shade of red. "Probably not," he answered honestly. "But you see, I had to try you. That's the way it is. Hell, if you can cut a better deal, cut it. I know a lot of young men who would've let me get away with it.'' He took another swig of his drink. ''They would've cut the deal just to get my business, figuring they'd get me good the next time out, not stopping to think that there might not be a next time. I'm glad to see you can't be sucked in. Max has taught you well. Be at my office at eight A.M. We'll go over all the details then. Now, what do you say to going over to Time Out to mingle with a few of those pretty hostesses?''

Ken could barely keep from laughing. Nelson Warner was just another filthy rich, dirty old man. And he'd had the nerve to call Max a sly fox. ''Thanks for asking, sir, but I've got a beautiful young woman expecting a phone call from me.'' Smiling, Ken got to his feet and picked up the tab.

Nelson removed the bill from his hand. ''This is on me, son. You run along and call your little lady. I hope she knows she got herself a respectable young man.''

''She does, Mr. Warner. She does. Thanks for everything.'' After shaking Nelson's hand, Ken made a hasty departure, grateful they'd had dinner in the dining room of his hotel.

Ken let himself into the room, then emptied his pockets and laid his keys and loose change on the nightstand. Unable to wait another second to hear Omunique's voice, Ken sat on the side of the bed and dialed her number. When he got the answering machine, he left a message so as not to alarm her with a hang up.

He then dialed Mamie Gordon's home number, smiling when Mamie answered. ''Hello there, Ms. Gordon. It's Kenneth Maxwell. How are you?''

''Hello, Kenneth.'' she responded, sounding wide awake. ''I'm doing just fine.''

''I know it's late. I hope I haven't disturbed you, but I just returned from a business dinner. Has Nique made it there yet?''

''Now, why did I think you called here to talk to me?'' she teased. ''Yes, she's here, but she's sound asleep. She was so tired when she arrived I insisted on her going straight to bed. I promised to wake her up when you called. If you'll hold on, I'll get her for you.''

"I don't think we should wake her. She was really tired when I talked to her earlier. I'll call her in the morning. You young ladies take care of each other. I know Omunique thinks her troubles are over, but please warn her to be cautious. The person who's responsible for turning her life inside out is unpredictable. Goodnight," he said, hiding the disappointment he felt at not being able to speak to the woman who held his heart in her hands.

Raking his hand through his hair, he looked around the room, feeling an overpowering emptiness. Decorated in autumn colors, the room wasn't all that spectacular, but it was comfortable and the furnishings were of good quality. Had Omunique been with him he would've surrounded her in the lap of luxury, but when alone all he needed was somewhere clean and comfortable to lay his head.

A round table and four leather armchairs sat in one corner of the room. A king-size bed covered in an awning stripe bedspread was in the center of the room. Matching drapes hung from the windows and sliding glass door. A desk and two nightstands completed the mediocre decor. A small balcony overlooking the ocean was the room's best feature.

Ken was tired, but he knew that if he got into bed all he would do was toss and turn. Taking the laptop computer from its case, he sat down at the desk and began working on the figures for his early morning meeting with Nelson Warner.

He worked diligently until midnight, and his fingers ached from punching in the computer codes. After shutting the computer down, he placed it back in its case. He turned the television on, only to turn it off a few seconds later.

He walked into the bathroom, where he turned on the shower, stripped himself bare, then installed himself under the brisk flow of hot water. As the hot water filled the room with steam, steamy memories of the fiery shower he'd taken with Omunique on their last night together made a willing prisoner of him. Suddenly, anxiety tore at his peace of mind with an uneasiness that had him worried as he lathered his body. He was a man who listened to his inner voice and acted on natural instinct; his instincts seemed to warn him of impending danger. *But to whom?* he asked himself as he dried off. Was the danger to him, or Omunique? He prayed to God that it wasn't the latter as he dialed the office number of the security supervisor on duty.

A few minutes after his conversation, satisfied that everything was okay in California, he knelt down in a prayer of thanks. Still a little worried and concerned, refreshed but lonely, he climbed into bed. Though he tried hard to fight it, sleep apprehended him the moment his head hit the pillow.

Since it was much too early for even the birds to be awake, Omunique decided not to disturb Aunt Mamie. Quietly, she slipped out of the house, jumped into the Jeep, then backed it out of the driveway. Turning left at the corner, she headed the car in the direction of the ice arena. It was only five in the morning, but Omunique had been awake since three.

Disturbed and disappointed that Ken hadn't bothered to keep his promise of calling back, she took it out on the gas pedal, sailing the car through the darkened streets at an alarming rate of speed. She really had no way of knowing for sure if he'd called or not, because she hadn't spoken to Aunt Mamie since she'd arrived at her home the previous night, she had to admit.

About to make a turn, she looked in her rearview mirror and immediately noticed a car a good distance behind her. A tense fear chewed at her insides as she pressed down harder on the gas pedal. If she were being followed, they'd pick up speed, as well, she guessed. When the car disappeared out of view, her breath tumbled from her in one huge gush. As she got to the arena parking lot, a car pulled into another entrance—it appeared to be the same car. Fear and rage filled her at the same time.

As though she had lost her ability to reason, she jabbed the gas pedal into the floor. Catching up to the car, she swerved perilously in front of it, cutting off any path for escape. To avoid a collision, the driver brought the car to a screeching halt.

Omunique jumped out of the Jeep, ran over to the other car, and started pounding on the driver's window. When she saw there were two men in the car, one white, one black, her reasoning abilities quickly returned. Before she could turn around and run back to her car, one of the men loomed right in front of her, appearing larger than life.

She screamed, but it was soundless. With her body trembling, she backed away from the tall, stocky black stranger. "Why . . . why . . . are you . . . following me?" she asked, shaking like a leaf, her voice only carrying half of its normal strength.

The man seemed to be at a loss for words. He couldn't believe that she'd been brave enough to jump out of her car and confront strangers this way. The terror in her racking sobs tore through him like a dull razor blade. "Miss . . . Philyaw," he began . . .

He must be the stalker, she thought, *he knows my name.* Her breath now came in short gasps. Then hysterical screams came forth, drowning him out. The man felt so sorry for the terrified young woman he knew he had to do something to calm her down. Otherwise, she was going to suffer serious trauma.

"I'm not here to hurt you, Miss Philyaw. I'm here to protect you," he explained cautiously, inching his way closer to her, pulling out his badge for her to see. It took several tense minutes for his comments to register. When it did, her rage returned in full force. The white man was now out of the car, too.

"What do you mean, you're here to protect me?" she demanded angrily.

Avery Grayson, a moonlighting, off duty police officer, handed her his badge.

"We've been hired to keep any harm from coming to you, Miss Philyaw. I'm an active duty police officer, but I moonlight as a security guard." He pointed at the white man. "This is my partner, Officer Karl Hardin. We were recommended to your father by Captain Ralph Steel." Officer Hardin handed her his badge, as well.

She was now in a total state of shock. Ralph Steel? She racked her brain to remember where she'd heard that name before. While staring at the officers through dazed, glassy eyes, she handed them back their badges. Feeling completely out of sorts, she turned and walked away, only to turn and walk back to the men.

"How long have you been on my father's payroll?" she asked shakily.

Grayson exchanged indecisive glances with Hardin. "For a while now. I believe it was right after he learned of the danger you might be in. Miss Philyaw, your father was trying to protect you the only way he knew how. When you wouldn't agree to have someone with you at all times, he had to do what he had to do. That's not so unusual, especially when you love someone and you don't want to see them hurt," Officer Grayson said, pleading Wyman's case.

In disbelief, she shook her head from side to side. "So, I wasn't just imagining someone following me. You two have been watching my every move. Tell me, have you enjoyed scaring the daylights out of me? Is that what you call protecting someone? Did it ever occur to you that I might think you were the person who's after me? My father may have hired you, but I'm firing you. This very minute!"

She started to walk away, but she thought of one more question she desperately needed the answer to as she turned back to face the officers. "Who else is in on this atrocity?"

Grayson looked at his partner for some sort of support, but Hardin just shrugged his broad shoulders. "Captain Steel, as I already mentioned, a few other uniformed officers, and your boyfriend, Mr. Maxwell."

Bingo! Ralph Steel was Ken's godfather. "Correction. My ex-boyfriend."

"Miss Philyaw, his name, phone number, and address had to be placed on our security list simply because you spend time with him at his residence, and he at yours. Other than that, we don't know if he was directly involved in this. You're going to have to ask him that.''

She smirked. ''Oh, I intend to do just that, gentlemen. Now if you'll excuse me, I have a training session.''

Hardin finally spoke up. ''Ma'am, we're going to have to continue to do our job—that is, until your father tells us otherwise.''

She bristled with indignation. ''Like hell you will! If I see you within five feet of me, I'm filing harassment charges. You two terrorists have frightened me enough.''

''No disrespect intended, ma'am, but you'll have to file charges,'' Avery grumbled. ''We're going to stick to you like white on rice until we talk to your father. We'll alert Captain Steel and apprise him of the present situation. He'll be the one to make contact with Mr. Philyaw.''

Angrier than she'd ever been in her life she turned on her heel and stormed back to the car. Inside the Jeep, she started the engine and drove recklessly to the other side of the arena, the two men watching after her in disbelief.

Grayson laughed. ''I'd sure hate to be in Maxwell's shoes. Her father's probably not going to come out smelling like a rose either. That's a tough little sister they got there. I'm concerned about the way she confronts dangerous situations.''

Chapter Fifteen

As her mind turned to Brent's call of last evening, her rage increased. Uncertainty filled her at the same time. The more she thought about the accusations that he might spew at her, the angrier she got. Determined to fight like hell where her personal rights were concerned despite her intention to kick Ken to the curb, she swerved into a parking spot near the front entrance.

By the time Omunique entered the arena her body trembled all over. She burned with an anger that made her want to annihilate Wyman and Ken. How could they have done such an underhanded thing? Keeping her in the dark about hiring security was the worst thing they could've possibly done. They should've told her about this. It would've saved her a lot of grief and pain.

Those two were much safer right where they were, out of town, out of reach of the damaging acid that laced her tongue, out of reach of the perilous hands that longed to strangle them both, she decided. *Brent should be out of town, too*, she thought churlishly.

Brent was drinking coffee when Omunique entered his sparsely furnished office. The small cubicle was a mess, with books and papers strewn all over the place. As usual, he didn't seem the least bit bothered by all the clutter.

She nodded at him as she took a seat. "Before we get into this meeting, Brent, I need to know if we're really here about my poor performance. Or is this about my relationship?" Waiting for his answer, she moved forward to sit on the edge of her seat.

"Good morning to you, too, Nique." He took a gulp of his coffee. "Both." She sucked her teeth. "You knew we'd get into this sooner or later. You also know how I feel about you dating your sponsor, but that's not the issue I'm most concerned with."

Omunique jumped up. "I think it's the only issue. This is the first time you've come right out with it, but it's been spelled out for me on more than one occasion, the insinuations constant. And your bad moods are just another indicator," she accused with prevailing calm. When her legs began to tremble, she sat back down. "For the life of me, I just don't understand any of this, coach. I guess I'm confused about a lot of things these days."

Brent sighed, rearing back in his chair. "Then I haven't made myself clear. Nique, all I'm trying to say here is that you've got too many things going on at one time. You're preparing for one of the biggest competitions of your life, being threatened by some psychopath, and you're working on a new routine for an upcoming ice show. Then you go and fall head over heels in love with your sponsor." He shook his head. "A career in figure skating is hard enough on its own to maintain. Trying to manage all these other demands on your time is eventually going to get you into big trouble. Why can't you see that?" he asked, throwing up his hands.

Impatiently, Omunique tossed her hair over her shoulder, hating the fact that he was right about her situation being hard. In fact, keeping it all together was getting even harder. What was she to do? Even though she was highly exasperated with Ken at his decision to help deceive her, not to mention her disappointment, she loved her man beyond reasoning—and she'd been born to skate. How could someone ask her to give up either? She somehow got the impression that there was something more behind Brent's opposition to her love life than he was willing to admit. She was almost sure of it.

She pressed her back into the chair. "Why are you really so bothered by my seeing Ken? I've always performed at top level, haven't I? Sure, I've had a few mishaps during training, but when it comes to competing I'm right on the mark, and you know it. What's the real reason behind all this nitpicking nonsense, coach? I don't think you're coming clean with me."

Omunique fumed as she waited for his reply. When Brent came from behind the desk and threw his empty Styrofoam cup across the room, she involuntarily flinched. Not at all intimidated by his display of anger, her eyes remained glued to him.

"That was really professional. Did I hit a sensitive nerve?" she asked, feeling as if she could take the whole world on right then . . . and win.

Glaring, he stood right in front of the chair she sat in. "I resent your attitude, Nique. I resent everything that's gone on over the past months. I've worked hard trying to get you prepared for future competitions. I don't have time for someone who doesn't appreciate my efforts." Feeling himself losing control, he took a deep, calming breath. "Your priorities are all mixed up. You, young lady, must decide what's more important to you—a spot on the Olympic team or your precious love affair. You get to make the call."

Omunique swallowed her anger . . . and it tasted bitter. "Don't I get any credit here? In case you've forgotten, I'm the one who goes home with sore muscles and aching feet." For someone who'd just seconds ago thought she could take the world on, the apathy she heard in her voice actually scared her.

She then recognized what she'd heard in her voice: the distinct sound of defeat. "I know I've been a little ragged lately, Brent, but that's when I need your support the most. All you do is growl at me and tell me how lousy I'm doing. Instead of ripping my confidence to shreds, I need you to help me through all these things," she challenged. Not wanting him to see her cry, she jumped up and ran out of the office.

As she laced her skates, she thought about all that Brent had said. While it took several minutes for all his comments to sink in, when they did she knew he'd been justified in his concerns. She'd either have to shape up or find herself without one of the best coaches in the business. Either way she was going to have a tough time of it, especially when her love for Ken was the heart and soul of the entire controversy.

Her racking sobs tore through her like an icy stream. Brent had never made her cry before. It hurt like hell, but she'd just have to get a grip on her emotions. She'd have to grow up and face reality. Her future depended on it.

She knew she had what it took to make it big in the sports world. By making it big she'd be making a name for Brent, as well. Her phobias had become all-consuming, and she just had to find a way to conquer them; fear had become her archenemy. There was too much at stake for her to allow fear to take her over completely, yet how was she going to control what seemed larger than life?

Skating to the Ohio Player's seventies tune "Fire" Omunique became merciless atop the ice as she took to it like an angry hurricane. As she dug her blades into the smooth surface in a flurry of twists and sharp turns, ice chips sailed through the air. Transforming herself into a whirling tornado, she pounded the ice like a torrential rainstorm. Resembling tiny hailstones, the flying ice chips fell quietly back to the surface. A rumbling earthquake sounded beneath the ice as she executed several jumps and inexorable landings that created the acrimonious sound of thunder as they cracked inflexibly against the ice. Beads of sweat dotted her forehead. Her fawn-brown complexion was flushed with the nuance of hostility as her eyes torched a three-alarm fire.

Normally, she was a quiet storm on the ice, but the tempest had effortlessly escaped the fragile teapot. Every natural disaster known to man was reflected in the way she skated. Sparks of blue fire and tiny bolts of golden lightning shimmered beneath the ice as she completed the melodramatic presentation with a breathtaking pirouette.

Hearing loud applause, she turned in the direction from which it came and saw Brent standing there with a look of infinite pleasure on his face. His topaz eyes gleamed with pride, but she was still too emotional to appreciate his obvious reverence.

Smiling, he skated over to her, careful to keep some distance between them. The sparks of blue fire that had shimmered beneath the ice mirrored the dangerous glint he saw in her eyes. "If you skate like that in the finals, Nique, you're a sure win," he praised. When she didn't respond, he shoved his hands in his pockets. "I thought I'd just about seen all the brilliant skills you possess, but I've never seen you skate with that type of passion. You've been holding out on me, kid."

She shot him a scathing glance. "Anger is more like it," she remarked flatly. "Brent, I don't want to have to be angry to skate well enough to please you. Anger is an emotion I can easily live without. And I can't believe you're acting as if everything is hunky-dory between us. You're the reason I *am* so angry."

Sensing that she wasn't going to be easy to placate, Brent chewed on his lower lip. "I don't feel you need to be angry to skate well, Nique. I simply saw your performance as extremely passionate," he patronized unwittingly.

"A person can be passionately angry, you know. I don't like feeling this way. It goes against my nature, not to mention the damage it does to my spirituality. Being angry takes a lot out of me, just as fear does. What has you so fearful, Brent?"

Her question stunned him. "I'm not fearful of anything,

Nique. I just worry that things might turn out bad for you if you continue this unpopular love affair.''

She looked puzzled. "What are you talking about now?"

"Our plans, Nique. Our dreams, our hopes, and all that we've worked so hard for," he conveyed to her, his tone less condescending than earlier. "Think about all the bad press you could get, Nique. You're the sweetheart of the African-American communities."

She slapped her forehead with her right hand. "Oh, Brent, don't even go there. I can't stand for any more guilt to be heaped on my sagging shoulders. I'm not going to disappoint them, or you, or myself. Why do you keep on trying to convince me that professional sports personalities are not supposed to fall in love? I've been stalked in past weeks, and I don't ever hear you mention it. In my opinion that's a much more serious threat to my well-being than a love affair. For the record, the press doesn't seem to be at all interested."

The hairs on the back of his neck stood up, and he bristled. "You think not, huh? When you see your name smeared across the headlines of one of those disgusting tabloids, don't say I didn't warn you. I've never known you to be so unreasonable about something so damn important. It's your reputation, but it would be nice if you'd remember that mine is on the line here, too!" With that said, he skated off in a huff.

As though she hadn't created enough natural disasters for one day, uncontrollable tears flooded from her eyes as she watched Brent's angry departure.

Unsuccessfully, Omunique had been trying to work a half-decent program for hours now, but her skates and the ice just didn't seem to be able to make their normal body and soul connection. Without Brent there to set the pace for her, she had tried too hard, had pushed herself far too much. It was time to quit, she decided. Skating over to the metal bench, she sat down and practically ripped the ice skates from her feet.

After covering the blades she tied the laces together and tossed the skates over her slumping shoulders, thinking with disquiet that it would take a miracle to get her out of this big mess.

Omunique felt overwhelmed as she slowly walked to the locker room, as if her entire world had suddenly come to an end. Instead of Brent praising her for training on her off days, he'd reduced her to a pile of guilt and shame. Something had happened she would've never thought possible—her confidence was shaken. Over the years Brent had helped her to build rock-solid confidence. Now it seemed as if he was trying to totally dismantle it. The morning's tirade had nearly worn away her tough resolve.

Had she really gotten that bad? she wondered, sitting down on a locker room bench. Brent had accused her of losing her nerve and her ability to concentrate, recalling the bad scene from a few days back. He'd criticized most of her jumps, and made numerous attacks on her technique. His remarks fell short of calling her lazy. Lazy she wasn't; of that she was sure. Brent had never demanded so much of her, nor had he ever belittled her as he'd done over the past few weeks, as if he was trying to break her spirit. He seemed hell bent on destroying her confidence in herself. The excuses he'd given for driving her into the ground didn't fit. He had cause for concern, but something else was at work here, she suspected, something sinister.

"Oh, no," she cried, looking down at her swelling feet. To have an arthritic attack was the last thing she needed. She couldn't afford to miss a single practice session, but if her feet continued to swell she might lose valuable time on the ice, she assessed in utter horror.

Grimacing from the pain, Omunique massaged her soles. Her feet felt painfully tender as she limped toward her gym locker. After retrieving her gym bag from the metal locker, she removed her toiletry items and a fresh change of clothing, laying them on a wooden bench. Instead of a hot shower, she turned on the cold water, hoping to reduce the swelling in her feet. Born of frustration, scalding tears mingled with the cold water pelting from the showerhead.

Omunique saw the flowers as soon as she stepped from the shower. Though surprised to find them there, she guessed this was Brent's way of apologizing. *He shouldn't be sorry,* she thought. He had a right to be concerned with her reputation. He'd put himself on the line for her so many times, had been there for her through thick and thin. She owed him, she figured; big time . . . and it was time to start showing her gratitude.

As much as it would hurt, she knew she had to put her love affair on hold, at least until the Olympic trials were over. She prayed Ken would understand, and that he'd agree to give her the time needed to complete her goals.

Picking a perfect white rose from the center of the bunch, Omunique put it to her nose and inhaled deeply. She felt something cold touch the tip of her nose, but when she tilted the rose to see if water had somehow gotten into it, a red liquid resembling blood splashed out of the flower, smearing her face and hands a bright red.

Terrified, she took flight, screaming at the top of her lungs. In her desire to escape the locker room she didn't see the puddle of water that had dripped from her body. Before she could take another step, her feet flew out from under her. As she tried to break her fall, she landed hard on her right ankle, slamming her backside against the concrete floor. Frantically, she screamed out again. The sound reached the outer rooms, startling Ken and the two officers who'd just entered the arena. Ken, having followed his instincts from the previous night had caught the first morning flight out of Seattle.

Ken and Officers Grayson and Hardin rushed inside the women's locker room. When Ken saw her face covered in blood, he nearly lost his mind. Thinking she'd been shot or stabbed, he ran across the room to where she lay.

"Nique, Nique!" he cried out, kneeling down beside her. "Oh, God, please let her be okay." With sweat running down

his face, Ken gently lifted her head and placed it in his lap.
"I'm here, Princess," he soothed.

The beautiful face he'd come to love was smeared with
blood, sweat, and tears. The anguish in her gray eyes reduced
his insides to jelly as he kissed her forehead tenderly. When
she didn't move a muscle or blink, he realized she was in shock.
As Ken looked around the room, he saw another uniformed
officer come into the room.

The wet towel had fallen away from her body, exposing her
nudity. Ken quickly picked it up and shielded her. Then his
dexterous fingers checked her face and body for cuts and other
wounds. "Call the paramedics!" he shouted to the other officer.
"I can't find an injury, but this blood is coming from somewhere." He brought his mouth level with her ear. "Are you
hurting anywhere?" She stared blankly at him, her eyes wild
with fear. "Omunique, talk to me, honey. I want to help you,"
he uttered, his heart breaking at the wild terror he saw in her
eyes.

When she finally blinked her eyes there was no expression
in them. While clawing desperately at his arm, she let out
another set of bloodcurling screams, reminding him of the night
at the restaurant. *Same scenario, different location,* he thought
with anguish. "Oh, God," Ken shouted, looking at the massive
swelling to her right ankle.

Police officers and medical personnel had invaded the room,
but he couldn't let go of her when he saw that her ankle was
terribly swollen, knowing that her career could very well be
over if it was as bad as it looked.

The pain was so great that Omunique nearly passed out. It
hadn't dawned on her that her ankle could be broken, but when
she heard Ken talking to the paramedics about the massive
swelling she felt as if she might throw up. Just thinking about
what it would mean for her to have a broken limb caused her
to flip out.

Pools of hot tears streamed from her eyes. "No, Ken!" she
screamed, shaking her head from side to side. "No, no, no.

I've worked too hard . . . for this to . . . happen now,'' she sobbed brokenly. ''Tell me this isn't happening, Ken. Please, God, help me,'' she cried over and over.

Brent was horrified. Watching her writhing on the floor in such pain made him terribly sick. When he looked at the swelling around her ankle, he closed his eyes, praying it looked worse than it was, yet he knew this could be the type of injury that might bring her long journey to a devastating end.

Had he caused an even bigger fiasco than the one he thought she was making of her career? Why had he let his personal feelings enter into their professional relationship? Why hadn't he trusted her to handle her own life? It was possible she could've handled hers much better than he'd handled his own. As he looked down at Omunique, Brent's shoulders sagged under the weight of his guilt. There was a good chance he could've stopped this from happening, he thought, staring at her bloodstained face. She'd been right when she'd told him he was more concerned about their love affair than the threat to her safety. How was she ever going to forgive him?

When the paramedics lifted her onto the stretcher, she let go of Ken's hand and reached out to Brent. He thought she looked like a broken china doll, yet he sensed she was taking it all in stride.

Taking her hand in his, Brent kissed the back of it. ''It's going to be okay, sport. Remember telling me that your Dad taught you how to accept the things you can't change?''

Slightly woozy, she nodded. Her eyes were glazed over from the pain injection she'd been given, which wasn't even coming close to controlling the pain in her ankle . . . and there was nothing that could mask the pain in her heart. Yes, she mused, growing drowsier, Wyman had taught her to accept the things she couldn't change. She couldn't change the condition of her ankle, but it was going to take a miracle for her to accept that she might never skate again. Her last coherent thought was of Ken, and how he'd react to her decision to leave him.

Knowing that there was still someone out there who intended

to hurt her had convinced her even more that she had to let him go. It was no longer about needing time to achieve her goals—no longer about her, period. She couldn't risk this maniac turning his sick attention on Ken. She'd rather die than have something happen to him because of her; she loved him that much. He had once told her he'd been afraid to love someone for fear they'd be lost to him the same way he'd lost his mother. Him losing her to death was becoming more and more a reality. The vicious acts had once again reared their ugly heads. Something terrible happening to him frightened her more than the threat to her own life . . . and she couldn't even bear the thought of someone hurting him.

With tears in his eyes, Ken closed his fingers around hers. Not wanting to upset her, he quickly dried them. "I'm so sorry, Omunique. We just have to pray that everything will turn out okay. I'm going to drive my car to the hospital. I'll be right behind the ambulance." He bent over and brushed his lips across her forehead.

It nearly killed Ken when Omunique didn't respond. He knew the pain medication had taken hold of her, but that didn't lessen the jagged pain ripping through his heart. She wasn't responding to Brent, either, he noticed, watching Brent closely as he tried to reassure her.

Something about Brent didn't sit well with him. He didn't know what it was, but he intended to find out. He relied on his instincts, and that's why he was standing in the middle of the locker room rather than in Seattle, where he should've been.

Brent knew that she had every right to be upset with him. He had treated her badly over the past weeks. When his past experiences had swooped in to haunt him, he couldn't keep from comparing his once perilous situation to the one Omunique was now in. He had no idea how she was going to handle all this. He prayed she wouldn't have a nervous breakdown—like the one that nearly caused him to take his own life. When Omunique finally managed to smile at both Ken and Brent,

Brent felt some relief, yet it didn't truly lighten his burden. Then she was quickly wheeled away.

Before Ken could follow the stretcher out to the ambulance two members of the local police department stopped him. Information was needed from him before they could file their report.

The first officer on the scene extended his hand to Ken. "I'm Officer Marcus Taylor. I patrol the area around the arena. This is my partner, Officer Kyle Thomas."

Ken had heard the name Marcus Taylor before, but he didn't know the circumstances under which his name had been brought to his attention. "Pleased to meet both of you. I'm Kenneth Maxwell Jr. Your name sounds familiar, Officer Taylor, but I know I've never met you before this moment."

The officer eyed Ken with something akin to suspicion. "I guess I have somewhat of a common name. I'm positive that we've never met before. I'm sure I would recall. Can you tell us what went on in here? I understand you were the first one to arrive on the scene." In painstaking detail, Ken explained all that he knew.

"What is your relationship to the victim?"

Ken bristled. "The 'victim' has a name, officer—Omunique Philyaw. If you don't mind, I'd appreciate it if you'd not refer to her as a victim."

"And if you don't mind sir, I'd appreciate it if you'd answer the question," Marcus countered, placing his hand on top of his nightstick. "We can't do our job if you're going to make this difficult for us."

Ken's eyes raked Officer Taylor over the hot coals of his anger. He felt threatened by the officer's gesture, but he decided he needed to remain calm. Getting into it with this arrogant officer wasn't going to help the woman he loved, nor was it going to get him to the hospital any sooner. "Miss Philyaw and I have a special relationship."

"How special?"

"What's this have to do with anything? I'm in love with the lady. Does that answer meet with your approval?"

Officer Thomas walked over to Ken and put his hand on his shoulder. "I know you're upset, but we need your cooperation. I'm sure they're taking good care of your lady friend at the hospital, but we need to catch the person who's doing this to her. Let's walk over here for a moment."

Officer Taylor stayed put. *Omunique Philyaw,* he thought, remembering the beautiful woman he'd given a ticket to a few weeks back, the same woman who'd embarrassed him in court.

Exhaling a breath, Ken nodded and followed the officer to what he referred to as the crime scene. The floor was still splattered with the blood from the overturned bouquet of roses, Ken noticed with dismay. It bothered him to be in the area where she'd gotten hurt.

Officer Thomas picked up one of the thin tubes. "It appears that someone filled these plastic tubes with this red stuff and inserted them into the roses."

"It's not blood?"

Thomas shook his head in the negative. "I don't think so." He stuck two plastic-gloved fingers in the red liquid and held it up to his nose. "It doesn't smell like blood. It's probably theatrical blood of some sort. It's easy enough to purchase." He wiped the fingers of the rubber glove off on a paper towel he'd removed from his back pocket. "I understand she's been receiving threats. When did it first start?"

Pulling out his wallet, Ken sucked in a deep breath, then removed two business cards from his wallet and handed them to the officer. "For starters, you need to talk to Captain Ralph Steel. His number is on the card I gave you. He can tell you everything you need to know. You can reach me at the number on the other card. I have a pressing engagement," he said, moving rapidly toward the exit.

"But, sir," Officer Thomas began, "we—"

"I'm out of here. I'm needed at the hospital. I can't tell you any more than I already have," Ken shouted in retreat.

Chapter Sixteen

It seemed as if hours had passed before someone finally came to talk to Ken. He stood up and rushed over to the man with the stethoscope around his neck who'd just called out his name.

Orthopedic surgeon Dr. Harrison King, a fairly young black man with marble-black eyes and a clear ebony complexion, told Ken he'd been called in to assess Omunique's case. Ken saw that he looked kind and sympathetic.

Dr. King sat Ken down to explain Omunique's medical condition. "Miss Philyaw has given me permission to discuss her case with you. Since you're not a family member, we had to have her okay. She tells us her Dad lives out of town. While her X rays don't show any fractures, we know her ankle is severely sprained. The possibility of a fracture can't yet be ruled out. The swelling has to be reduced before we can further assess its condition and come up with a prognosis."

Ken wrung his hands. "I know she'll be anxious about her career, Dr. King. Can you tell me anything at all?"

"I can't pass comment, not until the swelling has gone down.

These type of injuries are hard to diagnose,'' he sympathized. ''It could go either way. It takes time. We'll keep you informed, Mr. Maxwell.''

Dr. King left a severely disillusioned Ken when he had to go and respond to a demand for his expertise, but he'd promised Ken that he could see Omunique shortly.

When Ken walked into the cheerfully decorated room, she broke down and cried. He rushed over to the bed and pulled her into his arms, holding on to her as she cried her heart out, her painful sobs wrenching at his own control. The fact that her career might be over was so bitterly disappointing to her she didn't think she could survive it, she told him between sobs.

There wasn't a thing he could say to her that would bring her any comfort, so he kept quiet. In fact, he couldn't even bring himself to think about what a career-ending injury would do to her emotionally. Her career was everything, and now it could all be over, he mused with deep regret, dropping soothing kisses in her hair when she began to cry even harder.

''You warned . . . me, but I didn't listen. I thought it was all over. Now look at me. I'm a helpless sitting duck. He's eventually going to kill me. You know that, Ken, don't you? Oh, my God, he could've killed me today,'' she moaned, trembling all over. Holding her close to his chest with one arm, he used his free hand to press the nurse call button. Omunique was hysterical.

Her stroked her hair. ''It's okay, sweetheart. There's an officer posted outside your door. You're safe.''

He didn't blame her for being afraid. The person who was doing this to Omunique had already gotten around a whole team of trained officers, he thought with rage. Somebody would answer for what had occurred earlier, heads were going to roll!

Omunique's hysteria warranted an injection. A sharp prick to her backside, and the lights went out. Blackness arose to engulf her. Ken sat on the side of the bed, holding on to her lifeless fingers, fingers that had trembled in his hands only seconds ago. He watched as her eyes rolled back in her head, knowing there wasn't anything he could do for her. Sure that she'd probably sleep for the next several hours, he kissed her forehead and left the room.

Omunique was lying on her side, her right foot propped up on several pillows. Arrangement after arrangement of bright flowers had been placed all around the room, and several helium balloons hovered over the head of the bed.

She forced a smile to her dry, cracked lips. "Hi, Marion and Frank," she managed in a weak voice.

"Hello," they responded simultaneously. Frank pulled two chairs up next to the bed and he and Marion sat down.

Taking Omunique's hand in his, Frank lifted it to his cheek. "We're not going to ask you how you're feeling, Omunique. We think we already know. We're here simply because we care about you. We're also here in support of our dearest friend. We know how much he cares for you."

Marion stroked Omunique's hair. "I tried to call Ken this morning, but he wasn't in. Knowing him, he's probably on his way here. He called us last night to tell us about your accident. We'd already heard it on a special edition of the news."

Omunique closed her eyes and sucked in a deep breath. "It wasn't an accident. It was a act of pure terrorism," she said, imprisoning sobs.

Leaning over the bed, Frank tenderly kissed her forehead, wishing he could take all of her pain away. "We know it was, Omunique. And the person responsible for this will eventually pay. I know that's no comfort to you right now."

Fighting back the tears, Omunique swallowed hard. "It'll be okay. I just hope my injury is not as bad as what's been reported. The doctors really don't know at this point. My ankle is still too swollen for them to make a proper diagnosis. The media has reported that I'm out of the running for Olympic gold. Go figure, huh? I just don't know, guys. I've always known that I was the only person who could defeat me. It looks like I've managed to do just that. I've allowed myself to become sidetracked by too much, and I've given this terrorist my power.''

Frank sighed deeply. ''You shouldn't be talking about defeat. Like you said, there's been no formal diagnosis. Ken wouldn't want to hear you talking like this.''

Omunique frowned. ''Ken is my second biggest problem. I've been too preoccupied with him. My coach thinks our relationship distracts me. I think he's been right all along,'' she said, unable to hold back the tears any longer. As though it was a security blanket, she yanked the blue bedspread up under her chin.

Marion was totally confused. ''I don't think I fully understand. You two love each other, don't you?'' she couldn't help asking, knowing it was none of her business.

Omunique shifted in the bed, wincing in pain when her ankle turned over slightly. ''Yes, we do, but it's causing so much havoc. It seems I can't be competitive and in love at the same time.'' Omunique shook her head. ''It's all so confusing. Our relationship might be the key to what's happening to me. Besides, I'm very upset with Ken. He's been keeping things from me. His deceptions have been blatant.''

Now Frank was confused. ''Deceptions? Another woman?''

''It's much worse than that. I can compete with another woman, but I can't contend with dishonesty.''

''Whoa, Omunique, those are heavy charges. This is none of my business, but if you don't mind, I'd like to know what's really going on here,'' Frank said.

Omunique picked up a glass of water and sipped on it through a straw. She then placed it back on the tray table. ''It's a complicated story, guys. I can make it short, but not so sweet. My father hired a security team to protect me, without my knowledge. In fact, I had strongly voiced my objections to the whole idea. Ken knew what my father had done, but he didn't tell me. Someone was tailing my every move, even on the nights I spent at his house, but he never uttered a single word to me. I find deceit intolerable.''

There was no way she could tell them the truth of her deep fear for his safety, the crux of it all.

Frank looked perplexed. ''I see, and I don't see. I see why you feel you've been deceived, but I don't see how you can be angry at them for caring that much about you. And how do you know that your father didn't swear Ken to secrecy? You were in danger, you really did need the protection, and they did what they had to do to ensure your safety. I think Ken was in a no win situation.''

Omunique looked down at her ankle. ''A lot of good it did me,'' she said cynically. She smiled then at both of Ken's friends. ''I can understand why you'd think that. He's only your best friend. I'm not asking you to take sides. As far as things go with Ken and me, I think we've run out of time. With this injury, I'll have even less time for us than before. As it is, I'm going to have a hard road to recovery. And if my ankle is broken, and I pray to God it's not, it's going to take a lot of time for me to heal, physically and emotionally.''

Marion touched Omunique's hand. ''Sounds like you're trying to convince yourself to do something you really don't want to do, Nique. It sounds like you've talked yourself into ending the relationship between you and Ken. Am I right?''

''I don't . . . want it to be over . . . forever, just . . .'' she struggled to say, her voice drifting lazily in the air. Though she battled with the drowsiness, her eyes closed slowly. Frank and Marion grew silent as they recognized her drug-induced state.

''We need to go now, Frank. Besides the medication she's obviously under, she's emotionally worn out. We can talk this through another time,'' Marion told him.

With his eyes involved in a deep probe, Ken watched her from the doorway of her private room. Though she appeared to be asleep, he couldn't help wondering if she was at peace. After the horrific hand she'd been dealt, he seriously doubted it. As he stepped into the room, his breath caught. The sweet smell from all the beautiful flower arrangements teased his nostrils, causing him to inhale deeply of their scent. Another deliciously familiar scent tantalized him, making his entire body shiver with longing.

He slowly advanced toward the bed. When his lean fingers gently stroked her hair, her eyes fluttered open. As she looked up at him, her eyes filled with glistening tears, her lower lip trembling.

Time seemed to stand perfectly still as his smile for her came slow and easy.

For all the angry tirades she'd leveled against him, for all the plans she'd made to exile him from her life, she was at a loss for words, finding herself happy to see him. His caramel-brown skin was still just as creamy, his autumn-gold eyes just as devastatingly beautiful, his tall lean frame as powerfully masculine as ever.

At the moment she wanted him more than she'd ever thought possible. When he took her in his arms with such tenderness, she fell limp against him, deeply inhaling the sexy, very masculine scent of his aftershave.

He kissed her long and hard. She responded with fervor, loving the taste and feel of the honey-dipped lips that could reach in and warmly clothe the naked passions resting deep within her soul.

Laying her head back against the pillow, he teasingly brushed his index finger across the lips that were paler than normal. Fleetingly, he took possession of her mouth again. "I'm sorry, Princess," he whispered softly against her mouth. "So sorry. I should've never left you alone." He kissed her again, only this time it was more sensuous, deeply probing, and sexually arousing.

There was no way she could've kept from responding. Trying desperately to drown out the voices in her head reminding her of the terrible things she'd wanted to say to him, she clung to him.

Tears stung the back of her eyes as she finally willed herself to pull away. "Do I know you?" she asked, trying to sound indifferent and intolerant. When he smiled, she knew she'd failed. His smile had a way of illuminating her heart, no matter how grim the circumstances.

He pulled a chair up close to the bed, then rested his head on her pillow. "I hope so, considering how intimate we've become. How are you feeling, Princess?"

A sharp pain tore at her heartstrings. "Much better," she politely responded, sounding as though a stranger, not the man she loved, had inquired of her health. "I might have to ask you the same question when I get through with you." Though her tone was light, he got the feeling that she wasn't in an airy mood.

"Sounds like you've had a chance to formulate a plan. What's on your mind, Miss Philyaw?" he asked, unsure of whether he wanted to know the answer.

He lifted his head up. She looked so formidable to him as she eyed him with suspicion. She definitely had something on her mind. From all indications, it wasn't going to be favorable for him, he concluded.

Get right to the point, she told herself. *No matter how much it hurts, you have to do this. If something happened to him, you'd never be able to forgive yourself. If you truly love him, you have to put selfishness aside. Don't put his life at risk.*

Nervously, she cleared her throat. "You've deceived me. In a way that justifies dire consequences." Speaking of justifications, was she truly justified in what she was about to do? Yes, she decided, especially if it meant saving his life.

Bringing her eyes level with his, she sat up in bed. "I had decided not to see you at all. But I believe it's only fair that I tell you I think your integrity stinks," she charged unblinkingly. "I know about the security Dad hired. And I know that you were in on it."

Meeting her mutinous gaze with a defiant stare of his own, he sighed heavily. "It had to be that way, Nique. This incident has proved that much." Though he didn't call her Nique that often, she loved the way it tumbled from his lips. She hid the immense pleasure the sound of her name on his lips brought.

Unable to stand the melting heat his eyes engulfed her in, she diverted her gaze from his gorgeous face, but not before she sent a few icy daggers his way. "Maybe it did have to be that way," she half-heartedly conceded, " but I should've been told. If you knew how I found out who those jerks were it would scare you lifeless, but I'll let you find out the nightmarish details on your own, just the way I had to find out I was being followed."

He'd already heard the frightening details. While shifting his position in the chair, he gently covered her hand with his. Before speaking, he studied her face with an intensity that brought color to her cheeks. He was sure that out of frustration Omunique was using him for target practice, but he wasn't about to become the bull's eye.

"Are you saying you wouldn't have thrown a hissy if we had told you? Or are you conveniently forgetting your reaction when the subject was first approached? Before you answer, lady, let's get a couple of things straight here. I didn't fly all the way back here to stand trial for loving you, and I'm not about to sit here and defend myself on that count. I'm guilty. I'm here because I *do* love you, and I'm damn concerned about what's going on. I'm in this thing for the long haul. If you want to act like a stubborn brat, you just go right ahead and knock yourself out. How much is your ankle injured?" he asked, changing the subject purposely. "I've heard so many different reports."

She fought the urge to lose herself in his golden gaze. "Changing the subject is not going to make this go away, Kenneth. You're going to have to face these charges at some point in time. Now that you've so graciously given me a chance to respond, I want to address your first questions," she retorted.

He could see that there was one thing that hadn't changed. She could still read him like an open book, and she seemed hell bent on handing him a day in court. With her as the judge, jury, and executioner, it appeared as though she was going to sentence him to life, a life without her in it. He hoped he was dead wrong.

"I probably would've thrown a fit, and I do remember vehemently rejecting the offer of security when it first came up, but I still should've been told. My ankle is badly sprained. The prognosis is good. I'm going home in the morning."

He grinned. "That's wonderful news, Omunique!" With the intention of kissing her, he leaned over the railing of the bed. Hating herself, she turned her head away. She couldn't let him melt her heart with his warm kisses and sweet words of encouragement.

Her rejection hurt him, but he was determined not to let it show. "I'm so happy for you," he said, his tone absent of the excitement he'd felt only seconds ago as he stood up. "Something tells me it's time for me to leave. Call me when you get over whatever it is that's bothering you. I love you."

"I'm over it, and I have to get over you. It has to be this way, Ken."

"It has to be, Omunique? Why?"

She snatched the sheet back from her feet and pointed at her swollen ankle. "This happened because of my preoccupation with the things that are going on all around me. My relationship with you is one of those things, Ken. Things like this are going to keep happening as long as my attention is divided," she cried. "I have to refocus. I have goals to attain."

"First of all, this happened because some imbecile has waged a reign of terror against you. This has nothing to do with our relationship. What's happened to your courage, Nique? I thought you were determined not to let this person have control over you. You can't give up your power. You're starting to sound so hopeless, Omunique."

She threw her head back against the pillow. "You're right,

Ken. And these feelings of hopelessness are killing me. I'm lying here like a helpless kitten. I can't explain it, but I know I can't do this anymore, at least not right now. If you love me, you'll let me go for now. I can't have two lovers at the same time. My love belongs to the ice," she exclaimed, fighting a wave of nauseating despair, hating herself for lying to him, yet knowing she had to. If she told him she was sending him away to protect him he'd never remove himself from danger, she knew.

Every muscle in his body tightened, the color draining from his knuckles as he tightly gripped the metal bed railing. "I'm truly sorry you feel this way, Omunique. I realize it's a rarity, but this is one time you could've had your cake and eaten it, too. Because you've decided to choose one desire over the other, you just might not get the chance to fully enjoy the rewarding benefits of either. Winning is great, but when there's no one to share the triumphs with it quickly loses its flavor. I know. Except for the tragic loss of my precious mother, I've been winning all my life, but it never meant as much to me as it has since I've been with you. You make the born winner in me rejoice."

Her heart felt every ounce of his pain. "Wait a minute here, Ken—"

He jabbed his finger in the air. "No, you wait a minute!" he shouted, cutting her off in an agitated tone. "It's now clear to me that this has been a one-sided relationship. It offers about as much security as driving a car that only has wheels on one side. In other words, this relationship isn't doing either of us any good. Love shouldn't have to hurt." He touched her hair as though he'd never again feel its silkiness beneath his fingers. "I'm still positive that you'll attain all your goals, but are you going to be happy? For your sake, I hope so. Good luck, Princess."

Tears floated in her eyes. "Ken, wait," she cried as he turned to walk away. "I never meant for things to turn out this way. Please try to understand. For right now it has to be this way."

Until this maniac is out of our lives, she cried silently—*that is, if he doesn't kill me first.*

He laughed, but he found no humor in her refrigerator-chill comments. "I understand more than you give me credit for. But you'll have to suit yourself, Princess. If I haven't yet convinced you of how much I love you, then I guess I m pretty lousy at expressing myself. But I thought I'd done one hell of a job communicating to you everything that I am and ever hope to be, everything you are to me."

He knew there was nothing left to say, nothing that would convince her of his love. He turned on his heel and walked away, his shoulders slumping as he crossed the room. Each step he took toward the door brought their sorrowful farewell closer. At the door he turned back for one brief glance at the woman who was sending him away, the woman who was sending love away.

A love and a lover that belonged solely to her: simply, purely, honestly.

Of all the horrible things Ken had expected to find upon his return from Seattle he'd never expected to lose something, something as right as rain, something that meant the world to him. He certainly hadn't expected the Ice Princess to be so cold and distant. Whatever he was guilty of, the punishment hardly fit the crime. Omunique was responsible for him believing in the sun, but he could do without the dark forecast that now hung over his head. Losing her was like losing the sun forever. Without the light of his day, he figured the shadow of darkness would follow him the rest of his days.

At the same time that the door clicked shut, she felt an acute pain tear right through her bleeding heart. A lump the size of a cue ball got lodged in her throat. Love had come into her life on gilded wings, and she'd sent it flying away on the back of anguish and despair. At first she'd been so happy to see him, to feel his tender arms around her, to have his mouth crushing hers beneath its sweetness, to hear the sultry voice that turned her biological sirens on. Then, without prior warning, she'd turned on him like a lioness protecting her territory. Now her life would be devoid of all the wonderful things Kenneth Maxwell Jr. had brought into it.

Her heart had pleaded with her not to send him away, but she hadn't listened. The only voice she'd heard was the one that told her to fiercely protect the man she loved, the man she'd lay down her very life for.

As far as she was concerned she had already won the gold medal—a precious, golden heart: warm, loving, open, and honest.

Chapter Seventeen

Wearing a grim face, Ken sat in his godfather's office. "It's been well over six weeks now, but this department hasn't come up with a single clue. Is there any hope of catching this sicko that's been terrorizing Omunique?"

Handsome, tall, and paper-thin, Ralph Steel shook his graying head. "I'm not sure anymore. We haven't come up with any leads. It's like we're dealing with a phantom. The flower vase and the locker room have been dusted from top to bottom for fingerprints, but there were none. It's our guess the perpetrator wore gloves, a very common method of operation, you know. According to her father, the threats have ceased again. There was a barrage of calls, and we have possession of the most recent ominous notes that were sent through the mail. These cease-fires are deliberate. The perpetrator hopes to lull her into a false sense of security. The moment she lets down her guard, he's going to pounce. He sees this as a cat and mouse game. He loves the chase."

Ken grimaced. "What happens when he tires of the game?"

"That's the part we have to fear the most. And we haven't

yet established that it's a male. What if it's a female competitor? Everyone knows what happened before the last winter games. I can't believe anyone would be so stupid as to try something like this, not after seeing the outcome of that particular situation. But we can't rule out any possible scenario.''

Wearing a thoughtful expression on his face, Steel studied his godson closely. "Have you seen Omunique since she came home from the hospital? If so, how's she coming along?''

Ken clasped his hands together. "No, I haven't seen her. Per Dad, she's still on crutches, but she's healing nicely. There's even talk about her being fit enough to perform in the *Holiday on Ice* show. I don't know. Though it's been extremely difficult for me to stay away from her, I'm trying to honor her wishes. Dad says Ms. Philyaw is getting more and more frustrated with each day that she has to remain off the ice. He says she has become a bear to live with, and that nothing seems to please her these days.''

Ralph smiled. "Do you think her lousy disposition has something to do with the absence of her handsome black knight?''

Ken laughed. "That sure would be nice, but I'm not going to hold my breath waiting to hear from her. She's stubborn. And it just so happens she wants that Olympic spot more than she could ever want me. For a time there I had myself fooled into thinking otherwise, but I've let go of that foolish notion. However, I don't understand why we still can't be friends. I guess a friendship would be hard for me to handle, anyway, when I know in my heart that I want so much more than that.''

Steele came from around the desk and put his hands on Ken's shoulders. "What's stopping you from asking her to remain friends? That's better than nothing at all.''

He pondered Steele's question. "I don't know. Perhaps pride. She's very proud, too. But there're times when she has too much pride. We've even talked about it.''

Ken picked up a ceramic coffee cup and took a quick swig of the now lukewarm liquid. "I remember quoting her what I've heard Max say many, many times. Quote 'Pride won't keep your family fed, nor will it keep you company on a long, cold night.' Unquote.''

Ken got to his feet and walked over to the window, where he perched himself on the wide window ledge. ''I'm beginning to wonder if it *is* pride that's keeping us apart. Or is it something more than my having deceived her? I thought I'd fully explained my reasons for not telling her about the security team. I keep asking myself if I'm allowing pride to rule my heart and dictate my actions.''

Steel encompassed Ken in his concentrated, sable-brown gaze. ''Why else have you been flying back and forth between Seattle for the last several weeks? What other reason do you have for keeping yourself thousands of miles from the home you love?''

''Good questions. I just wish I had the answers. I hope pride isn't one of them. I don't blame her for being angry with me, or even disappointed in me, but to take things to such extremes as she has is unfair and insensitive. I never dreamed I'd be saying that about the most fair and sensitive person I've ever known.''

But in all the times they'd shared together, made love together, Ken thought, she'd never confessed to loving him. *Maybe that should've been a sign of things to come,* he thought, but until recently he hadn't given it much weight. He'd been taught that actions speak louder than words; her actions had spoken volumes. Deep down inside he truly believed that she did love him. Somehow he'd misinterpreted her actions. Then it was like old times again, times when they'd misread one another at every bend in the road.

His thoughts were disrupted when Steel's secretary popped her head in the doorway and handed Ken a message from his father. As she backed out of the doorway, Steele laughed. ''Did you see what she was wearing, Ken? That woman's clothes are AWOL from Halloween.''

Ken laughed. ''We had a similar problem with our secretary. But her clothes didn't create a morose atmosphere. They were just too darn provocative for the type of business we run, and I was the one who had to tell her.''

Ken got to his feet and extended his hand to Steele. ''This message from Dad needs my immediate attention. I'll be in touch, Uncle Ralph. Kiss Aunt Amanda for me. Tell her I'll be around there soon to see her.''

Steel stood up as he pumped Ken's hand. ''Listen to me, son. Do you remember why you fell in love with Omunique in the first place?''

Without the slightest hesitation, Ken nodded.

''Then there's no reason why you can't pursue her friendship. Sometimes we have to go back to basics. There comes a time when we might have to take a step down before we can take a step up. Don't fool yourself into believing that you haven't gone to see the woman you love out of nobility, as you've suggested. I understand your decision to give her the space she's requested, but in this instance, I think you're the one who's taking things to the extreme. Space is space. An empty space is entirely another matter—An empty space is what's found in the heart when its needs aren't met.''

Ken smiled warmly. ''Thanks.''

Omunique crept out of bed. Using crutches, she made her way to the front of the house. After depositing herself in a chair in front of the window, she watched the rolling tide wash ashore and crash against the sunlit coastline. As though in a daze, she began to imagine the ocean as one large ice formation that connected the entire world. Then she saw herself gliding across its smoothness, weaving her magic over the seven continents and the seven seas.

The crusted diamond ice blades shimmered and sparkled as she skated the globe, proudly exhibiting her artistic and technical figure skating talents.

Halfway around the world she saw a vision of powerful masculinity floating toward her.

The magnificent vision was like nothing she'd ever seen. As the vision drew closer, she saw eyes the color of autumn leaves, golden eyes whose radiance were brighter than the sun. The seductive male vision dazzled her, smiling with strong, even white teeth. When the vision engulfed her in a whirlwind of soft caresses and bouquets of sweetly scented kisses, they became as one.

As they whirled over the ice with the speed of lightning and the power of thunder, they created a rapturous melody that could be heard throughout the universe. As they healed the world with the power of their love, skaters from every corner of the globe joined them in celebration of their glorious union.

A light touch on her shoulder tore her away from her fantasy. Discreetly, she brushed the tears from her eyes. "Good morning, Dad," she greeted emotionally, swallowing the massive lump in her throat.

Tilting her chin, Wyman looked into the moist eyes that appeared awestruck. "Why didn't you wake me? I don't like seeing you all alone."

Laughing lightly, she caressed the back of his hand. "Oh, I wasn't alone. I was side by side with the world," she responded breathlessly.

He chuckled as he sat on the arm of her chair. "And just what were you and the world doing, Nique?" he asked, sliding his arm around her shoulders.

She looked up at him and smiled. "Celebrating, Dad. Celebrating the union of a lonely Ice Princess and the handsome Prince of her fairy-tale dreams. Skaters from all over the world were there to wish them well." Wyman's eyebrows shot up as he cast her a concerned glance. Her laughter sparkled. "No, I'm not insane yet, Dad, but I'm getting closer by the minute. Can't you just imagine a wedding on ice, with skaters from all over the world in attendance?"

His loving smile warmed her heart. "No, but I think you just did. Why don't you share it with me?" he commanded softly, moving over to the chair opposite hers. Omunique made herself more comfortable by placing a pillow behind her back and resting her injured ankle atop the leather hassock.

For the next few minutes Omunique enchanted Wyman with the fantasy story she'd conjured up in her mind. Her eyes shimmered as she talked about the Prince of her imagination, the Prince whose heart matched the color of his golden eyes.

As he listened patiently, Wyman didn't need to be a genius to know that the vision in her story was Ken. Adding more and more details as she went along, she continued her highly colorful journey around the world. At the story's conclusion, she would've given anything to have her fantasy come true.

"Nique, that was a beautiful story. It touched me in more ways than I can tell you. Your mother used to write me little fantasy stories." His eyes watered up. "My fantasies are all buried with your mother. But Nique, you are still very much alive."

"I'm not so sure anymore, Dad. I'm just not sure."

"Don't bury yourself alive the way I have, sweetheart. Without the power of love in our lives, we may as well be dead. Don't make the same mistakes I have. I'm sure your mother is disappointed in the way I've handled her death. I know she'd want me to love again. Who knows? Maybe someday I will. If you never hear another word I say, hear me out on this. I think it's high time for atonement. Love's ultimate goal is reconciliation. Don't ever forget it."

Omunique sighed. "You know this subject is taboo between us."

Wyman eyed her with concern. "Nique, you don't have to rekindle your relationship with Ken entirely, but you do have to break the silence. It's imperative."

Omunique didn't wince at all when she walked the entire length of the weight room under her own power. Raising her arms in triumph, she smiled at her physical therapist.

Winston Laughlin smiled back "You did just great, Nique.

Let's do the whirlpool treatments. Afterward, we can see how you do without the crutches.''

Outfitted with all the latest state-of-the-art equipment, the weight room in the Philyaw home was only a few years old. It had been added on for the sake of convenience. Omunique had welcomed the new addition.

While Winston readied the whirlpool jets Omunique stripped away the cover-up she wore over a modest navy blue swimsuit. As she slid into the tub, the hot swirling waters—pre-treated with aromatherapy salts and other relaxing herbs—caressed and soothed her injured ankle.

"Slide your foot over here to me," Winston instructed.

Winston massaged Omunique's ankle for twenty minutes. After drying her feet off with a sterile white towel, he applied a cool, soothing balm to each ankle, paying special attention to the injured one.

He helped her to her feet. "Okay, let's move on to the exercise phase. I want you to take things slow and easy, Nique. You're way ahead of schedule as far as the healing process goes. We don't want to do anything that might cause you to regress.''

"I know that's right," she responded.

"Do your stretches first. That's it. Continue to go lightly, Nique.''

"It seems that those who thought I was down for the count were badly mistaken," she quipped. "Some reporters out there are going to look very stupid when I'm back on the ice in far less time than they'd reported.''

Winston laughed. "Don't you just love those reporters who reported your injury as career-ending?''

"Whatever sells papers, Winston. I guess.''

Excited over her progress, Omunique, using the crutches, walked Winston to his car. She then took a quiet stroll on the beach. The security guards weren't visible, but she knew they watched her every move. She had gotten an idea of what the President of the United States felt like when surrounded by secret service agents. Unlike before, she now welcomed their comforting presence.

As Omunique took the metal clasp from her hair, the wind skipped through her long tresses. While maneuvering the crutches through the sand, she thought about all the times she and Ken had walked hand in hand on this very same path. Though he wasn't there beside her, she still felt the warmth of his hands imprinted in her flesh. She admitted to herself that Wyman had been right. Losing someone she loved was devastating. The devastating consequences of pushing Ken out of her life were hers and hers alone to bear. He wasn't dead, yet she mourned him. To keep him alive and well she'd commit to mourning him for the rest of her natural life, and she vowed to do whatever it took to keep him safe.

When Wyman answered the door he was surprised to find Ken on the other side. He'd thought Ken was back in Seattle. From the way Ken looked, Wyman could easily see that paradise had somehow forsaken the young man he'd come to admire and respect.

Wyman extended his hand. "Good to see you, son. I'd heard you were still out of town. Come on in."

Forcing a half-smile to his lips, Ken firmly pumped Wyman's hand. "My plane landed a few hours ago. I had to come here to see how Omunique is coming along. I could no longer stand not seeing her for myself. How is she doing?" Ken's eyes mirrored the anxiety he felt as they moved into the living room.

A slight frown creased Wyman's forehead. "It's hard to tell. Her ankle is coming along just fine. She's actually able to walk without using the crutches. Besides being frustrated and sulky a good bit of the time, I think she's doing okay. Nique is good at accepting the things she can't change, maybe too good at it. You can go on in to her room if you'd like. She's awake. I was just in there."

Nervously, Ken raked his fingers through his hair. "Maybe

you should tell her I'm here first. She may not want to see me.''

Wyman frowned again. "How interested are you in seeing her, son?''

Ken bit down on his lower lip. "More than I can express, sir. I've been just plain miserable without her. I desperately need to see her, but I'm not here to press her about our relationship.''

That's too bad, Wyman mused, his smile sympathetic. "In that case, you'd better go in unannounced. She might get a little huffy. But one thing is for sure, she won't be able to run away from you.''

Ken appreciated Wyman's humor. "You've got a point there. Do you think I should wear full body armor and carry a shield?'' Ken joked.

"Just smile at her and be your usual charming self. I get the feeling my daughter is defenseless against those two warheads of yours.'' The two men had a good laugh before Ken moved cautiously down the hallway, toward Omunique's bedroom.

Before knocking, Ken stood quietly at the door, wondering what he should say to her. More importantly, he wondered how she'd react to seeing him after such a long absence. Did she miss him as much as he missed her? He hoped so. When he finally got up the courage to knock, he held his breath, waiting for her response.

He stepped into the room upon her soft command. As usual, her inescapable beauty astonished him. "Hello, Omunique,'' he greeted, trying not to sound as nervous as he felt. "I just dropped by to see how you're doing.''

In a state of shock, Omunique could only stare at the man she'd just finished praying over, the man she dreamed of every minute of the day and night. Did God really answers prayers that quickly?

Ken read her silence to mean that she didn't want him there, so he backed himself against the door. "If this is a bad time for you, I can come back later.''

Omunique panicked at the thought of him walking out that door. "Oh, no. Your timing is just fine."

Instant relief was his to claim. "I merely came by to see how you're doing. Max has kept me informed of your progress, but I thought it was time for me to find out in person. How *are* you doing, Omunique?"

Omunique moved from the bed to a chair. "I'm doing okay. How about yourself?" The quaking sound of her voice displeased her.

"I'm fine. Just working hard. How's the ankle coming?" The unnaturally polite conversation between them drove him mad.

Looking down at her ankle, she rubbed her hands together. "It's coming along beautifully. My physical therapist is thrilled about the progress I'm making."

Male or female therapist? he wondered, hating the thought of any man other than himself touching her with tenderness, remembering all the times she'd asked him to massage one area or another on her silky body. If it was a male, he hoped she didn't think he was great in any area other than his profession.

"That's good to know, Nique. Were you resting before I came in?"

No, she thought, *I was praying for you to walk through that door. Now that you have, I don't know what to do about it.* "Kind of meditating," came her reply. "All I seem to do is rest these days."

She suddenly remembered her manners. "Ken, why don't you have a seat? I apologize for my rudeness."

He looked at the antique rocking chair—it had been purchased when her mother first found out she was with child, Omunique had told him. "Well, maybe just for a minute. I don't want to tire you out." *But I'd stay here forever if only you'd ask.* Nervous as a bird around a hungry cat, Omunique trembled inwardly as she launched questions at him about his work in Seattle.

The conversation was still too polite for his liking, but neither of them seemed to know how to change their stuffy demeanor. He missed the days when they'd rambled on endlessly to one another, never running out of interesting topics to discuss.

It made her ill to learn that he'd only be home for a few days. Had he found someone new in Seattle? She thwarted that thought immediately.

When he got up, she thought he was ready to leave. She wanted to grab him and hold onto him for dear life. She battled the urge to tell him how much she loved him, how much she missed having him in her life, how empty she felt without him. But to confess her true feelings to him would only place him in danger. A look of deep regret came into her eyes.

He walked over to where she sat. Bending over, he placed a kiss in the center of her forehead, then kneeled down in front of her. "Would it be too much for me to ask that we remain friends? It doesn't seem right for us to act like polite strangers. We do have a history, Nique." *A wonderful history.*

Friends? Is that all he wants from me? Oh, God, she cried inwardly. *I want forever with him, and I can't even tell him. The man I love deeply and lust after wantonly wants to be my friend.* Knowing how much she'd hurt him, she was sure it had cost him dearly to even ask her to be his friend.

"Friends," she said, extending her right hand to him, hoping her tears wouldn't surface. Her heart wanted so much more from him. Needed so much more of him.

Woman, can't you see it in my eyes that I want you back as my lover? Please don't let me walk out of here with no hope for the future, he pleaded in silence. *I can hear my heart crying out loud for your mercy. Why can't you hear it, Omunique? Why?*

"Friends," he echoed, backing out of the room.

Throwing herself across the bed, Omunique cried bitterly. She cried for the man with the golden eyes and the luscious mouth, for the absence of his all-empowering love, for all the unconquerable sexuality packed into that one beautiful body.

Ken's most precious gift to her had been himself. It was

only to her that he'd given his love, so unselfishly, so willingly, he'd once told her. And because of some unidentifiable demon she'd been forced to throw it all back in his handsome face.

As the image of one of their very special nights assailed her mind, she closed her eyes. There, in her mind's eye, the romantic saga bloomed resplendent.

She could almost touch all the wild emotions she'd experienced, feel the titillating warmth from the fireplace on her nudity, taste the feverish passion that had swelled between them. In no hurry to rush the inevitable, they'd napped in front of the fireplace, after sharing a quiet dinner at his place. They were going to make heart-stopping love as sure as the sun would never fail to rise. Short of death, there'd be no plausible intervention.

Ken had awakened her with a kiss that bewildered, exhilarated, and sensitized her beyond reality, all at the same time. As he torridly undressed her with flaming eyes, his scorching hands had gently swept away her satin gown. His kisses had been erotically fierce. Her uninhibited responses to his eroticism had been irrepressible. When he'd asked her to sheath him, she had nearly come unglued at the prospect of sharing something so far beyond what she understood as intimacy. In fact, it had gone beyond anything she could comprehend.

"Yes, yes, Nique. I love you." were the last recognizable words he'd uttered that night.

Even now Omunique felt his hips undulating wildly beneath her, felt each upward thrust as he careened into her with reckless abandon, with her returning each power stroke in the same wild manner. Tiny pinpoints of blazing lights had shattered their very existence. In unison, they'd ridden out the sweetly tormenting waves of ecstasy.

As his heat spilled into her, she had moved over him like a storm raging on and on without direction. As her own fulfillment staggered and billowed through her, she felt hot tears scalding the back of her throat. Realizing that the tears belonged to the present, she opened her eyes, feeling that which had nothing to do with surrealism. She was every bit as aroused as she'd been on that glorious night. Only this time Ken wasn't there to put out the fire that burned deep within the furnace of her sexuality.

Just as she'd felt when she'd awakened the morning after she'd sent him away, she could once again touch the bluish nuances of her emotions. Would the sadness ever be replaced with unmitigated joy? Would she ever be in his arms again, consumed by his love? Would she ever be back in his life, back in his hotbed of passion?

Chapter Eighteen

Omunique was back on the ice. The past few weeks had kept her busy as she trained physically and mentally for the Denver showing and the *Holiday on Ice* performance. It seemed to her that there weren't enough hours in the day, but her nights were interminable. Missing the intimacy she'd once shared with Ken, she thought of him constantly.

It didn't matter that they weren't together any longer—Ken's life had been threatened, anyway. In another sick note recently delivered to Omunique he'd been accused of robbing her of the sunshine in her smile.

No comfort had come from it, but she felt she'd been justified in keeping him away. But what good had it done? Now it seemed he was in danger with or without her. She *was* glad he was away. In Seattle he was out of danger.

Her concentrated thoughts turned to Denver as she continued to furiously pound the ice. If she had any hopes of getting her confidence back, she needed to skate, needed to feel the fire beneath the ice seep into her feet, needed to have its heat course through her body, needed to have it light up her insides like a warm summer day. She desperately needed to taste the fire of her desire and the delicious twinges of joy that were hers when her blades made contact with the hardened surface.

Checked through by security but unnoticed by her, Ken entered the ice arena, his autumn-gold eyes feverishly searching for the woman he couldn't seem to shake himself free of, the woman who owned his every thought. Then he saw her skating forcefully over the ice, leaving behind her a long trail of steaming grooves. His heart melted at the sight.

While adroitly skating the magnificent program that had been choreographed for the *Expressions on Ice* show, the one she'd been sidelined from, she thought about all the things that had occurred over the past few months. Fearful and desperate thoughts of the death threat that had been made against Ken had triggered a staggering panic attack that hurled her across the ice, landing her hard on her backside.

Discreetly watching her every movement from behind the seating tiers, Ken's first reaction was to rush to her side. When she picked herself up and dusted the ice shavings from her pink leotard, he sighed with relief. Would she give up? Or would she work through whatever caused her spill? He agonized, waiting with bated breath to see what her next move would be.

Omunique just stood there, looking bewildered, looking as though her world had caved in, looking as though she couldn't take another step. Then, impetuously, dazedly, as though she warded off evil spirits that only she could see, she rapidly whirled into a spin that seemed without cessation, around and around she went spinning and turning like a tyrannical whirlwind. She stopped abruptly when a rush of dizziness nearly caused her to topple over.

Trying to calm his heart, Ken inhaled and exhaled a steady stream of breath, smiling when she moved further into her program, seemingly undaunted by whatever had caused her to stop. Positioning himself on a back seat, one that kept him well out of view, he watched in awe as she manipulated the ice artistically and technically.

Fascinated by her sensuality and the seductive swaying of her delicate hands and body, he longed to shout *Bravo* at the top of his lungs. Fear of the show coming to an abrupt halt should she discover him caused him to sit back in his seat. Quietly, he enjoyed the rest of her emotionally draining performance.

Had Ken not heard the words of "The Greatest Love of All" he could've easily deciphered them through the graceful language her impassioned body movements communicated. Although she had a bit of trouble skating to the faster paced "Another Sad Love Song," it was barely noticeable to him. Amused by her jazzy style of ice dancing, dazzled by her capricious flirting atop the ice, he grinned. As he'd done so many times before, especially of late, he slipped out of the arena with her none the wiser.

Returning to Seattle without speaking to her was going to be hard, but he wasn't going to do anything that might interfere in her progress. She'd been through enough already. He loved her too much to risk jeopardizing all she'd accomplished thus far. Dealing with him wasn't what she needed right now.

As though she'd somehow felt Ken's presence, she looked around the arena, to no avail. Disappointment sliced into her as she exited the ice. Her natural instincts had somehow deceived her. She could've sworn that he'd been there. She would've bet money on it. She had felt the familiar warmth that often came over her when he was near. Before heading for the locker room she took one more look around the arena. When she saw that he simply wasn't there, she blamed it all on wishful thinking and the fact that she missed him terribly.

When the doorbell rang, Omunique had just settled herself into one of the living room chairs. She couldn't imagine who'd been bold enough to brave such nasty weather. The skies had spilled buckets of rain over much of Southern California. Not wanting the visitor to be out in the inclement weather any longer than necessary, she hurried to the door. Even though security was extremely tight around the premises, she looked through the viewing window.

His clothes soaked through and through, Brent stood there. Omunique quickly pulled him into the house, watching him closely as he got out of the lightweight raincoat he wore over dark brown casual slacks and a tan, pullover sweater. She couldn't help noticing how puffy and red his eyes looked. He was unshaven, which she thought was odd since Brent was the clean-cut, Ivy League type.

Brent shoved his hands in his pants pockets as he rocked back and forth on the balls of his feet. "I hope I haven't come at a bad time, Nique. I wanted to see how you were doing. I'm happy to have you back on the ice. I missed having you at the arena. Everyone else there missed you, too."

Omunique motioned for him to follow her into the living room. She sat down, but he refused her offer to have a seat. "Thank you, Brent. That's nice to hear. I don't think I could be doing any better." *Physically, that is,* she thought, knowing she was in emotional turmoil over Ken. "I've been pulling out all the stops at practice."

Brent nodded. "Yeah, I know. I guess that's what has me worried. I don't want you to overextend yourself, Nique. You don't want to reinjure that ankle. Complete recovery is essential for your return to competition. You need to be well enough to work as hard as you've always worked in the past."

His comment genuinely surprised her, since he'd bitterly complained about her lack of drive before she'd gotten hurt. "I promise not to overdo it, Brent, but I am strong enough to work in the same way I'm accustomed to." She chewed on her lower lip. "Something tells me that that's not the reason you've come out here in this dreadful weather. Is there something else you want to discuss with me?" He looked at her briefly, then turned back to the window.

Seconds later he turned around and took a seat. "You know me well, don't you, Nique?" He blew out a ragged breath. "Nique, I can't stand the tension between us. I know I've been totally unreasonable about your relationship with Maxwell, but I just can't find the right words to explain my actions. If I had done my job, you probably wouldn't have had to hobble around on those crutches. That's something I have to live with. The guilt has really taken its toll on me."

Trying to clear her mind, Omunique shook her head from side to side. Despite his weariness, sitting before her was the old Brent, gentle and soft-spoken. The Brent she was used to. The man she loved and respected.

"You shouldn't feel guilty. There is absolutely nothing for you to feel guilty about. You had nothing to do with me getting hurt. Someone deliberately caused what happened, and that same someone is still out there on the streets. Brent, can you tell me why you really objected to me seeing Ken? I somehow sensed that there was more to it than what you'd said."

He stood up again, rubbing his hands together. "It's personal, Nique. Please don't push the issue. My bones are chilled right down to the marrow." He shivered to prove his comment. "Could I trouble you for a hot cup of coffee before we talk about the decision I've made, which is the reason I came here today?"

Omunique was embarrassed. "It's no trouble at all. I'm just sorry that I didn't think to make the offer. Do you want to come into the kitchen with me while I make the coffee?"

Brent looked over at the window. "You go ahead. I'll follow in a couple of minutes. I want to get another peek at that magnificent panoramic view you have out there, though I've seen it hundreds of times."

Omunique shrugged her shoulders. "Okay. You know where the kitchen is."

Omunique was scared stiff when she entered the kitchen. *What decision?* she wondered. Was Brent going to dump her? Was he just going to up and walk out on her? He had threatened to quit, she recalled with clarity, but would he be so callous as to drop her on such short notice? It was true that their relationship was terribly strained, but she didn't think it was so bad that it couldn't be worked out. She hated her thoughts, yet she couldn't help herself. Brent's somber mood hadn't made it any easier for her.

That he'd been offered another coaching position was her last fearful thought, which brought forth the rain from the storm clouds in her gray eyes. She just might be jumping to all the wrong conclusions, she decided as she measured out the coffee and dumped it into the filter. She then filled the glass container with water and poured it into the top of the coffeemaker.

While the coffee brewed, she set out the cream and sugar and arranged some lemon drop cookies, compliments of Aunt Mamie, on a small tray. Small tasks had become easier and easier for her, she noted happily. A few weeks back she could barely walk. Now she was back to doing all the things she loved to do. Except for the one thing she might never do again—make sweet love to Ken.

Just as she removed a ceramic coffee mug from the cupboard Brent strolled into the room and took a seat. "Smells good. Too bad you can't stomach the stuff. It's a good equalizer for a bad case of nerves."

The look she gave him was fraught with anxiety. "Why are you so nervous, Brent? I've heard that word coming from you a lot lately. I always thought you had nerves of steel. Is everything okay with you?"

Not quite meeting her inquisitive gaze, he rested his elbows on the table. "What can I tell you, Nique? I guess I'm just a nervous kind of guy." *Hardly,* Omunique charged silently, setting the coffee mug down in front of him. "I worry too much about everything, and sometimes nothing at all. That ankle of yours has caused me a lot of worry, though I'm sure it can't compare to the worry it's caused you." Brent stirred sugar into his coffee. "Really, Nique, there's nothing for you to be concerned about. How's your father?" he asked, hoping he'd quelled her curiosity.

Omunique dug her nails into her palm. Brent's nervousness had rubbed off on her. "Dad's good, despite the fact I've been one big pain in his neck. He's out with a client. I know he can't wait to go back to San Francisco, but he would never admit that to me."

He glanced at his watch "Well, I guess it's time for me to tell you about the decision I've made, Nique. I've put it off long enough now." He reached for her hand. "I think it's time for me to move on, Nique. It appears I've done more harm to your career than I've done good," he announced, looking down at her right ankle.

Too stunned to speak, she looked at him with incredulity, horrified at the thought of what his next words might be.

He let go of her hand. "You need a coach who doesn't let his personal feelings get in the way. I hope you'll be able to forgive me for allowing that to happen. I came here today to resign my position as your coach."

Fighting back the immediate tears that sprang to her eyes, Omunique picked up a cookie and broke a piece off, feeling as though she had to do something with her trembling hands before they shook loose from her wrists. "Why, Brent?" she cried. "Why do you have to do this? Why now? What's this really all about?"

Brent stood up. Towering over her chair, he shuffled his feet nervously. "I once had a nervous breakdown, Nique. Things were so bad that I tried to kill myself." Glad that that was over, he blew out a jagged breath. "My self-control has been threatened a lot lately," he commented, looking down at the floor. "I feel unstable." Embarrassment reddened his cheeks as he cleared his throat. "I'm sorry you had to find out the truth about me like this, Nique. I should've been honest with you from jump street. I'm trying to be honest now. I really tried to pull it together so you wouldn't have to deal with my problems, but it looks like I haven't been too successful."

She asked him to return to his seat. He was happy to oblige her, since his legs felt like lead. "Brent, you could've shared your problems with me. I wouldn't have condemned you. We all have weaknesses," she asserted with genuine understanding. "Gosh, we're only human, you know. I'm just glad you survived your ordeal."

He leaned over and kissed her forehead as he got to his feet again. "Thanks, Nique. I can always count on you to be the light at the end of the tunnel. I knew if I was going to stay sane, I'd have to come clean with my star athlete." *As clean as I'm capable of right now,* he mused. There were still serious issues to be addressed. "I'm sure you have a lot of questions."

She smiled back. "I do, but I only want you to answer those questions you're comfortable with. How long ago did this happen, Brent? Why do you feel that you're losing self-control?" she asked, hoping she wasn't getting too personal.

Brent sat back down and slid his arm around the back of her chair. "Many, many years ago, Nique, when I failed to make the Olympic team. Sometimes it feels as though it only occurred yesterday. It haunts me still. I guess it always will." His expression spoke to pain as he pondered her second question. "I started losing control when I saw so many distractions befall you. I knew what was happening to me when I began to magnify minor concerns regarding your performance level. Then, right after one of my major tirades, you hurt your ankle. I felt responsible for it. I felt I'd taken you down with me. That's when I decided it was time to resign. I hope I haven't caused too much damage to your confidence. I'm sorry I let my personal experiences get in the way of the job I was hired to do, Nique."

Proud of the way he seemed to handle the matter, Omunique smiled at him. Taking responsibility for his actions was important to him, she guessed. But he was no more responsible for this disaster of a situation than she herself was.

"I need you, coach. So much," she remarked truthfully. "I had to take time off to heal. So why can't you do the same?

Why can't you just take some time for yourself, rather than up and resign? Why not take some time to heal?"

Unable to believe what she'd just asked, he stared at her. How could she still want him as her coach, especially after what he'd just told her? Besides, there were things he hadn't been able to tell her—in his opinion, unforgivable things, things he knew he had to tell her. It was inevitable, with no way around it.

"You shouldn't even consider keeping me on as your coach, Nique. I don't think I can do it," he said, amazed by the degree of empathy she'd shown him. "It just wouldn't work," he lamented with deep regret, massaging his thighs. "I still have to tell everyone in our camp about my problem. I'm sure they'll all be furious with me, and I imagine Lamar Lyons will probably want to sue me for breach of contract. No, Nique, it's just not in the cards for me to stay on. You're better off without me."

Omunique took his hand. "No one will be furious with you—no one is going to sue you. I'm sure everyone will understand what you've been through. I understand, and I'm the one with the final say-so regarding your position as coach. If you're worried about Dad, he'll feel the same as I do. No one has the right to pass judgment on you." She touched his cheek. "This is not the time to pressure you about anything. It seems you've had too much pressure on you as it is. Take time to pull it all together. Just know that I want you back when you're ready. We're a team."

You wouldn't feel this way if you knew the whole truth, he thought. *I've kept it to myself for far too long, and I have to keep it a bit longer.* Brent knew he couldn't tell Omunique any more than he'd already revealed, not until after the Olympic trials were over and she reigned victorious. Her success had been sabotaged enough.

Brent fought hard to hold back his emotions. "I can't believe you, Nique. I've always known you were special, but I just didn't know how special. Can you give a jackass a hug?" he asked, laughing through his tears. She pressed her face against his and hugged him fiercely. His hold on her was so fraught with desperation she felt it in spades, along with the tremors that shook his body as he returned her affection.

"Whether I decide to return or not to return as your coach, you've provided me with the strength I need to move on with my life. There isn't a remedy in the world that is more effective at healing than a good dose of love and a few understanding friends. I admire your humanity. You have a beautiful spirit."

Brent took a handkerchief from his pocket and dabbed at her moisture-filled eyes, then wiped his own tears away. "Don't ever change, Nique. God has blessed you with so many special gifts. Use them all. You're fearless. You're Olympic material!"

His encouraging words warmed her through and through. "Thanks. Does this mean you're going to consider staying on, coach?"

"I'm going to give it some serious thought, Nique." He glanced at his watch. "I have a meeting to attend in about forty-five minutes. Is there anything else you'd like to discuss with me before I leave?"

Omunique licked her lips and swallowed hard, afraid to ask the most important question of all, the question about his private life. Would his answer be synonymous with what she'd been thinking for a long time now?

Brent sensed her reluctance. "You can talk to me about anything, honey. I'm going to the right place, should it cause me any anguish." He laughed. "A support group meeting. It's where I learned that 'denial' isn't a river in Egypt."

Laughing at his comment, she took his hand again. "It's about love, Brent, and the hurt it can sometimes inflict without warning." Nervous about the subject matter, she inhaled a deep breath. "I need to know if part of the problem we've had could be centered around love. A lost love, perhaps? Did you lose your heart to love, only to lose that love, Brent?"

Brent suddenly felt hot and clammy, beads of sweat popping out on his forehead. Quietly contemplating her words, he stared at her in bewilderment. Did he dare tell her the truth? Did he dare tell her of the undying love that was responsible for all his torment—and just as responsible for hers?

Recognizing the pressure she'd put on him by posing such a personal question, she saw the need to rescue him. "You don't have to answer that. I'm sorry for asking. It's just that I love Kenneth Maxwell with every fiber of my being, but I'm scared to death of something I can't even explain to myself." *And scared for him,* she mused fearfully. "I've been miserable ever since I sent him away. I keep asking myself if I really sent him away for the reasons I've been telling myself. Perhaps because I fear losing myself to love, only to lose that love forever. I'm not sure I could survive that, which is exactly what happened to my father, and to Ken's."

Grateful for the reprieve, Brent got up from the chair and paced the floor. He suddenly stopped and stood over Omunique, drying his sweaty palms on his slacks. "If you love Maxwell the way you say you do, Nique, don't fight it. Conquer your fears before they conquer you, especially if he feels the same way about you. If you're anything like your father, you'll only love this deeply once in your lifetime." *If you're anything like me, you'll never love this way again,* he added in his thoughts.

Brent pulled her up from the chair and gathered her in his arms, the sorrowful look in his eyes taking her hostage. "I completely lost control of my life when I lost the bid for a spot on the Olympic team. That loss left me destructively bitter. Don't end up like me, honey. Once you've experienced true love, there's nothing else like it." *Even if it's not returned.*

"I said you couldn't have both, but I didn't know what the hell I was talking about. My bitterness did the talking for me. Go for the gold, Nique. Go for the man you love. You might not win the gold, but from what you've been telling me you've already won Ken's love. True love is far more precious than gold."

Though she thought he'd left out an important element, Brent's story had been fraught with fear and uncertainty, not to mention hopelessness, all the same things she'd encountered since she'd sent Ken from her life. If only she could listen to her heart and not her fears, she probably could have both her love and her career.

Though she'd taken Brent off the hook where his private life was concerned, she still felt that his conflict about her and Ken's relationship was somehow connected to a lost love. She had seen the pain in his eyes, which spoke of grief—the same constant grief she felt. Ken was every bit as much her destiny as figure skating. She couldn't tell the future, but she was almost sure she could've had forever with her handsome Prince Charming. It seemed all so clear to her now. Some of her fears had mirrored Wyman's. Wyman had loved someone. He had lost. So had Max.

And she now feared losing the only man she'd ever loved— to death. Somebody out there was out to exact revenge on her, for whatever reason, and Ken could become a target of that vengeance. No one should ever have to live in fear. Life was all about taking risks. Sometimes you won, sometimes you lost. No one could win all the time. In competition there was always a loser, and the same often applied to love. Kenneth Maxwell Jr. had loved her unconditionally, as she loved him, but fears had torn them apart, fears that neither of them had created.

Was it too late for her to risk it all for the man she loved? Wouldn't it be terribly unfair to put his life at risk so that she might have that love? she wondered from the doorway, watching Brent as he dashed out in the rain.

Though Brent hadn't promised to stay on as her coach, he hadn't made the decision to resign, she thought, as she closed the door. Just another fear to add to the existing turmoil. Just another unanswered question.

Chapter Nineteen

The Ice Palace arena was magnificently decorated with all the trimmings of a White Christmas. Fluffy snowbanks of glittered cotton covered the outer perimeters of the ice. On a movable raised dais stood a massive, snow-sprayed Christmas tree adorned with large white doves, gold angels, red velvet bows, and hundreds of twinkling lights. With the arena filled to capacity, the crowd buzzed with excitement as they waited for the show to begin.

As "Jingle Bells" rang out, the stunning cast of skaters swirled onto the ice. Cheerfully dressed in red and white sequined costumes, with Santa hats atop their heads, they circled the arena and waved at the crowd as they passed by. The group then treated the audience to a scintillating performance, which included plenty of playful banter and well-executed ice dancing.

Back in rare form, Omunique flitted across the ice alongside her brilliant peers, scheduled for two solo performances and one with Ian. Her single performances would include two festive songs. The performance with Ian had been slated at the last minute.

In the next number Mr. and Mrs. Santa Claus appeared together. Dressed in the traditional attire, the couple painted a delightful Christmas story on ice as they performed to "Santa Claus Is Coming To Town."

Garbed in sparkling emerald green outfits, the entire cast reappeared. They would skate to "Here Comes Santa Clause," "Oh Holy Night," and "Away In A Manger." The captivating choreographed program was accomplished with perfect precision and superb synchronization as the skaters fluttered across the ice.

As the angelic chords of music stole into the hearts of the audience, the group paired off in twos. The skaters then formed a circle and linked hands as they skated around the Christmas tree, which now stood in the center of the ice.

Suddenly the lights took a bow, darkening the entire arena. As they slowly came back up, clouds and clouds of white smoke drifted from the rafters, a multicolored spotlight igniting the center of the ice. As the smoke cleared, Omunique emerged, wearing a short, formfitting tuxedo with long white tails. A red sequined bow tie and cummerbund sparkled against her crisp white shirt. Omunique dazzled and effervesced as Nat King Cole lustfully sang "The Christmas Song."

No one would've guessed that Omunique had recently recovered from an ankle injury had it not been all over the media. Neither could anyone see the joyful tears glistening in her eyes as she put everything she was and hoped to be into her earth-shattering performance.

The spirit of Christmas had created a cheerful atmosphere of Yuletide that was felt throughout the arena.

Several other festive programs included pair and solo skating performances filled with emotional drama and comical animation. Skaters costumed as animals and fairy-tale favorites brought rousing cheers and laughter from the children in attendance.

In Omunique's final tour de force she skated dexterously to "White Christmas." During her short program with Ian, they skated harmoniously to "I Saw Mommy Kissing Santa Claus" and "Silent Night." The two skaters brilliantly executed another dazzling sequence of jump combinations, double and triple axels, salchows, toe loops, and a variety of spins.

Costumed in a variety of colorful attire, the other participants joined Omunique and Ian on the ice. The grand finale was executed in perfect synchronization to the tune of "Joy To The World."

While dressing for the semi-formal cast party Omunique chatted enthusiastically with her female peers. Everyone was excited about how successful the show had been, and all looked forward to the party.

When several vases of flowers were delivered to the dressing rooms, to various skaters, Omunique was very cautious with the ones she'd received. There were the usual heartwarming yellow roses from Wyman, but the red roses sent by Ken put her on top of the world. Her smile dazzled with happiness as she tore open the card. Her dazzling smile quickly soured as she read the card: Happy Holiday Skating, Princess.

She was happy that he'd thought enough of her to send flowers, but the closing broke her heart into millions of pieces. It read: From your dear friend, K.M. Jr.

"Dear friend," she moaned. Of course she wanted his friendship, she anguished, but more than that she wanted to be his lover again, his wife, the mother of his children. *You know it can't be that way, Nique, not as long as there are lives at stake. Stop torturing yourself,* she scolded in thought, wondering if he was still in Seattle. The roses could've been sent from anywhere in the world. Would he have come to her performance had he been home? Probably not, she decided. There was nothing that could be done about her broken heart, yet she remembered when it looked as though she could've had both of her heart's desires.

All she could do now was see her other desire through to the end. The Olympic trials were so close, and she simply had to continue to drive herself toward achieving what she'd set out to achieve many, many years ago. Long before Ken. Long before love.

Her heart nearly stopped when she saw him from across the room at the cast party. *He's not in Seattle,* she thought. *He's here.* Addressing wealth and position, the fabulous tuxedo he wore looked marvelous on the handsome Prince of her fairy-tale fantasies. He wasn't alone. He held the arm of a woman with a beautiful figure, but she couldn't see the woman's face. It felt as though her heart had stopped when the woman turned around—Thomasina Bridges, his secretary. *What's that all about?* she cried inwardly.

Quickly recovering from the devastating blow to her heart, Omunique cast Ken a beautiful smile. Not only had he cared enough to send her roses, he'd cared enough to come and see her perform, she enthused, soothing her hurt. She was glad she'd done well.

He was dazzled. Her smile rarely failed to dazzle him, to bewitch him. Her eyes were on him, and he couldn't do anything but smile back. She had that kind of effect on him. He hadn't touched a drop of alcohol, yet he felt drunk, drunk with passionate desire. Acutely aware of his deep love for her, for one brief moment he got completely caught up in her, forgetting all about the woman who stood beside him. There was only one woman in the room for him, the only one that mattered.

He was inebriated by her inner and outer beauty, missing the effervescent personality heightened by a dash of witty sarcasm and the flippant sense of humor that brought his laughter to life. He missed the inferno of their combined passion.

The strapless, emerald-green chiffon dress was a stunning compliment to her fawn-brown complexion. She looked so bewitching he found himself wanting to kiss her bare, creamy shoulders. When she suddenly turned to someone who'd called out her name, a tall gorgeous someone, jealousy ate right through to the core of his being.

What's he doing here? Why is he with Omunique? Ken

wondered, shocked and confused, remembering that Marcus Taylor was the officer at the arena.

Lifting Omunique's hand to his lips, Officer Marcus Taylor kissed the back of it. "It's been a while," he told her, charming her with a warm smile.

She smiled back. "Yes, yes, it has. How have you been, Officer Taylor?"

Realizing he still held her hand, embarrassed, he let go. "I've finally recovered from our past encounter. You made an absolute fool out of me in court, Miss Philyaw. My ears are still burning from the judge's scathing comments."

She arched an eyebrow. "Just stated the facts, sir. You couldn't have possibly seen me run a stop sign. After I checked it out, I realized what you had to have known all along. There isn't a stop sign within a two-mile radius of the arena," she kindly reminded him. "Off the record, why did you really stop me?"

He grinned. "I plead the fifth. Being made a fool of once is quite enough for me, thanks," he said, tugging at the arresting designer tuxedo he wore so wonderfully well.

She shot him a smug glance. "Did you really believe I wouldn't show up for my court appearance, prepared to do battle?"

"Let's just say a prayer went unanswered," Marcus remarked, laughing. "Can I get you something to drink?"

"Thank you, but I'm just fine."

"Then how about a dance? The music is live."

She stretched out her hand. "As you wish, my friend," she flirted innocently. No matter how innocent her flirting may have been, Ken glared at her from across the room, hating the attention Officer Taylor showered on the woman he loved.

When Omunique and Marcus moved onto the dance floor, Ken cursed, wondering if Omunique had gotten the wrong idea. He had only escorted Thomasina to the cast party because Max had asked him to. Her car was in the repair shop. Max had also arranged for the staff Christmas party to be held in conjunction with the skating event party, which was the only reason Thomasina was even there.

Without considering the personal interest Thomasina had once shown toward him, Ken whisked her onto the dance floor. Two could play this game, he mused, thinking that Omunique had used Marcus Taylor to show him that she had no interest whatsoever in mending their relationship. Realizing he'd been unfair to Thomasina, he promised himself not to ever use someone in that manner ever again. Deep down inside he knew that Omunique wasn't capable of using someone in that way, either. She was probably dancing with Officer Taylor simply because he'd asked her to.

Omunique learned that Marcus was a personal fitness trainer in his off duty time, which explained why he was in such good physical shape, and why he was at the party. A lot of people from the world of sports had attended the ice show and the party. Figure skating had become extremely popular in recent years.

Marcus smiled at her. "I'm for hire."

A puzzled look stirred in her eyes. "For hire? What's that supposed to mean? Are you involved in an escort service of some type?"

He laughed. "No. I'm interested in becoming your personal bodyguard. I hear your people are looking for someone to work the Olympic trials. If so, I'm the best."

She was surprised to hear him speak of the Olympic event. Backing slightly away from him, she scowled. "Where in heaven's name did you hear that?" She threw up her hands. "Forget the question. I don't want to know. It'll only spoil my evening."

She strongly suspected that her father was the culprit, but now wasn't the time to discuss it. She would deal with Wyman in due time. Besides, security had been doing a wonderful job since the last incident, and she saw no need to fix what wasn't broken. At any rate, the security in Denver would be extremely tight.

Marcus whirled her around the dance floor. "In that case,

it's forgotten. But if you change your mind, give me a call.'' She nodded, but she had no idea what she'd done with his number, nor did she have any intention of calling him.

Omunique thought Marcus Taylor had all the qualities she liked in a man, but she was totally unaffected by him. Marcus's cool blue eyes had glowered at her all during her stupendous presentation in court, yet she'd calmly presented the facts as she knew them. To prove her point to the judge, she'd also taken pictures of all the intersections around the area where she'd been stopped. There was not a posted stop sign anywhere in the vicinity of the arena.

Embarrassment had been his lot. Victory had been hers.

After court, all those weeks back. he had tried to talk to her, but she'd made a hasty retreat. Marcus was nice enough, but her heart was taken, her soul was engaged to another. Looking over the room for Ken, she noticed that he wasn't where she'd last seen him and prayed that he hadn't left because of her.

When Max cut in on Officer Taylor, Ken smiled. He watched for a few minutes more, then got out of his seat and walked onto the dance floor. With his head held high, he quickly approached Omunique and Max.

Ken tapped his father on the shoulder. ''If you don't mind, Dad, I'd like to dance with Omunique. That is, if it's okay with you,'' he said to her.

Dumfounded, Omunique couldn't believe that he actually wanted to dance with her. Desperately wanting to be held by him, she went straight into Ken's arms, into the arms where she longed to be, into the refuge of the arms that she should've never left.

Dying to kiss her breath away but not daring to, he encircled Omunique in his arms. *I love you,* his heart whispered to her.

I love you, too, her heart whispered back.

She looked up at him. ''What's going on with you and Thomasina?'' she asked, hating herself for allowing those tell-tale words to leave her lips. She couldn't let him know how jealous she was of him being there with Thomasina.

His thumb itched to run itself across her smooth cheekbone and downward to her luscious lips. Purposefully, hoping to burn his desire into her flesh, he seductively pressed his muscular thighs against her petite body. When his desire snapped to attention, he moaned inwardly. Pulling her in even closer to his burgeoning fervor, he deeply inhaled the titillating scent of her perfume.

He refused to allow himself to be encouraged by the possessiveness he thought he heard in her voice. "We're having our Christmas party here tonight. Max wanted to kill two birds with one stone," he said, leaving her curiosity unfulfilled.

That didn't explain why he'd come waltzing through the door with Thomasina on his arm, she thought, seriously agitated at his response. She then decided she was better off not knowing. She couldn't bear it if Thomasina had become more to him than his personal secretary.

He was just about to escort Omunique back to her table, when the band began to play the music to "Hero."

"Our song!" Omunique and Ken exclaimed simultaneously. The thought had come to their minds at the same time, they realized, embarrassed that they'd spoken their thoughts aloud.

Without either of them daring to analyze what had just occurred between them, Ken drew Omunique back into his arms. They had never let this song go to waste, and he wasn't going to let it go begging this time around, either. He'd always think of himself as her hero. Maybe she'd begin to think that way again, too.

With renewal of hope flashing in her gray eyes, she looked up at him. "Are you back in town for good? Or are you just home for the holidays?"

For an eternal moment he lost himself in her smoky gaze. Home. Home was supposed to be where the heart was, but his heart no longer had a home. He doubted that it ever would again, at least not the type of home he'd been foolish enough to think he'd found with Omunique.

Tossing his troubling thoughts aside, he returned his attention back to her. "I only came back for the Christmas party. Max insisted on it." *I only came back because I wanted to see you give yet another riveting performance, because I wanted you to mesmerize me one more time. I wanted to feel the warmth of the fire you magically create on ice—even if only from afar.* "Tomorrow morning I'm leaving on the first flight back to Seattle. However, I won't be alone Christmas day. I have an invitation to dinner. It's crucial that I attend."

Her heart shattered. The two families hadn't gotten together for Thanksgiving, as was planned, because of her injury. Though Max had already accepted the invitation for Christmas dinner, she knew it wasn't going to be much of a celebration for either of them with Ken absent.

The song came to an end all too soon for him. The moment he released her a cold chill ran up and down his spine. *Lady, you've just stolen the heat right out of my body, and I don't know how I'm supposed to stay warm without it, or without you.*

Ken escorted Omunique back to the table she'd occupied with Sara, Ian, and several other skaters. He pulled her chair out. "It was nice to see you again, Omunique. Take care of yourself. I'm sure we'll see each other around."

Ian's eyes seemed to bore right through Ken, which made him uncomfortable. When Ken looked directly into Ian's eyes, Ian quickly averted his gaze, as though he were guilty of some wrongdoing.

With her eyes fixed on Ken, Omunique remained standing. "Are you leaving the party?"

"Yes. It's time for me to go."

Her eyes grew choppy with doubt. "You're not leaving because of me, are you? I hope I haven't done anything to make you feel uncomfortable." Though she didn't feel an ounce of joy, she laughed gently. Her laughter caressed his soul and ignited his passion.

His expression softened. *Princess, I do have to leave, but not for the reason you think. I'm leaving because I desperately want you all to myself. I want to touch you in places I can't possibly touch you in here—not without getting arrested.*

"Don't ever think like that, Nique. We're friends. Remember? I'm simply tired, and I've got a busy tomorrow ahead of me."

Friends! She cringed inside at the word that hardly described the intimate relationship they'd once shared. They'd been so much, much more than friends, physically and emotionally. *Oh, yes,* she thought, remembering the physical part of their relationship.

Her eyes followed him as he walked back to his table. There was an aura about him, a fascinating and powerful aura, she thought, her eyes embracing him with a warmth that she herself could feel and then she quickly turned off the thoughts in her head, the type of thoughts that would only add to her grief.

Brian Terry walked up to the table where Omunique sat alone, having purposely waited for this moment. He quickly dropped down in the chair closest to hers. His sudden appearance startled her, but she quickly recovered and then smiled at the young man whose arm Ken had nearly broken off.

"I haven't seen you around in a long time. You look nice tonight, though I detect a little sadness. What's going on, Brian?"

Swallowing hard, he ruffled his shaggy blond hair, nervously drumming his fingertips on the tabletop. "Nique, I have something to tell you. I know you're going to hate me for this, but I hope one day you can forgive me."

Her face grew somber. Something in his voice chilled her to the bone. Trying to hide her feelings, she smiled encouragingly. "I could never hate you, Brian. What did you do, put a dead frog in my locker?" Brian was well known for pulling lighthearted pranks on the skaters, but a few of them had been a little on the scary side. She couldn't help remembering the rubber snake incident. She could hear the dryness in his voice as he attempted to tell her what he'd done.

"Nique, I'm sorry about the bad things I've done to you.

Although Coach Masters told me not to tell you until after the Olympic trials, I can't keep it to myself any longer."

A stunned silence prevailed as she looked at him with raised eyebrows. "What are you talking about, Brian?" she finally managed, praying he hadn't said what she'd thought he had. "And what does Coach Masters have to do with anything?"

Brian lodged his tongue under his top lip and pressed hard against his gums, his eyes filling with water. "I was ... the one who made ... those ... awful phone calls," he stammered, tiny beads of sweat popping out on his forehead. "Are you going to have me locked up?" he asked, turning pale from fear. "It started as a joke, Nique. I swear."

Astonished, Omunique couldn't find the right words to adequately express herself. Out of the blue, she began to laugh. When her laughter turned hysterical, she was sure she'd gone over the edge, but she had to get a grip. There was so much she needed to know. As she fought hard to bring her hysteria under control before she drew unwanted attention to herself, she gave Brian a murderous look, causing him to slouch in his seat.

"Brian, that was a horrible thing for you to have done. Do you realize how much trouble you've caused? I'm glad you came to me with this, but you're going to suffer the consequences of your actions," she threatened, suppressing her relief at finding the culprit. She needed to know the reason why.

Ken had seriously suspected him of involvement, but she'd convinced him that he was on the wrong track. "Brian could never do something like this, regardless of the type of crowd he hangs out with," she remembered telling Ken.

Brian squirmed in his seat. "I'm sorry, Nique," he said timidly. "But I don't want to go to jail. I don't want to be locked up. Jail sucks."

A look of surprise crossed her features. "How do you know that, Brian? Have you been to jail before?"

"Juvenile Hall. It's the same thing. When I was twelve, I put sugar in one of our neighbor's gas tanks. Then I got into writing obscene graffiti all over some of our other neighbor's garages. My mother thought I was out of control, so she sent me to Juvenile Hall. I was there for two months, then she let me come back home. But, Nique, I haven't been in any trouble since. Not until now,'' he said, diverting his shame-filled eyes to the floor.

"Big trouble, Brian. Let me ask you something. What do you think I should do about this? It's real serious, you know.'' He belonged in therapy, she knew. The only reason she was even talking to him about this was her desire to know every minute detail. He'd implicated Brent. That alone had kept her glued to her seat.

He gave her a thoughtful look. "Give me another chance, Nique. I won't ever do anything like this again. I promise. I could do some work for you. Whatever you want. But please don't turn me in to those people haters,'' he pleaded, referring to the police. "Coach Masters says he's going to help me become a better person. He's even had me talk to someone about the things I did. I don't remember the guy's name, but he works with troubled young men like me.''

Listening to him talk about Brent caused a sick feeling to chew at her insides. She just couldn't figure out what this all meant. In fact, the whole thing was ludicrous. "Are you telling me that Brent knew you were the one who was harassing me?'' Brian nodded. "Why wouldn't he want you to tell me? And how did he find out it was you?''

"I made one of the calls from the payphone outside his office. He heard everything. He pulled me into his office and jacked me up pretty good. When I offered to confess all of it to you, he said you had enough to deal with right now. And he wanted to be the one to tell you when the time was right. In the meantime, he said, I'd get the help I needed to straighten my life out. He even got me more hours at the arena. When Mr. Maxwell brought some money and clothes to our house one day, I felt so bad I started to tell him the truth about everything, but I got scared. That guy probably would've killed me. He's already tried to break my arm off.''

This was too much truth for her to even begin to believe. She had to come up for air before she suffocated to death. Brent, an accomplice to a malicious crime against her? It didn't add up. But if it were true, he had been an accomplice and he'd tried to cover up the crime. She thought back to some of the things he'd said when he'd visited her at home, the very same visit when he'd talked of resigning his position as coach.

She knew she couldn't stand to hear anymore right now. Her heart wouldn't survive any more disappointment. She stood up. "You listen to me, young man, and you'd better listen good. I don't want you to mention our conversation to another living being. I'm not through with you yet. You have a lot more to explain. If you talk to anyone else, I won't even consider keeping the police out of this. Don't you as much as breathe a single word of this to anyone. If you do, you'll go to jail, and that's where you'll stay for the next twenty-five years or so," she added through clenched teeth, hoping to put the fear of God in him. He deserved much worse than that. He deserved to have his bloody neck broken. But until she got to the bottom of Brent's involvement, she wasn't going to screw up her chances of getting all the facts. However, Brian would be punished for his unlawful deeds. She'd see to that.

Without uttering another word, she picked up her purse and headed for the nearest exit. She had seen the others coming back to the table, and there was no way she could hide the turbulence she felt inside, especially from Ian and Sara. There was no way she could face any of her colleagues right now. The knowledge she carried inside was too explosive to be explored in the presence of others.

Something had to be emotionally wrong with Brian, for him to have done all the horrendous misdeeds he'd spoken about. She quickly came to the conclusion that he was emotionally disturbed, and that he needed some serious help. Of all the different emotions that Brian had evoked from her during their brief conversation, relief was at the top of the list—relief in knowing that there wasn't someone out there who actually wanted to harm her or the man she loved.

Although she didn't have all the facts, she had to wonder if Brian was solely responsible for all that had happened. Could someone else have been in on it? Did someone other than Brent know about this? She cringed as the incident with the vase of roses came to mind. Well, for sure, as a part-time employee Brian certainly had access to the locker room, nor was it impossible for him to gain access to her personal information. With all the latest computer technology in existence, privileged information was a thing of the past. The privacy act was practically null and void.

But the restaurant bathroom and the coffee shop incidents didn't make sense. As tears pooled in her eyes, anger, hurt, and frustration assaulted her sanity. She had a lot of homework to do, she figured, but she'd have to keep it all together. She couldn't fall apart now that she was so close to solving the puzzle.

Chapter Twenty

The Philyaw home was filled with holiday dinner guests. All of Wyman's local employees had been invited, but only six had come. Aunt Mamie's dearest friend, Teresa Banks, had been invited, as well. Frank and Marion and Ian and Sara had also come.

Omunique's suspicions about Sara being involved in the crimes against her had been removed long before Brian had confessed. When Sara and Ian had become romantically involved, a motive ceased to exist. At one point, she'd even suspected Ian. In fact, there weren't too many people that she hadn't come to suspect. Omunique hadn't been able to reach Brent at all, and she couldn't wait to do so. He had a lot of explaining to do.

Max had assured them of his presence, but Ken was still in Seattle, which distressed Omunique to no end. They'd been looking forward to the holiday for months. Now they'd be spending it apart—all because she'd been so heartless, she thought as she made sure all the tables were set properly.

The formal dining table and several portable tables were

lavishly decorated with fine linens, antique china, and crystal stemware. Crystal vases of red and white flowers served as centerpieces. On each side of the flowers tapered candles nestled in magnificent silver candleholders. Tantalizing everyone in their wake, the delicious smells of Christmas floated throughout the house. While Mamie and Wyman put the finishing touches on the superb meal they'd prepared, Omunique kept pretty busy, acting as the temporary hostess.

In the kitchen Wyman slid the huge turkey from the roasting pan and transferred it to a large silver platter. He then removed prime ribs from the upper and lower ovens and set them on the tile counter. He removed the dressing from the turkey and placed it in a ceramic casserole.

When Max sauntered into the kitchen, Mamie was busy slicing the sweet potato and pumpkin pies. "Hello," Mamie exclaimed cheerfully. "We're glad you were able to make it. You're looking quite dashing there, Mr. Maxwell."

As Mamie smiled, her dusky brown complexion glowed. Her eyes, the color of fine bourbon, sparkled like the North Star. At fifty-five she didn't look a day over forty, her body still shapely and firm. Done up in a neat French roll, her once mixed-gray hair was now rinsed a deep chocolate-brown. Max hugged Mamie. After Wyman wiped his hands on a paper towel, Max shook hands with the host.

"It's good to see you both," Max said, eyeing the mouth-watering pies.

"It's good to see you, too, Max. Please tell me that son of yours is with you. Despite her denials this won't be much of a holiday celebration for Omunique without his presence," Wyman remarked without reproach.

Max frowned. "I wish I could, Wyman, but I can't. He's still in Seattle. I talked to him late last night. His mood was so foul I didn't dare give him a crash lecture in Manners 101. I could tell that he didn't care much for spending Christmas Eve away from home. Actually, this is our first holiday apart.

However, Omunique seemed just fine to me at the *Holiday on Ice Show*. I wish I could say the same for my son.''

"She's doing just great, Max. At least her ankle is. But I've been thinking of having her see a cardiologist. That daughter of mine is suffering from a broken heart.''

"That daughter of yours *is* not,'' Omunique objected from the doorway. When everyone turned around to look at her, she turned on a smile that made them seriously doubt Wyman's statement.

Looking gorgeous in a royal blue silk dress and shoes of the same color, she stood on her tiptoes and kissed Max's cheek.

"Hello, sweetheart,'' Max greeted with genuine affection. "You look like a million bucks. I hear you're feeling like a million, too. How close are you to being ready for your next competition?''

Omunique looped her arm through his. "The most important competition of my life,'' she corrected. "I'm more than ready, Max. I'm going to make Maxwell a proud sponsor. You can bet the firm on that.''

He grinned. "We're already proud. Those television spots we decided to run from the initial video session are going to pay off big-time. You did a marvelous job on the speaking parts, which we've already dubbed in. And you're skating great. I saw your performance in the holiday show. I enjoyed it tremendously.''

She smiled. "I'm glad you did.'' She wanted to ask if Ken had come home for the holidays, but she decided against it. The answer could hurt too much.

Once all the food was placed on the table Wyman made a brief speech that welcomed all of their guests. Name cards marked the seating arrangements, and everyone took their assigned seat. There was only one place setting left, which would've been Ken's. After giving the blessing, Wyman excused himself.

Omunique eyed the name card wistfully, feeling an overpowering urge to break down and cry. *Couldn't he have put his feelings toward me on hold?* she asked, knowing she hadn't afforded him the same consideration all those interminable weeks ago. *But today is Christmas,* she wailed inwardly.

Just as the food was passed around the table, Wyman returned.

Then, wearing a red Santa hat, Kenneth Maxwell Jr. walked into the dining room right behind Wyman, bearing a cache of brightly wrapped gifts. "Merry Christmas! I can't believe you all were going to eat before Santa Claus arrived," he joked with ease, removing the bright red hat from his head.

The food was momentarily forgotten as all eyes were on Ken, but he seemed to pay no attention. Everyone's eyes widened when he headed straight for the empty chair next to Omunique. Frank and Marion exchanged knowing smiles.

As usual, his stride was confident, Omunique noted, her heart working itself into a frenzied state. He briefly touched her hand as he sat down, causing her heart to race at an even faster pace. Her lips and throat felt parched, her eyes burned with unshed tears.

Ken looked around the table. "Is everyone going to just sit there and gawk, or are we going to eat? Marion, pass the mashed potatoes, please. This meal looks fit for a king."

Omunique had lost her mind in a time warp, with him acting as if everything were perfectly normal, and she couldn't believe he was actually sitting next to her. The urge to pinch him to make sure he wasn't a vision was overwhelming. When his arm accidentally bumped hers, she felt the sizzling contact that confirmed his presence.

Within minutes buzzing conversation once again filled the room. Omunique seemed to be the only one who hadn't quite gotten over his sudden appearance, but she could see that Max was proud that Ken had decided to mind his manners. All Max could do was smile as he chatted with Teresa Banks, who sat next to him. She sensed that Wyman was thrilled, yet worried about how she'd handle Ken's unexpected presence.

A short time into the meal Omunique excused herself and

went into the kitchen. Feeling dizzy from all the emotional stress, she leaned against the counter for support. Ken hadn't said one word to her, which made her feel sick with emptiness. "So much for friendship. Why did he bother to come here if he was going to act like such a juvenile?"

"Because he was invited. And it was crucial that he be here," he responded, walking up behind her. She'd heard him say those very words the night of the cast party, which meant he'd intended to come to dinner all along. Or so it seemed.

He leaned over her shoulder. "I'm sorry. I didn't know I'd acted like a juvenile. I didn't come here to upset you, Omunique. That was never my intention." She turned around to face him, but her eyes began to blur and her head suddenly felt like chopped cotton. The dizzy spell hadn't quite passed, and she began to fall.

Catching her before the floor could rise up to meet her, he pulled her into the safety of his arms. "Are you okay? Is it your ankle again?" he asked with grave concern. As she looked up at him, her world swayed crazily, but not from the dizziness. She merely felt the heated contact; right down to the ends of her painted toenails.

Quietly assessing their feelings about being in one another's arms, they stood motionless. The atmosphere hissed with tangible tensions: mental tension, physical tension, sexual tension. Their breathing came in uneven spurts, short gasps. As she tried to move away, he held her tighter, then bent his head and consumed her mouth with a fire hotter than Hades had ever been described. Hunger, deprivation, wantonness, all the things they'd experienced over the past weeks, seemed to belong to the past as they devoured, and recklessly gleaned what they so desperately needed from one another. As she clung to him, he gently pushed her back against the sink and molded his hips against her trembling body.

As though he still hadn't gotten close enough to her, he lifted her up, sat her on the counter, and positioned his hips between her parted knees. All the while, he gorged himself on the honey

Linda Hudson-Smith

taste of her luscious lips. "Omunique, tell me . . . this is for . . . real. Tell ¯. . . me . . . I'm not . . . dreaming," he said over and over again, without giving her a chance to respond. "Oh, Princess, how I've missed kissing you this way, missed you touching me the way only you can."

Omunique didn't want to respond; she was afraid that if he let go of her she just might wake up. If it wasn't real, she needed every bit of what seemed like reality that she could get—him being there with her, him seeming to want her every bit as much as he had before they'd split, their love. She wanted him desperately, but if he were to leave after what they now shared she knew she'd never be able to face reality again.

Lifting her down from the counter, he guided her toward the back entrance. Snatching a blanket from the laundry room shelf, they headed for the beach. Neither of them spoke as they raced against the wind. They reached the shore just as the sun was about to set. After spreading the blanket on the cool, damp sand, Ken pulled her down onto his lap and buried his lips in her perfume-scented hair. Mindless to everything but the love they felt for one another and the joy of being together again, they shared the sunset, the moon, and the stars.

Conversation simply wasn't necessary. Apologies weren't needed. Explanations weren't called for. They could see, feel, and hear what each needed to say to the other. Their eyes saw, their bodies felt, their hearts rejoiced.

Later, Omunique and Ken slipped in through the same door they'd exited from. Ken joined the others while Omunique went to her bedroom to repair her disheveled looks. On cloud nine, she floated down the hallway.

From the looks on their faces when he walked into the room, Ken could tell that everyone who'd been privy to their situation knew that the undying embers of their love had been rekindled.

After a discreet period of time had passed Max pulled Ken off to the side of the room. Ken smiled when Wyman went in search of his daughter. He sensed that both fathers were eager to know all the details of their children's possible reconciliation, but there were some very intimate details that would forever remain a secret between himself and Omunique.

The second Omunique walked into the room Ken excused himself from Max, eager to dance with her while the slow songs played, figuring it wouldn't be long before the faster paced music would be requested since several people had expressed the desire to boogie the night away.

He held his arms out to her. Smiling, she drifted into his space. They clung to each of as though there'd be no tomorrow while Boyz to Men soulfully crooned "On Bended Knee."

When everyone else paired off to dance, Ken saw that Max and Teresa were the only ones without partners, but he knew Max was too much of a gentleman to allow a classy woman like Teresa Banks to become a wallflower.

Ken softly sang in Omunique's ear the words to the song that was filled with anguish over losing a lover. Omunique thought she should've been the one singing to him, since she was the one who almost caused them to lose forever.

He was there with her now, but she needed to know if he was back to stay. Tilting her head at an angle, she looked into the eyes that spoke to her heart. "Will you come back to me?" she asked, positive that their lives were no longer in danger.

His eyes seemed to fall deeply in love with hers. "I never left, Princess," he whispered against her temple. "And never again am I going to let you leave." His eyes said so much more to her than he'd voiced. Both responses left her weak as a newborn kitten.

She smiled into his eyes. "That sounds like a promise. Is it?"

He kissed her deeply. *A promise of forever,* his heart chimed. "We'll talk about that later. I just want to hold you and feel your heart beating next to mine. That's all I want to hear for now. Wrap your arms around me, woman, and we'll soar back to the moon."

When the song "I'll Make Love To You" came on, also by Boyz to Men, his eyes made promises that he couldn't wait to live up to. Tightening his arm around her slender waist, he brought her nearer to him. With the message in his eyes clearly understood, she relaxed her head against his inviting chest. It felt so good to be in his arms, so good to feel the steady beat of his heart, so good to taste the sweetness of his mouth on hers. *Sooo good,* she marveled.

There was a lot they had to talk about, so many things to be settled, but it all would have to wait. Once she had all the facts, she'd explain it all to him. Tonight was their night to rediscover the mystery and the magic of love.

Once all the guests had left, Omunique and Ken made themselves comfortable in their usual spot in front of the fireplace. They were completely alone, since Wyman had taken Mamie and Teresa home.

He nestled her head in his lap. "How are you really doing, Princess? Physically and mentally."

She looked up at him. "Physically, I'm doing just great. Mentally, I've been a few bricks short of a load, and I've nearly driven my father crazy. He even tried to get me to see a psychiatrist, during the time I'd become really depressed. He was so happy when I felt well enough for him to go back up north. Everything is fine now, especially now that you're back in my life. I can't tell you how much I missed you."

He smoothed her hair back. "Why don't you give it a try? I'd love to know if you missed me as much as I missed you. Speaking of depressed, I gave that word a whole new meaning. But maybe we shouldn't talk about this now. There'll be plenty of time for us to talk about all that we've been through. This is Christmas. A time for sharing lots of love and happiness."

She felt relieved. She was so sure the conversation would've gotten around to all of the terrible things that had happened to her. She felt as Brian did. If Ken knew that Brian had been responsible for hurting Omunique and ripping their lives apart in the process, he would've gotten himself into serious trouble. There was no doubt in her mind that Ken would've done something that he would've ended up being sorry for. She certainly didn't want to see him end up in jail. As it was now, she'd have to approach the matter with extreme caution and with loads of sensitivity. And she'd have to find the right time. Now wasn't it. Enough light hadn't been shed. Brent had to bring more illumination on the truth to the table. Until she could see the entire situation clearly, she vowed to keep her silence.

"Oh, sweetheart," he moaned, taking her into his arms, "I'm so happy to be here with you like this. I prayed fervently for this moment. I love you, Omunique Philyaw. I love you with all my heart."

She used his hand to brush her tears away. "I guess I really failed at communicating my feelings to you. I guess I held back a lot of things. To make up for all the times I couldn't tell you I loved you, I promise to tell you every single day how much you mean to me. Should I forget to do so, will you kindly remind me of my promise?"

She did love him, though she hadn't exactly said the three words he longed to hear. Still, Omunigue's confession had shaken his world as he imagined a ten-point earthquake would rock California. She was still capable of making the stars collide, and the universe tilt.

"I will, Princess, but I doubt that you'll forget. The kind of love we share doesn't come along every day. I love you, Princess. And I hope you don't get tired of hearing me say it, because I'm never going to stop."

"I love you, Kenneth. I love you so much!" she confessed breathlessly. Any doubt that he might have about her feelings for him were washed away the moment she said those three magical words. As she brought her lips feverishly to his, it was just like he'd imagined it would be. The stars in the sky collided and the universe tilted, leaving him dizzy with longing.

He tilted her head back and nipped gently at her throat. "I can't tell you how I've longed to hear you say you love me, Princess. Now that you have, don't ever stop. It sounds like heaven to my ears. I deeply regret that I wasn't here to see you through all your trials and tribulations. I'm sorry that you had to go it alone.''

She pulled his head down for another kiss. ''That's so sweet of you, but you're not to blame. You told me how you felt, but I refused to hear it. Maybe I needed to go through all this alone. I'm much stronger because of it, and it's helped me to understand myself a lot better. It has also reaffirmed my purpose for the upcoming competition. Thanks for being so patient with me, Ken.''

Ken didn't leave the Philyaw home until the morning sun blazed across the clear blue skies. They'd spent the entire night talking and reacquainting themselves with each other. It was like starting their relationship all over again. Ken seemed as eager as she to do just that. They'd set new boundaries for their relationship, and they'd promised to always communicate their feelings.

To confess her love for him in the midst of them finding one another again was most appropriate, Omunique thought as she snuggled her petite body under the blush-pink comforter. For all their talk of starting over, she was painfully aware of the unfinished business she had to take care of before she could look forward to their future. Before catching a few hours sleep, she promised herself to make sure he'd always feel her love, in the same way he'd made her feel his.

Lying in bed, Ken thought about all the things he and Omunique had discussed during the course of the night and the early morning hours. He remembered telling her that he wanted her to fulfill her lifelong dreams as much as she needed to fulfill them. He'd wait for her for as long as it took, give her as much space as she needed. He'd made that vow to her, a vow he fully intended to honor. Once she accomplished her mission, he'd be there to share in her triumph.

He had an important mission in life, too.

Omunique Philyaw.

Chapter Twenty-one

With her teeth chattering and her body shivering, Omunique skated onto the ice. Trying to generate some heat, she vigorously rubbed her arms. Although the California weather had cooled considerably and the rains had been constant, Omunique wasn't only shivering from the cold as she warmed up. She had a case of the jitters. She only had a few weeks left to practice before heading to the skating competition in Denver, which would send her to the Olympics or send her back to the old drawing board to come up with a fresh routine. Adding more stress to her already existing anguish, Brent hadn't returned to his duties.

The replacement coach he'd arranged for her was doing a tremendous job. Possessing a quiet confidence in his ability to coach her, Jim Schmidt was gentle in his teachings and his criticisms, firm and committed to how things should be done. He didn't want to hear from her that Brent did it this way or that way. He'd made it clear to her that he was in charge now, and he wanted it done his way.

She was only too happy to oblige him. She wanted to become as confident in his abilities as he already seemed to be in hers.

Under Jim's savvy administration her confidence had been restored by leaps and bounds. No longer intimidated by all the things that had gone wrong, she now focused on all the things now going right. However, she hoped for many reasons that Brent would return. The matter of bringing Brian to justice couldn't be achieved until he provided her with the rest of the facts. In her opinion, Brent had the key that would open the lock to the truth.

By the time she reached Denver she'd be a force to be reckoned with. By the time the competition was over she expected to be a member of the United States Olympic team— the second African-American female ever to make it to the big show.

Omunique worked through her long program, timing herself to ensure that she kept the program to exactly four minutes. She worked several different jumps into her program, using the landing edge of one jump as a takeoff edge for the next one. The triple axel was always the hardest for her, the only jump executed from a forward position, considered to be one of the most difficult jumps in figure skating. She made many valiant attempts before finally making the type of jumps that she could be extremely proud of.

Dropping her head and shoulders backward, she arched her back, executing a nearly flawless layback spin. She then practiced the same move over and over again before moving into the technical portion of her program, which had to be completed in two minutes and forty seconds and had to include all of the eight required elements.

After several falls and slides across the ice Omunique became frustrated, but she refused to doubt herself. To allow doubt to creep in was like inviting disaster to come along for the spin. Doubt had no place in any sport, and she certainly wasn't going to allow it to earn a spot in her head.

It was well after 10:00 P.M. when Omunique finished her practice session, exuberant over how well she'd executed her short and long programs. If she did as well at the competition, she could make the Olympic team, especially if the judges gave her the marks she truly deserved. She had a few aces up her sleeve where her artistic program was concerned, but she knew that she needed to work much, much harder on the technical portion.

Dancing joyously on the inside, she flitted across the parking lot. She couldn't have been happier. Everything was going to be okay. Ken, she thought warmly, would be eagerly awaiting her at his condo. She tingled all over as she thought about all the ways he'd show her how much he'd missed her. She couldn't wait to rush into the safety of his loving arms, the arms that held her security tight.

As she opened the door to the Jeep, a dark shadow fell across the lighted parking lot. Icy fingers wrapped around her wrist, twisting it until she thought her hand would break off and fall to the ground. Then a gloved hand muffled her screams before they could escape her throat. When she turned around to face her attacker, she was spun back around so fast she had no chance of identifying her assailant.

"You beautiful, ungrateful witch," a raspy voice charged, "I gave you so much of my attention, but you never knew I existed. I've supported you and I've loved you, but you took your smile away and gave it to someone so undeserving."

Though numb with trepidation, Omunique tried to wriggle free from the strong grasp, but her attacker grabbed her hair. "If you move again, I'll snap your neck like a dry twig. I've got nothing to lose. You've already taken it all away."

The large hand repositioned itself over her mouth. Holding her from behind, her assailant dragged her to a blue van and forcefully pushed back the sliding door. Lifting her off her feet by her neck, the assailant shoved her inside and slammed the door shut.

Omunique could barely breathe. Her heart was in her mouth, and her brain felt as though it had been wired with dozens of explosives. She rubbed at her swollen, twisted wrist, trying to massage the throbbing pain away. Scared to make a sound, she crawled into a corner, hoping and praying that she wasn't going to die.

She couldn't die now, not when she had so much to live for, not when all the pieces of her life had begun to fall into place. Brent held the last piece of the puzzle, just waiting to be inserted into the slot that would complete it. She just about had everything she'd ever hoped for.

Now it appeared that the ice wasn't the only thing under fire, she thought in sheer terror.

Her very existence was under fire!

When the van engine backfired, she nearly fainted. It sounded so much like a gunshot being fired into the night. Why had she stayed at the arena so late? Jim had left long before dark. Hadn't she been warned about this very thing? Time and time again. So determined to stay focused on her dream rather than the nightmares she'd been plagued with, she'd disregarded all other warnings. So confident that she knew who her personal terrorist was—a silly misguided teenager named Brian Terry—she'd insisted on discontinuing the security surveillance.

It had been a hard sell to Ken and Wyman as to why she no longer wanted security all around her, but she'd somehow managed to wage a convincing argument, accomplishing it without giving them all the facts as she knew them. A long time had passed since the last incident, and it shocked her to realize that she'd once again lulled herself into believing it was all over and that the men in her life were still just a bit too reactionary.

The van moved now, but very slowly. Then it rapidly picked up speed, tossing her around like a rag doll. It was then that she spotted the rear door of the van and began to inch her way toward the back. It would be suicide to jump out at this high rate of speed, she knew, but surely the van would be caught at a light before it reached its final destination. If she didn't try to jump out, the final destination could very well be death. Jumping out would probably break every bone in her body, but she thought it better for that to occur than to never feel anything ever again.

Reaching the rear door, she waited for the chance to act. So many things passed through her brain she thought it would simply die from sheer exhaustion. Every nerve ending in her body was painfully alive. Even at the height of competition, she'd never felt such an incredible adrenaline high. Unwittingly, she'd now entered the biggest competition of her life, the fight for her very existence.

The van careened around a corner, throwing her away from the rear doors and slamming her into the back of a seat. Before she could inch her way back to the rear door, the van came to a screeching halt. *Death is imminent,* she thought, though she continued to pray for a miracle, a miracle that would set her free, a miracle that would save her precious life.

As the heavy door slid back, she heard the asthmatic breathing of her kidnapper. The breathing grew closer. Then a dark figure loomed over her, snatching at her hair once again. She screamed, and was punished with a sharp blow across the face which practically rendered her senseless. The next blow nearly caused her to black out, but she fought hard to remain conscious. For what she thought her attacker might have in mind, unconsciousness might have been kinder, in the sense that she wouldn't feel a thing.

As she was dragged from the van, the cold night air further assaulted her senses. Unmitigated fear robbed her of the ability to think about escape, of all the strength needed to physically or mentally do battle, of her courage.

Suddenly, a gunshot rang out, followed by another warning shot.

"Hold it right there," a police officer's deep voice commanded. "Let her go or I'll blow your brains all the way to hell!"

There was a flurry of motion, then Omunique felt cold metal against her neck. "If I die, she goes with me. Back off or force me to end it for her right this minute. And don't bother trying to kill me. I'm already dead.''

The rasp was now gone from the attacker's voice, and Omunique immediately recognized it. It was a voice she'd heard a lot in recent weeks, a voice that at one time had soothed her and innocently flirted with her—at least she had believed his friendly demeanor had been innocent. A voice that had asked for employment as her personal bodyguard. The voice of Officer Marcus Taylor.

"Oh, God," she screamed as a cold dose of reality knocked her for a loop. "Why? Why are you doing this? I don't even know you. Why would you want to do something like this to anyone?" She began to sob brokenly, wondering what she'd done to make this man attack her in this manner, a man who was supposed to uphold the law, not break it.

The look on his face said that he didn't care that she now knew the identity of her personal terrorist. He wanted her to know. And he was ready to meet Satan face-to-face, ready for anything and everything that might come his way.

He pulled her head back. "You want to know why, do you? I'll tell you why. It'll be the last thing you'll ever hear from me. I've been there every day to watch you skate. I've adored you. I've watched over you day in and day out. When I got off duty, I came there and waited. I was there on my off days. I followed you home every night, keeping you safe from hurt, harm, and danger. Then you failed me. You turned to someone else. You took your smile away. Yet I still adored you.''

Sticking the cold steel under her chin, he spun her around to face him. "Now you tell me why you couldn't return those feelings. I stopped you and gave you that ticket, hoping you'd come to notice me. You tell me why you stopped smiling at me. You tell me what Maxwell gave you that I couldn't. Was it wealth and power?''

Glaring and snarling like a rabid animal, he turned the knife blade sideways and meshed it against the side of her neck.

"Was it what he did for you in bed?" he asked, placing the blade back under her chin. "Answer me, Omunique," he demanded.

Her eyes blinked uncontrollably. It was difficult to speak with the cold metal under her chin—She feared the blade would penetrate her skin if she opened her mouth. But his eyes demanded a response from her.

She tried to swallow the bitter taste of fear, but it wouldn't go away. "I . . . had no . . . idea . . . of . . . the things . . . you've been talking . . . about . . . here," she stammered. "I'd never . . . seen you . . . before the . . . traffic stop. I didn't even . . . know your name . . . before then."

She could see the other officer edging closer. It caused her more fear than the steel blade at her flesh, since it appeared he was working solo.

"It wouldn't have mattered if you had. The minute the wealthy Mr. Maxwell entered your life I would've become extinct. I was only trying to make you see what a big mistake you were making by choosing him over me. You seemed willing to give up all your dreams for someone so unworthy of you. You became spineless."

The vacant stare in his blue eyes chilled her to the bone. "I followed your every move, hoping you'd think it was someone in his life, hoping that you'd give him up and return your smile to me. A few lousy mishaps caused you to freak and go soft.

"When your coach talked to me about the kid who was making threats against you, he had no clue. He thought he was helping out you and the kid. But he played right into my hands, and I took up the battle from there. Your coach knew as well as I did that your involvement with Maxwell was a mistake. Everyone takes a friendly officer into their confidence."

The area was now crawling with his colleagues, but Taylor remained undaunted. He ignored the shouts from his fellow officers, including the pleas from his own partner, Officer Kyle Thomas. All he could hear were the voices inside his head that told him to destroy her, the same voice that told him if he couldn't have her no one else would.

The swat team had taken up position. Omunique saw the discreet flashes of movement out of the corner of her eye, but Officer Taylor didn't seem to notice. He was completely lost to his own mindless ranting.

"Taylor," Officer Thomas shouted through a bullhorn, "give it up, man. This is not worth it. Let us at least negotiate a deal with you, Taylor," Officer Thomas pleaded. "You already know you're not going to be able to get away with this. What would you like us to do for you? Just name it. The department will help you in every way they can."

Taylor backed Omunique up against the van door. "There's nothing you can do for me," he responded to his longtime partner. "I have all I've ever wanted in life. I have the rapt attention of the Ice Princess."

Kenneth Maxwell Jr. seemed to appear out of nowhere— the worst thing that could possibly happen, as far as the police were concerned. His presence only added to the serious problems they were already faced with.

Ken thought about the call he'd received from young Brian Terry, who had seen Officer Taylor abduct Omunique from the arena parking lot. After he'd contacted the police, he'd called Ken, who had given Brian his phone number the day he'd gone to their house to lend the family a helping hand. When Brian saw that Officer Taylor was the same man that Brent had asked to help him, he had called Ken and told him everything. Ken had learned the location from his godfather.

When Taylor's arm pressed into Omunique's throat, almost cutting off her air supply, the cops yelled for Ken to clear out. Ominously, Ken moved on toward the demented officer.

"Don't come any closer, Maxwell," Taylor shouted. "You're the reason she's in trouble. You've ruined her career and her life. She was all mine until you appeared. She was as pure as silent snow until you soiled her. You're to blame for all of this."

Ken moved forward, then came to an abrupt halt. Omunique was turning blue right before his eyes. Slowly, he began to back off. "This is all for nothing, Taylor. Omunique cares about you." Ken heard his own voice, but he had no clue why he'd been compelled to speak those particular words. "She recently broke off our relationship. She's not interested in anything but skating. Are you going to take that away from her? Achieving her goals means everything to her."

Ken gulped greedily at the air, his lungs on fire. "Are you ready to give up her attention now that you have it?" Ken continued, feeling scared that he seemed to have no control over what came out of his mouth.

Taylor suddenly loosened his arm. His expression seemed to soften as he looked down into her eyes, watching her intently as she gasped and sucked in the fresh air she'd been deprived of for far too long. He then removed the cold metal from her neck.

In that fleeting moment, before Taylor had a chance to take further action, a barrage of shots rang out. In a split second, without a thought to her own safety, Omunique pushed Officer Taylor backward into the open door of the van, hoping to save him from the torrent of bullets aimed at taking his life.

There was a moment of deadly silence, and then Omunique's screams shattered the moon and scattered the stars. Ken rushed forward, enfolding her crumbling body in his arms. "Oh, God, Nique, I thought you were going to die!" he cried out in anguish.

She hadn't heard anything he'd said, because she couldn't control her screams. The reality of the entire scenario had set in on her like rigor mortis as she clung to Ken in desperation. She then fell to the ground, taking him down with her. As she screamed and wept, he held onto the most precious life in his world, a life that had nearly been lost to him forever.

"Om . . . u . . . nique," came the strangled cry from Marcus Taylor.

Taylor was calling out for her, and she felt compelled to respond. In a daze, she lifted herself up from the ground and moved slowly away from Ken.

"No, Nique," Ken shouted as she moved toward the van, "don't go near him. He's out of his mind!"

The swat team still had their guns trained on their fellow officer as they waited for the paramedics to arrive. Knowing he was armed was what had kept them a safe distance back. As if the situation weren't tense enough, Omunique had now placed herself right back in the direct line of their fire and Taylor's. For sure, he was armed and dangerous.

She cast Ken a look that caused his heart to break. The look in her eyes told him that she had to do this—she had to confront the man who'd tried to kill her, the sick man who somehow believed he loved her and that she'd failed him—though there was no way she could've known. Ken couldn't believe the depth of her compassion.

It appeared to her as though an adoring fan had turned into a homicidal maniac, a crazed fan that she hadn't even been aware of, a fan who desperately needed help.

Inside the van, Omunique knelt down beside Marcus, but she couldn't bring herself to touch him. There was a good deal of blood on him, but she didn't freak out. Tears fell from her eyes as she looked down at the handsome man with the cool blue eyes. *So handsome,* she thought. *He probably could've had almost any woman he wanted.*

He looked up at her, pitiful adoration shining in his dilated eyes. "Was Maxwell telling . . . the truth? Do you . . . care about me?"

This is so pathetic, she thought, tears running down her cheeks. There was no appropriate answer to his question, yet she could see how desperately he needed one. She didn't even know him. How could she care about him in the way that he spoke of?

"Yes, I do," she responded honestly. In accordance with the word of the Heavenly Father, she cared for everyone. Sighing heavily, Taylor smiled.

Unable to deal with the danger she'd placed herself in, Ken rushed inside the van, quickly lifted Omunique up, and carried her out into the night air. As he ran toward the nearest officer, he heard a shot ring out. When he looked back, it appeared that Taylor lay dead inside the van. Horrified at the tragic scene before him, he set Omunique down and covered her eyes with his hands. It looked as though Officer Marcus Taylor had shot himself straight through the head with his own service revolver. Omunique tried to turn around and look back, but Ken propelled her on toward the waiting officer who was the first one on the scene.

Luckily for Omunique, Officer J.T. Dailey had been patrolling the area around the arena when the radio call was first dispatched. He'd gotten to the scene just as the blue van, which met with the description of the suspect's vehicle, had pulled out of the parking lot. He had tailed it at a safe distance, calling for backup as he did so.

After running a check on the license plates he learned that the vehicle belonged to a Marcus Taylor. Because the suspect's name wasn't at all uncommon, he'd never dreamed it could be their very own Marcus Taylor, a ten year veteran of the police force.

"Is she okay, sir?" Officer Dailey asked Ken.

"That's a stupid question, don't you think?" Ken responded acidly. "She just witnessed a man being shot, not to mention the living hell she'd already been through. And you want to know if she's okay! Hell, no, she's not okay."

Ken dropped his head in shame, then looked up at Officer Dailey. "I apologize for that, man. I thought she was going to die. I'm just not myself right now. I should be thanking you instead of taking your head off."

Officer Daily placed a calming hand on Ken's shoulder. "It's okay, Mr. Maxwell. I understand. I'll try to get clearance for you to take her home. She's in no condition to be questioned right now. I'm sure the supervising officer will authorize it." The officer turned away and moved toward the on duty supervisor.

While watching her trembling like the ground during a major

earthquake, Ken noticed that Omunique's skin had no color to it whatsoever. He removed his jacket and placed it around her shoulders, then engulfed her in the warmth of his body. "I'll have you home in just a few minutes, Princess. Just lean on me, sweetheart."

She circled his waist with shaking hands. "Ken," she uttered weakly, "how could something like this happen? I never would've suspected a police officer of doing something so horrific, especially not an officer who was involved in the investigation. What is this world coming to?" she sobbed.

"An end, unfortunately, sooner than most people think. The one altercation I had with Taylor made me a little wary of him. Just as you'd mentioned, he was too quick to draw his baton. When I first met him, that day in the locker room, I couldn't remember where I'd heard his name. I just knew that I had. It didn't dawn on me who he was until much later. I would've never named him as a suspect, not even after I saw him with you at the holiday show cast party. However, that's when I thought about the bogus traffic citation issued by him. Brian and Brent were the two people I suspected more than anyone else. Though somehow they're both involved in this, Officer Taylor cast himself as the rogue cop."

She thought about Brent's part in all this. His silence was as much to blame for this as anything, or anyone. Why he'd kept this from her made no sense at all. It was as if he'd purposely tried to sabotage her dreams. But why?

"Oh, God, how sad," she moaned. 'We were so close to realizing our dream. How could Brent be in on something like this? How could he help sabotage our success in this manner?" *We worked so hard to get where we are, and now it could all be over.*

"I can't hope to win in Denver without Brent there to encourage me. He always knows how to motivate me, no matter what. Jim is a great coach, but he's not Brent Masters."

Ken gently pressed her head into his chest. "I'll be there for you, Princess. All of us who love you will be there. We'll get through this. Trust me, sweetheart?"

She brushed her lips across his. "Trust you? You bet I do. Can we go home now?" she asked, choking back a sob.

"Until you hear Brent's side, I don't want you to jump to any conclusions. We don't know why he chose to handle things the way he did. We don't know what he was thinking at the time. Although I was suspicious of him, I honestly don't think he knew about Officer Taylor's sick intentions. That's something I just can't fathom." Wiping the tears from her eyes, she nodded. "Let's go see Officer Dailey. He should have an answer for us by now. I can't wait to get you out of this dismal atmosphere."

Another cold dose of reality claimed Omunique as she showered. She dropped down on her knees to the floor of the tub as hysteria tried to force its way into her throat. She bravely fought the urge to scream until no more screams could emerge, but her entire body felt limp and lifeless. *Life is a cruel game,* she thought. If one didn't know how to play it, there wasn't a chance in hell for survival. Cold chills of dread raced up and down her spine as she thought about Officer Taylor stalking her every move.

Ken walked into the bathroom, and the haunted look in her eyes distressed him as he reached his arm around the shower curtain and turned off the water. Kneeling down beside the tub, he put the drain plug in place and turned the water back on.

"I think a hot bath will do you a world of good," he said, sprinkling scented bath salts in the water. "The shower water had turned cold, but you didn't seem to notice."

Picking up the bath sponge, he trickled the hot water down over her neck and shoulders. "I know this has been tough on you, Princess, but you have to try to put it out of your mind.

We need to get a good night's sleep. We can sort out everything in the morning.''

Expressionless, she nodded her head.

While lying in bed Ken watched Omunique as she tossed and turned. One minute she was pulling the covers over her body, the next minute she was kicking them off. A terrorizing inquietude had crept into her once peaceful world, and it seemed to be turning her every way but loose. As much as he wanted to make love to her, in hopes of pushing her fears aside, as well as his own, he knew the timing was all wrong.

He felt helpless and inadequate, very aware that there wasn't any amount of solace that would quell the raging storm within her. No human in the world could take away the unmitigated fear that Marcus Taylor had willingly placed in her heart. Her fears could only be removed through divine intervention.

Turning over on her back, she pulled Ken's head onto her chest and crushed his satin curls between her fingers. The tension began to melt away from both of them as he smothered her breasts with gentle kisses. ''Is there anything I can do for you, Princess?''

''Make love to me,'' she whispered softly. ''I need to be reaffirmed.''

Looking deeply into the smoky-gray eyes awash with tears, he tilted her head back. ''Are you sure that you want me to, Nique?'' he asked, a hoarseness replacing the sultry baritone in his voice.

She kissed his throat. ''I've never been more sure of anything in my life. I want so desperately to feel the intimate connection that I'm only able to feel with you.''

An hour later, deeply satisfied by the ultimate connection she'd made with Ken, Omunique fell into a restful sleep, nestled in the arms of one of the only two men she felt safe with.

Just before dawn Omunique bolted upright, her loud screams awakening Ken. He reached for her with tender arms and she flung herself into him, and he rocked her back and forth as she sobbed brokenly. As the sobs turned to low whimpers and painful moans, Ken stroked her back. After several minutes had passed, she fell back to sleep, cradled in his soothing arms, cradled in the protective arms of the man she would've sacrificed her life for.

Chapter Twenty-two

Sitting in the living room of her home, Omunique eyed Brent suspiciously, not knowing whether to believe his story or not. Some of it made sense, but she still wasn't completely satisfied. Something was missing from his woeful tale.

Brent softly touched her hand, cutting into the preponderant thoughts in her racing mind. "I swear I didn't know about Taylor. When I told him what Brian had done, I thought I was soliciting the help of an upstanding pillar of the community. For God's sake, he was a police officer. I had no idea he was a fan of yours, let alone an obsessed one. This guy could've gotten an Academy Award for such a believable performance.

"Brian was only guilty of making the first threatening phone calls, but I assumed he was guilty of everything else, just as you did. Taylor simply continued on with the same method of operation that Brian had told him he'd used. I guess I spurred Taylor on by confiding in him about your personal affairs. Hell, I'd even grown to like the guy."

Agitated, Omunique threw up her hands. "That doesn't explain why you didn't tell me what you knew about Brian. A lot of things have happened since the first few phone calls, a lot of terrible things, Brent, like my concussion and ankle injury. Would you mind explaining why you kept quiet after those things happened?''

Looking worn down, Brent shook his head. ''Nique, that's when I realized that someone else other than Brian was involved in this. When I talked to Officer Taylor about my suspicions, he told me the department would handle it. He already knew the extent of Brian's involvement. He knew he was that *someone else.*''

Brent pounded into his knee with a closed fist. ''I would've told you before I left town, but Taylor convinced me that telling you would only put you in more danger. He said that the detectives had a good lead on a suspect, and I just might blow the case for them if I said anything to anyone. That's when I decided I'd done more harm than good.''

Astounded, she got up from her seat. ''This is too incredible for words. It's almost impossible. Let me see if I have this straight,'' she said, pointing at her temple as she sat back down. ''Brian initiates the threatening phone calls. You catch him at it, then you get Officer Taylor to help a troubled youth turn his life around rather than see him end up in Juvenile Hall. Brian tells Officer Taylor about all the things he did to frighten me. In turn, Officer Taylor takes up where Brian left off when I'd started seeing Ken. When the phone calls didn't seem to work, that's when the letters and the stalking began. How am I doing so far?''

Brent blew out a ragged breath. ''Sounds like you've put it all together. I couldn't have summed it up any better than that. I take full responsibility for not telling you about Brian. If I thought for one second he'd really intended to bring harm to you, I wouldn't have gone about it the way I did. I knew the kid was troubled, but he assured me that he never intended to hurt you. I believed him, Nique. I hope the community service the judge sentenced him to will help.''

Omunique sighed. ''We all knew that Brian was troubled.

Some practical jokes he'd played around the arena were evidence enough of that. A few of his jokes bordered on schizophrenia. I'll never forget the rubber snake incident. His family problems were more than one young man should ever have to try to handle.''

Brent grimaced. ''He did try, but no matter how bad his life was it didn't justify his actions. And speaking of schizophrenia, that's probably what Taylor suffered from.''

Omunique frowned. ''When I was told about all the pictures Taylor had of me in his place it made my flesh crawl, pictures of me pasted all over the house. Ken's godfather said it looked as though his entire bedroom had been wallpapered with photos of me. What I don't understand is why someone didn't see this obsession. Didn't any of his colleagues ever visit him?''

Brent shook his head. ''He was a loner, from what I've been told. Didn't associate that much with others in the workplace, or outside of it. Very little socialization.''

Unwittingly, he'd just given her the opening she'd needed to discuss his private life. His life wasn't that different from Taylor's. Only this time she wouldn't let him off the hook. Her questions needed answering if her curiosity was ever going to be satisfied.

She looked him straight in the eye. ''I know we've discussed this before, but I need to discuss it with you again. It's centered on the question I posed to you before. Did you lose yourself to love, only to have it fly far away?''

As he had the last time she'd asked about his love life, he suddenly felt hot and clammy. It was time for the truth, he knew, but it would be hard for him. He took a couple more seconds to pull it together as he made a huge withdrawal from the bank of courage that lay deep within him. Looking extremely nervous, he wiped the sweat from his forehead.

''In response to your question, Nique, yes, I lost myself to love. Then I lost the love I'd lost myself to. I loved Kelly Cheyney back then. I love her now. Kelly was as obsessed with the ice as I was with her. When I asked her to marry me, she turned me down. She said there wasn't any room in her life for a serious commitment, yet she professed her love for me. She loved the ice more than she loved me. I was devastated when she told me she'd never make a permanent commitment to me, or anyone else. Her commitment was to the world of figure skating.''

He reached for Omunique's hand. ''I lost my heart and soul to a woman that couldn't love me in the way I needed her to. Then, when I lost my bid for a spot on the Olympic team, I completely lost control of my life. You already know the rest. It was the devastating impact of both losses that made me so bitter.''

Her eyes filled with a compassionate look. It seemed to her that Brent had allowed his relationship gone bad to usurp his confidence on the ice, which was probably why he hadn't been effective in his final competition. His broken romance had turned him against love, and had stopped him from seeking a new one. It appeared to her that he'd never found a way to deal with his insecurities and his fears. In doing so, he'd given in to defeat. She'd come close to the same fate, she knew. Omunique could now see why he'd been so against her relationship with Ken.

She kissed his cheek. ''Thanks so much for sharing with me. I can see that it still hurts. Things are so much clearer to me. I now understand why you feared my relationship with Ken. Fear can be destructive.''

She lowered her lashes. ''I almost allowed my fears to consume me. I purposely sabotaged my chance at happiness with Ken because of the things I feared. But that's all behind us now. I'm glad I'm straight on the part you played in this whole weird scenario. Of all the people I've doubted, like Ian and Sara, I'm sorriest for ever doubting you.''

He hugged her. ''You had good reason for your doubt. I'm glad I've been able to come completely clean with my star athlete. Now that this nightmare is over we can get our minds back on that competition we're going to win.''

Excited about what he'd said, she clapped her hands together. "I heard you say 'we'. Does this mean you've decided not to resign?"

"Exactly. That is, if you still want me as your coach."

"That goes without saying. Now that you've come clean with me, I have to do the same with Ken. Just as you couldn't tell me a lot of things, there are a lot of things I couldn't tell him. At least not until I had all the pieces of the puzzle. Just as you've come clean with your star athlete, I have to come clean with my superstar lover."

"As I told you before, Nique, go for the man you love."

The sun had already set behind the mountains as the moon and stars dazzled the heavens with light. The air that blew in through the patio door was crisp and clean from the rain showers that had lasted for several days.

Stretched out on the sofa with his feet propped up on the coffee table, dressed in a paisley robe and boxer shorts, Ken was engrossed in the latest edition of the *California Sun* newspaper.

Missing their quiet intimate evenings together, he had tried to reach Omunique several times, but to no avail. He hadn't laid eyes on her in the last seventy-two hours, and it was beginning to get to him. She'd asked him for some time to pull herself together, mentally. He deemed it necessary to honor her request of having some time alone. However, he hadn't expected their time apart to become so prolonged. When the doorbell rang, Ken rubbed his stomach, in anticipation of eating the pizza he'd been waiting for.

Omunique stood on the other side of the door. To him she looked and smelled more delicious than any pizza he'd ever seen. Clad in deep plum wool slacks and a pale lavender angora sweater, she looked good enough to be the appetizer, the main course, and the dessert. His appetite was ravenous enough to handle all three courses.

Unable to believe his eyes, he blinked hard. When she floated into his arms, her fiery touch and lilting laughter authenticated her glorious presence. While offering her lips to him, she stood on tiptoe, gladly receiving the full power of his mouth crushing against hers. As their tongues met in a deeply probing kiss, he wedged his knee between her thighs, drawing her in closer to his burgeoning virility.

Suddenly, the doorbell rang, causing them to abruptly pull apart. His first thought was to ignore the urgent ringing, but Omunique had the door open before he could get a tangible hold on his turbulent mind. Ken's breath caught at the bewitching smile she turned around and gave him before she accepted the proffered box from the deliveryman's hand.

Omunique snapped her fingers at Ken. "Money, please! This guy deserves a tip despite the fact he just interrupted our intimate rendezvous." The three of them laughed as Ken handed over a wad of balled up cash, closing the door as the deliveryman took leave.

With their hunger completely satisfied by the pizza and sodas, they made themselves comfortable on the sofa. Omunique settled back, ready to tell him everything that she hadn't yet shared with him. As she explained things, she went through a range of emotions, her story fraught with exasperation, shed tears, and voiced regrets. Though she kept her lamentations minimal, she loudly expressed a few expletives.

Ken found himself sharing in all of her emotions, glad that she was finally able to get everything off of her chest. When she talked about Taylor it was obvious that she'd come to terms with the horrendous things he'd put her through, but he was stunned by the scenario of painful truth that Brent had painted for her.

Truly astounded by her willingness to forgive, he could also see that Omunique wasn't holding any grudges. If Marcus Taylor had lived, Omunique certainly wouldn't want to sit down to dinner with him, but she would've forgiven him. Ken also had a big heart, but not nearly as big as hers.

"If I'd gone through what you've been through, I would've

exploded all over everyone the moment I first became suspicious of their motives. Any considerations for forgiveness would've come last. I don't know how you held it inside of you. I would've had to tell somebody just to keep my sanity. As for Brian, I could see that your heart was on your sleeve as you talked about his part in all this. When you ended the story on a burst of laughter over the teenager's foolish and thoughtless pranks, not to mention the cruelty of it all, I felt as relieved as you looked.''

"I welcomed the laughter, Ken. It felt great. I simply needed to get the intense portions of the story out of the way first.''

He leaned over and kissed her full on the mouth. "I'm glad this is all over for you. It's sounds as if you've got it all together now. About the Terry kid, I'd like to talk to him. Along with the therapy he's getting and the community service hours he has to do, maybe I can help him sort out some of his less serious problems. It sounds like he needs some positive influences in his life. For sure, he needs a good male role model.''

She cupped his face in her hands and took another kiss. "That's really sweet of you. Thanks. I think Brian would enjoy having you to talk to.'' She laid her head in his lap and looked up at him. "Interested in going to Denver to watch a fabulous black female figure skater do her thing?''

"Anyone I know?''

"Yeah, big guy. Intimately.''

"Just how intimately do I know this fabulous black female figure skater?''

She threw her arms around his neck "How about her giving you a sample?''

Laughing, he got up, walked across the room and turned on the CD player. He then returned to her and lay down alongside her. "I don't *do* samples, but I *do* give certain figure skaters the full treatment. Listen,'' he said, "this is the perfect song for this night. The one that had us going crazy Christmas day, but there were too many people around for us to do anything about it. Do we have all night?'' he asked as Boyz to Men's

"I'll Make Love to You" charged the room with a heady dose of sensuality.

She kissed the tip of his nose. "That all depends on how well you *do* what you *do*!"

Lifting her up from the sofa, he carried her into the bedroom, confident that they'd have all night long.

Tangling his legs around hers, he smothered her neck and arms with moist kisses. Just to drive him wild, she resisted his advances, but he held her captive with the strength of his legs. The more she squirmed against him, the more aroused he became. When she finally decided to surrender, she lay perfectly still in his arms, allowing him to lure her into his fiery lair, moaning as he trailed hot kisses over her bare stomach. When his hands heatedly caressed her inner thigh, she felt an intense heat cascade through her entire body.

The silk of his boxer shorts felt smooth under her touch as she crushed the material between her fingers. Slowly, she inched them off his waist. As his hands worked feverishly to remove the rest of her clothing, she freed him of his silky attire. He groaned against her lips as her delicate hands made searing contact with his more than adequate physical endowment.

While crushing his mouth down over hers, he whispered into the stream of her warm breath, "The fire in our kisses tells me we've been apart far too long. Don't ever stop wanting me, Nique."

"Not ever!"

"Denver is only a short time away and we'll have to be apart again, but right now we have all night. Let's make every second count," Ken whispered huskily. Her response was quick and decisive as she drew him inside of her, ready for an all night affair. For days now she'd been putting the ice under fire, now it was time for her to put her man under fire. . . .

Just as they'd promised, they gave each other the entire night and the morning after. Their lovemaking had been frantically fulfilling. Knowing they wouldn't have this chance again, not until after the competition, they made every fragile second count.

After a long shower and another bout of heated contact, Omunique had dressed in the clothes she'd worn the night before. At the door, they kissed and held one another until they somehow found the strength to break free from their desperate embrace.

"Good luck! See you in Denver, Princess," he shouted as she stepped into the cool morning breeze.

"In Denver, Ken!"

Chapter Twenty-three

Poised in a softly seductive stance was the stunning African-American Ice Princess who possessed the figure and the gracefulness of a ballerina. Styled in a thick French braid, Omunique's almond-brown hair hung down the middle of her ramrod straight back. While highlighting her silk-n-satin fawn-brown complexion, the bright lights dazzled in her smoky-gray eyes.

As soft, sweet chords of "Songbird" strummed the cool air, the brilliant spotlight skimmed across the shimmering ice and came to a final rest on the center of the arena. Her white sequined costume sparkled like diamonds as it flowed softly about her shapely legs. Her luminous eyes overflowed with a quiet passion as the Ice Princess waited patiently for the cue that would send her into another stratosphere.

Taking the ice with the gracefulness of a cygnet, Omunique covered the outer perimeters of the arena in a smooth gliding style. Her gentle moves and fluid body language conversed easily with the universe. The audience looked on in complete awe of her sweet, tantalizing movements. When she spun into a triple axel, the crowd rose to their feet, shouting and cheering their approval as she completed a perfect landing.

Tears slid from Omunique's eyes in sheer gratefulness as she blocked out all other thoughts and locked her mind onto the task at hand. The technical program would count for one-third of her final standing. The next two minutes and forty seconds would seem like a lifetime, but she couldn't dwell on that, either. Omunique knew she had to successfully complete each of the required elements. Otherwise, the judges would penalize her on technical marks. While tuning out everything but the eight elements required for completion of the short program, she became acutely aware of the fact that her spins, step sequences, and the set combination of jumps had to be picture perfect.

More importantly, a brief landing could only interrupt the jumps. If she were to kiss the ice with her rear . . . God forbid! she thought, scolding herself for even thinking like that. In what appeared as slow motion, Omunique continued working her short program. The audience seemed to hold its breath as she went through each of the required elements with calculated precision.

Every element came up roses, and Omunique grew more and more confident with each passing minute. Unless her imagination had run away with her, she had captured the hearts of the audience and the judges, but she couldn't let that go to her head. There were other singles skaters to perform, all of them exciting. Then there was the long program to get through, which counted for sixty-six and two-thirds percent of the final score.

The crowd was on their feet as she made her way to the *kiss and cry area,* where the skaters and their coaches waited for the final scores to flash on the scoreboard. A lot of kissing and crying took place in this spot—tears of joy, and tears of sorrow.

At the moment Omunique's were tears of joy.

Omunique had stood in this area in many arenas. Over the past several years Brent had always been there with her. It would've seemed eerie without him, but he was there for her.

Jim would've given her the same encouragement she received from Brent, but she needed Brent to be there should she take an emotional spill.

When Brent had watched Omunique run through her short program at practice, he'd told her that a winner resided inside her soul. When she actually performed the short program, he found himself laughing and crying at the same time. He now thanked the good Lord that he hadn't resigned his coaching position.

When Omunique had exited the ice, she could see how proud Brent was of her performance from the huge smile on his face. Inside the *kiss and cry* area she received several bear hugs from him.

"Great job, Nique. Your best performance ever, honey."

She nearly fainted from joy and relief when the scores finally flashed upon the scoreboard. "Oh, Brent," she exclaimed, dizzy from excitement, "the high scores they've given me are much more than I could've hoped for. This is so hard to believe."

He smiled broadly as they embraced. "Believe it, Nique. And you've earned every single one of them." Somehow she already knew that. Deep down inside she felt it. After all, she'd given the performance of her life.

Although Omunique had given her best performance ever and her scores were extremely good, she'd been slightly edged out of first place, which landed her in second place on the short program. Second place was nothing to shun in this grueling sport, but Omunique knew that her long program needed to be close to flawless. *Completely flawless is more like it,* she told herself, not wanting to feel so confident as to think she'd walk away with a spot on the team if she didn't take a first place win.

In the hotel coffee shop Omunique and Brent discussed the earlier performance and what their strategies would be for the next day. When Brent went over their early morning practice schedule, he gave her the time she was expected on the ice.

Brent sipped a bit of his orange juice and put the glass back down. "In the long program, you'll be the next to the last performer, Nique."

She clapped her hands. "Oh, I'm so grateful for that," she sang out on a sigh. "That will give me a good chance to study the other performers."

After finishing a light meal that consisted of green salads, vegetable soup, and iced tea, Omunique and Brent went to their separate living quarters.

Omunique headed for the bathroom. A relaxing bath was in order, and she couldn't wait to stretch out in the queen-size bed. She laid out her night clothing and practice attire for the next day, then submerged herself in the tub of hot, foaming water. The water was so relaxing she could hardly stay awake. Slowly, the tension eased out of her as the hot water tenderly massaged her muscles, making her feel warm and languid.

With her mind clear and relaxed, she gave deep thought to her earlier performance, trying to pinpoint why she'd been edged out of first place. If she recalled correctly, the skater who'd taken first place had made a couple of shaky landings, which should've been noticeable even to the untrained eye. It was apparent that the judges didn't think it was significant enough for penalties, since they hadn't taken any points away. Omunique had been around the skating circuit long enough to know that the judges saw things from a totally different perspective.

Satisfied that she'd done her very best, and determined to top it the next day, she let her mind stroll down other avenues. The first stop—Kenneth Maxwell Jr. Omunique thought about the promise they'd made not to see one another until after the long program to take place tomorrow afternoon. She'd felt his presence all through her program. He'd somehow tapped into her psyche, and she'd felt the positive energy that had flowed from him and into her. His presence had been encouraging and spiritually uplifting.

After quickly drying herself off, she slipped into black silk pajamas and practically dived into bed. The book she'd begun to read was interesting enough, yet she fell asleep in minutes.

Brent waited for Omunique as she made her way to the area he'd chosen for practice, wearing a red, white, and blue gym suit over her white leotard. They hugged one another, then Brent sat her down on a nearby bench.

He gripped her hand lightly, smiling gently at his star athlete. "I don't want you to work yourself too hard this morning. Take it easy, and don't get caught up in producing a flawless workout session. Save all your brilliance for the competition."

She smiled back and gave him the thumbs-up sign. "I've got it, Coach. It's going to be hard not to give it all I've got, since I'm used to doing just that, but I understand the need to take things slowly. Do you know where I went wrong on the short program, Brent?" she asked, wrapping her arms around her knees.

"You didn't, honey. These things just happen sometimes, but it doesn't hurt your chances of taking it all. Now you go ahead and take a quick run-through of your program. I'll be right here to see that things go well," he said, winking.

"Thanks for all your encouragement, Brent." She took to the ice, to do what she did best, taking it slow and easy, but with the same precision as always.

Later, she brimmed with confidence as she entered the hotel room. The time for the final performance was drawing near, so near she could almost taste the fire. In just two short hours her fate would be decided.

Omunique rested, but her mind was filled with thoughts of the competition.

Later, she skated in her dreams to the all instrumental songs that she'd chosen for the short program, which had been taken from Kenny G's Duotones. It seemed as if she'd only been asleep for seconds, but she'd been asleep for forty-five minutes, she realized as she looked over at her travel alarm clock.

After a quick freshening up, she unpacked another stunning costume. Black with gold sequins, sheer sleeves, bustline, and back, the beautiful outfit was fashioned with a triangle of sheer sequined ruffles cascading from the low cut back to meet up with the upper portion of her thighs. As she held the costume up to her and looked into the full-length mirror, she felt a rush of electricity wash right through her, her eyes sparkling with an astonishing glimmer of anticipation.

She met up with Brent outside the hotel, where they boarded the shuttle that would take them to the arena. All through the short ride her mind churned and chewed on the program she'd trained so hard to perfect. Never for one second did she allow doubt to rise, but all the same, butterflies were deeply nestled inside her stomach. She would've been worried had they not been. Omunique never, ever, wanted to be too confident about anything so utterly important. Smug confidence had led a lot of athletes down the road to total disaster.

From the onset of the competition Omunique closely watched the other skaters perform, making mental notes of the things she'd need to be extremely careful not to do. At one point, she scanned the tiers of seating for her loved ones, but it was much too difficult to find them in the sea of endless bodies packed into the arena seats.

Brent stood up and pulled her to her feet. "It's time, champ. You need to get into position." He gave her a hug, watching her intently as she moved into place.

As she turned and looked to him for one more ounce of encouragement, he gave her the thumbs-up sign. Smiling nervously, she returned the gesture. When her name was announced over the loud speaker, she skated to the center of the ice. Once she was on the mark, the lights came up slowly, outlining her in the dim shadows.

"Calm down," she whispered softly to herself. "You can do this. You have to do this."

She had chosen "Hero" as her musical selection, which she thought to be the perfect song for inspiration. The second song

selection would be short and snazzy, which would allow her
to showcase a charismatic modern dance routine. While doing
several deep-breathing exercises, she prayed fervently that
she'd be able to reach way down deep inside of her and give
every ounce of what she knew she was capable of.

On this day she became her own hero, bewitching the ice
and the audience as she spread her jumps throughout the life
of the program. The chosen choreography was as brilliant as
the skater who effected it with such elegant finesse.

As though hypnotized by her alluring movements, Ken
watched and repeatedly gasped as she worked him and the rest
of the audience members into a nearly uncontrollable state of
euphoria. The audience's reaction to the skater's performance
was often an important factor in the judge's minds, he knew.

"If I Ever Lose This Heaven" was a jazzy piece of music
selected from Quincy Jones's Body Heat album, but Omunique
listened to the rhythm of her skates as she performed to the
second number. "Take it to the ice," she soothed. "Give it all
you've got. This is your one big chance, possibly your last.
You're not getting any younger."

Omunique had never won a first or second place spot at the
senior level of competition. This was her chance to take it all,
and she knew it. Unless there was a tie, a third place win would
be good enough to secure her a spot on the U.S. team.

Although there were no required elements, Omunique indeli-
bly worked her long program, effecting easily the lutz, salchow,
double and triple toe loops, double and triple axels, and a
set combination of astounding jumps. The air crackled with
apprehension when she slightly muffed one of her triple jumps,
but she recovered quickly and quite nicely, hoping no points
had been taken away.

Omunique arched her back and dropped her head and shoulders backward to effect the layback spin. As she executed the
sit spin, she drew her body low to the ice, with the skating
knee and the non-skating knee extended beside it, effecting
the perfect mesmerizing finish to an unbelievably intriguing

program. The long program proved to be a breeze for her, despite the earlier muff on one of the triple jumps and the resident butterflies.

Ken hardly contained his excitement as he thought about how she'd worked him and the blades of her sparkling skates, seeing that Max and Wyman were also stunned by her awesome performance. Ken couldn't describe the enormity of what he felt, just that it felt sensational.

Along with the crowd, Ken got to his feet as she made a sweeping tour around the perimeters of the arena, waving and smiling. Skating backward, she stayed in a bowing position until she exited the ice. *Such a magnificent outward show of humility,* Ken thought, his heart swollen with pride.

Apparently the judges were just as enthralled as he was by her extraordinary performance, Ken noted. Seven of the nine judges had given her five-point-nines. The other two had awarded her perfect sixes.

Ken turned to address Max and Wyman. "She's on her way to the Olympics! Those last scores clinched her a spot on the team. I just know it. It's happened. I can feel it in my bones. She's one incredible athlete," he gushed with pride. "I saw the reflection of my dreams in her silver eyes the moment I held her in my arms. But I think she had me, hook line and sinker, at hello."

Max smiled. "That must have been a powerful reflection, son."

"We need to get down there to where she is after the last performance," Wyman interjected excitedly. "She'll be expecting us." The moment the last performer exited the ice, the three men hurried out of the stands. For security reasons, an usher escorted them to the waiting Ice Princess.

Wyman was the first one Omunique embraced as the others looked on with deep sentiment. After all, Wyman was her loving father and number one fan. Had it not been for him, she wouldn't be where she was today.

She drew her head back and looked up into his walnut-brown

eyes. "Daddy, I'm so happy. Thank you for everything. You've believed in me, and you've supported me from the onset. I can never repay you ... and I know you don't expect me to."

Wyman kissed her forehead. "You're right about that, sweetheart. You don't owe me anything. You just stay focused on your goals. That will be enough for me. A thousand congratulations on your win!" Wyman kissed her again before turning her over to Max, who then showered her with warm affection.

Tears glistened in her eyes as Ken gathered her into his arms. "You were incredible!" he whispered in her ear, his voice hoarse and trembling. "You took this competition to a level never reached before. Those fortunate enough to have shared in it will never forget it. You're a winner, Omunique Philyaw. Your dreams are destined to be golden."

She kissed him softly on the mouth. "Thank you, Ken," she enthused, tears running down her face. "I'm so proud I could burst." Her eyes were suddenly shadowed with disappointment. "Oh, if only Jim could've been here for this moment. He deserves a lot of the praise, too. He's another fantastic coach," she cried. "I owe him, Ken."

"He is here," a quiet voice came from behind her. "And your imaginary debt has been paid in full. Congratulations, kid! You certainly wowed all of your fans this time out. Congratulations on a stupendous performance!"

Omunique screamed as she threw herself at Jim Schmidt. "Oh, I can't believe this. You *are* here," she exclaimed, pinching him softly. "You're here in the flesh," she cried, hugging him to her. Jim held onto her briefly, then stepped aside for Brent to take his rightful place.

Omunique saw that Brent was in shock, but it didn't stop her from bowling him over when she leaped into his arms. After finally managing to offer his congratulations, he lifted her off the ground and spun her around. While including Jim in the circle of champions, Brent set Omunique back down on her feet.

She then fell back into the arms of the man she loved. Ken

stroked her back and wiped the tears from her eyes with a
handkerchief, dabbing at his own eyes before placing the handkerchief back in his pocket.

"Omunique," Ken said, his voice thick with emotion, "this
is your time to bask in the glory of it all, but you don't seem
to realize what's happening here, Princess. You're a bonafide
member of the Winter Olympic Team!"

As though the realization had just hit home, she squealed
loudly, throwing her arms up in the air as she jumped up and
down, dancing around in circles. "Yes!" she shouted. "I'm a
member of the United States Winter Olympic Team!"

She looked up toward heaven. "Did you hear that, Patrice
and Ava Philyaw? I'm Olympic bound. I know you're sharing
in my joy. Mommy and Grandma, I love you both. Thank
you for watching over me from up there on high." When she
promised Julia Maxwell that she'd love her son through all
eternity, she saw Ken's deepest emotions reflected in his eyes.

The emotion packed moment was interrupted when she heard
her name blaring over the loudspeakers.

"It's time for me to acknowledge and to be acknowledged
now," she said, blowing kisses as she backed away and returned
to the ice.

As she skated around the perimeter, she placed her hand
over her heart and bowed her head in silent prayer. She'd been
so excited after her performance she hadn't been able to sit
still long enough to watch the last performer, nor had she paid
close attention to the other scores. When it finally dawned her
that she'd indeed placed first, Omunique became emotionally
overwhelmed. She had a hard time containing herself for the
next few minutes.

As a bunch of red roses were placed in her arms, sweet tears
of victory gushed from her eyes. The tears kept on coming as
the National Anthem played. As the gold medal was placed
around her neck, she wept openly and audibly.

The moment the official ceremonies ended, she joined all
the men in her life, smiling brightly through her tears. "No

longer is the *ice under fire*. It's been extinguished. A new and even more exciting fire has now been ignited. I now know that I can have it all. My man, my career, and my own ice arena," she sang out joyously.

Ken brushed her lips with his. "Princess, you *do* have it all. Together, *we* have it all."

"Yes, yes," she breathed, "we *do* have it all!"

The elevator came to a smooth halt on the ninth floor of the fabulous Twin Tower Hotel. Taking the key from Omunique's hand, Ken guided her down the hall, then opened the door to the suite and flipped on the light. Boasting an Oriental flair, the elegant furnishings in the grand suite were magnificent, done in ivory damask trimmed in gold braid.

Omunique loved the warmth that engulfed her. Stepping out of her shoes, she kicked them aside and walked into the sitting area, where she dropped down on the sofa.

"Like it?" Dropping down beside her, Ken gathered her into his arms.

She looked into his eyes. "It's fantastic." As she gripped his hand, she felt his trembling. "You suddenly seem so nervous, Ken. What's that all about, sweetheart?" she asked with concern.

He smoothed her hair back from her forehead. "Us! It's all about us, Omunique." He cleared his throat. 'I've been so worried about us, Princess. Sometimes I'm afraid I'll wake up one day and you won't be around anymore. I don't think I could bear for that to happen again. For the longest you weren't able to tell me you love me, but when we were together, when we made love together, I felt deeply loved by you. I felt everything I needed to feel from you—and more. But then one day you were gone. I really don't have to ask this question, but I'm going to anyway. Do you love me, Omunique Philyaw?"

He knew she loved him. It was there in her eyes every time she looked at him.

"Oh, God, how I love you! I love the very air you breathe." She touched his cheek. "I'm no longer afraid, Ken, afraid that you'll somehow be taken away from me, no longer afraid of growing old with nothing left but memories of you deeply etched in my heart, no longer afraid that I can't have a fulfilling love life and my career. Nor do I want to wake up without you. I want us to have as much time—"

Silencing her with a finger to her lips, he stood up and took his jacket off, then removed a tiny velvet box from his inside pocket, flipping open the box to reveal its brilliant content. "Is forever time enough for you, Omunique?"

Astounded, flabbergasted, her heart was so full she couldn't speak. All she could do was watch the emerald-cut diamond as it winked its sparkling facets at her.

"Well," he urged, "are you going to say anything?"

Throwing her arms around his neck, she burst into tears. "Yes . . . yes . . . yes!" she cried, gasping wildly to gain control of her emotions.

With tears in his eyes, he removed the ring from the velvet padding and slipped it onto her finger. "This time I hope I'm reading you accurately. Are you saying you'll marry me, Miss Philyaw?"

"Are you asking, Mr. Maxwell?"

"Are you not as perceptive as I've always given you credit for? Will you marry me, Princess Philyaw?" he asked on bended knee, looking up into her wondrous eyes.

With her arms around his neck, she drew him to her. Pressing her lips to his mouth, she breathed a sensuous "yes." Feverishly, his mouth closed over hers.

Trembling, he held her away from him and looked deeply into her eyes. "I guess this means you love me."

"Consummately! I've loved you longer than I dare to reveal. She tenderly caught his face between her delicate hands. "I love you, Kenneth Maxwell Jr. I love you," she cried breathlessly.

He felt ecstatic, felt as though his life was just beginning to be utterly fulfilled, fulfilled by the only woman he wanted to sculpt his future in ice with. Unlike the ice, the solidarity of their love would never melt away.

With Omunique stretched out alongside him, utterly fulfilled, Ken lay in the center of the bed, savoring the quivering and jerking movements that told him he'd unequivocally fulfilled her. Rolling over closer to her, he placed her head against his broad chest.

She felt like a limp, broken doll, but she was all his. Her eyes closed, she, too, savored every drop of their intoxicating love, remembering how they'd kissed one another until both were breathless.

Ken stroked her hair. "Princess," he whispered, "are you still awake?"

"No," she moaned. "I'm alive! Yet I can only breathe through you. Tell me I'm not dreaming?" she pleaded, her voice husky with passion.

He did one better. He showed her.

By the time the erotic journey was complete, she knew there wasn't a dream she could possibly dream that was as wonderful as the ones her husband-to-be so magically created for her. She looked up into his eyes. "I think I'll have to write a book, Ken. The last several months have been a roller coaster of emotions, but for the most part it's been one incredible adventure."

He wrapped his warmth around her. "I think you should wait until you win the Olympic gold medal. Then you can share the details of your experiences on the Olympic circuit with all of your fans and readers. What do you think the title should be?"

"*Ice Under Fire*," they breathed concurrently.

Readers, this is my first published novel. I sincerely hope that you enjoyed reading *Ice Under Fire* from cover to cover. I'm interested in hearing your comments. I'd love to know how you feel about Omunique and Ken's story. Without the reader, there's no me, as an author. Please enclose a self-addressed, stamped envelope with all your correspondence.

Please mail your correspondence to:

Linda Hudson-Smith
2026C North Riverside Avenue
Suite-109
Rialto, CA 92377

You can e-mail your comments to:

LHS4ROMANCE@yahoo.com.

ABOUT THE AUTHOR

Linda Hudson-Smith is a native of Washington, Pennsylvania, and a 1968 graduate of Washington High School. After graduation, she pursued a business education at Duff's Business Institute in Pittsburgh. She continues her educational goals by taking a variety of classes on subjects of interest to her. Her current undertaking is screenwriting.

Married to a career meteorologist in the United States Air Force, Linda has called Japan, Illinois, and Germany "home." While living in Europe, she visited some of the most romantic spots on earth. After her spouse's retirement, Texas became home for six years.

Due to a debilitating illness, Linda was forced to give up her administrative position in public relations and marketing. She prayed for something to do at home to keep her mind occupied. In a short span of time, her prayers were answered and her talent to write revealed. She vigorously educated herself in fiction writing as she attempted to pen her first romance novel.

Because of her strong desire to serve romance readers of color, she wasn't discouraged when told "she might have little or no chance of being published if she didn't change the ethnic make up of her characters." An avid romance reader herself, she longed to read love stories about African-Americans. In 1994, she heard from a close friend that there was now a specific market for her works. By then, she had written several novels. Her extensive domestic and world travel allows her to place her characters in exotically romantic backdrops.

Linda supports the Lupus Foundation of America, the NAACP, and the American Cancer Society. She is a former member of the American Black Book Writers Association (ABBWA). Her interests include reading, writing, poetry, sports, traveling, and entertaining family and friends at home. One of her travel goals is to visit all fifty states by age fifty (only seven states to go). She tremendously enjoys the volunteer work she performs at a local nursing/rehabilitation center. Linda and her husband have made Southern California their permanent home for the past thirteen years, yet she still affectionately and proudly refers to herself as an East Coast kid. Linda has two sons and a son and daughter from her extended family.

Coming in February from Arabesque Books . . .